"*Leave It to Cleavage* is poignant, funny, romantic and sizzling hot. Miranda is a delightful heroine and Blake is the ultimate good guy who's almost too hot to handle. Wonderful secondary characters and a great plot make this book an uplifting winner. A very good read!"
—thebestreviews.com

7 DAYS & 7 NIGHTS

"This debut romantic comedy puts a clever spin on an age-old formula. . . . The novel's real strength is the witty clash." —*Publishers Weekly*

"Wax's first romantic comedy is a witty, battle-of-the-sexes tale and a perfect summertime read." —*Library Journal*

"Delightful! Don't miss this sexy, snappy, fun read."
—Haywood Smith, author of *Queen Bee of Mimosa Branch* and *The Red Hat Club*

"What a fun read! This story is a clever romantic comedy, in every sense of the words. . . . *7 Days & 7 Nights* is a fast-paced story that will have readers wanting more. It's the perfect summer book!"
—*Hawthorne Press Tribune/Lawndale Tribune*

"Entertaining, lively, and engaging, this is an excellent summer read." —*Booklist*

"*7 Days & 7 Nights* sparkles with wit and humor. . . . A mix of strength and vulnerability make Olivia a heroine with whom one can easily identify. Wax is an author to watch."
—*Romantic Times*

"[*7 Days & 7 Nights*] is a thoroughly satisfying read—funny, poignant, sexy, and real. This fresh, well-woven tale might teach you a thing or two about your own relationship! Put Wendy Wax on the top of your to-be-read pile." —Stephanie Bond, author of *I Think I Love You*

"Just what we've been looking for, a wonderful guilty pleasure, sweet, smooth, and delicious, with just the right note of tartness. And not at all fattening! *7 Days & 7 Nights* is a lovely new entry in that lovely genre, the romantic comedy. This is one box of truffles you won't be able to put down until you're done."
—Mira Kirshenbaum, bestselling author of *The Emotional Energy Factor* and *Too Good to Leave, Too Bad to Stay*

"Wendy Wax has a hilarious take on men and women and relationships. She has a gift for creating characters and situations that are real. Readers will enjoy getting to know the different characters, and are sure to identify with many of them. I found myself laughing out loud more than once as I read Ms. Wax's first romantic comedy, and I'm looking forward to reading future books by her."
—*Old Book Barn Gazette*

"*7 Days & 7 Nights* is the delightfully funny, yet very emotional, debut contemporary romance by Wendy Wax. The bickering and bantering dialogue between Olivia and Matt is delicious, as are their 'on air' personalities. This is a fast-paced and intriguing story, guaranteed to keep you turning pages long into the night."
—America Online's Romance Fiction Forum

"A romantic comedy that is sure to please . . . Wendy Wax proves that she has a knack for showing us what makes her characters tick and keeping it light yet fascinating. It's been quite a while since I've enjoyed a contemporary romance this much. It was a shock to see that this is Wendy Wax's first romantic comedy, and I look forward to more from the lady in the future. Pick up a copy of *7 Days & 7 Nights* today and settle in for a read that I guarantee you'll enjoy!"
—*Romance Reviews Today*

"Debut author Wendy Wax throws her hat into the proverbial romance writing ring with a surefire hit. *7 Days & 7 Nights*, with its quirky but lovable characters and its positively refreshing plot, is a definite winner in this reader's opinion. Kudos to Ms. Wax for her ingenuity."
—thewordonromance.com

"A *hilarious* and romantic romp that is unforgettable! I laughed all the way through it. Highly recommended!"
—*Huntress Reviews*

SINGLE
IN SUBURBIA

Wendy Wax

Bantam Books

SINGLE IN SUBURBIA
A Bantam Book / July 2006

Published by Bantam Dell
A Division of Random House, Inc.
New York, New York

This is a work of fiction. Names, characters, places, and incidents either
are the product of the author's imagination or are used fictitiously. Any
resemblance to actual persons, living or dead, events, or locales is
entirely coincidental.

Bantam Books and the rooster colophon are registered trademarks
of Random House, Inc.

ISBN-13: 978-0-553-58897-2
ISBN-10: 0-553-58897-4

Printed in the United States of America
Published simultaneously in Canada

www.bantamdell.com

OPM   10   9   8   7   6   5   4   3   2   1

This book is for Kevin and Drew, whose love of baseball is a beautiful thing. I love to watch you play. It's also for the coaches who give so much of themselves and all the other moms with whom I've shared bleachers, blankets, and peanuts.

There's nothing quite like a baseball field on a perfect spring day.

Acknowledgments

Heartfelt thanks to critiquers Jennifer St. Giles and Sandra Chastain, and especially to Karen White, who did not run screaming into the night the second time she was asked to read this manuscript.

Thanks also to attorneys Amy Kaye and Barry Wax for their insights into the law as well as the people who practice it. And a large merci beaucoup to Louise Legault, baseball mom and bleacher friend, for checking my French. Any mistakes in this regard are mine, not hers.

I also want to thank my husband John for his ongoing support and encouragement. Twenty down, thirty to go.

SINGLE
IN SUBURBIA

In the car lot of life, Amanda Sheridan decided, she was a Volvo station wagon with about eighty thousand miles on it.

People said a woman should look at how a man treated his mother when deciding whether to marry him, but Amanda now knew, from painful personal experience, that a man's car-buying habits were a much better indicator.

In her family men bought good quality cars and drove them until they stopped running; they racked up the miles and bragged about their odometer readings. And in most cases, their marriages lasted just as long.

In Rob's family, which Amanda had been a part of for almost twenty years, the men traded up. Every year they chose a new car and passed the year-old vehicle down to their wives. Occasionally a car might last a little longer if there was a teenager in the family; but as a rule, if you were a Sheridan, when your car's ashtray got dirty it was time to trade that sucker in.

Which went a long way toward explaining why Rob was test-driving a BMW Z4 convertible named Tiffany while Amanda, whose bench seats were sagging, appeared headed for the used car lot.

Amanda scooped Wyatt's baseball socks out of the clean-clothes basket and tossed them on his bed then stashed a fresh stack of towels in the kids' linen closet. Pithy car metaphors notwithstanding, Amanda had no idea how she was supposed to get Rob, who appeared to be in the throes of a monumental midlife crisis at the age of forty-two, to come to his senses, and even less idea of how she'd go on alone if she failed.

It was now almost two and a half months since that morning in mid-December when her husband admitted to lubricating another woman's carburetor; two long months since he'd moved out on New Year's day to park his, er, car, in a strange garage.

Amanda had spent the first month in denial and the second in a semi-comatose state from which she roused only long enough to take care of Meghan and Wyatt. She'd stead-fastly kept her chin up in public, had even managed to adopt a "men will be boys" attitude that belied the gaping hole she felt in her heart and the knife wound in her back.

Still, despite the evidence to the contrary, she simply could not believe that Rob had stopped loving her when she wasn't finished loving him; could not believe that he'd looked her in the eye and told her that his feelings for her had died. Died! As if they were living breathing things that she'd somehow managed to kill.

Her chest tightened.

Rob had moved out to "look for" himself but as far as she could tell, all he'd found was a fancy town house in a singles complex and the zippy little Tiffany.

In the kitchen she brewed a pot of coffee and pulled out a thermos to take to the ball field. She'd let too much time slide by without resolution and had been spectacularly unsuccessful at forcing Rob to discuss the situation. But she'd been wrong to let Rob call all the shots; wrong to continue living in limbo at the mercy of Rob Sheridan's libido.

If there was one thing she knew about her husband—and given his current behavior it might be the ONLY thing she knew about him—it was that he would be at Wyatt's season opener tonight. Which meant it was time to straighten her backbone and stop being such a wimp; time to give Rob an ultimatum: her or us; alone or together.

She'd just have to find a way to make him realize what he was giving up and she'd do her best not to include the word "asshole" while she was doing it. But by the end of the evening, one way or another, she intended to regain control over her life.

"Are you ready, Wyatt?" She took a last look in the hall mirror and tried to squelch the butterflies tumbling in her stomach. She refused to dwell on the small wrinkles that radiated out from her eyes, the deepening grooves that now stretched across her forehead and bracketed her mouth. When you were facing forty, you no longer hoped for perfection.

Better to focus on the unexpected weight loss that made her jeans fit the way they were meant to and the new cashmere sweater that she'd bought for the occasion.

"Just have to get my bag and cleats." Wyatt clattered down the stairs behind her and went into the garage. At twelve, he was tall and lanky, already matching her five feet eight and on his way toward his father's six feet two.

Outside, the sun was setting and the temperature had started to drop. In Atlanta, the end of February was tricky; some days felt like spring, other days bit like midwinter. She poured the entire pot of coffee into the thermos and took an extra moment to add cream and sweetener, though the way those butterflies were cavorting, she wasn't sure she'd be able to drink a drop.

"Last chance, Meghan!" she called up the back stairs.

Her daughter's door opened and a cacophony of what was supposed to be music billowed out around her. Meghan leaned over the balustrade, her dark hair falling forward to obscure her face. At fifteen, sarcasm was her friend. "Normally I'd love to go freeze my butt off for two hours just for the thrill of watching Wy play. But I've got a project due tomorrow." She offered a flip smile and a shrug. The beat of the music pulsed behind her.

"Your dad will be there."

Meghan went still. The flip smile fled and was replaced by a look of hurt so stark that Amanda had to look away. "Do you think I should come so he can pretend like he cares about me for a minute or two?"

"You can drive." She held up the car keys offering the ultimate temptation. "And your father loves you no matter what." It was just her he didn't love anymore.

Amanda made herself meet her daughter's pain-filled eyes. She watched Meghan's gaze sweep over her, taking in the new sweater and carefully made-up face.

"I'm not coming, Mom. And I hate to tell you this, but you're wasting your time. He's moved on and I, for one, am not planning to run after him."

Shrugging into her leather jacket, Amanda picked up the thermos and blanket. "No, no running," she promised as she said good-bye to Meghan and headed for the door.

And no begging, she added silently to herself.

Rob was the one who needed to beg their forgiveness and ask to come home.

And if he didn't?

Then she'd find the backbone to tell *him* to get lost. Right after she shoved his dipstick where the sun didn't shine.

The ball field parking lot was almost full by the time Amanda and Wyatt arrived. It was seven PM and the smell of hot dogs and burgers cooking on the grill outside the concession stand reached them as they got out of the van. There was no sign of Rob's car, but from one of the far fields came the crack of the bat and a huge cheer. Amanda smiled remembering the first time Wyatt had knocked one over the fence. Even all these years later, she could still remember the thrill of amazement at her son's ability, the high fives from the other mothers perched beside her in the stands. Wyatt had been playing at this park since the age of five, and had been madly in love with the game from the first time he stepped up to the tee and made contact with a ball.

Amanda gathered up the blanket she'd brought and cradled the thermos in it while Wyatt put on his cleats and lifted the equipment bag from the back of the van.

"I'll see you down there, sweetie." Amanda watched him

walk down the concrete stands toward the dugout, keeping him in her sights until he disappeared from view.

She was tempted to leave and not come back until warm-ups were over and the game had begun, when attention would be on the field, but she was here and she suspected running would feel even worse. She leaned against the side of the van trying to build her courage, but all she could think of was all the hours they'd spent together in this place. They'd always come here as a family and had been part of the crowd whose kids played not only fall and spring but well into summer. They'd spent countless hours in these stands and others just like them, munching peanuts, cheering their children on, and inevitably picking over the latest gossip.

Gossip. She'd watched other baseball families come apart, seen the children walking around wounded, shuttled back and forth.

At games, the parents, and ultimately, their new significant others, would stake out opposite ends of the stands and try to act as if nothing had changed while everyone else tiptoed around them trying not to declare too obvious an allegiance to either side.

She'd observed all this. Selfishly, she'd hated how it complicated the pure joy of baseball, but she had never for a moment imagined it happening to them. She'd never imagined any of the things that they were living through.

Amanda snorted at her own naiveté. Straightening her shoulders, she walked directly toward the knot of women already seated in the stands.

"Hello, Susie," she said. "Helen." Amanda knew when the entire row of women stopped talking exactly who they were talking about. Helen Roxboro, whose son Blaine had gone to school with Wyatt since preschool, gave her a small wave. Karen Anderson, with whom Amanda shared team mom duties, gave her a tentative smile. There were some other nods and murmurings, but mostly the other mothers watched her face, their own eyes wide, as if they could hardly wait for the entertainment to begin.

Through sheer force of will, Amanda kept a smile affixed to her lips. As normally as possible, she placed her blanket on the far end of a row and went about settling in as if she weren't suddenly the most fascinating thing in these women's world.

Out of the corner of her eye she saw a flash of sympathy on the face of the statuesque blonde who was now dating the boys' coach. At any other time Amanda might have found the idea of such a sweet man dating such an apparently sophisticated woman intriguing, but today all she could think was at least Dan Donovan had waited until he was divorced before he started going out with other women.

Scanning the crowd for a glimpse of Rob, she caught Brooke Mackenzie, Hap Mackenzie's dewy-skinned trophy wife, assessing her with interest. Amanda's heart lurched as she realized that this was probably what that Tiffany business looked like—all pampered and polished. Amanda's eyes teared up, and she dropped her gaze, unwilling to give anyone the satisfaction of seeing her falter. As Tom Hanks said in *A League of Their Own*, and as she'd often reminded Wyatt, there was no crying in baseball.

Swiping the moisture from her cheeks, Amanda checked her watch and then did what she hoped was another casual scan for Rob. She caught Wyatt's attention and sent him a thumbs-up. Wyatt smiled briefly but then his gaze moved past her toward the parking lot. He flinched and turned away.

Unable to stop herself, Amanda turned to glance over her shoulder. Rob was crossing from the parking lot and heading toward the field, his gaze locked on his son. She watched him bypass the stands altogether—he didn't even bother to check for her presence—and trip happily down the concrete steps toward the dugout.

He looked like Rob, but not. He had the same blond hair, the same even features, the same lanky build, but the hip-hugging, bell-bottomed blue jeans, the spotless white T-shirt, and the red sweater knotted around his neck were new. And so was the skip in his step.

The heat rose to her face and her hands clenched at her sides. The rush of blood to her brain was so loud she barely heard her own gasp of shock or the sudden silence that now surrounded her. Because trailing along behind him was what could only be the new Z4 in all her tight-chassis, glove leather glory.

Speechless, Amanda watched them go by. The girl—calling her a woman would have been a stretch—actually looked like she'd stepped off the cover of a magazine. In this case, probably *Teen People*.

She had a cloud of blonde hair that moved with her as she walked and a body that made you look even when you didn't want to.

She had perfectly sculpted limbs, high jutting breasts, and an absurdly tiny waist. Her stomach was unfairly flat above her low-slung jeans; it had never been stretched by childbirth and then expected to snap back. Her silk blouse was white and the burgundy leather blazer was beautifully tailored, but it was her face that sucked all the breath out of Amanda's lungs as she passed. It was the most perfect face Amanda had ever seen.

"Holy shit!" The expletive left the mouths of the group

of women seated around Amanda; it was torn from their lips and infused with both wonder and horror. Several made the sign of the cross. In their sweats and sneakers, wrapped in their blankets, and bedraggled from an afternoon of shuttling their children all over creation they were a set of serviceable pearls, chipped and unpolished; Tiffany was a four-carat diamond in an antique platinum setting sparkling in the sun.

The theme song from *Jaws* began to play in Amanda's head. "Da dum . . . da dum . . ."

The appropriately named Tiffany grabbed Rob's arm as they reached the dugout. Stopping at the chain-link fence, Rob leaned forward to say something to Wyatt and the hot flame of anger ignited in Amanda's stomach.

Leaving them had been unconscionable, but showing up here with this . . . *child* . . . was beyond belief. Amanda's anger built; every move they made, Rob's laugh, Tiffany's flick of her hair, the fact that they were breathing when she could not, stoked that flame into a billowing inferno.

How could he do this? How *dare* he do this? No longer caring what kind of show they put on for those assembled, Amanda rose and walked down the steps and directly toward her husband. It was hard to see him, what with the red haze before her eyes and all, but she continued to move forward as if some unseen hand pushed from behind. She could not let this travesty continue.

Suddenly understanding the concept of second-degree murder, Amanda imagined the headlines if she were to give in to the bloodlust she felt right now:

DISCARDED WIFE GOES BESERK AT BALL FIELD.
BASEBALL MOM BATS CHEATING HUSBAND
OVER LEFT FIELD FENCE.

No jury with a married woman over thirty-five on it would convict her.

Every eye in the stands was focused on Amanda's back, but she told herself it didn't matter because this couldn't possibly be happening. As she reached the ground and began to move toward the dugout, the whole situation turned surreal; this was not just her facing down Rob, but WonderWife facing down every dastardly husband who had dared to spit in the face of his family.

"This is completely unacceptable!" she hissed when she reached them. "How could you bring her here?"

Tiffany flushed with surprise and Amanda wondered exactly what the girl had expected.

From the corner of her eye, she saw Wyatt swivel around on the dugout bench to watch them. His face was white, the freckles across the bridge of his nose stood out in stark relief.

"It's OK, Wy," she said, though of course it wasn't. "You just focus on your game, you hear? We're going to work this out."

The coach stepped up next to Wyatt. He placed a hand on her son's shoulder and gave Rob a steely look. Thank God for Dan Donovan. "You all right, Amanda?"

"Yes, thanks."

Donovan led Wyatt to the other end of the dugout out of earshot. She looked Tiffany in the eye.

"You're dating a married man and you come to a place where his wife and child will be?"

"Oh, Robbie's going to . . ."

Amanda stepped closer, needing to invade their personal space in the same way they'd invaded hers. "Shame on you!" she said, angered anew by the inadequacy of her words. "Shame on both of you!"

"But, Robbie, you said . . ." the girl began.

"It's not *Robbie*." Amanda put every ounce of disdain she was feeling into the nickname. "His name is Rob, and at the moment he's still married to me. He and I need to have a conversation. We're not going to have that conversation here in front of an audience. You can go sit down until we're done, or you can go play on the slide, I don't care which. But if I see your face again tonight, I'm going to rip every one of those blonde hairs out of your head and stuff them in your mouth."

Tiffany gasped and stalked off. Without looking to see if Rob followed, Amanda marched in the other direction. She walked until she reached a tree beyond the stands and out of the others' line of sight. When she turned around Rob was standing in front of her.

"I didn't mean for her to come tonight. She just couldn't wait to meet Wyatt and all . . ." His voice trailed off.

"You didn't *mean* for her to come?" She shook her head in disgust. "But big bad Tiffany didn't listen to little Robbie?" She delivered the last in the most offensive baby talk she could manage. "What a crock!"

"Amanda, I . . ."

"No." She looked into his eyes searching for the man she'd fallen in love with all those years ago. "I don't even know who you are anymore. The person I married would never have run away from his family like you have, or humiliated them like you have tonight. What *happened* to you?"

Rob ran a hand through his newly coiffed hair. "You don't know what it's like to wake up one day and realize that the best part of your life is over; that all the rest is just an unavoidable downhill slide."

Amanda took the blow and flinched. All they'd become to him were a symbol of the downhill slide.

"I just felt so trapped." He put a hand out toward her and she noticed that his fingernails appeared to be freshly manicured. "Things started getting out of control. I could barely get up in the mornings."

OK, so knowing the truth was definitely overrated. His reasons didn't change the destructiveness of his actions; his total lack of concern for them.

She looked him straight in the eye. "And where do love, honor, and commitment fit into your little scenario? What about us?"

He sighed as if this was something to be weighed and considered. "I don't know."

She studied her husband for a long moment, took in the new polish and salon-styled hair, the stupid red sweater knotted at his throat. And she realized that it didn't really matter what either of them said now. Even if she wanted him back, and she didn't know that she did, what was she supposed to do? Yell him into sending the lovely Tiffany away? Force him to burn the clothes and never let another woman shop for him again?

And then what? Then she'd be waiting every moment for

his next attempt to break free. She'd know that even if he was there, he'd be wishing he were somewhere else. She and Wyatt and Meghan weren't exciting enough for him? Well, then he didn't deserve them.

"Well, I know what's going to happen now."

He looked up, surprised.

"I'm going to the ladies room and then I'm going to go back and watch the game." She raised her chin a notch. "You're going to leave."

His mouth opened but she didn't give him a chance to speak. "Before I come out you and that . . . girl . . . are going to be gone. And you are not to bring her to this field again until we're divorced."

"Divorced? But . . ."

She stopped him with a look. "That's it, Rob. Your dick has drained all sense from your brain if you think you can go out and have a good time and wave it in our faces and then just come home as if nothing's changed."

"Well . . ."

Amanda looked down at her watch. "You've got ten minutes to leave; ten, and not a minute more. You don't *deserve* to watch Wyatt play baseball."

Amanda stayed in the bathroom for the required ten minutes. This was not easy given the primitive nature of the ballpark's ladies room. The bare concrete walls and floor, overflowing trash bin, dripping faucet, and cracked funhouse mirror afforded no distractions. She spent the first five minutes pacing, the last five perched on top of a cracked toilet lid, and an extra three staring at her distorted reflection in the ancient mirror.

When she couldn't put it off any longer, she left the bathroom and walked slowly toward the stands unsure of what she'd do if Rob and Tiffany were still there. She felt some measure of relief when she confirmed that they had, in fact, left. But the way everyone made a point of NOT watching her as she took her seat spoke volumes. And even though all the eyes that had been glued to her earlier were now fixed on the field, Amanda knew the spectacle on the field was nowhere near as interesting to the assembled adults as the one she and Rob had just provided.

Resolute, she, too, fixed her gaze on the field and sat in silence for the remaining forty-five minutes as Wyatt's team got pounded into the dirt—an experience with which she could completely relate.

When the game was over, the stands emptied quickly but whether it was due to the loss, the plunging temperatures, or the desire to avoid having to speak to her, Amanda didn't know. Wyatt, too, stood apart from his teammates, completely focused on stowing his equipment in his bag while the other boys jostled and joked.

The cold bit through her leather jacket and useless cashmere sweater, and she hugged herself for warmth and comfort. Hearing the crunch of shoe on dirt, she turned. Hap Mackenzie's new wife stood beside her, her gray eyes assessing. "Are you OK?"

"Yeah, I feel great."

The other woman sat down uninvited, ignoring the sarcasm. "He won't stay with that one, you know."

Nonplussed, Amanda took a closer look at Brooke Mackenzie. She was somewhere in her late twenties with thick auburn hair and creamy *unwrinkled* skin. Last spring when the recently divorced Hap had married a girl nearly half his age, they'd all been scandalized. Amanda had never said more than a polite hello to her.

"Too flashy," the new Mrs. Mackenzie said. "She's perfect for running around, but sooner or later he's going to expect someone to cook and clean and take his shirts to the dry cleaner. That one's not going to be able to pull it off."

"And that's when I get him back?"

The redhead studied her. "No, that's when he picks a slightly more domesticated version of her and marries *her*."

"Gee, now I know why we've never talked before."

Brooke shrugged. "Sorry. I could tell you the statistics but they're even more depressing."

"Thanks."

"Don't mention it." She smiled and it changed her whole face; the careful gray eyes lit with warmth and the Angelina Jolie lips twitched upward. "If it'll make you feel better, it won't take him long to start treating her exactly like he's treating you. They only seem to have two settings." She flicked an imaginary dial. "Wife or girlfriend."

Amanda smiled back. "Now there's a real day brightener."

"Of course, the wife gets more of his time plus the accompanying perks and status. But, frankly, I think the girlfriend gets a whole lot more respect and consideration."

"You can say that again."

They both looked up to see Candace Sugarman standing several rows in front of them. The coach's girlfriend was tall and blonde with a carefully preserved face and figure. She had an innate elegance that belonged on the pages of *Town and Country*, but Amanda couldn't tell on which side of forty she fell. "I've been both and unless she's got a great attorney, the wife always comes out the loser."

"Boy you two are just what a wounded woman needs. What are your nicknames: Sweetness and Light?" Amanda looked around. The coach was shepherding his son and Wyatt and Brooke Mackenzie's stepson out of the dugout. Everyone else had gone.

Not one of her so-called friends had stayed around to console her.

Candace raised a perfectly shaped eyebrow. "Anyway," she said, "I think you handled yourself really well tonight. And I figured you might need this." She handed Amanda a business card. "I used her for all three of my divorces; she's not afraid of anyone or anything."

The field lights snapped off. Coach Donovan and the boys started up the concrete stands toward them. Amanda looked down at the card. It read, *Anne Justiss, Attorney at Law.* And underneath her name, *Get them where it hurts; in their bottom line.*

Dan Donovan reached them first. He slipped an arm around Candace's shoulders and waited while Amanda and Brooke stood and dusted themselves off.

"If you need any help getting Wyatt to practice or anything, Amanda, just give me a call." He ruffled Wyatt's hair and gave Brooke a nod. "I hope Hap will be back in town for Saturday's game."

"That's my understanding." Brooke smiled tentatively at her stepson, but he walked right by her without responding.

Amanda fingered the crisp white business card as they made their way up to the parking lot, their voices echoing in the late night emptiness. Clutching her jacket around her, she repeated Anne Justiss's tagline to herself. She didn't actually know what Rob's bottom line was; finances had never been her thing.

But she could definitely use someone who wasn't afraid of anything. She only wished the same could be said for her.

chapter 3

Anne Justiss didn't look like a man-eater. In fact, with her short stylishly wispy blonde hair, cornflower blue eyes, and upturned nose, the attorney looked kind of like Cameron Diaz. Or the wholesome girl next door your mother would want you to hang out with.

"I understand Candace Sugarman referred you to me," she said as she met Amanda in the doorway of her large corner office in the pricey midtown high rise and showed her to a seat opposite her desk.

"Yes."

The attorney settled in her chair and folded her hands on the top of her glass and lacquer desk. "Candace is an unusual client. Completely proactive. We worked together a number of times."

Amanda shifted uncomfortably in her seat. The idea of even one divorce made her palms sweat.

"Why don't you fill me in on your situation."

"It's nothing particularly novel, I'm afraid," Amanda said. "My husband moved out a couple of months ago in order to find himself."

"And has he?"

"I don't know, but he, um, seems to have found a girl named Tiffany. I got to meet her at our son's baseball game the other night."

The attorney's eyes narrowed. "I hate that they think they can just run off and do whatever they like. How many children do you have?"

"Two."

"How old are they?"

"My daughter's fifteen, Wyatt's twelve."

"Do you work outside the home?"

Amanda shook her head. "No."

"Is he still paying all the bills?"

"I, um, think so."

One blonde eyebrow went up. "But you don't *know*?"

Amanda swallowed and wiped her hands on the sides of her skirt. "Rob's always deposited a certain amount in the household account each month and that hasn't changed. I assume he's still paying the mortgage and the car payments. He's, uh, always written the checks for the bigger stuff."

"And your savings? Stock portfolios? Other joint accounts and assets?"

"I don't know."

Anne Justiss held Amanda's gaze with her own. "If your husband came home tomorrow and told you he was sorry, would that be enough for you?"

Amanda thought about that one. Her wounded pride shouted absolutely not, you can't let him get away with this!

But the frightened part of her, the scared, shaking part deep inside, wasn't so sure. "I don't know."

"May I be brutally honest with you?"

Amanda swallowed. "Do you have to?" she joked, but Anne Justiss didn't smile back.

"In my experience once a man moves out and starts another relationship, especially if he's rubbed his wife's nose in it as yours apparently has, the marriage is over."

Amanda's mouth was completely dry. She swallowed again but all the moisture seemed to have moved to her eyes.

"I'm not a marriage counselor. I'm not here to help you fix your relationship. I'm here to protect you." She pulled two Kleenex from the black lacquer dispenser on her desk and handed them to Amanda.

"Normally, I advise my clients to file for divorce immediately because it freezes the joint assets and allows us to access financial information. It also gives you a psychological advantage, because when you take action you stop feeling like a victim."

Amanda thought she nodded, but she wasn't sure. She was concentrating all her energies on not allowing the tears to spill down her cheeks.

"You can't bury your head in the sand, Amanda. The longer you wait the greater the opportunity he has to hide or shift assets. Even if you're not ready to file, you want to start gathering financial documentation."

Amanda dabbed at her cheeks. The tissue came away sopping wet.

"Has your husband retained an attorney?"

"He *is* an attorney. He's a tax attorney with Powell Newman."

Anne Justiss sighed. "The bad news is he can get the divorce guy in the firm to handle it and he won't be worried about running up the hours." She cocked her head. Amanda imagined she could see the mind racing inside. "The good news is he's probably not going to want to look too bad in front of a judge; he'll have his reputation to consider."

The attorney considered her carefully. "I know this isn't easy," she said. "But I can promise you it's better to take action than to live in a continued state of emotional limbo."

Amanda nodded, but her heart wasn't in it.

"Traditionally after a divorce, the man's standard of living improves. The ex-wife and children's standard of living drops dramatically. I do my best not to let that happen to my clients. Candace may have mentioned my belief in the Green Giant school of divorce."

"Green Giant?" Amanda tried to blink away her tears even as she tried to follow the conversation. "As in the vegetables?"

Anne Justiss smiled a very tight smile. "There's a very old joke that asks what do you have when you've got a large green ball in one hand and a second green ball in the other?"

Amanda shook her head, thrown by the insertion of veggies into the conversation.

"Complete control of the Jolly Green Giant."

Anne Justiss's blue eyes were now more like steel than cornflowers. Her delicate features had also hardened. "I can help you get your husband by the balls," she said with complete certainty. "But the time to act is now. We want to sue

for subpoena and get hold of all relevant financial information as quickly as possible."

Amanda studied the woman in front of her. She'd
wanted someone who wouldn't be afraid and she'd found
her. But she would have given all she owned to be able to
turn the clock back to just before everything fell apart;
would have given anything not to have to make this decision.

She'd spent the last months praying for a miracle that
would somehow put their lives back the way they were. But
Rob was airbrushed and he had a girlfriend named Tiffany.
No amount of wishful thinking was going to alter that
reality.

Amanda straightened slowly and met the attorney's gaze
straight on. She'd waffled long enough. She had nothing to
gain from waiting and everything to lose. It was time to act.
"It might take me a few days to put together the deposit,"
Amanda said carefully. "But I'm ready for you to go ahead
and start squeezing."

The drive home from Anne Justiss's office was an out-of-
body experience. Like the near dead who claim to watch the
efforts to resuscitate them from above, Amanda saw her
minivan traveling north on Highway 400 toward the suburbs, saw it change lanes, merge, and exit the interstate, but
the specifics of how it reached her home were hazy.

Leaving the van in the garage, she stepped into the
kitchen. With the kids still at school, the house was pin-
drop quiet. The only thing breaking the silence was the re-
frain "You're getting a divorce, you're getting a divorce" that
echoed in her head.

Trying to elude those thoughts, she left the kitchen and moved through the house. In the dining room she paused behind a Chippendale-style chair and tried to see the room as a stranger might. But her mind moved right past the carefully designed mix of antiques and contemporary art to the Thanksgiving and Christmas dinners, the countless turkeys and hams she'd served to her family there.

Passing through the formal living room, she crossed the foyer and hesitated in the entrance to Rob's former home office. The antique desk and leather wing chair were gone, the shelves emptied of books and mementos. Bright squares and rectangles dotted the chocolate brown walls where Rob's gallery of fame—the carefully arranged shots of Rob glad-handing local politicians and the occasional sports figure—had once hung.

Turning her back on the empty office, she moved to the family room and breathed in its essence. The room was both chic and comfortable, just as she'd intended. The couch, covered in a cheery cranberry chenille was flanked by club chairs with ottomans in a bold cranberry and black pattern.

The remnants of a bowl of popcorn sat on the edge of the massive wrought-iron coffee table, which could, and had, hold an entire meal.

Stepping toward the big screen television, Amanda ran her gaze over the built-in bookcases that surrounded it. They were packed with books and magazines and small finds from arts and crafts shows. Framed photographs from family vacations and holidays dotted the shelves. Amanda lifted each photo in turn, studying the poses and faces like an anthropologist might, searching for what lay behind the entwined arms and happy faces of her family.

In the photos, Meghan and Wyatt's gap-toothed smiles gave way to braces; their baby smooth skin to the marks of adolescence. Rob looked the same in every shot: tall and blond, his smile one of supreme confidence. She'd thought him straightforward and uncomplicated, even downright predictable, but she'd been wrong on all counts.

She reached for a photo of the two of them in Vail just over a year ago. Holding it up for closer examination, she looked for signs of his discontent. Had he already begun feeling trapped? Started plotting his escape?

And what of her?

She remembered handing the camera to a sulky four-teen-year-old Meghan, still angry that she hadn't been al-lowed to bring a friend on their family vacation. She'd been trying to soothe her daughter's ruffled feathers, bargaining for a smile, trying to manage her family's reactions and feel-ings as she always did even as the picture was snapped.

As a result her brow appeared furrowed and her eyes telegraphed her concern. Dismayed, she noticed that none of the shots of her reflected enjoyment. In picture after pic-ture she saw the careful, overly organized woman she'd prided herself on being; a woman preoccupied with the de-tails of their lives.

Had she never been carefree? Unconcerned about what everyone else felt and wanted? What had she felt and wanted then? She couldn't remember.

Opening a set of cabinet doors, she began to rifle through the stacked photo albums, searching for a shot that reflected her *real* self. But even the shots of their early married days, when she'd been all of twenty-one, showed the preoccupied smile and furrowed brow.

Worried now, she rooted through the cabinet, finally pulling out a battered imitation leather album whose binding was cracked from age and neglect. Clutching her prize to her chest, she plopped down onto the sofa and opened it.

The photographs were dated and dog-eared; the captions scrawled beneath them were written in the spidery cursive she'd affected in college.

The first one read, *Me and Jean-Claude in front of Eiffel Tower.* And sure enough there they were, too tiny in the foreground, the passerby Jean-Claude had gotten to snap the picture clearly more concerned with including all of the landmark than the expressions on their faces. But she could actually remember the feel of the smile that had split her face that day. Could still remember the way her jaw ached from smiling and laughing as he gave in to her mad insistence to see every site, every museum, every worthwhile café that Paris had to offer.

"Tu es enchanteur et électrifiant." You are enchanting and electrifying, he'd said as he'd stared down into her eyes on the steps of the Louvre. *"Tu es mon beau papillon."* You are my beautiful butterfly.

Mon beau papillon. He'd called her his beautiful butterfly so many times that she'd finally come to believe it.

For almost the entire year she'd studied in Paris, she'd flitted and flown like the butterfly he'd named her, embracing the freedom like a prisoner suddenly and unexpectedly set free from her cell.

In every picture her face declared her adoration of Jean-Claude and her fascination with all things French. For a moment, she heard his voice whispering intimately. *Mon beau papillon.*

Her gaze flew around the beautifully decorated family room and she saw it for what it was; a carefully designed cocoon into which she'd retreated and where she'd traded in her wings for a perpetually furrowed brow.

Stung, she slammed the photo album shut and shoved it under a pillow. Searching for a distraction, she strode into the kitchen and began opening cupboards, but she was too agitated to eat and too scattered to cook. Beneath the sink she spotted a bucket and a jug of vinegar and before she knew what she was doing, she'd filled the bucket with warm water, added a healthy dollop of vinegar and located the mop. Moments later she was mopping the wood floors, finding unexpected comfort in the repetitive rhythm of a chore she'd always paid others to do. She finished the kitchen floor quickly and then moved into the dining room, where she swabbed carefully around the Oriental rug on which the mahogany table sat.

As she worked, another, more private snapshot surfaced in her mind. She and Jean-Claude in the bare student apartment he'd maintained on the Left Bank, discovering what making love actually meant.

"*Tu es incroyable.*" You are incredible, he'd breathed as his mouth moved over her naked breast. "I can't get enough of you."

She was dumping the dirty water down the laundry room drain when the phone rang. "*Oui?*" she said, unable to pull her mind from Jean-Claude, his lips, or the wonderful sense of abandon he'd stirred in her.

"Amanda?" Her mother's voice brought her back to the good old U S of A more quickly than a speeding bullet.

"*Oui*," Amanda said. "Um, I mean, yes." She set the still damp mop outside the kitchen door to dry and crossed to the bay window that overlooked the backyard.

"Are you all right?"

Amanda cleared her throat. "Yes, yes, of course. I'm fine."

"And Rob and the kids?"

Amanda winced. Her parents had been married for forty-five apparently blissful years, a record she had hoped to meet and possibly even exceed.

Which went a long way toward explaining why she'd never mentioned Rob's desertion. Telling her parents would have made the demise of her marriage all too real; it would have been a one-way ticket out of the Land of Denial.

But she now had an attorney whom she'd instructed to "start squeezing." Rob's financial records would be subpoenaed any day now. It was time to tell not only her parents but her children. Oh, God, how was she going to do that?

Amanda opened her mouth determined to come clean. She'd simply tell her mother the truth and then somehow she'd find a way to tell Meghan and Wyatt. This would actually be good practice; a dry run of sorts.

She drew a deep breath, but none of the words she knew she should say actually came out. She told herself it was because she didn't want to spoil her parents' cross-country trip; the one they'd been planning for as long as Amanda could remember.

"Everybody's fine," she said in her perkiest good-girl voice. Then without meaning to, she repeated it in French, the translation popping into her head unbidden as if unleashed along with the memories she'd kept so tightly tucked away. *"Ils vont très bien."*

She'd just lied to her mother in two languages.

"Goodness," her mother said. "I haven't heard you speak French in ages. Are you planning a trip?"

"Not exactly," Amanda heard herself say. "I just seem to have France on the brain right now." This at least was true. Maybe she wouldn't burn in Hell after all. "How's your trip going? Where are you right now?"

"We're in Arizona, right outside of Sedona. We're going to stay here for a few more days. It's beautiful, Amanda, the sun setting over the red rock is just glorious. Your father's been trying to photograph it for days."

Amanda could picture them there together, soaking it all in. Sharing the days and nights in the cozy motor home they'd purchased.

"We thought we'd sort of work our way toward Atlanta. Maybe end up at your place."

"That'd be super, Mom." Maybe by then she would have worked up the nerve to tell them the truth.

"Hey," her mother said as they began their good-byes. "Maybe Rob will surprise you with a trip for your anniversary. Maybe I need to put a little bug in his ear."

"Wouldn't that be great?" Amanda asked as she bid her mother *au revoir*.

It would certainly be a whole lot greater than the girlfriend he'd surprised her with for Christmas.

chapter 4

Trying to ignore the stares of the other adults she passed, Candace Silver Bernstein Sugarman picked her way over the gravel path toward the ballpark concession stand.

She had to concede that the Prada jacket might have been a mistake. Ditto for the Italian calfskin demi-boots with the three-inch heels.

"Damn." Her ankle turned yet again and she windmilled to regain her balance as red dust flew and pebbles scattered around her. She was NOT going to land on her rear end in the middle of the Saturday morning crowd. A pint-size ballplayer with a bulging equipment bag slung over his tiny shoulder pointed a finger at her as he and his mother approached.

"Look how fancy that lady is, Mommy!" He piped at the top of his voice. "How come she's all dressed up?"

The mother, who was dressed in jeans and sneakers like every other woman Candace had seen so far, shot Candace an apologetic smile and pulled her son along beside her. "I don't know, honey. Maybe she's going somewhere nice after this."

If only. Actually, Candace thought the child's question a good one. An even better one might be: What was a nice Jewish divorcée with no children doing spending an entire Saturday afternoon at a Little League ballpark? And why would said divorcée offer to sell snacks while she was there?

The answer was tall, dark, and Irish. And his initials were DD.

By the time Candace reached the concession stand she had a red dirt smudge on the front of her jacket, a large chunk of gravel wedged inside her left boot, and absolutely no desire to explore this strange new world into which this Sugarman had never gone before.

Too bad she couldn't get Scotty to lock onto her coordinates and beam her up.

Brooke Mackenzie also wished she was somewhere else. Like on her way to the East End Day Spa for her weekly mani and pedi instead of wending her way through a throng of Little Leaguers to a broken-down concession stand. But Hap was out of town yet again, and the former Mrs. Hap Mackenzie, who claimed to have the flu, had called to ask whether Brooke could take Tyler to the ballpark and then work her scheduled shift.

Brooke, whose cuticles and psyche were clamoring for attention, had picked up her stepson from his mother's, driven the totally hostile and completely silent preteen to the field, and watched him stomp off to the batting cages where his team awaited. Tyler got to play baseball. Brooke got to spend the next three hours in a concession stand with two other women who would probably make her stepson look like Mr. Friendly.

Tossing her hair over her shoulder, she tilted her chin upward and headed up the gravel-strewn hill reminding herself as she walked that she was exactly where she wanted to be.

Married to a successful man with a home in the suburbs, she had come a long way from her trailer park beginnings. Making the rent on a doublewide had been her mother's crowning achievement. But Brooke had been born with her mother's looks and a calculator of a brain—undoubtedly inherited from the father her mother had been unable to identify—and she had used them both to get her accounting degree, which had led to a position at Price Waterhouse. Which in turn had led to Hap.

Keeping her gaze fastened forward, Brooke ignored the admiring looks of the fathers she passed. The hostile looks their wives aimed her way were harder to duck.

Brooke's smile slipped a notch. Her single friends, who treated a trip to the suburbs like a trek to Siberia, had largely abandoned her. The wives of Hap's friends and the women she met here weren't planning to welcome her into the fold any time soon. She was their worst nightmare and the fact that she'd refused to go out with Hap until after his divorce was final was a hair they weren't interested in splitting.

At the concession stand she spotted Candace Sugarman and hid a smile as the older woman leaned against the concrete building and yanked off her boot. When she turned it upside-down and shook it, a landslide of dirt and pebbles poured out.

Brooke looked down at her own black suede mini boots, which were now covered in dust. "This place isn't exactly high heel friendly."

"No, it's not." Candace gave her the once-over then went back to clearing the debris from her shoe. "But I don't *own* Levi's or sneakers. And I don't think I want to."

Brooke considered the blonde. The woman was much too sophisticated and independent to fit in with the mothers from the team, but there were things to be learned from a woman like this. Like how to carry herself and how to look like she didn't give a damn, without giving offense—not the sort of thing one picked up around the trailer park. Or even in an MBA program.

Amanda Sheridan arrived for concession duty dressed like the other mothers, for comfort not show. Brooke couldn't help feeling sorry for her, being dumped like she had after almost twenty years of marriage.

But Brooke didn't think the woman was finished. Not by a long shot. In fact, she could probably learn everything she needed to know about being a suburban wife from Amanda Sheridan. As Brooke had discovered at a very young age, there were lessons to be learned from everyone. She'd just have to figure out the holding on to her husband part by herself.

Amanda knew just how far her stock had dropped when she discovered that she'd been assigned to work the concession stand with Brooke Mackenzie and Candace Sugarman.

Ushering them into the boxlike structure, she stowed her

purse under the counter and considered her coworkers. They looked like aliens plopped down on earth with no idea of the local dress or customs.

Brooke's auburn hair cascaded down her back in carefully orchestrated disarray and her black suede man-tailored shirt nipped in to a Scarlett O'Hara–sized waist. Low slung jeans and pointy-toed boots in the same black suede as her shirt completed the ensemble. Her diamond studs were big enough to double for doorknobs.

Candace, too, looked more suited to a lunch date than an afternoon flipping burgers. Amanda tied an apron over her own faded sweatshirt and tried not to stare at the blonde's Prada jacket and string of perfectly matched pearls. Not even the layer of ballpark dust that now covered her could detract from the woman's smartness.

"So," Amanda said, "which one of you wants to get the grill going?"

The two stared at each other obviously waiting for the other to volunteer. Brooke caved first and went outside with the lighter.

"I could cut up the tomato and lettuce, maybe make an arrangement of crudités to decorate each plate," Candace offered.

Amanda opened the refrigerator and pulled out industrial-sized bottles of ketchup and mustard and slapped them into Candace's hands. "These go outside on that picnic table. They can have their burgers plain or with cheese. These are the plates." She reached for the roll of aluminum foil and ripped off a square. "The only crudités here are the men."

With a knowledge born of long experience, Amanda directed Brooke and Candace through the opening checklist. She'd been team mom more times than she could count and had headed up the park concession committee for three years in a row. She was known at this ballpark, respected as a hard worker who played well with others. Now she was tainted with Rob's indiscretion, pitied as a discarded wife, and stuck here on a Saturday with an overdressed crew of outcasts.

Amanda checked the cash drawer and straightened the display of candy bars realizing as she did that she'd forgotten to eat again. She considered having a Snickers bar, but couldn't work up any enthusiasm for it. Rob had even ruined chocolate for her; the man had a lot to answer for.

Leaning on the counter, she stared out toward the playing fields and did a slow scan for Rob. Wyatt's team was warming up in the flank of batting cages to her right. To her left, a game was already underway; the fielders' hazing chatter to the batter carried up to her on the breeze.

Keenly aware that Rob might appear at any moment, she busied herself educating Brooke and Candace on concession stand procedures then sent Candace over to their sister stand to get more ice. Brooke got window duty.

When the first customer appeared, Brooke stepped forward with a big smile. Amanda waited behind her prepared to help, but Brooke didn't turn to her for assistance. She simply got out a cardboard holder, retrieved a slew of items from the warming tray, the refrigerator, and the chip and candy rack and began piling them into it as she'd been instructed. "That'll be twelve sixty-five," Brooke said with another smile then reached her hand out for payment. Taking a twenty, she opened the register, made change, which she passed through the opening and sent the bulging holder after it. "Thanks so much. Hope you enjoy it."

Still smiling, she turned to Amanda. "What?" she asked, noting Amanda's expression. "What did I do wrong?"

"You didn't ring anything up or use the calculator," Amanda said. "How did you know what his total was?"

Brooke looked startled then tapped her forehead with her index finger. "I just do it in my head." She shrugged, her expression self-deprecating. "Numbers are kind of my thing."

Amanda considered the younger woman. "OK." She stepped past Brooke and began gathering items. When she had twenty things, she laid them out on the counter careful not to put them in any particular order then picked up the handheld calculator and began punching in prices.

Before she could hit the total button, Brooke said, "Fifteen dollars and ninety-five cents."

A moment later the same number appeared on her screen.

"One more time." Amanda removed four items and replaced two. She hadn't even turned the calculator back on when Brooke said, "Ten dollars, twenty-five cents."

Amanda slid two more items off the counter.

"Eight fifty."

Amanda nodded and wondered what, besides a calculator-like brain, Brooke Mackenzie was hiding behind her pretty face. "All right," she conceded. "You keep the window. I'm going to sit back here"—she gestured toward the lone chair near the refrigerator— "and work on my math skills."

A steady stream of gaping men eager to purchase whatever Brooke was selling made their way to the concession stand window. Brooke never once wrote anything down or touched the register except to deposit or withdraw money. But as the line grew, Brooke began calling out each order so that Amanda could help fill it.

During a lull at the window, Amanda checked the till. "Good grief," Amanda said as she examined the piles of bills. "I can't total it in my head like you do, but it looks like we've sold more food and drink in the last twenty minutes than we normally do in an afternoon. Maybe I should send you out into the stands like the Pied Piper and let all the men follow you back."

Brooke laughed. "Thanks, but no thanks." Her expression grew thoughtful. "But it might make sense to upgrade some of your offerings. I bet we could increase the per transaction total two to three percentage points immediately just by adding a few items."

Amanda blinked.

"Your client base is upscale," Brooke continued. "I mean they may be at the ball field, but these people are used to double lattes and Macchiatos from Starbucks. Has anybody looked at the idea of adding some designer coffees? Or maybe even just purchasing a cappuccino maker?"

There was the sound of wheels on gravel and Candace staggered in clutching two large bags of ice to her chest. Her jacket was rumpled and had wet stains across it. "I have a cart out there with three more bags." She looked down at her boots and groaned. "My shoes are finished, but I think I've taken care of the gravel problem. I just stashed all the loose stuff in my shoes and brought it with me."

She limped over to the freezer and stuffed the bags of ice inside. "Did I hear someone say double latte?"

"I bet Candace would pay extra to have one here," Brooke said.

"I'd pay three times as much to be allowed to go have one somewhere else," Candace retorted. "If I'd realized how far that other stand was, I would have driven my car and kept on going."

Candace turned and stomped back outside. Amanda and Brooke followed. Each of them grabbed a bag of ice and hefted it inside.

When all the bags were in the freezer, Candace sank down onto the chair.

"So how'd you end up on concession duty today?" Amanda asked as Brooke turned back to the window.

"I'm not sure," Candace said. "I think this is one of those drawbacks that you read about in magazines to dating a divorced man. When they're taking you to fancy restaurants and trying to get you into bed, they're not necessarily mentioning that they eat and breathe their kids' sports. Dan's actually full of surprises." She blushed, and Amanda thought about the thoroughly sweet man who coached her son. He was tall and well built with an attractive smile and a truckload of patience, but she'd never thought about him naked. And certainly never pictured him in bed.

"One minute I was buttering his . . . toast," Candace said. "The next I was offering to do this." She fingered her pearls, the only part of her outfit, Amanda noticed, that didn't bear signs of the ball field. "I am *so* out of my element here. I feel like Steve Irwin at a cocktail party."

Amanda knew all about treading on unfamiliar ground. She'd been a wife for eighteen years and a full-time homemaker for fifteen of them. Now she stood on the threshold

of a whole new life that she didn't want and hadn't asked
for. The only current bright spot was that Rob didn't appear
to be coming to today's game.

As if reading her mind, Candace asked, "Have you seen
Anne Justiss yet?"

"Yes." Amanda leaned against the prep table. "I found
her whole Green Giant philosophy pretty unnerving.
Doesn't she seem a little . . . scary . . . to you?"

"Absolutely." Candace smiled. "But I've been divorced
three times now, and I can promise you this: when you walk
into court, you don't want to go there with Miss
Congeniality at your side."

chapter 5

That Monday morning, Amanda sat in front of Meghan and Wyatt's computer, a steaming mug of coffee forgotten beside her. She'd gone online to check e-mail as soon as the kids left for school, but although her in-box indicated she could add inches to her bust (pointless at the moment) or get a penile extension (Rob's had already extended far enough, thank you) there was nothing to which she needed to respond.

The day stretched ahead of her. She had no volunteer shifts scheduled, her appointment with Anne Justiss wasn't until tomorrow, and although none of her friends and acquaintances had formally cut her, their calls had tapered off over the last weeks and she felt uncomfortable about calling them.

With a click of the mouse, she opened a newly created file she'd labeled "cleaning projects" and spent a few minutes perusing the list. Her hands on the keyboard belied her rapidly growing cleaning compulsion—she'd begun to wonder if the spirit of Martha Stewart had somehow invaded her body. They were dry and cracked and her fingernails were jagged. If she was going to scrub her way through this downturn in her life, she was going to have to wear gloves while she was doing it.

Logging on to Google, she typed in the words "rubber gloves for cleaning."

Ten pages of possibilities popped up on the screen. Scrolling through the listings, she chose a pair of rubber gloves that had an embossed palm and were guaranteed strong enough for both polishing and waxing. Intrigued by the variety of offerings, she typed in "cleaning" and ten more pages of listings appeared. She followed the link to householdcleaningtips.com then clicked eagerly from site to site, printing out the most interesting products and cleaning tips and dragging them into her cleaning file.

Imagining Martha urging her on, she printed out the list of projects and pulled on her raggediest, most comfortable clothes—probably not at all what Martha would have worn to hunt down dust bunnies. After getting out her supplies and equipment, Amanda started to clean.

Vacuuming her air vents led to wiping down her baseboards, which segued into dusting the wooden blinds on every one of her thirty-eight windows. Shortly after lunch, she took a toothbrush to the grout in the master bathroom.

She poured herself into these domestic tasks, seeking the mental numbness that was supposed to accompany hard physical labor. What she found was a comforting sense of accomplishment that actually freed her brain from the loop of panic it had fallen into, and allowed it to travel at will.

At first her thoughts tumbled from one thing to the next in an odd sort of freefall. One minute she was remembering something one of the children did when they were little, the next it was naming the things she was cleaning in French, as the language she'd learned and then buried rushed back to the fore.

Le tapis beige est très beau. The beige carpet is quite lovely.

Les fenêtres miroitent comme des diamants au soleil. The windows sparkle like diamonds in the sun.

Sacre bleu! If she cleaned long enough she might actually become fluent in French again.

Without warning, her brain latched onto a less welcome image of Jean-Claude. Though she didn't want to, she could actually see his face as he sank down on one knee—the goof—and asked her to marry him.

Sparing her nothing, her brain also allowed her to see the look on his face when she said no. And made her relive his withdrawal when she'd admitted that she didn't trust in their love enough to leave everything she knew to spend her life with him in France.

It was afternoon and she was in the pantry alphabetizing her canned goods—a fact she intended to keep to herself—when her thoughts settled on tomorrow's appointment with Anne Justiss. Although she hadn't heard from Rob, she knew that her attorney had contacted his. She couldn't put off telling the kids any longer.

Placing the final can on the shelf, she tried to figure out how she was going to do it. How did you set the scene for a conversation that no one wanted to have?

Cushion it with food, Martha's voice advised. And then it added, *And make that food French.*

"Wow!" Wyatt's gaze took in the boldly colored tablecloth covering the kitchen table and the vase of cut flowers that sat in the center of it. He inhaled deeply and his eyes lit up like he'd just discovered a new big barrel bat under the Christmas tree. "Is it somebody's birthday or something?"

He looked to Meghan who stood stock-still inside the kitchen door. "I'm definitely in the wrong house." She made a show of turning to leave. "What, exactly, are we celebrating?"

Amanda's heart thudded uncomfortably in her chest as she realized that the table did, in fact, look awfully celebratory. Much too celebratory for the news she was planning to reveal over dessert.

Had her subconscious, which now that she thought about it seemed oddly French, decided that since a divorce was the only logical next step it should be celebrated?

"Nothing," she said quickly. "I just thought we should take advantage of this one night we don't have to be anywhere. And I was in the mood for something French." Now there was an understatement. If she didn't watch out, she was going to turn into a total Francophile.

Wyatt and Meghan tore into the Beef Bourguignon and crusty French bread she'd prepared with an enthusiasm that shamed Amanda. They ate as if they were starved, which she supposed they were. Even Meghan, who normally picked at her food and meticulously counted every calorie, ate with an abandon that turned the gourmet meal to ash on Amanda's tongue.

Long before Rob left, her cooking had become strictly utilitarian. Since his departure, Meghan and Wyatt had been lucky to get something that wasn't delivered to the door or carried home in a sack.

The meal she'd fussed over most of the afternoon, and about which she'd felt so proud turned to lead in her stomach as she thought about the speech she'd been rehearsing while she cooked.

Surreptitiously she studied the faces of her children; Wyatt's younger, rounder version of Rob's blue eyes and sandy eyebrows, Meghan's dark eyes and sharply angled cheekbones that were so similar to her own.

Picking at the food on her plate, she waited while they finished.

"So, *mes enfants*," she said, striving for a light tone and a French accent. "I think eet ees time for zee dessert."

"Cool." Wyatt was still basking in his good fortune, his twelve-year-old brain unable to join such great food with the possibility of bad news.

Meghan got up to help clear the dishes without being asked—an event Amanda would have documented and photographed at any other time—then came back to the table and reclaimed her seat. Her expression turned wary, though whether it was due to the approaching calories or her instincts about what was to come, Amanda didn't know.

Drawing in a steadying breath, Amanda picked up the crème brûlées from the counter and carried them to the table. "And now," she said, "*zee pièce de résistance*." She set the individual ramekins down with a flourish.

Wyatt's smile broadened and he lifted his spoon and immediately dug in. Meghan shot her mother a look, the look of a Christian about to be fed to the lions.

Amanda retrieved her own dessert and forced herself to take a spoonful.

"So what do you think?" she asked, stalling, suddenly wishing for a knock to sound on the door or the phone to ring. She would have sold her soul for a single telemarketer.

"It's great, Mom. Do you have any more?" Wyatt, so sunny and grateful, wiped his face with the back of his sleeve. She didn't have the heart to tell him no.

"Sure. You can have the rest of mine." She pushed the dessert gently toward him.

Meghan set down her spoon and pushed hers toward Wyatt too. "Here, Wy. I have a feeling you're going to need it."

The barb flew right over his head and hit Amanda as it was intended.

"Are we like totally fattened up for the slaughter now?" she asked. "Or are you hoping we'll be so full we'll be comatose and miss the bad news?"

Wyatt stopped eating.

Amanda folded her hands on the table and swallowed painfully. "Meghan's right," she said. "I do have some news and it's, uhm, not particularly good. Though, I, uh, think in the end it will actually turn out to be for the best."

They braced; Meghan, who was trying to sound so tough, clenched her body in an obvious way. Wyatt looked like a puppy who'd spotted the rolled-up newspaper coming toward it, but had no idea how to get out of the way.

Amanda knew that if she let herself look into his eyes, she'd be lost.

The carefully worded speech she'd practiced flew out of her head, forever lost and irretrievable. "I'm filing for divorce," was all she could come up with. "I've hired an attorney and your dad and I are going to get divorced."

There was a long silence, which Meghan finally sliced through. "Well, *duh*," she said, her voice dripping with sarcasm. "He *is* dating someone else."

Amanda felt the pain behind her daughter's bravado; it was an angry slash of hurt she'd never be able to forget. A tear slid down Wyatt's cheek.

"What did you think, you baby?" Meghan said to Wyatt, though Amanda noticed she couldn't face his tears either. "Did you think they were going to kiss and make up?"

She stood and shoved her chair in. "Hey, at least we got a meal out of it."

Wyatt didn't move. He might have been a statue except for the tears sliding down his cheeks.

"That's enough, Meghan. Please," Amanda said. "Sit down so we can talk about this."

"What's there to talk about?" Her daughter's voice was so brittle, her body so rigid, that Amanda was afraid it might break. "You couldn't hold on to him," Meghan said, "and he found somebody younger. It happens all the time."

"Not to us." Amanda reached for Wyatt's hand and squeezed it hard. She reached up toward Meghan, but her daughter wanted none of her.

"I know how hard this has been," Amanda whispered. "And I'm so, so sorry."

"Right." Meghan aimed her words at Amanda like bullets. "Should we start packing now? Or maybe we get to wait until the divorce is finished? He'll probably want to give our house to Tiffany."

"Meghan!" Amanda held on to Wyatt's hand as if it were some sort of lifeline. "That's enough!"

"Is that true, Mom?" Wyatt sounded dazed. "Chris Matthews had to move when his parents got divorced. His mom told him they couldn't afford their house anymore."

"No," Amanda said, "that's not going to happen."

"Yeah," Meghan scoffed, "like you have anything to say about it."

Amanda stood on unsteady legs. Still clutching his hand, she drew Wyatt up with her then slid her other arm around Meghan. Her daughter didn't shrug her off, but her shoulders were so stiff with anger that Amanda couldn't shake the mental image of her shattering into pieces that could never be put together.

"I'll have plenty to say about it," Amanda said. "I'm meeting with the attorney tomorrow morning and no matter what happens, the one thing I can promise you is that we are not going to give up this house. I absolutely will not let that happen."

She stared into her children's eyes; Wyatt's blue ones telegraphing his urgent need to believe, Meghan's brown ones silently shouting her disbelief. In that moment, Amanda vowed to herself that she'd keep that promise she'd just made so blithely. She'd hold on to this house for her children no matter what it took. They were the innocent parties. Their entire world had shifted on its axis and they deserved something familiar to cling to.

They did the dishes together in silence, each retreating into the inner turbulence of their own thoughts. Amanda's were filled with the pledge she'd just made. She'd have to make it clear that the house was not a negotiable item. She would not allow their home—and all that it represented—to be taken from her children.

No matter how hard Anne Justiss had to squeeze.

The Children's Hospital Gala was underway by the time Candace and Dan arrived. It was early March and the theme was Spring Fling. The women's gowns reflected that, the pastel shades and muted jewel tones providing a sophisticated accent to the grand ballroom's sherbert décor.

"Remember," Candace said, straightening the bow tie of Dan's rented tuxedo, "there are all kinds of heavy hitters here tonight. This function could do a lot for your accounting practice."

"My practice is doing fine." Dan took her hand and guided it gently from his throat. "Why don't we just enjoy ourselves?" He smiled impishly. "You look like a bonbon in that dress. Definitely good enough to eat." He brushed his lips across her cheek. "And the orchestra sounds great."

"You never liken a woman to a piece of candy," she admonished, nonetheless pleased by the compliment. "Too fattening." She scanned the room trying to determine the best place to start mingling. "And besides, I don't think Christian Dior was going for 'bonbon' when he designed this gown."

She made a subtle adjustment to her gown's strapless bodice and slipped her arm through the crook of his. Then she led him toward a knot of couples on the far side of the dance floor.

"That's Todd Williams on the left," she whispered as they

crossed the room. "He builds shopping centers. Walter Green is next to him. His family has always owned banks. They were just bought out by Bank of America."

She drew him along with her enjoying the picture she knew they presented, but unsure how Dan would handle himself with this crowd. So far most of their time together had been spent in casual pursuits or in bed. She'd enjoyed both immensely, with the possible exception of the ballpark. But this was her milieu and, she assumed, as alien to him as the concession stand had been to her.

"Hello, darlings." She went up on tiptoe to peck Walter Green on the cheek then slipped an arm around his wife's waist for a social hug. "This is my friend, Dan Donovan. Dan, this is Walter and Tessa Green."

The men extended their hands and shook. Candace was poised to facilitate conversation. If necessary, she could promote Dan and his company without him speaking a word.

"I know you, don't I?" Walter said to Dan. "Is it from the club?"

Candace prepared to step in and save both men any embarrassment, but Dan was smiling easily. When he spoke it was with the same comfortable tone he used with the boys on his team and the clerk at the convenience store.

"I helped with an audit you were conducting before the merger. And then I strong-armed you into making a donation to the inner-city baseball program. We put your money to good use."

"That's right." Walter's smile was equally genuine. He turned to the man beside him and said, "Todd. Want you to meet Dan . . ."

"Donovan." Dan put out his hand and shook comfortably. A moment later, the men were discussing the inner city baseball program and then moved on to the Braves' current lineup. Candace accepted a glass of wine from a passing waiter and tuned in to Tessa, surprised to realize that Dan didn't need her to run interference or help him through any social awkwardness.

Conversation among the women began with their offspring then turned, as it often did, to their "help."

"I'd give anything for someone I could give instructions to in English," Sandra Williams said. "Our maid is Brazilian, and she's absolutely lovely, but I don't speak a word of Portuguese and she has about ten words of English. We use sign language and charades in order to communicate. You can't really get what you want when you can't express the details."

"Tell me about it." Tessa leaned closer. "Have you ever tried to act out toilet paper?"

Laughing, Candace glanced over Tessa Green's shoulder and spotted Brooke and Hap Mackenzie. The redhead looked lovely, but uncomfortable, in the only black gown in a sea of pastels. It was also a tad too revealing, with a plunging neckline that revealed creamy white breasts. It was too bad, Candace thought. With Brooke's thick auburn hair and her elegant figure, the right sort of dress would have made all the difference.

The men's conversation continued. Reassured by Dan's easy participation, she tuned them out. Listening to the ladies with half an ear, she smiled at the appropriate pauses in conversation and subtly scanned the room.

In a distant corner, she spotted Rob Sheridan, the louse,

with the sparkly Tiffany on his arm. Tiffany looked even less comfortable than Brooke, or maybe that was just wishful thinking. Amanda Sheridan had spent most of her adult life focused on her husband and family and she'd been supplanted by an empty head of blonde hair and a perky set of breasts. Candace shook her head, resenting the girl on Amanda's behalf. Women of a certain age needed to stick together. She made a mental note to check in with Amanda tomorrow. Maybe she'd like to do lunch or go out for a drink.

Realizing the conversation flowing around her had come to a halt, Candace pulled her attention back to Tessa and Sandra.

"I'm sorry," Candace apologized. "What did you say?"

Tessa nodded to a group of women to their left. "Isn't that your mother?"

Slowly, so as not to call attention to herself, Candace turned her head and followed Tessa's gaze. She loved her mother and knew that in her own way she meant well, but tonight the words "isn't that your mother" filled her with the same sort of dread she might have felt if someone had said, "isn't that Typhoid Mary?"

"Yes," she said, "it is, isn't it?" Which was very surprising since her mother was supposed to be in Florida right now.

As subtly as she could, she slipped her arm back through Dan's and squeezed gently. "I, um, wondered if you could come with me for a minute?" she asked quietly as he turned to her. To the group, she offered a smile and said, "Will you excuse us? There's someone on the other side of the room I want Dan to meet."

They extracted themselves and without comment she

propelled them to the right, away from her mother. Though she wanted to, she was very careful not to actually cut and run. Instead she walked sedately—OK she might have been tiptoeing—while she tried to figure out how to slip out without being noticed. And how to explain to Dan why she suddenly wanted to leave.

"What's the matter?" Dan looked down at her, his eyes telegraphing his concern. "You're trembling."

She was contemplating feigning a headache when she heard her mother's voice behind her.

"Candace?"

Candace froze, bringing Dan to a stop with her. She let go of his arm and barely resisted the urge to shout, "Save yourself! Run, get away as fast as you can." Slowly she turned. Dan turned with her.

Hannah Bloom was short by anyone's standards, but she was mighty. Possessing incalculable quantities of will and determination, she was a force of nature. In hurricane terms, Hannah Bloom was a category five.

"Mother!" Candace didn't have to feign her surprise. "I thought you were out of town." Which was why, of course, she'd felt safe bringing Dan to this function.

"Ida asked me to stay to help with Myra Mench's daughter's bridal shower, so I decided not to go. You look like a bonbon in that dress." She said it with none of the affection that had filled Dan's voice.

"Yes, I was telling her that earlier. It's fabulous, isn't it?" Dan wrapped an arm around Candace's bare shoulder, clearly offering his support. "I'm tempted to start calling her Candy."

"Don't." Candace and her mother uttered the word in

unison. Her mother's tone was adamant, Candace's automatic. At the age of three, when she was preparing to enter preschool, "Don't call me Candy" was the phrase her mother had taught her to share with her classmates.

Candace would have explained that to Dan now, but all of her mother's formidable attention was focused on him. Candace's goal now was to minimize casualties and get out alive.

"And who is this?" Her mother asked Candace the question, though her gaze remained on Dan.

"This is Dan Donovan, my date for the evening." Candace felt Dan flinch as she relegated him to the level of paid escort. But she knew her mother too well to think that Dan Donovan was going to pass muster. The tall, dark, good-looking part might fly; the not-so-ambitious and definitely-not-Jewish part would not.

"Oh?" Hannah Bloom's tone was icily polite. Candace knew what was coming. As her mother liked to say, all she wanted was what she thought was best for her only daughter; the words "what *she* thought best" being the operative ones.

Candace knew what sort of men her mother deemed best for her; she knew because she'd married—and divorced—three of them. Dan Donovan wasn't one of those kind of men.

She straightened her shoulders and battened down her mental hatches, wondering just how old she'd have to be before she stopped trying to win her mother's approval. Then she threw Dan an apologetic look as Hannah Bloom, with the surgical precision of a trial attorney, commenced the third degree.

"So, Daniel," she said in a deceptively friendly voice. "You don't mind if I call you Daniel, do you?"

"Of course not."

"Where are your people from?"

Dan smiled and Candace thought she saw a twinkle steal into his eyes, which told her he had no idea who he was dealing with. "Originally, County Cork. Ireland, ma'am. More recently, to be sure, we're from Boston."

Candace turned slowly to consider Dan Donovan who, if she wasn't mistaken, now had a distinctly Irish lilt in his voice.

"How interesting," the Grand Inquisitor said. "And what do you do, here in Atlanta?"

"I'm an accountant."

Hannah brightened a little at that. "Oh. Are you with one of the large firms?"

"I'm afraid not," Dan replied. "'Twould be a fine thing of course. But I'm a sole practitioner. It allows me my freedom, don't you know."

Candace had a bad feeling the next words out of his mouth were going to be "faith and begorra."

She nudged Dan gently, but his attention was focused on her mother. He didn't look the least bit worried. Or apologetic.

"Dan is very involved in charitable works, Mother," Candace felt compelled to point out. "And he coaches his son's Little League baseball team, the Mudhens."

"How nice that you have the time for that." Her mother's tone made it clear that she believed only the underemployed would have time for that sort of thing. "How many children *do* you have?" Here the assumption was that someone named Donovan would have a truckload.

"Just the one," Dan said easily, the smile and the lilt firmly in place, "which was a sore disappointment to me sainted mother. I was one of seven." He winked. "I'd love to have more, meself. And I don't think it's ever too late."

Candace told herself Dan hadn't really said "me sainted mother" or "meself," except of course he had.

She shot her mother an appraising glance, but saw no sign that she realized how thoroughly she was being had. Candace knew for a fact that it was time to beat a retreat, but it was beginning to occur to her that they weren't necessarily going to be leaving with their tails between their legs as she had expected.

"I always think it's a shame for the only child." Dan was still on the subject of children, a subject Candace had given up on a long time ago. "They have no one to squabble with. No character-building issues over hand-me-downs or lack of personal space. And just think of all that parental attention and adoration aimed solely at them. Imagine what that can do to a child."

Hannah Bloom flinched. It was a small movement, not much more than a blink, really, but Candace saw it. The unimaginable had happened. A mild-mannered, unassuming accountant had thrown himself in the path of an oncoming train and somehow managed to alter its course.

"Well then," Candace said much too brightly, "I'm so glad you two had the chance to get acquainted." With Dan's arm still around her shoulder, she leaned forward and gave her mother a peck on the cheek. "There's someone else we need to say hello to and then we really have to be going. I have a, um, headache. And I think we should go lie down for a while."

Her mother gasped.

"I mean, *I'm* going to go lie down. At home. By me . . . myself. Dan is just going to drive me there." She finally clamped her mouth shut to halt the babbling.

Dan just smiled his good-bye and followed along without comment. But his blue eyes twinkled merrily.

chapter 6

H ave a seat," Anne Justiss said as she ushered Amanda into her office the next morning. "Would you like some coffee? A Danish?"

Goosebumps shot up Amanda's spine as she took in the attorney's tone of voice and the look of concern on her face. The offering of food felt especially inauspicious.

"No thanks." She braced herself, much as her children had done the night before, barely able to wait for the attorney to walk around the desk and take her seat.

"What's wrong?" Amanda asked, not really wanting to know, wishing for about the thousandth time since her life had spun out of control that she could turn back the clock. This time she'd settle for right before she'd walked into this office. Right before her alarm had gone off this morning might be even safer.

"It turns out that your husband's financial balls are much smaller than we expected them to be." This time there was no accompanying smile or hint of laughter. "In fact, they appear to be nonexistent."

Amanda's stomach dropped somewhere around her knees. The one thing she'd been counting on was the cleansing effect of taking her husband to the cleaners, of leaving him up a creek without a financial paddle.

"Actually, he seems to have been living beyond his means for some time."

Amanda was trying, but she simply could not get her brain around this. "Beyond his means? But he has a huge salary from the law firm and he's made all kinds of investments over the years."

The attorney's eyes telegraphed her regret. "Oh, he's made investments all right—all of them ill advised. Each one of them has weakened his position even further."

"Are you sure?"

"Unfortunately, yes. I put the best forensic accountant we have on it because something felt off."

She studied Amanda as if trying to determine whether she needed to call the paramedics. "And I'm afraid it gets worse."

As if anything could be worse than Rob's lack of money at this particular point in time; money she'd been counting on to smooth the transition for the kids.

"He's apparently been dipping into client trust accounts to cover his personal losses."

Amanda stared at Anne Justiss hoping against hope that she'd misunderstood her. "But he's an attorney. That's illegal!"

"It most certainly is. And it happens far more often than most people realize." Anne Justiss looked down at the file in front of her then back up at Amanda, her gaze unwavering. "We do have some leverage. Depending on how we handle this information, your husband could be disbarred or end up in jail. But, of course, with either of those scenarios his earning potential is cut off for good. That's not in your, or the children's, best interests."

Stunned, Amanda tried to take it in. She'd promised the children they'd keep the house. But that was when she'd assumed the house was just one of many assets available to divide. And as angry as she was with Rob, did she really want to send Meghan and Wyatt's father to prison? Tying him in the basement and torturing him, yes, letting him languish in a real prison with hardened criminals, no.

"I can't lose the house," Amanda said. "I promised the kids it would be ours."

"I'm going to get you the house, Amanda," Anne Justiss said. "That I promise. The payments are low and you've got a good bit of equity in it. If you sell it and scale back, you should be able to buy some time to get on your feet."

Amanda shook her head slowly. "But, I told the kids they wouldn't have to move."

"Unfortunately, they're going to have to get used to a lot of things they shouldn't have to. Your husband has a lot to answer for."

But Amanda was the one who'd have to face Meghan and Wyatt; she was the one who would be held accountable. Somehow she'd have to find a way to keep her promise to them. Anything less was completely unacceptable.

Anne Justiss's smile was apologetic. "I'm sorry, Amanda. I'd hoped to do so much better for you. We need to give some serious thought about how to proceed. Your husband's firm isn't going to want this made public, so he may not end up disbarred. Still whatever happens, he's not going to be of any financial help for a long time to come, if ever."

She closed the file on her desk and stood to shake hands. "I have a meeting scheduled for Monday morning with his attorney. We'll see who's still standing after this little bomb gets dropped."

Once again, Amanda drove home from Anne Justiss's office in a fog. One minute she was stumbling toward the law office's parking garage. The next she was pulling into her own.

When the kids got home, she put on her mother smile and heartiest good humor and ferried them to where they had to go, grateful that they were both sleeping over at friends. She might have been a drama major but at the moment acting normal was a real stretch.

When she got home again, she picked up the telephone and punched in Rob's number. She needed to know how this had happened, needed to have some sense of perspective on how their lives had gotten so flushed down the toilet.

"Rob Sheridan's office." His secretary answered on the third ring.

It was a challenge to keep her voice steady. "Is he there, Cindy?"

"Sorry, Mrs. Sheridan," the secretary said. "He's out of town for the day taking a deposition. He's due back early this evening."

Hanging up, Amanda punched in her parents' cell phone

number but hung up before the call went through. For months she'd failed to offer so much as a hint that there was a problem. How could she call now and admit to total defeat?

She stared at the phone searching her brain for the right person to call, but the hard cold truth was there was no one. She knew lots of women through her volunteer commitments and the kids' activities but she'd been so wrapped up in her family and her responsibilities that she hadn't pushed very far beyond the surface with anyone; had never gone the extra mile necessary to establish and maintain that kind of closeness. She had had pleasant social relationships with many women, but there wasn't a single one she felt she could share all of this with now.

She was still clutching the phone when it rang.

"Hello?"

"Amanda? Is that you?" Candace's voice was firm and smooth with none of the wobbliness Amanda felt in hers.

"Yes. How are you, Candace?"

"Fine. I just called to check in and say hi. Dan and I were at the Children's Hospital fund-raiser last night, and I saw some of your favorite people there."

"Oh. That's nice."

"Amanda? Are you OK?"

That simple question from an almost stranger opened the floodgates. "I'm fine." Amanda choked on the word. A sob escaped despite her attempts to hold it back. "Everything's . . . good." Except, of course, for her life in general and her future in particular.

"I'm coming over."

"That's not necessary." She suspected her protest would

have sounded more convincing if it hadn't come between sobs.

"Don't argue. We can be there in fifteen minutes. Brooke Mackenzie is already on the way here. We ran into each other at the fund-raiser and Hap's out of town. Do you mind if I bring her?"

At the moment Amanda didn't care if Candace brought the man in the moon. It was human contact and she would take it right now any way she could get it. "OK." She sniffed. "Thanks."

"And if you're not dressed get some clothes on. You sound like you need a drink—maybe lots of drinks. We'll take you out. The last place you need to be right now is sitting at home."

Brooke and Candace led Amanda out of the car and into Chili's. As they were shown to their table, Brooke couldn't help noticing that they were the only women over the age of twenty who were there without children or men. The suburbs were not designed for single women of any age. It took a strong woman to operate alone within its borders.

As far as Brooke could see, Candace managed by holding herself apart from it all; she might be dating the coach of a Little League team, but she wasn't concerned about communing with the moms. Nor was she scrambling for position like a lot of the women were. How grand it must be to feel so sure of oneself, so not in need of others' approval.

Amanda was different. She was a baseball mom/suburban hausfrau down to her toes and she didn't appear to have any desire to be anything else. Her husband's desertion had obliterated the world as she knew it.

Brooke thought about how different their lives had been from hers and how shocked they would be if she told them exactly where she'd come from and how hard she'd worked to create the woman she presented to the world.

Except, of course, that she'd never even told her husband and suspected she never would.

As soon as they were seated, Candace called the waiter over. He appeared to be about twelve. "What are we drinking?"

"Nothing for me," Brooke said. "I'll be the designated driver." She saw Amanda's face fall. "But Amanda deserves to take the edge off, and I doubt she wants to do it alone."

Candace turned to Amanda. "I'm thinking margaritas. Are you with me?"

Amanda simply nodded.

"A pitcher of margaritas," Candace told the server. "Anybody interested in food?"

Nobody was.

The waiter scurried off and the three of them looked at each other expectantly. They knew each other, but didn't, and as far as Brooke could tell, they didn't have anything in common. Still she wanted to help Amanda if possible and she could tell that Candace did too. It was a place to start.

"OK, Amanda," Candace said. "I think you need to tell us what happened today. We are taking an absolute vow of silence, a pledge of confidentiality." She looked to Brooke who nodded in agreement.

"This"—she motioned to the table at which they sat— "will be your confessional in the Temporary Church of Chili's. And you can think of me as your . . . sister confessor . . . one of the few Jewish women to ever hold this position."

Even Amanda smiled at that.

The waiter arrived and set the frosty glasses in front of them then poured Amanda and Candace a drink. "Thank you, Sister Candace, for the offer of spiritual guidance," Amanda said. "And for these margaritas which we are about to consume."

Amanda and Candace drank their margaritas down and slammed the empty glasses onto the table. Candace poured a second round.

"I can't go into the details right now," Amanda said licking the froth from the corner of her mouth, "but the bottom line is Rob doesn't *have* a bottom line."

"Has he managed to hide it all?" Candace asked, her eyes narrowing. "One of my husbands tried to take two of his companies offshore, but Anne Justiss headed him off."

"I wouldn't exactly call the money . . . hidden," Amanda said, sipping on her margarita. "But I'm going to be lucky to get the house. And even if I get the house, I'm not sure how I'm going to be able to afford to hold on to it."

Amanda turned her glass up and emptied the rest of it in one long gulp. Candace followed suit.

That was, Brooke noticed, two down in about as many minutes.

"Well that sucks." Candace picked up the pitcher and held it out toward Brooke. "Are you sure you don't want a taste? I really don't think half a glass is going to impair your driving."

"No thanks. I don't drink," Brooke said.

"At all?" Candace's surprise was evident. Amanda's attention was pretty much fixed on her empty glass.

"No," Brooke repeated. And if their mothers had climbed into a bottle each night after getting home from cleaning houses, they wouldn't either.

The waiter came back to suggest chips and salsa. "Food might be a good idea," Brooke pointed out. "It can't hurt to soak up a little of that alcohol." Neither Candace or Amanda were interested, but Brooke ordered for them anyway.

While they waited, Amanda finished her third margarita. Her eyes were starting to look glassy and her words came out more slowly than usual. "Candace is right. Everything sucks big time."

The near profanity sounded strange coming from Amanda's lips. She took another drink and once again, tipped her glass up and drained it.

At this rate, Brooke thought, the two of them were going to be under the table before the chips even arrived. She wondered how she'd get them back into her car.

"I feel so helpless. All these horrible things keep happening and I never get to strike back." Amanda hiccupped then giggled in surprise. "Rob just keeps dishing it out and I just keep taking it." She shot a look of longing at the now empty pitcher. "That doesn't seem at all equitable." She turned to Brooke, her gaze unfocused. "Do you think it's equita . . . babble? Equita . . . bubble?" She shook her head as if trying to figure out what was wrong with her lips. "Fair?"

"No, it's not," Brooke conceded. "And if *you're* not safe from this kind of thing, I don't know who is. I mean you must be pretty close to forty and all, but it's not like you've totally let yourself go or anything."

"Gee, thanks." Amanda tried to roll her unfocused eyes.

"What I mean is," Brooke amended, "at what point is a woman safe? Now that I'm a wife, how do I keep someone like me from coming along?"

"If you can figure that one out, I'll bankroll your run for president." Candace ran a finger over the remaining salt on the rim of her glass and licked it off. She sounded just as forceful as she had earlier but her words seemed to be coming out more slowly too. "I personally think that striking back is very important," she said. "It cleanses the soul and helps you blow off some of the anger. It can help you move forward." Candace took another sip of her drink. "In fact, now that I think of it, I'm a big proponent of revenge as a self-help tool." She sat up and set down her glass. "I've always been attracted to monetary punishment, but I think any form of revenge would probably help."

Brooke thought food would help even more. Lots of food to soak up the alcohol they'd consumed.

"Well, I'd like some revenge right now," Amanda said. "And I don't even care in what form I get it." She waved to their waiter. When he arrived, finally bearing the chips and dip, she leaned forward and whispered conspiratorially, "I don't think we need those chips after all. We just need the check. I have to go punish somebody. And my two new friends are going to help me."

They piled into Brooke's car. Well, actually Candace and Brooke piled, Amanda sort of oozed in. She wanted to come up with something scathingly brilliant that Rob would never forget, but she had neither the resources nor, at the moment, the mental abilities required. She knew she should be worried about her lack of mental acuity, but the alcoholic fog that now enveloped her was too comforting to object to. It was warm and fuzzy inside there, like being in a big protective bubble. Amanda didn't want to come out any time soon.

"OK, so what do we have in mind for Rob? Should we slash his tires? E-mail naked photos of him to his clients?" Candace asked.

Amanda didn't really care what she did to him as long as she did something. For at least one moment in the midst of all this mess, she wanted to be the one acting rather than the one being acted upon. No matter how small the gesture, she simply had to make one.

Brooke put on the brakes at a stoplight and a small drugstore bag sitting on the seat beside Amanda slid to the floor. Its contents spilled out and as she picked them up, she noticed the word *Trojan*. "What have we here?" She giggled— her, Amanda Sheridan, who had not giggled for at least a dozen years. "We have condoms." She stopped laughing as the realization hit her. "But I don't need condoms." Stricken, she held the box aloft and slid forward in her seat so that she could talk to Brooke and Candace. "I may never need condoms again." Her eyes teared up.

"Amanda, there are plenty of other men out there. I know. I've been out with what feels like millions of them." Candace's words were slightly slurred, but they were still reassuring. "I'll buy you some condoms for your birthday if you want. We'll get you a whole truckload of them."

Candace smiled crookedly at her. "Because that's what friends are for."

Amanda smiled through her tears. "That's one of the sweetest things anyone's ever said to me."

"Good grief," Brooke said. "You two are completely wasted."

"But I don't need anyone to buy me condoms," Amanda continued. "I'm not officially poor yet. I can buy my own condoms. And I can buy as many as I want."

She opened the box in her hands and took one out. "I've always thought they looked kind of like balloons. Do you think they look like balloons, Candace?"

"Nope."

"I wonder if they blow up like balloons." Amanda stretched the condom several times. Drawing in a deep breath, she brought the rubber to her mouth, placed her lips over the rolled edge, and blew mightily. Only the tip expanded.

"You're right." She expelled the words along with the air she'd been holding. "They don't inflate."

"They're thicker than balloons," Candace said. "And, of course, they are designed for a slightly different purpose. I don't suppose you have a bicycle pump in your car do you, Brooke?"

Even Brooke giggled. "I can't believe you're sitting in my backseat trying to blow up prophylactics. Which I can't believe I left sitting where you two nutcases could play with them."

Amanda raised the condom to her lips and made one last futile attempt to inflate the thing.

"What size are they?" Candace asked. "Not that it probably matters."

The condom flew out of Amanda's mouth with her laughter. "So you're saying size *is* a factor?"

Candace's tone was droll—drunk, but droll. "Well, you can bet they don't come in small. I've never met a man who would admit to needing anything less than an extra large."

"Oh God, now I'm picturing a whole row of cocktail wieners stuffed into oversized buns," Brooke groaned.

There was more laughter.

It was then that the synapses in Amanda's brain fired and made the connection. Or at least something did. Later she wouldn't know what possessed her, but at the moment the thought seemed a completely logical progression of everything that had come before. "Pull into that Kroger," she directed Brooke, "and let me run in. I think Rob deserves to see at least one of the things he's taken away from me. I'm going to buy every single condom I can get my hands on and whether they inflate or not, I'm going to hang them on the tree in front of his town house. It'll be a little reminder gift from me to him."

chapter 7

Trying not to weave too noticeably, Amanda walked through the grocery store past the office supplies to the pharmacy and closed in on the rack of condoms. Without stopping to analyze their features or to contemplate whether ribbing and/or mint flavoring, did, in fact, increase pleasure, she pulled all thirty-odd boxes from their holders and dropped them into her basket.

Buoyed by the soft haze of alcohol, she pushed her booty back to the front of the store and wheeled into the checkout lane. A few moments later, she'd piled the lot of them onto the conveyor.

"Wow." The male voice behind her was deep and laced with laughter. "It looks like you're taking the 'be prepared' credo awfully seriously."

Amanda turned and looked up into a pair of clearly amused green eyes.

"Think you have enough there?"

Amanda contemplated the man in front of her. He was well over six feet and had an interestingly craggy face. It took her alcohol-deadened brain a little longer than it might have otherwise to register the wide shoulders and rock-hard build.

Normally, she would have blushed and stammered and searched for some sort of plausible explanation like a children's science project or some novel cleaning technique.

But he was looking at her in a way she hadn't been looked at in years and it was a balm to her unappreciated and completely rejected soul.

"Gee." She found herself teasing back. "I don't know. Maybe I should run and pick up a few more."

His smile grew wider.

She smiled back. "Unfortunately this purchase is not exactly what it seems."

"No, I'm sure it's not." He was clearly trying not to laugh. "Because that would be way too good to be true."

He winked at her then. God, he was yummy. And she was fairly certain it wasn't just the alcohol that was saying so.

"Are you ready, ma'am?"

With real regret, Amanda turned her back on the stranger and stepped up to the register.

The checkout girl blushed as she scanned each box of condoms and slid it down to the bag boy who also blushed each time he dropped a box into the waiting grocery sack.

Amanda barely noticed. She was much too busy basking in the green-eyed stranger's attention and congratulating herself on her boldness so far.

She wished she had the nerve to give him her name and

number. Or at least the wit to exit with a truly racy comment that he'd remember long after she'd gone.

Unable to do either, she reached for her bags and prepared to depart. Once again, his voice reached her from behind. It was deep and casually masculine with that truly attractive hint of laughter.

"You're not going to leave without telling me what they're for?" he asked.

She turned then and smiled—a full wattage affair that showed each and every one of her pearly whites to full advantage. And then, because she'd definitely had too much to drink and because the occasion seemed to demand it, she turned her voice all husky and growly, like a modern day Mae West. "I am stunned that you don't know what they're for by now, big boy," she purred as she turned to leave. "I only wish I had the time tonight to show you."

Amanda woke Saturday morning to complete quiet. Slightly, but not unbearably hungover due, she was sure, to the two aspirin Brooke had forced her to swallow before she dropped her at home, she lay in bed reliving last night's margarita-fueled evening.

She, Amanda Sheridan, had not only flirted with an incredibly attractive man she'd never seen before, she'd tied three hundred plus condoms to the branches of Rob's Bradford pear tree.

She smiled as she remembered Candace and Brooke's whispered words of encouragement and the muffled laughter that had accompanied them. It had, of course, been a totally stupid and futile gesture, but even now with her head throbbing and her financial future still bleak, she was glad that she'd made it.

Pulling on a robe, she put on a pot of coffee and went outside to retrieve the morning paper. Around her, the neighborhood slept. Garage doors remained down. Houses were shuttered, drapes still drawn across windows. The sun was up, but not yet making much of a statement.

Barefoot, Amanda walked gingerly down the driveway and out onto the dew-draped grass to pick up the paper. The only sounds cutting the silence were the occasional chirp of a bird and the honk of a duck from the nearby pond.

The phone was ringing as she entered the kitchen and she didn't need the caller ID to tell her who it was.

"Whoever tied all those condoms on my tree needs to have their head examined. There must be two hundred of them." Rob sounded a lot less mellow than usual.

"Three hundred and twenty-five, actually," she said. "And I think you've got bigger problems than a condom cleanup."

"What does that mean?"

"That means your attorney will be hearing from mine on Monday. She found the trust account fraud, Rob. You're in serious trouble."

"Shit." He sounded as deflated as the condoms currently dangling from his tree.

"Is that all you have to say?" she asked. "What happened, Rob? What's going on? The man I married would never have treated his family or his clients this way."

Amanda stared out the kitchen window of the house they'd shared and which she now had to find a way to hold on to. "And what are we supposed to do now? Did you give any thought at all to us when you were stealing from your clients and throwing away everything we had together?"

"It wasn't like that, Amanda. I didn't mean for any of this to happen."

She waited in silence, her anger building.

"I had an investment go south and I had to cover the debt. But I put the money back in the account and swore I'd never do it again. Then I was short again, I was always short somehow, and I just couldn't see any other way out."

"Why didn't you say something? I thought we were supposed to be in this together." She could hear the hurt in her voice and hated it. She preferred the anger that accompanied it, so hot and fluid.

"Jesus," he said, and she could picture him raking his hand through his hair. "I'm so completely screwed."

Amanda couldn't believe it. He'd trashed all of their lives and jeopardized his children's futures and still he was thinking of himself. The only one who might walk away unscathed was Tiffany.

"We're all screwed, Rob," she said, struggling to keep her voice even when all she wanted to do was shriek out her rage and fear. "And I'm just curious what you would suggest I do about this? How am I supposed to support Meghan and Wyatt when I've been a stay-at-home mom for fifteen years? What kind of job do you think I'm going to be able to get that doesn't require me to say 'do you want fries with that?' "

There was no answer from Rob and she realized as she slammed down the phone, there wasn't going to be. She was on her own whether she wanted to be or not. And she was going to have to find a way to accept that.

Acceptance might have come more easily if the Sunday classifieds contained even a single salaried position for an exceptionally experienced multitasking carpool driver. Or if Meghan hadn't presented herself dressed and ready, wanting to know when they could leave to go shopping for her prom dress.

By two that afternoon, she and Meghan were picking their way through the throng of Sunday shoppers at the mall. Meghan was practically vibrating with excitement as they moved through the crowds. Amanda was expending most of her energy trying to squash down her panic; the last thing she should be doing right now was spending money they didn't have.

"So, what kind of dress do you have in mind?" Amanda asked. It was hard to get in the proper acquisitional mood when her biggest concern wasn't style, but price. Clearance priced would be good. Drastically reduced even better.

"Oh, I don't know," Meghan said. "I kind of figured I'd know it when I saw it."

Amanda looked at her daughter. Meghan rarely talked about the coming divorce, but her moods had begun to change with the unpredictability and intensity of a supercell thunderstorm. Not for the first time, Amanda wished there was some manual for divorce: a set of guidelines for navigating the uncharted waters.

"Let's start at Nordstrom and then move on to Parisian and Macy's." Amanda considered her daughter's tall, lithe body. "I see you in something simple and classic that screams good taste." She couldn't help adding, "And doesn't cost an arm and a leg."

Meghan stiffened. "Lucy Simmons got a designer gown from a trunk show at Saks." Meghan's tone swelled with envy. "Her mother said it was worth every penny."

"That's nice." Amanda swallowed her irritation. "But Lucy's pudgy and doesn't have a waist. She *needs* designer help. You'd look great in a sack."

Meghan rolled her eyes. "Nice try, Mom. Maybe you should tell me our budget before we start so I don't fall in love with something I can't have."

Unfortunately, the amount they could afford was much too close to zero to share with Meghan. Because, really, they shouldn't be here at all. "I kind of figured I'd know it when I saw it," she said, copying Meghan's nonchalant tone.

"OK," her daughter said, reluctant to let the conversation go. "But I sure hope we both know and see it at the same time. Everybody else already has their dresses."

"I'm ready," Amanda said, banishing the worry, wanting desperately to enjoy the shopping rituals she and Meghan had developed over the years. "Are you?"

Meghan gave a thumbs-up. "Yep!" Her smile turned less brittle and her eyes gleamed with enthusiasm. Amanda would give a lot to keep that look in her daughter's eyes.

"OK, then," Amanda directed. "You start over there. I'll take this side. We'll work toward each other."

"Check."

"On your mark, get set . . ." Amanda brought her hand down like the flag before a race.

At the nearest rack of size sixes, they began to pan for

gold, looking and assessing, rejecting and considering as they slowly narrowed the gap between them.

"Oooh, look at this!" Meghan, the first to find a nugget, held up a turquoise taffeta ball gown with a nonexistent back.

"Interesting," Amanda conceded, careful not to point out the lack of a back or ask the price. Meghan might take a dozen gowns into the dressing room. There was no point in worrying about specific dresses this early in the game. "I'm not sure about the drape though. I'd definitely try it on."

For the next few hours, Amanda pushed aside the panic and gave herself up to the joy of seeing her daughter preen in front of mirrors and whirl in gowns that clung and caressed her newly feminine curves. Everything looked good on her, everything brought color to her cheeks and a sparkle to her eyes, but nothing swept them away until the very last store a very few minutes before closing time.

"Oh, Mom, look!" Meghan turned slowly from the mirror to face Amanda. Her dark hair swirled around her bare shoulders and her face shone with delight.

The strapless silver sheath was the simplest of the gowns she'd tried on; just a column of silk that slid down her body, molding to each curve, revealing but subtle, a dress that called attention to the girl wearing it rather than the dress itself.

"It's perfect," they breathed in unison. Tears welled in Amanda's eyes at this glimpse of what her daughter already was, and what she would become.

Meghan closed her eyes as if in prayer. "I'm afraid to look at the tag." She looked to Amanda, hope and fear showing in her eyes. "It's so simple. Does that make it more or less expensive?" She turned back to study herself in the mirror. "You come look. I can't do it."

Slowly, Amanda moved to Meghan. She didn't want to look, either, didn't want anything to ruin this moment.

Rob's desertion, his betrayal, the divorce, their financial ruin, all of it had been thrust, unbidden, on her children. Her daughter deserved this moment of joy. And she deserved to go to her prom in a dress that made her feel fabulous, not in a dress chosen solely for its price tag.

Standing next to Meghan, Amanda looked at the two of them in the mirror. Her daughter was already as tall as she was. Her build, the slash of her cheekbones, the slight upward slant of the brown eyes, were identical to her own.

Reaching out, she grasped the tag poking out from beneath Meghan's arm and flipped it so she could read the numbers.

Stifling a gasp, she looked down again, hoping she'd misread it. Surely someone had added an extra place value by mistake. Or they'd accidentally hung a couture gown in the junior's eveningwear department.

"It's too much, isn't it?" Meghan's shoulders drooped and the light in her eyes dimmed.

Her gaze locked with Amanda's and Amanda, who'd been expecting anger and frustration saw regret and a sad understanding instead.

"It's OK, Mom. We'll just take one of the other ones." She turned to the gowns hanging on the hooks. "The black one was nice. And I kind of like the blue satin."

Amanda noticed that Meghan didn't look in the mirror again. But Amanda couldn't take her eyes off her daughter in the perfect silver dress.

Meghan's resignation tore through her. In that instant Amanda knew it didn't matter how much the dress cost. The silver sheath was perfect, and Amanda was going to buy it for her even if she had to go out and rob a bank to pay for it.

"No," Amanda said, reaching out a finger to lift Meghan's chin. She turned her slowly so that she could see herself once again in the mirror. "You don't walk away from something that perfect no matter what it costs."

"But . . ."

"No buts. It's yours. Fortunately it doesn't need accessorizing and we can dye a pair of heels to match, so there'll be no other expenses."

She kept her voice calm and matter-of-fact despite the pounding of her heart and the mocking voice in her head that said, "Don't do it, Meghan will understand. Don't add more debt when you have no way to pay for it."

Amanda ignored all the reasonable things the voice said. Instead, she focused on her daughter's joy, listening with a brief stab of happiness as Meghan called her friends from the car to describe in agonizing detail the incredible dress her mother had just bought for her.

At home, Meghan raced into her room to try the dress on one more time.

Amanda raced to her bedroom clutching the classifieds, hoping she'd find something she missed earlier, trying to still her growing horror at the amount of money she'd just spent. First thing tomorrow, she was going to have to start looking for a job.

chapter 8

By eleven Monday morning, Amanda had put in applications at two art galleries, one ladies' clothing boutique, and a trendy little coffee shop/bookstore in the quaint historic shopping area near her home.

No one was dying to hire her, but no one told her to get lost, either, which given the current state of her ego was a definite plus. Leaving the historic district, she spent the next several hours cruising through the strip malls and shopping centers in the northeastern Atlanta suburb where she lived, stopping anywhere that looked remotely possible to fill out an application and inquire about work. As she had when she'd condomed Rob's tree, she found comfort in the act of taking action. She could no longer afford to sit and wait for things to improve; if there was a job to be had within a ten-mile radius of Chandler's Pond, she intended to have it.

It was close to three PM when she pulled the van to a stop in the Steinmart parking lot. For several long minutes,

Amanda sat and stared at the familiar storefront. Of all the places she'd stopped this morning, this was the one in which she'd be most likely to run into friends and acquaintances.

"It's no big deal," she said out loud. "Don't be such a wuss. You're just going to ask about employment opportunities and fill out an application, just like you've done everywhere else."

Getting out of the car, she walked across the parking lot and stepped up onto the curb. "You know their inventory as well as they do," she reminded herself as she pulled open the door.

Inside, a line of customers with returns waited for help at the service desk. Unable to force herself to ask for a job in front of an audience, Amanda strolled through the women's section, pausing occasionally to look through a rack or finger a fabric.

Although Amanda knew women who continued careers or worked to bring in a second income, most of the women in her circle were full-time mothers who dabbled at enterprise.

They took spaces in cute little antique malls or sold things on eBay. Some gave jewelry and Tupperware parties, or sold gifts or imported things from their homes. A few taught exercise classes, but it was tacitly understood that they did this from choice not necessity. They were simply trying to pursue an interest or pick up some extra money. They weren't punching a time clock at a minimum wage job.

The few times she'd run into an acquaintance working on the floor of a neighborhood store, they'd both flushed with embarrassment that they'd been very careful not to acknowledge.

She could hardly believe that she was hoping to become one of those women.

After completing a pass through clothing and another through accessories, Amanda staked out a spot behind a rack of new summer blazers. Eyeing the desk, she waited for her opportunity, but every time the line cleared, someone else stepped up for help.

Amanda pulled a multicolored linen number from the rack and held it up in front of her. Peeking around the left sleeve, she cased the service area carefully.

"Would you like to try that on?" A saleswoman materialized beside her and reached for the blazer. "I'll be glad to put it in a dressing room for you."

"No, thank you," Amanda said, taking her gaze off the front counter in order to deal with the saleswoman.

Though white haired and willowy, the clerk proved surprisingly persistent. "It's no trouble," she said, grasping for the garment. "I'll hang it on the dressing room door so you'll know which one is yours."

Amanda couldn't bring herself to let go. Clutching the shoulders of the jacket in both hands, she ducked down behind it, keeping the blazer between her and the customer service area, wishing the stupid line would clear so that she could step up and get an application. In private. Without witnesses.

Surely that wasn't too much to ask.

A quiet, but determined, struggle followed.

"I need this blazer *here*," Amanda said finally, wrenching it out of the woman's grasp, "so that I can match things to it."

"N-no problem," the saleswoman stammered as she re-treated, keeping her gaze trained on Amanda.

Amanda stayed where she was until the line finally broke up. Then she hung the jacket on the rack and moved toward the service desk as nonchalantly as a woman who had been cowering behind clothing could.

At the counter, Amanda said, "I'd like to apply for a job."

The young woman, who'd cheerfully refunded a small fortune to Amanda over the years, raised her head from her paperwork with a questioning smile. "I'm sorry," she said much too loudly. "What did you say?"

Amanda looked furtively around her. "I, um, wondered if you had any openings."

Understanding flashed across the woman's face at the same time Amanda sensed someone approaching from be-hind. Glancing quickly behind her, Amanda recognized Susie Simmons drawing near. She, too, was divorced but lo-cal gossip had her settlement so large she'd never had to work. They'd known each other forever and saw each other regularly at the ballpark but had never been friends.

"Did you say you want to apply for a job?" The customer service woman's voice rang loudly enough to reverberate off the walls.

Amanda's whole body tensed. "Yes," she whispered, not wanting to be overheard.

The young woman reached beneath the counter, pulled out a printed form, and pushed it toward Amanda. Someone stepped into line directly behind her; she fer-vently hoped it wasn't Susie.

"If you'd like to fill this out, I'll make sure it's put on file," the clerk seemed to shout.

Amanda grabbed the form and stepped backward, eager to get out of there. There was a crunch as her heel landed on something decidedly un-floorlike.

"Ouch!" Susie Simmons yelped in her ear.

"Oh, my gosh! I'm so sorry!" Amanda turned around while trying to whip the application behind her back. The form shot out of Amanda's hand and fluttered toward the floor. She and Susie knelt down to retrieve it. Their foreheads knocked together.

"I've got it." Susie reached the paper first then glanced down to see what she held. The flash of pity in her eyes was quick but unmistakable and hit Amanda like a punch to the solar plexus.

They helped each other up and Amanda, fighting the urge to flee, stayed to chat while Susie filled out her return slip, as if she had no problem with going to work for minimum wage in a place where she would in all likelihood wait on legions of her former friends. But her stomach—that unflinching barometer of her true feelings—churned with embarrassment.

"You take care now," Susie said as they parted with little air kisses.

"You too." Amanda smiled. "I'll see you at the ballpark. We really have to do lunch one day soon."

The meaningless words tripped off her tongue, but she knew there'd be no lunch. There would, however, be gossip. Unless she missed her guess, word of her dire straits would be all over the neighborhood before Amanda backed the van out of its parking spot.

The suburban drums were already pounding.

* * *

Amanda spent the next two days waiting. She waited for Anne Justiss's office to call and tell her where things stood. She waited for one of the stores at which she'd applied to call and offer her a job. She waited for Meghan to stop treating her as if she'd intentionally destroyed her life.

Most of all, she waited for something that might be construed as a positive indication of anything. But all she got was a house so clean it practically shouted "Get a life!"

In fact, if there were a prize for floors most possible to eat off or windows that most looked like they weren't there, she would win hands down. It was just too bad there was no cleaning equivalent of the Pillsbury Bake-Off. Or a national circuit for cleanaholics like the professional eaters went on. Or a reality show pitting compulsive cleaners against each other with a catchy kind of name like *This Old Rag*.

When she couldn't wait another moment, she picked up the phone and began placing calls, once again feeling that any action was better than none.

She called Anne Justiss's office and was told that they hoped to have a tentative agreement by the beginning of next week. Then she called all the stores where she'd applied. The only nibble of interest came from Steinmart.

"I see that you've been in retail for the last fourteen years," the human resources person said.

"Oh, yes," Amanda said as a tiny seed of hope blossomed in her chest. "I've been in retail stores on an ongoing basis most of my adult life."

She pictured herself on the sales floor selling so effectively that they'd be clamoring to move her into management. She had the very powerful motivators of fear and desperation on her side; all she had to do was make the most of them.

"Which retailer were you with?" the woman asked.

"Oh, I didn't stick with just one," Amanda said. "I'm a firm believer in accumulating a diversity of experience." She'd always been an equal opportunity shopper.

"That's great. We have very few applicants who've worked for more than one retail chain." The interviewer's tone was genuinely enthusiastic. "Who were you with and what positions did you hold?"

Amanda's foot slipped out of the rung of her fantasy leap up the retail ladder as the woman's words sank in.

"Um, I was a . . . shopper," she said carefully, trying to figure out how to regain her footing.

"You were a personal shopper? We've actually been considering offering that service to our customers—especially during the holidays when things get so hectic."

Amanda was dangling from that ladder now, unable to find a toehold. She'd shopped for herself and her family plus an assortment of other friends and relatives, but this woman wasn't looking for an itemized list of people Amanda had once bought something for.

She'd allowed her desperation to turn this woman's words into what she wanted to hear. For about fifteen seconds, Amanda considered lying. She could be a personal shopper with her eyes closed. All she needed was an opportunity.

She laughed and said as lightly as she could, "It seems we've misunderstood each other. The personal shopping I've done is just that: personal. But I do have a huge amount of experience at it. I'm practically a world-class shopper.

And I know and love your stores. I thought that might make me an attractive candidate. I mean you'd hardly have to train me."

There was an awkward silence during which Amanda imagined the woman picking her application up off her desk and dropping it into the trashcan.

"I'm sorry but . . ."

It took everything Amanda had not to beg; not to tell this stranger how incredibly frightened she was that she was going to fail her children.

"That's OK," Amanda said. "I understand. I hope you'll keep me in mind if something opens up. Thanks for taking the time to talk with me."

She hung up the phone. For a long moment, she sat in her silent kitchen and contemplated her reflection in the gleaming chrome fixtures. What she needed now was a bolt of inspiration; something that would buoy her up and keep her energies focused forward.

In the quiet a line from *The Sound of Music*, in which she'd played the role of the Mother Superior in college, formed in her head. "When God closes a door," she repeated now as she had so long ago, "somewhere he opens a window."

Getting up from the table she offered up a small prayer that this was true. And just to be on the safe side, she got out the Windex and a clean cloth and went to work determined to make sure her windows would stand up to His scrutiny.

Late that afternoon Rob came to pick up the kids for the weekend. He looked decidedly less cocky than he had just a week ago, and every one of his forty-two years showed.

"Why don't you guys go ahead and put your stuff in the car?" he said after he greeted Meghan and Wyatt. "I want to talk to your mom for a minute."

They stood together and watched their children scuffle off to the car. An argument ensued over who would ride shotgun, with Meghan dominating the taller Wyatt through sheer force of will. It appeared that Tiffany hadn't come along for the ride.

"Is it me, or does Meghan seem especially angry?" Rob's gaze was on the kids. He winced slightly when she slammed the passenger door of his BMW.

Amanda bit back the "duh, really?" that sprang to her lips. She could hear it echoing in her head in Meghan's perpetually surly tone. "She is angry, Rob. We all are. And hurt. And disappointed. You pick the negative adjectives and we're them. Meghan's just a little more verbal about her feelings than the rest of us."

He turned from the car to face Amanda. "I met with the managing partners at the firm today. I'm out, but they're not going to report me to the bar association or press charges. They won't take the chance of damaging the firm's reputation." He spoke quietly, whatever emotion he was feeling kept tightly in check.

"So you'll be able to keep practicing law?"

"I don't know. I won't have a reference so none of the big boys will touch me. But I might be able to find something with a small one- or two-man firm. If I had a penny to my name, I could put out my own shingle." He sighed. "I can't believe it's come to this."

That made two of them.

"It seems to me you're lucky not to be going to jail." She

looked into Rob's eyes, searching for the man she'd married.

"Yeah. That's what your attorney said. She made it clear to the judge that if I wasn't able to get a job in my field, I'd better get something else so that I could help support you all. I believe she mentioned working on a garbage crew as a possibility." He smiled a tired smile that didn't reach his eyes. "Once all the dust settles, I'm hoping to do better than that."

"Oh, Rob." Despite her hurt and anger, her heart ached for him and for all the promise that he had wasted.

"I'm really sorry, Amanda. I don't even know what else to say. I juggled things for so long. I never imagined I'd drop so many balls at one time."

"What about the house?" Amanda asked. "I've been waiting to hear from Anne Justiss's office."

"The mortgage payments are up-to-date. And for the time being the house will stay in both our names. Unfortunately, I'm not going to be able to help with the payments. Or much else for that matter. I don't even know how I'm going to keep up with the town house."

He looked at her and she realized with some surprise, that he was waiting for her to suggest that he move back in so that they could consolidate their expenses.

"Maybe Tiffany can help you pay the rent."

He studied her for a long moment then turned from her to consider the house. She had the sense that he'd finally realized how much he'd given up. "Yeah. Maybe so."

Amanda watched him gather himself and when he spoke again it was of details. "I deposited five thousand dollars in the household checking account earlier this week right before everything got shut down. That should get you through the next month. I'd suggest we sell the house so that you can buy something less expensive, but given our appalling lack of income you'd never be able to buy anything else. And without an income you can't refinance."

"I wouldn't sell anyway," Amanda said. "I made a promise to Meghan and Wyatt. I won't disrupt their lives any further. I'm just going to have to find a way to hang on."

Rob nodded and squared his shoulders. "I'll have the kids back Sunday afternoon," he said. "For what it's worth, I'll help you with them in any way I can." He smiled and the regret reflected in his eyes almost broke her heart. "If the garbage thing doesn't work out, maybe I'll pull an Eddie Murphy and open a Daddy Daycare."

chapter 9

Candace awoke on Saturday morning ready to purr. Lazily she stretched and yawned. The imported sheets were soft and sensual against her bare skin. The body heat of the man lying beside her was warm and comforting. She drew closer, turning on her side with her back against his chest so that she could tuck her bottom more firmly against him. He stirred against her.

"Mmmmmm." He slid an arm across her waist and reached up to cup a breast.

"Mmmmm yourself."

His fingers brushed lightly against her nipple causing her to arch against him. He pressed a sleepy kiss to the back of her neck. "Come here." He moved back and gently turned her over to face him. She opened her eyes and stared into his.

"Good morning." He kissed her cheek, the tip of her nose. His morning erection brushed up against the juncture of her thighs, not insistent or demanding, just warm and there.

Candace burrowed closer amazed as she always was by how easy he made things. With her husbands and the others she'd dated, she had always made a point of slipping out of bed before they woke up to brush her teeth and put on makeup so that she showed to best advantage. Dan had put an end to that the first time he'd stayed over when he'd padded naked into the bathroom behind her and shown her exactly how desirable he thought her just the way she was.

A glance over his shoulder at the bedside clock indicated ten AM. She should get up and get dressed. She'd promised her mother she'd go with her to look at fabrics. "Don't you have to be somewhere?" she asked.

"I'm headed somewhere right now." His penis pressed against her and he smiled lazily. "But I'm planning to take you with me. And I'm not in any rush."

When he'd taken her exactly where she was hoping to go, he flipped over onto his back and pulled her close so that her cheek rested on his chest. His breathing had slowed but his heart still beat quickly. She could hear its muffled rhythm under her ear.

"I need to get going," she said halfheartedly.

"I'd like to stay here all day," Dan said. "When's the last time you spent a day in bed?"

She checked to see if he was joking. All of the men she'd married and most of the men she'd dated would be seated at their desks or teeing up on the first hole by now.

"Um, that would be never."

"Well, we may not have the entire day, but we can get

close." He kissed her and pulled her tighter. "I don't have to be at the field for warm-ups until two. Why don't we start with the half-day layabout and work our way up to the full-day gig?"

He yawned and she snuggled closer. She noticed that he hadn't asked her to come to the game. He knew how out of her element she felt at the park and with the team mothers. But she also knew how much he liked it when she was in the stands.

Maybe she'd call her mother and see if they could start the fabric search another time.

"Why don't we catch a little snooze so that we can build up our strength?" Before she could answer, his breathing had slowed and his eyelids fluttered shut.

She hated to disappoint Hannah. Since her father's death five years ago, Candace had sensed a growing neediness underlying her mother's bravado.

Her last thought as her own breathing evened out was that she'd definitely reschedule with her mother so that she could make today's game. If Brooke were there she'd at least have someone to talk to. And maybe they could check on Amanda afterward. Rob was supposed to have the kids for the weekend, and Candace didn't like the idea of Amanda rattling around in the house all alone. She knew firsthand how lonely being single in suburbia could be.

Brooke lay in the chaise beside their backyard pool and stared up at the blue sky trying to ignore the slight spring chill. She'd been lying there most of the morning contemplating the clouds and her life, not to mention her marriage, which was turning out quite differently than she'd expected.

Idly she reached for the glass of iced tea on the table and drew a long sip through the straw. Her stepson was in the house playing video games on the big screen TV; he'd been planted on the couch since he'd woken up that morning. His father was out on the golf course, where he'd headed while she was still sleeping, and she had had to choose between her room, which was the only place in the house where the sound of MVP Baseball 2005 could NOT be heard, or out here in the late March sun, which wasn't really warm enough for sunbathing.

She gazed at the house and tried to feel the lovely little glow she normally got when she contemplated it, but she'd spent the entire morning alone avoiding Tyler's perennially pissy mood, and she wasn't feeling all that great about her marital accomplishments.

Looking for reassurance, she unzipped her coverup and studied her body in the new Gottex bikini. Beneath the goosebumps her stomach was flat, concave really, and a diamond stud twinkled from her belly button. Her legs were long and firm, without the slightest hint of varicose veins or cellulite.

Still, she'd made appointments to work out with the private trainer at the club, and scheduled a consultation with a highly recommended plastic surgeon. She'd always been a long-term planner, and as Amanda Sheridan's situation so clearly illustrated, a girl could never be too careful.

The truth was she was lonely and bored. At the Children's Hospital fund-raiser her isolation had become clear to her. Hap and Sarah's friends wanted nothing to do with her. The only people at that entire gathering who'd gone out of their way to talk to her had been Candace and Dan.

The cell phone beside her rang and she reached for it, but pulled back when she saw her mother's name and number appear on the caller ID. Cassie Blount was calling from Betwixt, Georgia, a place that could just as easily have borne the name "Back of Beyond."

Brooke felt the usual twinge of guilt that the only phone number she'd ever given her mother was her cell, but she refused to take the chance that some creditor, or her mother on a binge, might leave a message on the house phone that Hap might somehow hear.

When he'd asked her what family she wanted at their wedding, she'd answered truthfully that it was just her and her mother. And then when Hap had started to put her on the guest list, she'd hastily explained that they were estranged. What her mother would have called a high falutin' word for too embarrassed to acknowledge her.

With trepidation, Brooke picked up the phone.

"Hey there, sweet cheeks," Cassie Blount said with her take-no-prisoners cheerfulness. "How ya doin' down there in the big city?"

"I'm fine, Mama." No matter how hard she worked to lose her backwoods twang it always seemed to sneak back in when she talked to her mother. "How're you?"

"I'm good. I lost the Worleys. They hired them a imported maid. Let me go without any warning." There was a pause and then the relentless optimism. "But I think I can pick up some hours at the Holiday Inn."

"I can send you some extra in the meantime, Mama."

She'd set up a separate account from which she sent her mother's monthly checks. "How's the weather up there?"

"Oh, can't complain." There was a pause. "I went to an AA meeting, Brooke. Just like you asked me to."

"That's good, Mama." Brooke's enthusiasm was not as great as it had been the first couple of times her mother had made this pronouncement. "You need to stick with it this time, you hear?"

"Oh, I will. Don't you worry."

Brooke knew her mother meant it, at least for now. Her mother was chock full of good intentions; constantly turning over some new leaf.

"When you gonna bring your young man up here for a visit?" she asked like she always did.

Brooke thought how surprised both Hap and her mother would be to discover they were the same age. Not that she ever intended to let that happen. "Hap's awful busy, Mama," Brooke said, wishing this one truth were not. "I hardly see him myself during the week." And less and less on the weekends. "But we'll see what we can work out."

"OK, baby doll." Her mother pretended to accept the excuse, though even such a determined optimist must be realizing by now that it wasn't going to happen. "You take care of yourself."

"I will, Mama. You too."

Brooke made a mental note to send something extra in this month's check and had just settled herself back into the chaise when the phone rang again. Seeing Hap's cell phone number on the caller ID, she picked it up, brightening.

"Hey, doll." Hap's voice bore none of her mother's rural twang. The tinkle of glasses and the murmur of voices in the background told her they must be in the clubhouse. She wished she were there with him, about to have a post-round cocktail and not alone here at the pool covered in goose-bumps.

"Hi, Hap." She looked down at her watch. It was twelve fifteen. His note had said he'd be home by noon. "You all done?"

"We just finished the back nine, the course was packed today." She could hear him put his hand over the mouth-piece for a moment and speak to someone else. She strained to hear whether there were female voices, but couldn't make out anything over the general din. "I need to ask you a favor."

A favor? Like being gone the whole morning without a single complaint from her wasn't favor enough?

Hap didn't wait for a response. He just expected her to comply, like she always did.

"I'd really like to grab a bite with the guys." He covered the mouthpiece again, but she could hear him call out to someone that he'd be right there. Obviously it didn't occur to him that she might object. "And I wondered if you could get Tyler to warm-ups. I'll meet you all there in time for the game."

"But . . ." Tyler hated her and let her know it at every op-portunity. When Hap was around he turned the animosity down a notch. Being alone in a car with him was about as enjoyable as a root canal. "He'll be so disappointed not to go with you. You've been gone all morning, Hap." She said it gently, careful to keep the accusation out of her voice. No man liked to be nagged.

"I know, darlin', and I'll make it up to both of you. I'm

just asking for this extra hour. I haven't seen the guys in a month."

There it was, the subtle reminder that he'd given up his old life for her.

"If you'd like to go out with your girlfriends tonight, Tyler and I can order a pizza and bach it."

Her husband obviously hadn't noticed she didn't HAVE any girlfriends. The only women she'd shared more than polite chitchat with were Amanda and Candace. She swallowed back her hurt and irritation. "Of, course, Hap. You go on and have a nice time. We'll see you at the field."

Downing the last swallow of iced tea, she rezipped her cover-up. Inside she placed herself in front of the wide screen television, where Tyler could not ignore her. "Your dad asked me to run you to the field. He'll be there in time for the game."

Tyler grunted and then waited in impatient silence for her to get out of the way.

The roar of the baseball crowd boomed out of the surround sound speakers and followed her down the hall. She had to get undressed and step into the shower to drown them out.

Saturday afternoon Amanda donned her new rubber gloves and attacked the outdoor furniture with bleach and muscle, enjoying the feel of the sun on her bare shoulders as she scrubbed then sprayed away the residue of winter.

Hair riffled by the breeze, she put the earbuds in and strapped her iPod to her arm. With smooth French jazz swirling in her ears, she turned to the large wooden tub planters that she kept on the deck. After plucking the now limp mass of purple pansies, she added soil and conditioner, mixing them together in preparation for the summer annuals she intended to plant.

When her cell phone vibrated in her pocket, she removed one gardening glove and one earbud and braced the phone between her ear and shoulder.

"We're losing again." Candace was whispering, which meant she must be in the stands. "Is it normal to lose this many games?"

Amanda scooped the spent pansies off the ground and carried them to the garbage can. "We've been through a few rough patches in the past," she said, "but this does feel unusually bad." She walked back to the deck and leaned against the railing. "Who all's there today?"

"The usual," Candace said. "Susie Simmons is here going on about losing her cleaning woman and pouting about her son spending time on the bench. Meghan's sitting by herself with her nose in a book."

Amanda stared into the wooded backyard where a squirrel was busy stealing seed from a feeder. "You aren't really going to make me ask are you?"

"Sorry," Candace said. "Tiffany's here. She arrived during the first inning and it seems that however uncomfortable the other mothers are with you, they're ten times more uncomfortable with her. Of course that may have something to do with the fact that she's wearing a backless halter and shorts so short I think we're going to have to call them underwear."

"Gosh I'm so sorry I'm missing that."

"Yeah, well, Brooke and I miss you. It just isn't the same

with only two of us stooges. We thought we'd take you out to dinner tonight if you're available."

"Available?" Amanda laughed. "I'm not even going to pretend to check my calendar. But let's eat here. I'll make dinner if you'll help me brainstorm afterward. I've got to figure out a way to make a living and it's got to be something that doesn't require start-up capital or experience."

"All right," Candace said. "But I'll bring the wine. And if we're talking no money and no experience, I think we may need more than one bottle."

"The last time we drank together I tied over three hundred condoms to a tree. Let's take it easy on the alcohol. I don't want my new career to involve standing on street corners."

After riffling through her cookbooks for inspiration, Amanda laced up a pair of Nikes and headed outside for a walk. Around her, Chandler's Pond had sprung into full Saturday afternoon mode.

Across the street the garage door flew open and Myrna Hopewell buckled her three towheaded children—all under the age of five—into her Suburban and roared out of her driveway.

Two houses over, the Cotrell twins were setting up a lemonade stand. A gaggle of middle-school-aged boys milled around the base of Chad Hanson's driveway taking an occasional shot at the nearby basketball hoop.

The well-manicured lawns served as backdrop to the bright bursts of pink and white azaleas and fat fingers of purple wisteria. Flats of Gerbera daisies and zinnias sat near the flower beds they'd soon call home. It looked like anyone who could was out in their yard breathing it all in.

At the end of her street, Amanda turned left and continued toward the entrance of the subdivision. The clubhouse parking lot overflowed with cars and on the adjacent tennis courts mixed-doubles teams warmed up, while those waiting to play socialized.

When they'd first moved to Atlanta, she and Rob had played on the neighborhood tennis team. She'd been adequate, nowhere near as good as Rob, but she could still remember the pure joy of moving on the court in tandem with her husband while her children played on the nearby playground.

Everything had felt fresh and full of promise then. They'd had Saturday tennis followed by a Saturday date night every week so that they could be alone with each other. She tried to remember when all that had begun to change, but there was no demarcation date, no specific day she could point to on which the kids' activities had taken over the weekends and their time alone had somehow ceased to be.

Chatter and the lazy thwack of a tennis ball trailed after her as she passed the courts. Two streets ahead she rounded a corner and saw a sliver of the pond for which the neighborhood had been named. Two boys fished on the opposite bank and a family had spread out a blanket picnic next to the trunk of an ancient oak.

Amanda sank down onto a wooden bench shaded by the waxy green leaves of a massive magnolia. It was quiet and peaceful in her hidey-hole. Her thoughts skipped here and there, alighting briefly then moving on like the bee now buzzing around a nearby flower. The Rob she'd married versus the one she was divorcing; her life before and the one that stretched ahead of her.

Fear reared its ugly head and she mashed it back down. Everything about this day smacked of a new beginning; there was no room for fear in her new life.

Out on the pond a duck quacked. It was an angry, hostile sound that for some reason made her smile. "Oh, you," she said. "What do you have to complain about?"

"Yeah, that's a duck for you, never satisfied."

The voice was masculine and nearby and horribly familiar. Amanda sat up straighter and stole a quick glance over her shoulder. A flush of embarrassment swept over her as she recognized the hunk who'd been behind her at the grocery store.

"So how'd things go the other night?" He looked even better in the daylight than he had in the checkout line. He was over six feet tall and blond, well built in a non-gym-induced way. Intelligent green eyes glinting with amusement considered her from the rugged face. A black Lab sniffed the bushes nearby.

Amanda blushed again. The front of her camisole felt damp and clingy from her walk, she wasn't wearing an ounce of makeup, and he'd already introduced the topic of condoms. She prayed for the ground to open up and swallow her whole, but it appeared this was just one more in a long line of prayers that was going to go unanswered.

"What are you doing here?" she asked.

"We live over on Chandler Circle." He named a street on the opposite side of the pond in the newer section of the subdivision. "This is Fido's favorite spot."

"You actually named your dog *Fido*?"

"Um-hmm." He whistled and the dog's ears perked up. "Here, Fido. Come here, boy."

The dog crashed back through the brush, bounded toward the bench, and—just in case she wasn't already embarrassed enough—poked its nose directly between Amanda's thighs.

She gasped and shoved the dog's head away.

"Sorry." He reached for the dog's collar and pulled him back. "He sits and heels and he's got the first half of fetch down pretty well, but he's definitely not a gentleman."

Amanda smiled weakly and resisted the urge to look down to see just how wet the crotch of her shorts were.

"I'm Hunter James." He stretched his hand toward her and she responded without thinking.

"Amanda Sheridan."

Her hand disappeared in his and she felt the pleasant shock of warm skin and solid strength. His other hand remained clenched around the dog's collar. The Lab's tongue lolled out of its mouth and she wondered if after all these months of celibacy her crotch was sending out distress signals like those dog whistles that only canines could hear.

Hunter James didn't rush to fill the silence that fell between them, but she could feel his thoughtful gaze on her face.

"It's a nice spot," he finally said. "Mind if I join you?"

Amanda did a surreptitious check to make sure the picnicking family was still within shouting distance. After all, Ted Bundy had been attractive and personable.

"Sure." She slid over and he sat down beside her. Picking

up a stick, he sent it sailing through the air. Fido raced after it.

Trying not to imagine what she must look like, or what he must think of her after the condom encounter, she stared out over the pond wishing for some of the boldness the margaritas had given her the other night. *Chaud et sexy,* the French words for hot and sexy shot through her mind. If she were a *French* soon-to-be-divorced woman, she'd seize this opportunity, not shrink from it. He was one of the most attractive men she'd ever met. And then, of course, there was that smile.

"It's my favorite spot," her Anglo self managed. "It's a great place for figuring things out."

"Yeah," he said. "I can see that." He settled onto the bench and stared out at the pond too. The silence surrounded them, interrupted only by the occasional quack of a duck and muffled bursts of conversation from the picnic. He was solidly there, but somehow managed not to invade her space.

Fido galloped back with the stick and shoved it toward Amanda. After a quick scratch behind Fido's ear, she pulled the stick from the dog's mouth and flung it as far as she could. The Lab raced after it.

"What kinds of things are you trying to figure out?" Hunter James asked.

The words "nothing major" almost made it to her lips, but she surprised them both with the truth. "Oh, you know, small things like what I'm going to do with the rest of my life. How I'm going to support my children after what feels like a lifetime as a stay-at-home mom." She shrugged and looked up into his eyes. "Little things like that."

Fido trotted back with the stick. Stretching out at his master's feet, he began to gnaw on it.

Hunter placed a hand on the dog's head and rubbed gently. "Sometimes we get broadsided by trouble when we're least expecting it. But if there's anything that can help you do what has to be done, it's your children." He sighed and withdrew his hand from Fido's head, and for a moment Amanda wished he'd lay it on hers, not in a sexual way but as a gesture of comfort. "I'm sure it won't be easy," he said, the green eyes kind and sad at the same time. "But you strike me as exactly the kind of woman who'll figure everything out just fine."

"Thanks." Hoping that he was right, Amanda dropped her gaze. A glance at her watch told her it was time to get going if she wanted to make it to the grocery store in time to get home and make dinner for Brooke and Candace.

She stood and dusted off the bottom of her shorts, oddly reluctant to leave. If she hadn't known that there was probably a Mrs. James and a bunch of little Jameses waiting for him over on Chandler Circle, it would have taken an act of God to pry her from that bench.

"I have to admit I've been curious," he said as she leaned over to give Fido a good-bye pat on the head. "Did you have enough?"

His eyes lit with the same amusement she'd noted during that first condom encounter. Here in the dappled sunlight they seemed even greener.

Her earlier embarrassment forgotten, she found herself smiling back. "Truthfully," she said staring into them, "all the condoms in the world wouldn't have been enough for what I was trying to accomplish that night."

He laughed. A dimple creased his cheek. "I'll have you know I've actually lost sleep trying to figure out what you did with that many. My imagination's been running wild."

She couldn't stop her answering smile. Just sharing a bench with him had somehow lightened her mood. "Well, I'm afraid we're going to have to chalk it up as one of the great mysteries of the universe."

He laughed again, this time with appreciation.

"Because that's one bit of information I intend to take to my grave."

His laughter, which she really, really liked the sound of, followed her as she said good-bye and turned and left the park.

The day seemed brighter as she hurried by the tennis courts and made her way home.

chapter 10

For dinner Amanda decided on Chicken with Forty Cloves of Garlic and Moroccan Couscous which she found in her favorite Barefoot Contessa cookbook. She served it on the back deck on a patio table covered with a red checkered tablecloth. Flickering candles stuffed in empty Chianti bottles and a string of white Christmas lights wound through the deck railing provided light and atmosphere. A *Paris Combo Live* CD played on the boom box. If she tried hard enough, Amanda could imagine herself at one of the sidewalk cafés that dotted the broad avenues along the Champs-Elysées.

"Welcome to Chez Amanda!" she said as she took one of the bottles of white wine Candace proffered and set Brooke's prettily wrapped bakery box on the counter. She kissed them, European style, on both cheeks. Bringing the bottle of wine, she led them onto the deck.

"Wow! What a great setup," Candace said. "All we need

now is a Maurice Chevalier–type waiter. Or a piano player with a cigarette hanging out of his mouth singing naughty French love songs."

Amanda uncorked the bottle and poured a glass of the white wine for herself and Candace. "Brooke?" she asked.

"No, thanks."

Amanda smiled and reached for the bottle of Pellegrino. When they all had something to drink, she raised her glass and the three of them clinked crystal.

"Ooh la la." Brooke sipped her sparkling water and scanned the setting Amanda had so painstakingly created. "It's fabulous out here. I feel like a jetsetter."

"Have some brie." Slathering apple slices and crusty bread with the melted cheese, Amanda prepared them each a plate of appetizers.

"This is great." Candace snagged a bunch of white grapes and helped herself to a cracker covered with pâté.

They chatted for a while, just the inconsequentials of their day, but Amanda could sense them waiting for her to invite them into her life. For the moment she was content to play hostess—she'd enjoyed preparing tonight's meal even more than she'd anticipated. Still it felt incredibly good to know that they cared what happened to her. With some surprise, she realized that they no longer seemed like unlikely strangers. Their movements and facial expressions had become familiar; the details of their lives important.

"How did the boys take their loss today?" Amanda asked as she set an endive, pear, and Roquefort salad at each place.

"It wasn't pretty," Candace said as they sat. "If those parents don't stop blaming Dan for everything, I'm going to snap someone's head off. I don't know how he stays so calm. Even my mother couldn't rattle him."

"I know what you mean," Amanda said. "He always seems like a white sand island in the middle of a roiling sea."

Amanda finished her salad. Pleased, she watched Brooke and Candace finish every bite of theirs too. "How about you, Brooke?" she asked. "Is Tyler treating you any better?"

"Only when Hap's around." Brooke speared the last sliver of pear. "Which isn't anywhere near as much as I'd like. He's out visiting his restaurants almost every week now. So I'm on my own a lot. Good God, I miss my job at the accounting firm. And when he gets back, he either wants to play golf with his friends or we have some event of Tyler's. Or both."

They carried the empty salad plates to the kitchen and came back out with heaping servings of chicken and couscous. The garlic was sweet and tender with the faintest hint of Cognac and cream sauce.

"OK, now I know I've died and gone to heaven." Candace bent over her plate and inhaled. "Why don't we skip right over the brainstorming? I think you should train to become a French chef and open your own restaurant."

"Someday, maybe." Amanda smiled at the compliment as they began to eat. "Right now I know how to make two dishes and I have aspirations for a third. And I don't have time for a slow build. I've got to make money and I've got to make it fast."

The sun sank lower and the breeze that had felt balmy earlier began to feel cool as they finished the main course. "Why don't we have coffee and dessert inside?" Amanda suggested. "I've been dying to see what Brooke brought from the bakery."

They trooped in, carrying everything they could. Candace rinsed the dishes and loaded them into the dishwasher while Amanda brewed a pot of coffee. Brooke sliced three large wedges of the chocolate mousse cake and carried the plates into the family room.

Shoes off, their feet tucked under them, they settled in to drink coffee and moan over the sinful richness of the chocolate cake.

"OK." Amanda set her plate on the coffee table in front of her. "I need an idea."

"Maybe we should try stream of consciousness and see what we come up with," Candace suggested.

"OK, but it has to be something that will allow me to be home for the kids by dinnertime and doesn't involve a lengthy commute," Amanda said. "I don't want to be too far away in case of an emergency."

"What are your skills?" Brooke asked.

"Well . . ." Amanda thought about that for a moment. "I'm good organizationally. I've chaired a ton of committees and I know how to get things done."

"What's your degree in?" Candace asked.

"Drama."

"Have you tried the local theatre companies?"

"Yes." Amanda ticked off the negatives on her fingers. "Employees are mostly volunteers. Those who are paid, get almost no money. And you have to be there nights and weekends."

They all drooped. "Could you teach it?"

Amanda shook her head. "Not certified, and I don't have time to get a teaching certificate."

"What about substitute teaching? You don't need a degree for that," Candace said.

"Even less money. A substitute gets a whopping ninety dollars a day before taxes. And you can't count on it."

"Drama . . . makeup . . ." Brooke mused. "How about selling Avon? Or one of those multilevel marketing companies?"

"I'm not giving home parties. Even if I could count on my former friends and acquaintances, it takes forever to build those things."

"What about real estate?" Candace asked.

Amanda shook her head. "Every other divorced woman in the county has already beat me to it."

"Catering?"

"Like I told you, I make two really good dishes, both of them French. And it's another slow build." Amanda was starting to get depressed. "I need something I can make money at right away."

"Party planning?" Brooke said.

"Too festive."

"Personal shopping?" This from Candace.

"I thought I had a job doing that for Steinmart for about five minutes. But doing it on my own?" Amanda shook her head. "Most of the women I know are probably even more avid shoppers than I am. And it's another slow build."

"Decorating?"

"I'd need training and, again, you have to start with your friends. Right now you two are it."

Brooke sighed. Candace settled back into the sofa and

folded her arms across her chest. "There must be something you're good at that people need."

"Right now the only thing I excel at is cleaning my house." Amanda laughed, but there was little humor in it. "My grout and I are intimately acquainted. It started as a kind of therapy, but at this point I spend so much time cleaning we could have stayed inside tonight and eaten off the floor."

"You know," Candace said slowly, "the only thing the women around here talk about more than other women is their maids."

"That's true," Brooke said. "The other night at the ball-park there was a thirty minute dissection and comparison of cleaning crews. And nobody sounded all that happy."

"Just imagine what they'd give for someone who could speak English and actually understand what they want done," Candace said thoughtfully.

Amanda looked at Brooke and Candace. "I would have hated waiting on these women in Steinmart, I don't see how I could waltz into their homes, shoot them a smile, and excuse myself to go clean their toilets." She shook her head vehemently. "I don't think so." She got up to retrieve the carafe of coffee then freshened everyone's cup.

Candace raised an eyebrow. "My cleaning crew gets a minimum of one hundred twenty-five dollars a house and they do two houses a day, sometimes three, five days a week. That's . . ."

"A minimum of twelve hundred and fifty dollars a week," Brooke calculated, her voice sounding odd.

"Cash? In their pocket?" Amanda couldn't believe it.

"That's sixty-five grand a year." Candace did the math. "Cash. No deductions."

They looked at her, waiting for her reaction. Sixty-five thousand dollars a year would go a long way toward paying their bills and keeping them in the house. And if she did more than two houses a day . . .

"Bitsy Menkowski and Susie Simmons are both looking for a new cleaning woman."

"Oh, right, should I just call them up and tell them I'd like to come wax their floors?"

"I could book it for you, maybe use an alias," Candace suggested. "We could try to schedule you to clean when no one was home."

Go in their closets? Pick up their underwear from the floor? Amanda grimaced. Given the hours required to thoroughly clean the houses here, she didn't see how she could completely avoid the customers. And she wouldn't be the only one embarrassed. How would she feel if an old friend asked to clean her home? She might say yes at first out of pity, but it would be so uncomfortable. Like giving someone who'd been a frequent dinner guest scraps at the back door.

Amanda shook her head. "I don't think I'd actually mind the cleaning part. I don't understand why, but it seems to relax me. It's not the work, per se." She looked at Candace and Brooke, willing them to understand. "It's the humiliation. I'm not sure I could handle that. And I know Meghan couldn't. She can't bear the idea of being different or sticking out in any noticeable way. She would absolutely die of shame."

Brooke considered them from beneath carefully shaped

eyebrows. The curve of her cheek was lightly blushed, her skin taut and dewy. "I can completely understand that." She hesitated for a long moment, looked as if she'd thought better of speaking, and then blurted out, "My mother is a maid."

Brooke closed her eyes and tilted her head back as if seeing something she didn't want to. "And I'm not talking the waltz-in-and-out, part-of-a-service kind of cleaning woman. I'm talking the backbreaking, down-on-your-hands-and-knees-scrubbing-the-floor, belonging-to-the-customer-like-a-slave kind of maid."

Brooke shuddered. "She looked eighty at forty. And her hands are all crippled up," she whispered. "I still can't bear to look at them."

Amanda stared at this woman she'd thought she was getting to know. The one she'd originally written off as an empty-headed trophy. "Where does she live?"

"Oh, she's still back in Betwixt, Georgia, which is the booming metropolis where I was born. And she doesn't make anywhere near the kind of money Candace is talking about." She looked away. "I used to be so ashamed." Brooke still spoke in a whisper. "I got myself as far away from that as I could. All the way through college and into an MBA program. Anytime things seemed too hard or unobtainable, I'd think about my mother."

Amanda studied the beautiful young woman in the designer clothes and tried to picture it. "I never would have known."

"No," Brooke said. "I spend a lot of time and energy making sure no one ever does."

"Not even Hap?"

"Especially not Hap." Her look to Amanda and Candace was pointed. "He's never met my mother. I've let him think that we're estranged. You two are the only people on earth I've told."

"Well your secret's safe with me," Candace said.

"Me too," Amanda said. "Though I have to say my hat's off to your mother. She must have been pretty highly motivated."

"I guess so," Brooke said quietly. "I never really stopped and thought about *who* she was doing it for. All I ever saw was that it was the best she could do."

There was a silence as the three of them stared at each other, their coffee and desserts long forgotten. Amanda watched Brooke carefully but the younger woman didn't seem inclined to pursue the subject. Her shame seemed fresh and real—not a part of the past, but painfully current. Was this how Meghan would feel if she knew her mother was cleaning homes for a living?

"So where do we stand?" Candace finally asked. "I don't feel like we've found a solution. Do you want to table the subject and let us all give it some more thought?"

Amanda shook her head. "No. I don't have time to keep thinking about what I want to be when I grow up. And I can't afford to be picky. I need a regular income and I need it as soon as possible."

She knew then what she had to do. She really only had one viable choice that she could see. There was no point quibbling further about the pros and cons or the potential for embarrassment. "If you can get me clients, Candace, I'm ready to start cleaning houses."

"Are you sure, Amanda? I don't know if . . ."

"I'm sure," she said pulling up a picture of Meghan in the silver dress, rejecting the one of her on her knees in front of her ex-friends' toilets. "Just don't tell them that the maid you're booking is me. And if you can schedule me while they're out, that would be even better.

"In the meantime, I'm going to come up with some sort of disguise so that I can try to do this without being recognized."

"A disguise?" Candace asked, incredulous. "I don't think any of the women I know are going to welcome a maid in a stocking mask or fright wig into their home."

"Oh, I think I can do better than that," Amanda said, the wheels of her imagination already spinning. "I was a drama major after all, and I used to do local theatre before the kids' schedules got so hectic. I have boxes full of costumes and stage makeup from the shows I've done. You book the work, Candace, and I'll come up with the disguise."

As soon as Candace and Brooke had gone, Amanda hunted down her cache of wigs and costumes. At the bottom of the last carton lay her tackle box of makeup and specialty items.

Carrying them upstairs she sorted through the possibilities and finally took the most promising with her into the bathroom and began to experiment.

Slipping into a generic white uniform she'd once found at Goodwill, she tugged a dark curly wig onto her head, carefully tucked her own hair up beneath it, and teased the synthetic hair into multiple directions, liking the way the Brillo-like strands brushed the shoulders of the white polyester top.

Pulling out a pat of pancake makeup, Amanda dampened a latex sponge then rubbed it through the cake of color and spread it over her face to darken her skin. With an eyebrow pencil she sketched a heavier brow line then affixed a pair of false eyelashes, black and spidery, on top of her own. Nonprescription contact lenses transformed her brown eyes to a compelling blue.

Just as she'd hoped, the overall effect was more vivid, bolder than her normal self. Liking the new look, Amanda dug through her makeup case until she found a bright red lipstick, which she applied to her lips. A fake beauty spot at the left corner of her mouth became an accent mark.

Tilting her chin and making a moue with her mouth, she altered the timbre of her voice and tried out a succession of nationalities and accents.

At two AM she confronted her new persona. *"Mais, oui,"* she purred with a pronounced French accent. "Eet ees not too much trouble to add zee wax." She fluttered the spiky eyelashes; they looked a little like butterflies searching for a place to land. "I would be more than happy to fluff zee pillows for you, *Monsieur.*"

She smiled at her new French self and saw the resulting twinkle in the blue eyes. The flutter of her butterfly lashes made her think of Jean-Claude's nickname for her. *Papillon.* This was a bolder, more confident person than Amanda Sheridan had ever been. A husband would not walk out on this woman. And no other woman would pity her.

This woman would not take crap from anyone. Even as a maid, she would be bold and assertive. "Solange," she said experimentally. "I am Solange." The last name popped into her head formed and ready to go. It was absolutely perfect; an omen, she was sure, of the future.

"Amanda Sheridan," she said to the image in the mirror, "please allow me to introduce you to the vibrant and wonderful, Solange de Papillon."

chapter 11

A week later, the day of her first cleaning job, Amanda dropped the kids at the bus stop and drove to Candace's house where she stashed her van in the three-car garage and went into a guest bathroom to change.

It took her twenty minutes to complete her transformation. When she emerged Candace was waiting for her in the kitchen. "Hallo, *Candee ass*," Amanda said with her new French accent. "I am Solange. And I understand you are to give me zee ride to Mrs. Beetsy Menkowski's house."

Candace's mouth dropped open. "You're going to be a French maid?"

"*Oui*," Amanda/Solange said.

"But the only place I've ever seen an actual French maid is in France. Or *Playboy* magazine."

"Oh?" Amanda fluttered her papillon eyelashes at Candace and reminded herself that Solange's hand gestures would be more vivid and pronounced.

"In case you haven't noticed, all the maids in Atlanta and most of the Southeast are Hispanic," Candace pointed out. "I mean you could choose pretty much any Spanish-speaking country and get away with it. Why France?"

In the garage they picked up Amanda's vacuum cleaner and cleaning supplies and stowed them in the trunk of Candace's Mercedes.

"I don't know, *Candee ass,* it just feels right." Amanda tried out the new hand gestures and threw in a Gallic shrug. "I'm tired of being such a wuss. I don't want to walk into these houses feeling subservient and desperate. Even if I'm acting, I need to be brave and bold. Solange de Papillon is both of those things. Besides, I don't know any Spanish or Portuguese, but I do speak French fairly well. I think I can pull this off."

"All right," Candace said as they climbed into the front seat of the car. They'd agreed that Candace would schedule and drive her to help safeguard Amanda's identity. "This is your gig. I'm just the facilitator. But there is one thing."

"And what ees that my blonde-haired friend?"

"I don't let people call me Candy. Believe me when I tell you that *Candee ass* is not going to cut it."

A few minutes later they were heading for Bitsy Menkowski's subdivision. Amanda had known Bitsy for years. She and Rob had gone out with Bitsy and Herbert once or twice, but had thought the Menkowskis a little too straitlaced. "What did you tell her about her new cleaning woman?" Amanda asked.

"Not much because she didn't ask. She's been without help since Imelda quit four weeks ago. She doesn't care who comes."

"Good. That gives Solange more room to maneuver." Amanda's pulse quickened as it always had before a performance.

"It probably won't matter much today anyway," Candace said. "Bitsy's not planning to be back until three. I'll be here to pick you up at two thirty." Candace drove east toward the River Run subdivision where the Menkowskis lived. Amanda watched the familiar landmarks fly by, trying to see them through Solange's eyes. Her grocery store, the dry cleaner, Hong Wo's vegetable stand. It was all the same, yet imperceptibly different. Just as she was. A prickle of anticipation shot up her spine.

In the Menkowskis' driveway, Candace put the car in park and handed Amanda the list of instructions Bitsy had faxed over.

"She wanted you to do laundry, but I told her you'd only have time for sheets and towels. The key's supposed to be under the front mat."

"Good old Bitsy, not an original bone in her body." Amanda got out of the car and retrieved her supplies and equipment. They dangled against her legs as she strode up the front walk, located the key, and let herself into the house.

Amanda had been at the Menkowskis' for meetings and the occasional dinner party. Still, it felt incredibly strange to enter her house when Bitsy wasn't there; odder still to think she was about to clean it under false pretenses.

Like many of the homes in the Atlanta suburbs, the foyer opened onto formal living and dining rooms. A front stair led to the upstairs bedrooms and baths, a door beyond the stairs led down to a finished basement. Straight ahead was the eat-in kitchen and vaulted great room lined with windows that overlooked the wooded backyard.

Setting her supplies and vacuum on the kitchen floor, Amanda took stock of the situation. A stack of dirty dishes teetered in the sink and mounds of mail and the miscellaneous trappings of daily life covered the granite countertops. The kids' abandoned possessions littered the tabletops and lined the back stairs as if trying to make it to the next floor on their own. A fine coat of dust and neglect attested to Imelda's absence. It was clear Bitsy had never sought solace in scrubbing.

Upstairs, Amanda wandered through the bedrooms. The kids' rooms were pretty much what she'd expected, pink florals for Lori, a sports motif for Bitsy's eleven-year-old son. But the master had been done in what could only be called "early Bordello." Red damask, gold fringe, and mirrors abounded. The furniture was dark and heavy and faintly Mediterranean. It was also covered in dust.

Amanda felt an urge to pull down the heavy curtains and throw open the windows to let light into the room. But the clock was ticking. And she had been hired to clean not redecorate.

"OK." She caught a glimpse of herself in the ornately carved dresser mirror, took in the big hair, the bright red lipstick, and the blue eyes, so wide and assessing. "You are not Amanda Sheridan about to touch Bitsy Menkowski's dirty sheets and towels," she said to her reflection. "You are... Solange de Papillon... the much sought-after housekeeper. They are lucky to have you!"

Pumped, Amanda moved from bedroom to bedroom scooping up dirty clothes from the floor and stuffing them in the hamper she found in the laundry room. Then she began to strip beds and clear off surfaces. With no idea where things actually went, and with little time to figure it out, she opted for pile management, creating neat little mounds of similar stuff so that although the clutter remained it looked more intentional and less chaotic.

An hour later she'd washed and dried a load of sheets, remade one bed, and created a satisfying number of piles. But this was a five-thousand-square-foot home with a first floor and a finished basement. A glance at her watch told her she was going to have to work faster.

Three hours later she was forced to admit that cleaning her own house bore no resemblance to putting someone else's home in order. At home she could stop and start, do one task now and another later. But here the work seemed unending. Her carefully made-up face had begun to shine an hour ago and her back ached. Her feet, despite her most comfortable pair of Nikes, hurt. Throwing the last of the sheets into the dryer, she trooped downstairs to attack the kitchen and mop the wood floors.

It was two o'clock when the sound of the buzzing dryer reached her. Climbing the stairs for what felt like the thousandth time, she pulled the king-sized sheets out. Grappling them in her arms, she carried them back to the master bedroom and began to smooth them onto the bed. As she leaned forward, her foot hit something solid. She felt it again when she was putting the comforter in place. Crouching, she reached under the bed and pulled out a large unmarked cardboard box.

"Solange," she said. "You don't really need to know

what's in there. You already know Bitsy Menkowski is a messy person with bad taste. Isn't that enough?"

Evidently not. Because within moments she was holding a black leather whip and a pair of handcuffs in one hand and a black leather thong—please, God, let it be Bitsy's and not Herbert's—and a matching leather mask in the other.

Bitsy Menkowski and her husband were into whips and chains. Bitsy Menkowski, who had been Meghan's Girl Scout leader, was a dominatrix.

It was like finding out Mickey and Minnie Mouse were swingers. And that they'd had a threesome with Donald Duck.

A door slammed and Amanda froze. Bitsy's voice floated up the stairs. "Hello?" There was the sound of quick foot-steps on the wood floor below. "I'm home!"

"*Merde.*" Amanda threw the sex toys back in the box and shoved it under the bed. Taking a deep breath, she put on a look of surprised incomprehension, which wasn't difficult under the circumstances, then walked out of the bedroom, stopping at the top of the stairs.

"Yoo-hoo! Are you up there?" Bitsy stood at the bottom of the stairs craning her neck to see.

For a moment Amanda forgot who and what she was supposed to be. Her brain was still trying to wrap itself around the things she'd discovered under the bed.

"*Madame!*" Amanda said in French. "You have surprised me." Damn right, she was surprised. "I am Solange. Solange de Papillon."

She held her breath and waited for Bitsy to recognize her, but Bitsy's gaze barely skimmed over her before turning away to survey her kitchen as Amanda descended the stairs.

"Everything looks pretty good." Bitsy's tone was grudging. "Who do I make the check out to?"

Check?

Amanda followed Bitsy into the kitchen. A check was completely out of the question. One made out to a fictional person would be uncashable. One made out to Amanda Sheridan would be unthinkable.

"*Madame?*" Amanda stayed on the other side of the counter, not wanting to get too close, still afraid Bitsy might recognize her.

Bitsy was already pulling out her checkbook. A car horn sounded outside.

"No." Amanda laid on her fake accent and shook her fake curls adamantly. In careful English she said, "I do not accept zee checks. I believe Candace told you that I only take cash."

Annoyance flashed across Bitsy's face. "But I'll have to..."

The horn sounded again, more insistent this time. Thank God for Candace. Amanda waited, eyes locked on Bitsy, refusing to back down.

"Oh, all right," Bitsy muttered. "I suppose I can run by the bank later."

Still silent, Amanda looped her bucket of supplies over her arm and grasped the vacuum with her hand. She held the other hand out, palm up, for Bitsy Menkowski to count the money into.

"*Merci, madame,*" she said when the other woman had finished. "I appreciate your keeping the agreement."

Pleased that she'd emerged from the standoff victorious, Amanda turned to leave. She'd almost reached the foyer, when Bitsy grasped her polyester sleeve. "Wait."

Amanda didn't want to. She just wanted to get out of there, unrecognized, with her earnings intact. Staying in character she turned to face Bitsy, her shoulders back and her chin up. She looked down her nose at her client.

"What about next week?"

Amanda felt one eyebrow tilt up. "What did you say?"

"Next week. You come. Here." Bitsy pointed and mimed.

Amanda tilted her head to the other side, beginning to enjoy the show.

"Next week. The third week of April. You clean. Again." Bitsy took out another twenty and handed it to Amanda.

"Yes, of course." Amanda nodded and smiled, but not full out. Solange would stay a step removed. "You call Candace to schedule and I will come."

Then she swept out of there with all the bravado her tired self could muster, undaunted by Bitsy and Herbert Menkowski's sex life. Or the little algae problem they had developing in their master bathroom shower.

"So?" Candace asked as Amanda stowed her things in the trunk and climbed gingerly into the car. Her body was one giant ache and the white polyester pantsuit, now stained and sweaty, stuck to her body.

"Did she have an unsightly bathtub ring? Did you find dust bunnies under Bitsy's bed?"

Amanda rolled her neck from side to side, trying to work out the kinks, wishing that was all she'd found under the Menkowskis' bed. "Not exactly."

Candace, who was perfectly made-up, had the convertible top down on the car. Her hair stirred artfully in the wind. It was a gorgeous spring day, the flowers bulging with color, the sky a clear, perfect blue. Amanda had been so busy cleaning, she'd barely had time to glance out one of the Menkowskis' forty-some windows.

"What does that mean?"

Amanda felt a smile curve her lips. "Let's just say Bitsy's not as boring and unimaginative as we thought."

Candace pulled into her driveway and drove straight into the garage, where Amanda's van waited. She closed the garage door behind them so no one would see them unloading, or Solange transforming into someone else. "Can you be more specific?"

"I don't know." Amanda shook her head and stole a look in the rearview mirror at the wig, now even bigger and wilder after the ride in the convertible. "I'm wondering if there's some sort of cleaning woman's code of ethics. Because I now know way more about Bitsy than I ever wanted to. And I'm kind of horrified to think what my cleaning people knew about me."

"Oh, no you don't." Candace's voice was edged with disbelief. "If you have juicy info about Bitsy Menkowski you're definitely going to share it with Sister Candace."

Pulling off the wig, Amanda massaged her scalp and shook her hair free. "OK," she said as she spilled all. "But don't say I didn't try to spare you."

In the stunned silence that followed Amanda found a Kleenex in her purse and used it to wipe off the remains of the red lipstick. She'd enjoyed being Solange, but she could hardly wait to get home and get into the shower to scrub off the rest of her disguise, not to mention the dirt and grime.

"If I'm going to do this on a regular basis, I'm going to have to work out a system," Amanda said, climbing out of

the car. "I wasted a huge amount of time today trying to figure out where to begin and what to do next."

"I guess there has to be a learning curve just like with
anything else." Candace considered Amanda. "Are you OK
with this? I mean it sounded completely logical the other
night when we were brainstorming, but I'm sure the reality
of cleaning other people's houses is . . ."

"Eet's a dirty job, but somebody has to do eet," Amanda
quipped in Solange's accent. "I can't afford to be squeamish
right now. I'm keeping my eyes on the money."

Amanda went to the trunk of the car to retrieve her
cleaning supplies.

Candace's cell phone rang.

"Hello?" Candace waved Amanda to wait.

"Hi, Bitsy. Oh, that's great." Candace gave Amanda a
thumbs-up. "What time next Monday?" She cocked an eyebrow at Amanda and motioned her closer. "Just a sec."
Candace put her hand over the cell phone mouthpiece.

"Negotiate up," Amanda said. "It's going to take a jack-
hammer to get that place in shape and keep it that way. And
she'll like it better if she's overpaying. Solange *should* be
more expensive."

"Bitsy?" Candace said into the phone. "She can do
Mondays, but she needs one hundred and thirty-five dollars to do all the things we talked about weekly. If you drop
to every other week, the price goes up because she'll have to
clean deeper."

There was squawking on the other end.

"Yes, I know. But she'll only take on a job if she can put
in the time to do it right." More squawking. "Yes, yes, I
know." Candace winked at Amanda. "Solange is definitely

worth it. And you'll be the first in your neighborhood to have a genuine French maid."

Candace put her hand over the mouthpiece again. "Solange is a hit. Bitsy already told Susie Simmons about her and Susie wants to know if she's, um, you're available on Friday mornings."

Amanda smiled, pleased. She took off the uniform jacket and hung it over her arm then peeled off the beauty mark and stashed it in her pocket. "Tell her I'm going to have to check my calendar. Ask if you can get back to her tomorrow. The harder Solange is to get, the more they're going to want her."

Amanda took the cleaning supplies out of Candace's trunk and stored them in an empty corner of the garage. When Candace hung up, Amanda presented her strategy. "Give Susie Friday morning, but try to convince her not to be there. Maybe you can tell her that Solange works better uninterrupted, or something. She's more observant than Bitsy, and I don't want Solange exposed before I have a chance to build a client base."

"Got it."

"Are you really OK driving me? I hate to ask it, but . . ."

Candace put up a hand to silence her. "Don't even think about it. I'm glad to do it."

"Thanks. Thanks for everything." Amanda leaned against the passenger door. Peeling off a twenty from the roll of bills Bitsy had given her, she leaned over the door and handed it to Candace.

"What's this for?"

"It's your fifteen percent."

"Don't be ridiculous. I don't want . . ." Candace got out of the car and walked around it to Amanda.

"Look, if you're going to be Solange's agent and chauffeur—at least for the time being—you're going to have to let me pay you."

"But I don't need . . ."

"I know you don't." Amanda spoke quietly but firmly. Candace's help and support meant more to her than she could say, but she was NOT going to be a charity case. "I don't want to hear another word about it. You may not need the money, but I most definitely need to give it to you, *Candee ass*." She said the name in the heavily accented English she'd adopted and smiled at Candace's instant irritation. "And so does Solange."

Brooke stood in Macy's lingerie department trying to decide between a black silk teddy and a white lace thong with matching bustier. The black silk was sleek and slippery beneath her fingers and would accentuate the deep highlights she'd had put in her auburn hair. But the lace bustier pushed her breasts up and made them swell enticingly above the garment and the thong would leave her buttocks bare—all the better for encouraging Hap to go ahead and explore. With a heady little rush of pleasure, she bought them both.

But as she left the lingerie department and worked her way through the store, she thought about Amanda who would be getting home from cleaning Bitsy Menkowski's right about now. This led to thoughts of her mother, who was probably still making beds and swishing toilets at the Betwixt Holiday Inn.

Brooke's glow of pleasure faded. How could she waste an entire afternoon shopping for things she didn't really need while Amanda and her mother were performing hard manual labor, and only too glad to get it?

In the sportswear department she picked through a sale table of brightly colored long-sleeved T-shirts. At the bottom of the pile she found one in the very pale pink that her mother had always referred to as her signature color. Brooke held it up, imagining how excited her mother would be to own a brand-new garment like this; one that was in the height of fashion and newly purchased, not a hand-me-down gathered for the church jumble sale.

Not sure why, she took it up to the register and paid for it. Then she chose a pair of pink and white striped capris to go with it. And she paid for those too.

It was odd, she thought, as she rode the escalator up to customer service for a box to ship the outfit in. She'd sent gifts for Christmas and her mother's birthday—very generous monetary gifts that her mother could use for whatever she most needed. But this was the first time since she'd hot-footed it out of Betwixt that Brooke had thought to send her mother clothing for no other reason than because it was pretty.

chapter 12

On Friday morning Amanda crouched in front of Susie Simmons's front door, stuck a hand under the welcome mat, and felt around for the house key. It wasn't there.

Still crouched, she peered through the sidelights, searching for a sign of movement, but the foyer and the kitchen beyond were dark.

Swiping at one of Solange's curls, Amanda straightened and pressed a finger to the doorbell. A light went on in the kitchen and a moment later Susie Simmons, dressed in exercise clothes, her face already made-up, pulled open the door. "Solange?"

Amanda smiled, as if with delight. "*Oui, madame.* I am Solange de Papillon." God, she loved saying that. "I have heard so very much about you."

Susie's face suffused with pleasure. When her gaze flicked over her, Amanda braced for the gasp of recognition. She'd prepared an incredibly lame explanation of a drama exercise she was developing just in case she was recognized, but Susie was already turning to lead her into the house, yakking away as if Solange was exactly who she appeared to be. Either her disguise was even better than she'd realized or being a maid was the equivalent of donning Harry Potter's invisibility cloak.

In the kitchen, Susie moved toward the coffeemaker. A delicate china cup that looked like Limoges sat on the counter next to the creamer and sugar, its gold rimmed handle turned at a precise 90-degree angle to the coffeepot. Not a crumb marred the glossy sheen of the black granite countertop. Amanda could see Solange's reflection in it.

"Would you like a cup of coffee?" Susie asked.

"*Merci*. That would be wonderful," Amanda said in Solange's heavily accented English. Susie poured, then with Solange's direction, creamed and sugared the coffee while peppering Amanda with questions. Amanda was careful to answer in the same accented English. As she described the small town Solange had been born in and her years as head housekeeper for a famous French hotel chain, it occurred to her that she'd better write down the backstory she was creating so freely, so it didn't come back to bite her on her not-exactly-French derriere.

Ready to get to work and aware that too much face time could increase the risk of exposure, Amanda set down her coffee cup and nodded her head in a curt, businesslike manner. "So," she said. "You have seen me. I have seen you. Now I must begin."

A crease appeared on Susie's forehead. She didn't look at all happy about being dismissed by a cleaning woman, even one with cachet. She didn't move.

"I hope you are not going to stay here zee whole time," Amanda said. "Eet makes eet much more difficult for me to become absorbed in my work."

Susie's look of irritation turned into one of incredulity. This was undoubtedly the first time a cleaning woman had asked her to get out of her own house.

Amanda was kind of amazed herself. But for some reason she didn't fully understand, she could not back down. Cleaning homes might be her only option, but she was not going to hang her head while she did it. She raised a single eyebrow and pursed her heavily lipsticked lips. "If zees is going to be a problem for you, *I* will go."

Susie's eyes narrowed and Amanda realized she might have gone too far.

"But you look as if you are dressed to go somewhere anyway. *Non?*" Amanda smiled to take the sting out of her earlier words, but she didn't break eye contact.

"Yes." Susie folded first. "I am. If I don't hurry, I'll be late for my class." She picked up a list from the counter. "I explained what I wanted to Candace," she said, "but I took the liberty of preparing a list for you. In French." Susie looked quite pleased at her accomplishment. "My daughter, Lucy, is in honors French at *l'école*." She pronounced the French word for school so perfectly Amanda suspected she'd been practicing. If Susie Simmons needed to impress her maid, Susie Simmons needed to get a life.

"How clever zee girl must be." Amanda smiled and took the paper. It was written in careful cursive, the accent marks lined up just so. It looked like Lucy was going to be a chip off her mother's obsessive-compulsive block. "If you will just show me where you'd like me to start, I will commence with zee cleaning now."

Susie showed her the laundry room then led her to the master bedroom. Two minutes later a door slammed and the sound of a car backing down the driveway reached her. Now Amanda stood in the master closet, her mouth open in amazement, any pretense of cleaning completely forgotten. Because if her closet was any indication, Susie Simmons needed more than a life. She needed serious help, though apparently not in the area of organization.

"Color coded, huh?" Amanda and Candace were in Candace's car on the way home from the Simmons's. Amanda was dreaming of a bath, Candace was waiting for details.

"Color coded doesn't even begin to cover it. It was frightening. The woman had detected and allowed for shades of *beige*, Candace, *beige*. And everything was lined up with surgical precision. Susie's always been a little bit . . . controlling . . . but I had no idea."

"Was the whole house like that?"

"Pretty much. I mean have you ever seen underwear ironed and perfectly piled?"

"You looked in her underwear drawer?"

"Not on purpose. Something fell in and I had to get it out."

"Right." Candace sounded unconvinced.

"There was a pile of twenties on the dresser and I accidentally knocked one into the top drawer. I figured it was a test and that she probably knew exactly how much was there. I didn't want her to be able to question Solange."

"Was she there the whole time?"

"No, I got rid of her pretty quickly. But I think Solange may have pissed her off. Solange has a bit of an attitude."

Candace laughed. "You act as if she's someone else entirely."

"Yeah." Amanda thought about how easy it had been to speak up and get what she wanted as Solange; she could use a little bit more of that attitude in her everyday life. "I don't even know why she needs a maid," Amanda said. "There wasn't a piece of lint out of place. Even her son Chas's room looked completely unlived in."

"Status," Candace replied as she pulled into her garage. "I thought you were crazy when you decided to go with the whole French thing, but Solange is definitely unique. I'm sure this is the first time Susie has been ordered around by her maid."

Amanda giggled. "I have to admit I enjoyed it, but I liked it a lot better when I could take these people at face value. I don't *want* to know that Bitsy's kinky and Susie is obsessive-compulsive. Can't you find me some total strangers to work for whose neuroses I don't care about?"

Candace smiled. "I'll see what I can do. But right now Solange is the flavor of the month, and we should probably take advantage of that while we can."

"I think you're right, *Candee ass,* but I think maybe we should create a questionnaire for prospective clients with a place to mark off personal idiosyncrasies and fetishes."

"Absolutely." Candace laughed out loud. "I'll get right on that. And while we're on the subject, have I mentioned that I really don't like to be called Candy?"

* * *

Showered and de-Solanged, Amanda drove to The House of Dance to pick up Meghan. Slipping through the front door, she followed the sound of music to the main studio where Meghan's dance company was practicing for their upcoming recital.

Stopping in front of the plate glass window, she watched the eleven girls step into their positions on the scuffed wood floor. Long legged in pink tights and black leotards with lacy little camisoles over them, every one of them wore their hair in a bun and all of them moved with the grace that only came from long years of practice.

Meghan stood in the front, facing the mirrored wall, her arms gently rounded downward, her right leg extended behind her.

The instructor pressed a button on the CD player and the opening strains of Tchaikovsky's *Les Sylphides* filled the room. All of the girls began to move, but Amanda's eyes stayed on Meghan as her daughter's willowy arms floated upward and she began the opening movements of her solo.

Small delicate running steps, jeté, balancé, arabesque.

With fluid movements, Meghan danced through the line of other girls, her long limbs moving effortlessly, her chin high, her neck curved like a swan's.

Holding her breath, Amanda watched her daughter bend and gather herself then press smoothly up on pointe. Her mind flashed on the memory of the chubby five-year-old who'd first stepped into this studio with her hand clutched so tightly in her mother's and who had somehow metamorphosed into this graceful creature.

"Amazing, isn't it?"

The male voice so close beside her took her completely

by surprise. The fact that she recognized the voice was even more disconcerting.

Turning, she looked into the green eyes of Hunter James, who seemed to be making a habit of showing up at the most unexpected moments and places.

He nodded toward the girls who had separated into two lines and were passing each other in a series of intricate steps. "That's my daughter Samantha." He pointed to the tall blonde three girls to the left of Meghan. "She's addicted, can't seem to get enough of it. And her younger sister is dancing right along in her footsteps."

Amanda looked at the man in front of her. His shoulders were broad, his torso gently muscled, and he moved with a testosterone-fueled version of the grace their daughters were displaying on the dance floor.

Without thinking, she glanced down at his ring finger, something she'd forgotten to do the other day at the duck pond, and noticed he wore no ring. Nor was there a telltale white line.

He caught her at it, of course, and she blushed for what felt like the bazillionth time in his presence. But the absence of a wedding ring didn't confirm the absence of a wife. The fact that he was attractive and friendly didn't make him available.

Solange de Papillon would come right out and ask him his status and be prepared to act accordingly, but Amanda's tongue and brain didn't seem to be working in tandem.

"Sometimes I feel like they should rent out rooms here," she said.

One of his sandy eyebrows shot up and his green eyes

sparked with amusement. "I'm assuming you don't mean by the hour."

Amanda blushed yet again. She suspected she was setting some sort of record for cheek suffusion. "Because of all the driving. To, um, save on gas." She was blathering like an idiot and couldn't seem to stop herself. Where was Solange when she needed her?

"I've never seen you here before," Amanda said. And Lord knew, no woman would have missed him. "When did your daughter join the company?"

"About a month ago. But our housekeeper's been driving her. She left yesterday for Jamaica so I've got carpool duty."

Amanda was processing his answer when the girls began to pile out of the studio in excited little knots.

"Hey, Mom, guess what?" Meghan pulled Hunter James's daughter over in front of her. "Sam's going to the prom with Brent Means, he's Joey's best friend. So we're going to share a limo with Angie and Sandy and their dates. I asked them all to come over for a picture party before the prom."

"Gee." Amanda resisted looking at Hunter James, absolutely refused to check and see how those green eyes were reacting. "That's great." She swallowed. "The more the merrier."

If it had been any other parent, she would have invited them to stop by and be a part of the pre-prom gathering. But she was much too aware of Hunter James as a man to want to watch him in action with his wife.

"Mom?" Meghan nodded none too subtly toward Samantha's father.

Amanda gave a warning shake of her head, but her

daughter ignored her. "Lucy Simmons is having a bunch of kids *and* their parents over for their picture party," Meghan said.

"Well, I, um . . ." OK, this was ridiculous. She was NOT going to blush again. "Of course." Taking a step back, Amanda turned to face Samantha's father. "We'd love it if you and your wife could join us for pictures before the prom."

A look she couldn't decipher washed over his face, but it was Samantha who spoke. "My mother's dead. That's one of the reasons we moved here."

"Oh," Amanda said.

The girl's eyes welled briefly.

"I'm so sorry." Amanda reached out and placed a hand on Samantha's shoulder then turned back to Hunter James. "I'm sure the girls will want to get dressed together. Why don't you join us for the big send-off? And bring your camera.

"Will six work?" she asked Meghan.

Her daughter nodded and smiled her thanks.

They walked out to the parking lot with the girls chattering between them and got into their cars. Hunter James's was big and masculine like the man who drove it, but in reality it was a "mom mobile." Which was, Amanda decided, the way to treat the unnerving Mr. James—just like she would any other mother of her acquaintance.

She stole one last look as Mr. Mom slid behind the wheel of the black Escalade and knew it wasn't going to be easy.

Hunter James bore absolutely no resemblance to any other mother she'd ever met.

chapter 13

She'd heard it said that the eyes were the mirror to the soul. But after a little over a week in the cleaning business, Amanda was pretty certain that a person's closet was a much clearer reflection.

She stood now in the master closet of Sylvia Hardaway, one of Candace's neighbors, staring into a dressing room/closet combo that was large enough to house a small country. She was tempted to yodel into its cavernous depths just to see how long it would take for the sound to echo back.

With wonder she contemplated the burnished mahogany built-ins that covered every available inch of wall and in which Sylvia's clothing had been hung and folded in a rich spill of color and texture that delighted the eye.

A stand of custom-built dressers in the same deep wood and topped with dappled marble anchored the center of the space. At one end, a wall of shelves held a collection of designer shoes that would have made Carrie Bradshaw from

Sex and the City weep with envy. A sitting area with love seat and chairs cozied up to a minibar and refrigerator at the other end, presumably in case Sylvia worked up a thirst or appetite while dressing, which given the sheer number of choices seemed entirely possible.

The master bath lay through a door to the right. It, too, was divided into His and Hers and was separated by a carpeted hallway from her husband's slightly smaller dressing area.

Amanda circled Sylvia Hardaway's closet slowly, taking it all in, and noticed that many of the hanging garments still bore their tags. A glimpse at some of the price tags made her heart race—just returning one or two of them would make a large dent in the growing stack of bills on her kitchen desk at home.

As Amanda turned to leave, Sylvia Hardaway entered the closet, a hanging bag from Neiman's folded over one arm. She looked to be somewhere around fifty, but had the face and body of a woman who worked full-time on both. With apparent breaks for shopping.

"*Madame*," Amanda said in Solange's voice, "your closet ees *magnifique*. I am wondering if I might rent a part of zee space to live in it."

Her client's gaze was a bit vague, her smile heartbreakingly brittle. "Be my guest," she said, gesturing into the bowels of the closet. "And bring your family. I don't think Charles is home enough to even notice."

"Oh, no," Amanda/Solange said. "That cannot be true. I'm sure your husband notices *you*. You are a very handsome woman and if I may say so, you dress with a very French flair."

"Why thank you, Solange," Sylvia said, her smile warming. "That's very kind of you. I do spend considerable time on wardrobe selection."

This, of course, was like saying the Atlantic Ocean was damp, but Amanda didn't point that out.

"The right outfit can give a woman such a helpful . . . boost, don't you think?" her newest client said as she hung the new clothing without bothering to remove it from the bag.

As could alcohol, Amanda thought later when she found the empty vodka bottles buried in Sylvia's recycling bin.

The more she peered beneath the surface of other women's lives, the more she questioned the "happily ever after" tales that little girls were raised on. And the more attractive Solange de Papillon's marvelous sense of self-confidence became.

"Yes, Mother, I know. No, Mother, I won't." Candace sat at the desk in her home office, eyes closed in an attempt to ward off the headache that had threatened the moment her mother's phone number appeared on her caller ID. She allowed her mind to wander for a few moments, hoping that might stop the throbbing, but brought it screeching back when her mother's words sank in.

"I can't do lunch on Saturday." Candace rubbed her forehead, trying to loosen the knot there. "I have a previous commitment."

"But I promised Minna Jacobs we'd take her son to the club for lunch. He's only in town until Sunday morning."

"You shouldn't have spoken for me without asking." It was hard to talk with your teeth so tightly clenched, but

Candace had years of practice. "I can't do it. Other people are counting on me."

Any other mother would have given in then, but "no" was not a word Hannah Bloom accepted from others.

"Whatever in the world could be more important than lunch with your mother and an eminently suitable man?"

Candace knew before she spoke exactly how important her prior commitment was going to sound to her mother. Even she was having a hard time accepting how committed she felt about it. "I have concession duty at the ballpark."

There was a brief silence.

"I'm sorry," her mother said. "I must have misunderstood, because I thought you were turning me—and Stanley Jacobs, the podiatrist—down for concession duty at a Little League game."

Candace sighed. "No, no mistake." Looking up, she saw Amanda in the doorway. She'd removed all traces of Solange and had tucked her own straight dark hair behind her ears. Candace raised a hand and motioned her in then raised a finger to indicate she'd only be a minute. "I promised to help out. In fact, I want to help out. You'll have to take him to lunch yourself."

"This is all about that Donovan person, isn't it?"

Leave it to Hannah to cut right to the crux of the matter. "This is the second time you've canceled with me to do something with him."

Candace rubbed harder at her forehead, but all she managed to get rid of was makeup. "This doesn't qualify as a cancellation because I never agreed to the lunch in the first place." As if her mother was going to fall for semantics.

"Well, how can we make plans if you're always at that *ball field*?" She uttered the last words in the same way she might have said "den of iniquity."

Candace motioned Amanda to the chair on the opposite side of her desk.

"Listen, Mother," she finally interjected into Hannah's stream of complaints, "I've got to run. Someone just came in." She closed her eyes again and sighed at her mother's parting shot. "Yes, Mother," she replied. "I know *exactly* how old I am. And I realize that my eggs aren't getting any younger either."

"Wow." Amanda winced as Candace hung up the phone. "Does she bring those things up often?"

"You could say that. Doesn't your mother do the 'your eggs are drying up, why can't you hold on to a husband' spiel?"

Amanda shook her head.

"You don't know what you're missing. But then you already have children and your mother probably thinks everything you do is wonderful. What kind of torture does she have in mind for Rob?"

"She's always been very supportive, both my parents have." Amanda shifted uncomfortably in her seat. "And I, uh, assume they'd be totally on my side if I, um, ever actually admitted that Rob and I were having problems."

Candace looked at the woman seated across from her. She *looked* like a sane, normal person—except possibly for the whole Solange the butterfly persona—but then appearances were often deceiving.

"You mean you haven't told them about Tiffany? Or that you're getting a divorce? Or that you dress up as a French maid and clean houses?"

Amanda shook her head again.

"Wow." Candace sat back in her chair, trying to absorb it. "That could never happen in my family. If my mother even thought I was keeping something from her, she'd hire rogue CIA agents to capture me and inject me with truth serum. Hell, she'd probably cut out the middleman and inject me herself."

"I keep meaning to tell them," Amanda said. "But they're on this cross-country trip in their motor home that they've been planning forever. I don't want to ruin it." She sighed. "My parents have been married for forty-five years and are actually still in love with each other. I just can't bring myself to admit I've failed so badly at marriage."

"I don't think you're the one who failed," Candace said. "But won't your kids say something? Shouldn't you mention it before Meghan or Wyatt does?"

"Oh, I'm going to have to tell them sometime soon. I know that. I'm just trying to get up my nerve. I'm sort of hoping I can borrow some of Solange's."

"Ah, yes, the fabulous French one. How'd she do at Sylvia's? Isn't her closet to die for?"

"Yes." Amanda smiled, clearly relieved to move on to a safer topic. "I'm thinking about buying a bumper sticker for her Lexus that says, *I brake for Jimmy Choo*."

They shared a laugh over that one.

"But she doesn't look as happy as a woman with that many shoes should, *Candee ass*," Amanda said. "And that worries me. Because so far, from what I can see, no one's life is even remotely what it looks like it should be."

* * *

Brooke Mackenzie was not sorry to see the spin class end. Tired and sweaty, she jumped off her stationary bike, slung a towel over her shoulders, and gave a few nods of farewell to the other regulars.

Striding through the health club and out to the parking lot, she sorted through potential meal ideas as she walked. She'd never been much of a cook. In her single days, she'd existed on fast food and restaurant leftovers, but now that she was a married woman, she prided herself on the meals she presented to her husband. Of course, most of them came from the already prepared section of the specialty grocery stores, though she was very careful to destroy or hide the takeout evidence.

It was hard to set a romantic mood when she was playing the wicked stepmother for Tyler, but tonight it would be just her and Hap for dinner, and she intended to make the most of the opportunity. During dinner, she'd grab and hold on to her husband's full attention, a feat that was becoming harder and harder to accomplish. The meal would be a demonstration of how well she could fulfill her wifely role. Afterward, well, afterward Hap could have whatever he chose for dessert.

At the gourmet grocery Fresh Market, she picked up two salmon filets with a feta and spinach stuffing and the twice-baked potatoes that Hap favored.

At home, she showered and changed, preheated the oven, and assembled the salad ingredients in a beautiful ceramic bowl. By seven fifteen the potatoes were reheating, the salmon sat on the counter ready to pop in the oven, and a bottle of Hap's favorite white wine was opened and sitting in a cooler.

Running nervous hands down the sides of her tight black miniskirt, Brooke adjusted the low-slung waistband and figure-hugging black silk blouse she'd tucked into it to better display her décolleté.

At seven thirty the garage door went up. She'd just finished pouring his glass of wine when her husband came through the door.

Hap smiled, pecked her absently on the cheek, and took the wine she held out to him. "Thanks. Umm, smells good in here." He looked around the kitchen with the kind of appreciation he used to reserve for her.

"Salmon and twice-baked potatoes. We can eat in ten minutes."

"Great."

She'd pictured them chatting about their days—not that hers were all that full now that she'd quit work—while she got dinner on the table, imagined the exchange of meaningful glances that would make it difficult to get all the way through the meal before adjourning to the bedroom.

Her mind had conjured all kinds of elaborate scenarios for their childless evening, but Hap picked up the newspaper she'd left folded on the counter, and carried it and his wineglass into the family room. She trailed behind him and watched in dismay as he sank into his favorite club chair, put his long legs up on the ottoman, and buried his face in the sports section.

"Hap?" Brooke moved closer.

"Hmmm?" He grunted, but didn't look up.

Swallowing her disappointment, she stared at her husband. Hap Mackenzie's hair was beginning to show threads of gray and his once broad shoulders had begun to hunch slightly inward. His clear brown eyes were fixed on the newspaper at the moment, but she had seen herself in them; had seen the sparkle of interest, the burning of lust. When he'd asked her to marry him, she'd believed what was shining in their depths was actually love.

He was sixteen years older than her and was no longer the rock-hard jock she knew he'd once been. But she'd had enough rock-hard bodies in her life. Hap had something more alluring than muscle; an inner confidence that dwarfed her own and a firm understanding of his place in the world. The chain of fast food restaurants he owned didn't hurt either.

She'd never imagined that in just one short year he'd be able to ignore her so easily. Or that his sexual appetite, which had been formidable, would wane when she was no longer forbidden fruit, but ripe and readily available and hanging right there on his tree.

Back in the kitchen, she broiled the salmon and took the potatoes from the oven, taking great care to arrange everything attractively on his plate. Setting them on the candlelit table, she went back to the family room to retrieve her husband.

"Dinner's ready."

Reluctantly he folded the newspaper and set it down. Standing, he stretched contentedly and moved toward her. He was still strong and virile—and surely still interested in her?

She stayed where she was as he approached. Licking her lips, she pushed her shoulders back and her chest forward so that her breasts strained against the black silk blouse. When he reached her, she stepped forward until she was flush against him with her nipples pressing into his chest. Tilting her face up to his, she looked into his eyes and let her own smolder. "Hungry?" she purred.

Six months ago he would have slid his hands down to cup her buttocks, lifted her skirt, and pushed her back against the kitchen island. Now he looked down at her quizzically, as if he didn't understand what she meant.

If she didn't watch out, he was going to turn her into another Sarah—homey and comfortable and completely forgettable. Still, this didn't seem the moment to seduce him on the kitchen floor or chastise him for treating her like the wife she was.

"Now that I think about it," Brooke said, "I'm absolutely famished." She hooked her arm through his and made a show of being eager to get to the table, but the calculator that was her brain was analyzing the status of their marriage and thanking God that she'd already booked an appointment with Paul LaPrada, one of Atlanta's most prominent plastic surgeons.

Over dinner their conversation was desultory. She asked questions about his work and he answered. He asked about her day, and she did her best to give her workout and errands an interesting spin.

Brooke found herself wishing that she could tell him about Amanda's troubles. She would have loved to hear his thoughts and pick his brain a bit about the business aspects of Amanda's undertaking, but Amanda's secret wasn't hers to reveal. And a conversation like that could all too easily lead to questions that Brooke was nowhere near ready to answer. For the first time the wall she'd erected around her past felt like brick and mortar between them. She'd accused him of keeping her at arm's length, but she had no right to complain. How close could you get to someone you were afraid to share your past with?

She studied her husband, looking for clues as to what to do. He seemed perfectly satisfied with the past she'd created for herself. Even if she wanted to, how could she suddenly admit it was a complete fabrication?

No, she couldn't risk it. Better to simply be the woman he thought she was. Even if it left her on the other side of the wall, unable to get in.

chapter 14

In her rattiest jeans and one of Wyatt's old baseball jerseys, Amanda scrubbed her bathtubs, folded the kids' laundry and put every piece of it away. Then she cleaned out the refrigerator and both of her freezers, tossing out the science projects and rock-hard ziplock baggies that had been in the freezer since the last ice age.

When even she couldn't find anything else in the house that required her attention, she picked up the stack of bills that had been teetering on her desk and carried them to the kitchen table. Retrieving a legal pad, a pen, and a calculator from the desk drawer, she placed those next to the pile of envelopes then sat down at the table, scooted her chair closer. And eyed them.

She'd told herself that going through them would help her put things in perspective, but just looking at them— and acknowledging their existence—sent a shiver of dread coursing through her. They were visible, tangible symbols of how completely her life had changed.

Once her role had been clear-cut—she ran their home, saw to her family's well being and served as chief cheerleader, counselor, and organizer. She still had all those jobs, but now she was supposed to be the breadwinner too. Everything she did now produced all kinds of conflicted feelings and reactions.

Cleaning houses was hard physical labor; doing it while pretending to be someone else was both exhilarating and draining. And then there were Meghan's mood swings, which ranged from ecstasy over the coming prom to fury over her father's desertion. Too often Amanda felt as if she was tiptoeing through a minefield and that one wrong step would set Meghan off and cause them all to explode.

With a sigh, she opened the first bill, wrote the amount and the due date on the legal pad then moved on to the next. Thirty minutes later she knew exactly where she stood and wished that she didn't.

At the moment Solange earned a whopping total of $405 a week; not nearly enough to pay these ongoing bills and keep current on the mortgage, when the five thousand Rob had deposited to cover the month of April was gone.

Feeling old and not at all French, Amanda put the bills back in a pile, tied them and the dismal yellow sheet with a rubber band, and stashed them out of sight. She needed to call Candace to see if she had any more potential clients, but first she needed to pick up cold cuts for the kids' lunches and something she could cook for dinner. She'd best stock her pantry while she could. If she didn't start earning more money soon, she was going to be cooking

Casseroles d'Alpo instead of Beef Bourguignon and Coq au Vin.

At the grocery store the crowd in front of the deli counter stood three deep. Jockeying for position, Amanda wrestled a number out of the dispenser then angled her grocery cart over to the side. She had number 102. Eighty-nine was currently being served.

With a sigh she checked her watch then hunkered down for the duration. Wyatt had a ride home from an after school meeting and a house key. As long as she got to dance in time to retrieve Meghan, she'd be OK.

Behind the counter, two people who spoke more heavily accented English than Solange were slicing breasts of meat and holding the slices up—one at a time—for inspection. Their movements were slow and deliberate. Very slow and deliberate. They made oozing molasses seem fast.

Trying to control her impatience, Amanda scanned the crowd for familiar faces. She spotted Susie Simmons, impeccably dressed and in full war paint, edging closer to one of the few men in the crowd. He was tall and broad shouldered, the top of his sandy blond hair stood out well above the others. He'd just taken his bags from the deli person and was dropping them in his basket.

Susie inserted herself to his left, directly beside a nicely sculpted shoulder. In a completely calculated move, she opened her fingers and released her number, letting it flutter to the ground at his feet. She fluffed her hair, moistened her lips, and smoothed the arch of an eyebrow while he bent to pick it up.

The crowd shifted and Amanda got an eyeful of nicely rounded buttocks. She watched the man straighten and hand the number back to Susie, then recognized the angled jaw and ready smile of Hunter James.

Susie Simmons batted her eyelashes at him, touched her hair, leaned in closer. Like a fisherman casting her lure, Susie sent out every "come and get me" signal known to womankind.

"Number ninety-five!" a deli person shouted.

One of the customers yelled "Bingo" and stepped toward the counter. The remaining crowd shifted again and the press of bodies thinned.

Susie was decked out for "fishing." Amanda was still wearing worn jeans and Wyatt's old baseball shirts. Her hair had dried au naturel, which meant it was probably board straight with a funky frizz by now and she hadn't taken the time to put on the first drop of makeup. The best thing that could be said for her was that she wasn't presently clutching a gross of condoms.

She considered slipping away, but she needed the sandwich meat and something inside her absolutely refused to retreat. She inched close enough to hear while keeping a screen of people between them.

In a sea of minnows, Hunter James was one fine-looking fish.

"You look so familiar," Susie said to Hunter, her southern drawl thickening to alarming proportions. "Haven't I seen you before?"

He extended his hand, polite, and Susie latched onto it. "Hunter James. We're pretty new here, but I have daughters at Dickerson and Walton. Maybe we've passed in the carpool line?"

Amanda flushed at the predatory look in Susie's eyes.

Hunter's expression was harder to read. For all she knew, he liked being scoped out at the seafood counter, or dished up at the deli.

"Oh, no," Susie demurred. "I'd remember that. No, I've seen you someplace else. And your name sounds so familiar. I believe your daughter and mine are on the prom committee together." Susie hadn't let go of his hand yet; she appeared to be pressing her breast up against his arm.

"I know," Susie said. "Why don't I have my daughter invite yours to our picture party?" She looked him up and down, her gaze settling on the hand she wasn't currently clutching, presumably in search of a wedding band. "You and your wife are welcome too."

Amanda blushed on Susie's behalf. Or maybe on her own. God, she hoped she hadn't looked so . . . hungry . . . when she'd invited him to theirs.

"That's very kind of you." He withdrew his hand and took a small step backward. Turning away as he disengaged, his gaze collided with Amanda's. "But it's just me and my daughters and we've already accepted an invitation." He was looking directly at Amanda now. "From the Sheridans." That infernal look of amusement stole into his eyes. "Hello, Amanda," he said smoothly, leaving her no choice but to step forward and join them.

"Um, hi." Feeling like a kid who'd gotten caught with her hand in the cookie jar, and uncomfortably aware of her lack of makeup and the hole in her jersey, Amanda bobbed her head to Susie. "Hello."

Susie nodded back. Within a nanosecond she'd assessed Amanda, dismissed her, and refocused her attention on Hunter. "I'm sure you'll all have a wonderful time." Her tone said she doubted it. "I happen to be divorced myself, and I know what it's like to run a household on your own. But if there's anything I can do for you, Hunter, you be sure and let me know, you hear?"

Hunter didn't respond to the invitation in her voice. He didn't reject Susie, Amanda noticed, but he didn't encourage her either. As the crowd jostled around the trio, he addressed them both. "Actually," he said, "we've just lost our housekeeper, and I'm looking for someone. Do either of you ladies have anyone you can recommend?"

Susie perked up at the request. "I know just the person," she said.

Amanda had a bad feeling about what was coming next.

"Her name's Solange."

Shit. She might have fantasized about being in Hunter James's bed, she had NOT been fantasizing about making it.

"Your maid is French?" Hunter sounded understandably surprised.

"Yes, isn't that funny?" Susie batted her eyelashes at him again. "Have you tried her yet, Amanda?" Susie asked, not waiting for the answer. "She's quite sophisticated, though I do think her accent's a bit thick. My daughter's going to teach me French so I can communicate my *needs* more clearly." Susie looked Hunter right in the eye when she said the word "needs," and once again Amanda was tempted to blush on her behalf.

"And she is a little on the aggressive side."

Susie paused. Amanda bristled.

"She actually tried to tell me what to do, if you can imagine." Susie's tinkle of laughter grated. "But I'm sure you'd have no trouble keeping her in line."

Before she could stop herself, Amanda was leaping to Solange's defense. "Well, she is from another culture, Susie."

OK, so now she was defending a nonexistent person. "And I wouldn't call her . . . aggressive. I think she's just marvelously . . . self-confident."

Susie's gaze was still glued to Hunter James. She shrugged, clearly only interested in the subject as long as it interested him. "She does a good enough job. And she *seems* honest," Susie conceded, "though you really never know."

Her work was good enough? She only *seemed* honest? Amanda's back straightened. "*I've* been very satisfied with Solange," Amanda said. "But she's really in demand. I don't even know whether she has any openings left in her schedule."

Did she want to clean Hunter James's home? Like everything else in her life at the moment, the question elicited mixed emotions.

Susie stepped closer to Hunter. And she called Solange aggressive!

"I'm sure I can get her for you," Susie said to Hunter. "Why don't you give me your phone number? I'll pass it on to Candace Sugarman, who books her, and ask her to give you a call."

"Number one hundred two!" The voice of the deli person rang out.

"That's me." Amanda held her number aloft torn between staying to see if he gave Susie his phone number and wanting to escape before he turned out to be one of those guys who liked to be pursued by women like Susie.

He reached out as she stepped toward the counter. "Amanda." His touch was light on her arm. "When I leave here, I'm going to pick up Samantha at dance. Do you want me to pick up Meghan too?"

Amanda glanced down at her watch. She had other shopping left to do and it would be nice not to have to race through the remaining aisles. But the thing that really decided her was the ugly look that Susie Simmons aimed her way.

Amanda had been taught to turn the other cheek; Solange de Papillon had never even heard of the concept.

Amanda gave Hunter a slow smile, mostly for Susie's benefit, determined not to read anything into the warmth of the look he gave her. "Thanks," she said. "That would be great."

And then she turned her back on them and stepped up to get her honey maple ham and provolone cheese. While Susie Simmons glared daggers into her back.

By the Friday of the prom, that last weekend in April, Meghan and her girlfriends were in a fever pitch of excitement. Meghan, Angie, and Sandy, who'd been friends since elementary school, along with Samantha, who'd been happily added to the fold, had planned every detail of the evening with the ferocity of generals mapping out a campaign. Amanda was thrilled to see Meghan so happily occupied.

The girls' dates, on whom the intricacies of color coordination and restaurant evaluation were lost, had finally learned to nod their heads in agreement, if not understanding, and do as they were told.

Right now the girls, freshly manicured, pedicured, and coiffured, were upstairs in Meghan's room making up each other's face and helping each other dress. At six the boys and other parents would arrive for the picture party. At seven the limo would whisk the young couples out to dinner and on to the dance.

With the girls' happy squeals ringing in her ears, Amanda scurried about preparing the house for tonight's gathering.

In her bedroom she showered and dried her hair then spent a ridiculous amount of time on her own makeup and clothing.

She told herself this was because the night was so special for Meghan and would be commemorated in pictures forever. And because it was the first time she'd entertained on her own, not as part of a couple. Not because of Hunter James, who'd be arriving tonight on his own.

By five thirty she was downstairs heating hors d'oeuvres and putting out fruit and cheese. The white wine was chilling, the red open and breathing. A cooler of soft drinks awaited the kids.

She'd already done the alcohol lecture and the one about Meghan's body being her temple. But she was glad that the kids would be in a mostly supervised group and that none of the boys would be driving.

Promptly at seven the doorbell rang. Wyatt, who was on door duty, answered it and moments later Sandy's and Angie's parents were in the kitchen accepting glasses of wine, exclaiming over the food. The boys and their parents came next, the boys looking self-consciously stylish in their black tuxes and evening ties, each selected by his date to coordinate with her dress.

They carried plastic-boxed corsages in their sweaty

hands, and they huddled around the appetizers jabbing at each others' shoulders and whispering among themselves.

Nervous, Amanda busied herself serving drinks and passing appetizers while they waited for the girls to make their entrance. The doorbell rang again, and because she was closest, Amanda answered it.

Hunter James stood on the threshold looking very yummy in jeans, a crisp white button-down shirt, and a navy blazer. He had a bottle of wine in his hands and a younger version of Samantha at his side.

"Hi." Amanda stepped back to let them enter then reached out to shake the young girl's hand. "I'm Amanda."

"This is Julie." Hunter made the introductions, and waited while his daughter shook hands with Amanda. Footsteps sounded behind her and Amanda turned to see Wyatt approaching. "Hey, Wy," she said, "this is Julie James."

The girl's smile broadened.

"And this is . . ." Amanda moved to draw her son toward the Jameses, but he needed no encouragement. His gaze was already locked on Hunter's face.

"Mom," he said, "that's Hunter James. Hunter James is here!"

"Yes, I know, sweetheart. He's . . ."

"*The* Hunter James." Wyatt stepped forward and grasped Hunter's hand, shaking it up and down with all his might.

"First-round draft pick for the Baltimore Orioles in nineteen eighty-five. Went to Montreal in nineteen eighty-nine. Was with the Red Sox until he blew out his shoulder in two thousand three."

Amanda considered the man she'd been trying to think of as a ballet mom.

"He's a two-time Cy Young winner, Mom, and had one of the highest batting averages of any pitcher when he was in the National League." He was still shaking Hunter's hand, the words bubbling out unchecked. "I can't believe Hunter James is standing right here. In my house!"

Gently, Hunter grasped Wyatt's hand with his other and brought the handshake to an end. They stood, their hands still clasped, while the man looked down at the boy.

She saw the trace of amusement she was growing used to flicker in his eyes, but everything about his manner told her he would not embarrass her son. Which was a good thing, because hero worship shone from Wyatt's eyes like twin beacons of light.

"It's always great to meet a baseball aficionado," Hunter said. "Sam tells me you pitch too."

"Well, yeah." Wyatt flushed with both pride and embarrassment. He hadn't exactly been the strikeout king of late. "I've been having some problems with my changeup. It's hanging way too long over the plate."

"Giving up some runs, huh?" Hunter's tone was sympathetic. "I had a season like that in ninety-two; they were hitting me like crazy."

Wyatt nodded. "How'd you fix it?"

"Had to change my whole release. It was brutal."

Wyatt looked up at him.

"Maybe you can show me your stuff sometime. I'd be glad to try and help."

"Wow! Did you hear that, Mom? Wow!"

"I did, sweetheart. That's very generous." She was speaking automatically, saying all the usual mother things. But she couldn't quite absorb the fact that the man who'd had her fussing over her appearance for the first time since Rob had given her the heave-ho was a celebrity and one of Wyatt's heroes to boot. "Why don't you take Julie in and get her something to drink?"

"Sure, Mom." Wyatt led the girl away with a happy bounce in his step. Amanda turned to face her guest.

"Well, I feel kind of silly now. I suppose I should have known who you were."

He smiled, a dimple creasing his cheek, his tone self-deprecating. "Actually it's kind of a relief that you didn't. And *were* is the operative word. I'm too old to play baseball now, and way too old to be learning how to be a parent."

An upstairs door opened and there was the clatter of high heels at the top of the stairs. She and Hunter moved farther into the foyer and the rest of the group joined them. They stared in silence at the vision above them.

"Oh my God." He whispered it under his breath, but Hunter wasn't the only parent rocked by the sight of the four gowned beauties hovering above them.

The boys whistled in admiration, while every mother there blinked back tears. If Hunter was any indication, the fathers were worried about other things. Most likely their memories of what they themselves had been up to at that age.

Amanda had a brief stab of regret that Rob was missing this, but she shoved it aside. He'd made his choice and they weren't it. She was the lucky one. She was here to watch Meghan float down the stairs in the incredible dress, surrounded by her friends, alight with excitement. Another memory made in the home she'd refused to give up.

Digital flashes erupted and the groups were framed and

rearranged, until every permutation had been covered. Wyatt stood nearby, snapping pictures when she was too teary-eyed to do it. Then the limo driver rang the bell. Parents issued warnings while kids rolled their eyes and began their good-byes.

"Wait a second." Hunter grabbed Amanda by the arm and moved her next to Meghan. Then he motioned Wyatt over and took the camera from him. "Hold on while I get a last Sheridan shot. That's it, big smiles."

Amanda stood between her children and did as she was instructed.

"That's great," Hunter said, his smile genuine and his warmth contagious. "Let's get one more."

This time Amanda looked deep into the camera lens and by extension into Hunter James's eyes. The contact left her feeling slightly breathless and more than a little daring. In fact, she was in such a good mood, she didn't even scold Wyatt when he formed his fingers into bunny ears and raised them up behind her and Meghan's heads.

chapter 15

Hunter James is famous?" Candace, still looking much too well dressed for concession stand duty, stood beside the grill the next day while Amanda flipped burgers.

"Evidently." Amanda smashed the burger flatter and watched the flames flare up. "Wyatt knew all of his statistics from the moment he was drafted into the majors."

"I understand his personal statistics are pretty impressive too." Candace waggled her eyebrows and did a Grouchoesque flicking of an imaginary cigar.

"We are not even going to go there," Amanda said.

"Why not?"

Amanda rearranged the burgers on the grill. "Because Hunter James is too... attractive. Too... well known. Too... everything. And thanks to Susie Simmons, who has more than a passing interest of her own in him, he's about to become a client." She waved the smoke away from their faces with the spatula. "I don't think he's looking to get involved with his cleaning woman."

"That is one of the stupidest things I've ever heard you say."

"Stupider than worrying that the man you're dating is too kind and too easy to be with?" Amanda asked.

"That's different." Candace retrieved the platter of buns from the prep table and held it out for Amanda.

"In what way?"

"Well . . ." Candace waited while Amanda slipped the burgers inside the buns. "I'm worrying that he may not be enough for me. I'm not worrying that I may not be enough for him."

"Are you sure about that?"

"Here's the mustard." Brooke rushed up from the parking lot, clutching a large grocery bag. "I brought extra buns too."

Skittering to a stop, she followed Amanda and Candace into the concession stand, where a lone and very ancient box fan circulated air. At a back counter she unpacked the things she'd brought then turned to face Amanda and Candace, who were studying her carefully.

"What?" Brooke glanced down at the scoop-necked T-shirt she wore and double-checked the zipper on her shorts. "What are you looking at?"

"You," Candace said. "You were annoyingly perfect before. Now you're approaching nauseating. What did you have done?"

Amanda gave her the once-over, too, but didn't press. They all knew that was Candace's forte.

Brooke shrugged and crossed her arms over her chest. "Nothing major."

They continued to study her in silence.

"Just a chemical peel and a few injections. Collagen here." She pointed to the spot under her eyes. "Botox there." She traced her lip with the same finger. "The doctor thought I could wait awhile for the, uh, eye tuck."

"Why on earth would you need those things?" Amanda started wrapping the burgers in foil. "That plastic surgeon must have a child headed for college."

"I don't know," Brooke said quietly. "I was a little surprised myself at all the things Dr. LaPrada recommended. I went in thinking I was pretty solidly constructed and found out I was a fixer-upper."

Together they wrapped the burgers in foil and set out the condiments.

"Well, I think it's a waste of time and money," Amanda said. "You look great. So great that some of us don't even want to stand next to you."

Brooke smiled her thanks to Amanda. "I appreciate the vote of support," she said then averted her gaze.

"You're thinking it's money well spent," Candace said, and Amanda could tell from Brooke's start of surprise that Candace was right on target. The poor girl wasn't yet thirty and had only been married a year and she was already worrying about holding on to her husband.

"You have so much more to offer than your appearance, Brooke," Amanda said quietly. "Don't let Hap miss out on knowing the real you."

"That sounds great, Amanda. Your confidence in me

is . . . encouraging. But what if I introduce him to the real me and he prefers the me he married? What happens then?"

"Well, whoever she decides to be, there's nothing wrong with keeping up her beauty regimen," Candace said. "But you better be careful, Brooke. You start all this now and they'll be lifting your face from your knees by the time you're forty."

Candace's cell phone rang. Seeing her mother's number on the caller ID, she groaned aloud, but answered on the fourth ring. "Hello, Mother."

Amanda and Brooke shot her sympathetic looks and stepped away to give her privacy.

"No, I told you I was helping in the concession stand today." She braced herself for an argument, but her mother surprised her.

"I know, Candace. And I also know you wouldn't want to miss the opportunity to say hello to Stanley and Minna."

"But I'm—"

"I told them you had to help out your friends." The calm reasonable tone told Candace she must already be with the Jacobses.

"Mother—"

"And Stanley was able to rearrange his afternoon so that you could join us for coffee and dessert."

"But—"

"We've even met you halfway. We're at The Cheesecake Factory at Perimeter Mall. So it shouldn't take you long to get here."

"Mother, I told you—"

Candace never got to finish her sentence because Hannah Bloom had already hung up. And, she discovered after trying to redial her twice, had apparently stopped answering her phone.

Dan arrived at the concession stand just as Candace was getting ready to leave.

"How'd it go?" she asked as she removed her apron and hung it on a nearby hook.

"Another heartbreaker." He came into the stand and moved toward her. "When our defense is on, we can't seem to connect with the ball. When our bats come alive, we seem to have holes in our gloves." He shook his head in disgust then took the Gatorade Candace pulled out of the cooler for him. For the first time, he noticed the purse slung over her arm. "Where are you off to? I thought we were going out for lunch."

"My mother called. I have to meet her and some friends."

He cocked his head. "But I thought you told her you were busy."

"I did. But they moved their timetable back and they're sitting in a restaurant waiting for me."

His gaze was calm but assessing. "She doesn't want you to be with me and she's manipulating you."

"I know. And I know that should make it easier to refuse. But she's my mother and she needs me." She went up on tiptoe to give him a kiss. "I can't just leave her sitting there."

With a wave she was out of the concession stand and crossing the parking lot to her car. And then she was on the highway heading south, wishing that she wasn't.

Hunter James was the first client who actually looked Solange in the eye, which was very satisfying as a woman and very unsettling as an imposter.

She rang the doorbell of his impressive Tudor-style home at nine on Tuesday morning, clutching her pail of supplies and vacuum in front of her. She held her breath, hoping there'd be no answer and that she'd find the key stashed under the mat so that there'd be no need to pantomime and pretend. But the heavy hobnailed door swung open, and she had to crane her neck to stare up into the not-yet-shaven face of Hunter James.

He was wearing running shoes and shorts. A well-worn T-shirt advertising a baseball bat manufacturer stretched across his chest. And he was staring back, right into her artificially blue eyes.

Afraid to give him too much time to look and think, she juggled her things and stuck her right hand out in a briskly professional greeting. "Monsieur James? I am Solange. Candace Sugarman has sent me."

She clamped her mouth shut as their hands met. Tiny little sparks of awareness fired at the touch making her forget who she was. And who she was *supposed* to be.

Dropping her gaze and her hand, she tried to think subservient maid-like thoughts, as opposed to "this is a hot hunk of man" thoughts, but she was still working on it when he invited her in.

The smell of coffee and a lingering scent of syrup hit her. The morning paper sat open on the counter, a coffee mug anchoring it in place. Three plates and two glasses sat in the sink, rinsed but not yet in the dishwasher, and she thought how like her own morning kitchen it felt. She wondered if he got up and made breakfast for the girls or whether they were the ones who fed him.

She liked the kitchen. It was larger and newer than her

own, definitely more "gourmet," and yet the room was still warm and lived-in, cozily done. Not the bastion of male chaos she'd been expecting, but not obsessively neat and organized like Susie Simmons's either. If she'd been Goldilocks, she would have proclaimed this particular kitchen "just right." Ditto for the papa bear.

He offered her coffee, which she declined with as few words as possible. And then they stood there assessing each other for several long moments, which she knew was a very bad idea. Her disguise was a good one, and Lord knew she loved Solange like herself, but it was unlikely to stand up to serious scrutiny.

"Would you like for me to start on zee upstairs or zee bottom?" she asked in Solange's accent, though she couldn't help noticing that her attraction to Hunter James left even Solange feeling slightly off-kilter. Remember who you are, she cautioned herself. And remember why you're here.

"Your English is very good," he said.

Uh-oh. Had he already seen through her? Or was he merely offering her a compliment?

"Thank you. English is almost like my, how do you say, native tongue?" She shrugged and smiled, trying not to let her eyes lock with his like they kept wanting to. "Thees is such the land of opportunity. A person can become almost anything she chooses to be." Like a faux French maid, for example.

There was an exploratory bark from behind a closed door nearby followed by another, more frantic one.

"Fido's ready for his run." Hunter moved toward what she guessed must be the laundry room door and reached for a leash that hung nearby. "Why don't you start downstairs so I can shower when I get back? That way I won't mess up your work."

She was thinking that Solange would not at all mind being messed up by Hunter James, when he opened the laundry room door and Fido, the crotch-seeking missile, hurtled toward her.

The Lab's claws beat a tattoo on the wood floor as he closed the gap between them, barked . . . happily? then shoved his muzzle directly between her legs.

"Shit!" she exclaimed in a very un-Solange-like way. "I mean, *merde!*"

"Down boy!" Hunter grabbed Fido's collar and yanked him away. "No!"

Hunter snapped the lead onto Fido's collar and held him to heel. Sort of.

The dog kept lunging toward her, the leash stopping him just short of her promised land. Hunter James was looking directly at her, a considering look on his face. "He's wagging his tail like he's met you before."

The dog had an I'd-know-that-crotch-anywhere wag?

"How unfortunate that it is the dog rather than the owner who wishes to stick his face in my crotch," she quipped in French, while she put space between Fido and herself.

An expression of surprise passed over Hunter's face, but he made no comment as he led Fido toward the front door.

"The basement's down here." He stopped to point at a door just past the kitchen.

"Good," she said. "I weel begin." Still flustered, she turned and went through the door and down the carpeted steps. Above her the front door opened and closed.

"Phew!" Breathing deeply, Amanda looked around the basement trying to get her bearings. It was one large room that seemed to run the length and width of the house and had been arranged into separate areas. One featured a big screen TV opposite a corduroy pit group. Beyond that a regulation-size pool table stood near a pub table and chairs. The bar, which was made of gleaming wood, curved out of one corner and had a mirror with glass shelves behind it; not too flashy or overtly macho, but well stocked for entertaining.

The far area catered to the teen set. It had Ping-Pong and air hockey tables. Against one wall there was an old-fashioned pinball machine.

The posters and plexi-cased memorabilia were sports oriented and included a collection of old-time baseball gloves that Wyatt would swoon over, but there was nothing about Hunter James or his major league pitching career. The man evidently didn't feel the need to toot his own horn.

By the time she'd finished in the basement and moved back to the main floor, she was feeling a bit more relaxed and starting to hit her cleaning stride. She dusted and tidied the main floor, loaded the dishwasher, then headed upstairs to strip the beds and get the wash started.

In Samantha's room, with its telltale bulletin board covered in dance recital programs, a group of framed photos on the nightstand drew her.

The first was of Hunter James in a Baltimore Orioles uniform with a long-limbed brunette tucked under his arm, both of them achingly young and smiling brightly for the camera. The next was of the brunette, her hair pulled back, the top of a hospital gown visible at her shoulders, as she stared down into the squinched-up face of the newborn in her arms. The next was a family shot, years later, the four Jameses. Hunter was wearing a different uniform this time, and each adult balanced a toddler on one hip, a ballpark stadium she didn't recognize in the background.

The last was of the woman, older, but still beautiful, in a studio pose that showed straight white teeth behind a wide smile. Her warm brown eyes shone with what Amanda assumed was happiness.

The same studio photo sat on Julie's nightstand along with a different collection of shots, the first and last thing the girls would see when they went to sleep and woke up in the morning.

While she started the first load of wash, Amanda imagined the James family as it had been when it was whole. Had they been as happy as they'd looked in the photos? Had Hunter James been faithful to the hopeful-looking dark-haired woman? If his wife hadn't died, would he have traded her in like Rob had traded her? Or would they, even now, be living happily ever after?

In the master suite, the sound of the shower reached her through the closed double doors. Her imaginings took a different turn, focusing in very concrete terms on the man who slept in the bed she was stripping. And who even now was standing in the shower on the other side of the double doors. Presumably naked. While water sluiced down his body.

She was still removing the sheets and pillowcases when the shower stopped. The shower door opened and closed with a decided click. Which meant Hunter James was probably rubbing a thick, man-sized towel over his lusciously man-sized—and presumably still naked—body.

Mouth suddenly dry, Amanda tried not to picture it; told herself not to even imagine it, but she could think of nothing else. She could pretend all she wanted that she was bold and worldly and French, but in reality she was Amanda Sheridan, and the only man she'd seen naked in the past eighteen years was Rob.

Fido barked, mercifully from outside this time, the kind of mad barking that usually signified a mailman or a cat in the yard. The phone on the bedside table beside her rang and the movements in the master bath grew louder and more hurried.

It was then that she realized that Hunter James was probably going to rush into the bedroom to answer the phone. And that he might still be naked when he did it.

Frozen to the spot, she cast about for a means of escape. Or camouflage. She wished briefly that she could wiggle her nose like Nicole Kidman in the new *Bewitched* and disappear altogether.

But the bathroom door was already opening and Hunter James was striding through it. She squeezed her eyes closed and yanked the sheets up in front of her face. The air moved beside her, giving off a heady whiff of soap and man, and the phone stopped ringing in mid-shrill.

"Hello?" Hunter's voice sounded directly beside her. She was still cowering behind a wall of sheets and had no idea what to do.

"Oh, hey, Marty. Yes, that would be good. Yeah, I've got a game schedule. I'll e-mail it to you."

He was quiet for a moment and then he said, "No, not right now. I've got something I have to take care of."

Deprived of her sight, she could actually hear the amusement slip into his voice like it often did into his eyes. He was probably getting a good-sized yuck out of the fact that his flamboyant French maid was hiding behind his sheets in an effort not to look at him.

God, she hoped that something he had to take care of wasn't Solange.

She began to back up, but she couldn't see and the way the blood was whooshing through her veins left her disoriented and uncertain of her direction. She took another step. Her shoulder knocked into a wall.

Of hard naked flesh.

She froze. And hid behind the sheets like an ostrich with its head in the sand.

The phone was placed in its cradle. A hand touched one of hers and lowered it, bringing the shield of sheets with it until they were bunched in front of her waist instead of her face.

Because she really had no choice, she opened her eyes slowly. One at a time. And turned her head.

Her shoulder was embedded in Hunter James's bare chest where tiny droplets of water glistened in a fine mat of blond hair. She swallowed. His hand still rested lightly on hers. Despite the dampness of his skin, his body threw off an unbelievable amount of heat. Everything about him, including the green eyes, was warm and inviting.

"Are you all right?" he asked.

She didn't think about whether she was reacting as Solange or Amanda. It didn't matter who she was at all.

What mattered was that Hunter James was one of the most attractive men she'd ever met and his body was a Disneyland of hard angles and lightly sculpted muscles. And there seemed to be some sort of magnetic device implanted in it.

chapter 16

The tug of that magnet was powerful and almost impossible to resist. It pulled at her, teasing her senses, urging her to throw caution to the wind.

Kind of like Rob had probably felt when he first succumbed to Tiffany.

Abruptly her compass stopped straining north. One minute it was pointing toward the prize, urging her closer; the next it was spinning madly as if she'd just sailed into the Bermuda Triangle.

"Oh!" She jumped back, scalded by her own stupidity. Lowering her gaze, she took in the washboard stomach and silky blond hair that arrowed downward to . . . Relief and disappointment washed through her as her gaze encountered not a towel or bare skin, but blue jeans.

Her gaze flew upward. He was dressed!

She wasn't Catholic or French, but she made the sign of the cross anyway. *Thank you, God!*

"Are you OK?" He spoke softly and he was looking at her in a way that made her wonder just how deeply inside he could see.

"*Oui, monsieur*. I'm sorree. *Mon Dieu, tu me coupe le souffle*." My God, you take my breath away.

Surprise settled on his face, and she thought how much more surprised he'd be if he could understand her.

"My fault," he apologized. "I've been expecting a business call and when I heard the phone I didn't realize . . ." His voice trailed off. "I'm sorry if I frightened you." He took a step away to demonstrate his good intentions.

Amanda wanted to know what kind of business he was in now that he no longer played pro ball, how he felt about being a single parent, and whether his kiss would be as potent as she imagined. Solange just wanted to kiss him until he was as breathless as she was.

Both of them needed to get out of this room and back to work before she gave herself away completely.

"Ees not a problem, *monsieur*," she said backing her way out of the bedroom, the sheets once again clutched against her chest. "Really, I believe that eet was my mistake."

And this, of course, was completely true. She'd mistaken a perfectly clothed male for a naked one; mistaken a customer for a stud muffin; and come perilously close to launching herself into the arms of a man who'd done nothing more provocative than answer his phone.

If she was going to clean Hunter James's house on a regular basis, she and Solange were going to have to have a little talk. It was absolutely imperative that they get their respective shit together.

* * *

"Are you telling me he wasn't actually naked?"

It was Saturday afternoon and Amanda and Brooke sat around the glass-top table in Candace's sunroom. The table was littered with the remains of the appetizers Candace had put out. They were on their second bottle of Chardonnay.

"Nope." Amanda helped herself to a cracker slathered with cheddar. "But it took me a while to figure that out. All the blood had rushed to my head and I wasn't thinking too clearly."

Candace and Brooke laughed. "I can understand that," Brooke said. "From what you've said, Hunter James is really something."

"Well, he certainly brings out the Solange in me." Amanda sipped her wine. "If I don't watch out she's going to be jumping into his bed instead of making it."

Not at all liking how appealing that little scenario sounded, Amanda looked for a new topic. "This house is fabulous, Candace. How long have you been in it?"

"Two years. One with Nathan and one on my own." She ran a hand over the tabletop and glanced out toward the courtyard. "I objected like crazy when he told me that we were going to live out here in what I thought of as the boonies. My mother was even more horrified. But this house was completely custom-built. I put a lot of time and energy into it, and I didn't have the heart to start all over again. Again."

"You don't miss Buckhead?" Brooke referred to the prestigious area closer in to town that encompassed many of Atlanta's poshest neighborhoods.

"Every once in a while I have to go in for a shopping or

restaurant fix. Or to visit some old friends. Or at a royal summons from my mother." Candace shrugged as if it hardly mattered, but Amanda was learning to read beneath Candace's flip tone. "Anyway, I'm starting to get used to life in the suburbs; I'm even coming to terms with the ballpark now that I have you two stooges to hang out with."

Amanda let her gaze roam around the magnificent room. Afternoon sunshine poured in through expanses of plate glass and the bursts of color in the perfectly mani-cured courtyard garden were like candy for the eye. "Well, this stooge needs to earn more money. Right now, I've got the Menkowskis on Mondays, Hunter James on Tuesdays, Sylvia Hardaway on Wednesdays, and Susie Simmons on Fridays." She ran the math in her head—something she did almost hourly—and deducted the percentage she insisted on paying Candace. "I'm not even bringing home nineteen hundred dollars a month. That's not enough to pay the mortgage, which I'm responsible for as of this month, let alone our expenses. I'm afraid to think about what will hap-pen if there's an emergency of any kind."

"Could you handle more houses?" Brooke asked.

"Absolutely." Amanda turned to Candace. "I'm getting more efficient and if I pick up the pace a bit, I should be able to do two houses a day, at least five days a week. And maybe I could fit in a Saturday morning job. If we cut back far enough, we could squeak by."

"I could book you for all of that and more, Amanda," Candace said. "But I don't see how you're going to pull it off. Not alone anyway. Solange's attitude can only go so far. You've got to have time to *do* the jobs. And have some kind of life too."

"I can handle it," Amanda insisted. "I *will* handle it."

"It's not that easy." Brooke shook her head. "I have some money put aside for, well, just in case. Why don't you let me loan it to you to take a little of the pressure off? You can pay me back when things turn around. It's just sitting in the bank. I'd rather see it doing some good."

"Same here, Amanda." Candace's expression communicated her concern. "Or if you don't want a loan, why don't you let me invest in you? We could come up with some catchy business name and you could use the seed money to look for help that you could train to work with you. It would allow you to take your time and really build something."

Touched by their eagerness to help, Amanda considered the two women who not long ago had been total strangers. "You guys are great," she said. "And I appreciate your support more than I can say, but I can't take your money. I have to prove that I can do this. I need to know I can stand on my own two feet and take care of my family."

Amanda took a long sip of wine. It warmed her from the inside out, just as Brooke and Candace did. "Just book me, Candace. I'll do the rest. And whatever happens, I want you to know that I'll never forget the way you've been there for me."

Late that night, Brooke tiptoed into the bedroom and undressed in the dark. Naked she slipped into bed beside Hap and laid her head on his shoulder. She wished she were asleep like he was and not wrestling with her conscience, unable to shake her guilt for only offering Amanda money, when what she should have offered was herself.

Hap's breathing was loud, a heavy in and out with an occasional exhaled whistle that was surprisingly rhythmic. Other women complained about their husband's snoring, but Brooke welcomed the noise even when it kept her up. It was proof of all that she'd achieved; an audible affirmation of her place in the world.

Between snores and whistles, the sounds of the house settling reached her. Its creakings and shiftings provided harmony to Hap's melody. It, too, was a symphony of her success and she treasured each note.

She had a husband and a home, neither of which her mother had ever attained. And not just any man or home either. She was living the life she'd seen in magazines and watched on television—when they'd had one—as a child. She, Brooke Mackenzie, was living in the very sort of house her mother had spent her life cleaning.

She liked Amanda and valued their growing friendship. She'd always been too busy escaping her past to let anyone get too close; Candace and Amanda were the first people she'd shared her secrets with.

But how could she risk exposure of all that she'd worked so hard to bury? If she cleaned houses with Amanda and was found out, her whole sordid past could come tumbling down around her; it could be the end of everything. She didn't see how Hap could possibly love the real her, when he'd so readily accepted the self she'd manufactured.

Chilled, Brooke snuggled closer to Hap. Nuzzling her face into the crook of his shoulder, she rested her hand on his chest and pressed her breasts into his side. Maybe one day she'd feel secure enough to tell him about her mother. But the longer she waited, the harder it became. At the rate she was going, she'd be saving it for a surprise on their twentieth anniversary.

Hap stirred and pulled her closer. His face turned toward hers and without opening his eyes, he pressed a kiss against her forehead. "Why are you awake?" he murmured.

"Just thinking." She ran her fingers up Hap's bare chest and made a lazy circle around his ear. "I miss you when you're away. Everything feels so empty."

With one arm he lifted her on top of him and wrapped his arms around her back. "Well, I'm here now." He settled her more firmly on top of him. "Can you feel how glad I am?"

She cupped his erection between her thighs and rubbed gently against it. "I think I'm getting the idea," she whispered as she guided him inside her.

"Ah, that's good." He rocked against her, filling her as he moved, a great strong bear of a man who'd given her everything she'd ever wanted.

"Hold on, darlin'," he murmured from beneath her. "I'm going to give you a nice little ride."

"Oh, I'm holding on," Brooke said as he kicked things up a notch. "It would take an army to shake me loose."

Amanda attempted to pry Meghan out of bed at noon on Sunday. The extraction did not go well.

"Come on, sleepyhead." Amanda stood next to the bed and spoke softly. "It's time to get up. You don't want to sleep the whole day away."

"Yes, I do." The words were muffled by the layer of sheets and blanket under which Meghan burrowed.

Walking to the bank of windows opposite the bed,

Amanda opened the drapes. May sunshine spilled in, illuminating the piles of discarded clothing that covered the floor. "Well, I need you to pick up your room and help me with the laundry. Then we'll straighten the rest of the house. It's a beautiful day. If we get everything done inside, we can plant the annuals I bought." Amanda kept her tone purposefully cheerful, but she was starting to feel impatient.

There was a groan from the bed. "Sorry. Can't do it."

"Yes, you can."

"I'm sleeping!"

Amanda crossed to the bed and stared down at the talking lump under the covers.

"And when I'm done sleeping, I'm meeting Sandy and Angie at the mall."

"No, you're not." Amanda reached over to grasp the covers. With a decisive pull, she yanked them off exposing Meghan curled in a knot, her eyes tightly shut.

Meghan didn't reach for the covers, but she didn't open her eyes either. "Yes, I am."

"I need your help, Meghan. Now."

The sad truth was that the more houses she cleaned, the less time and energy she had for her own. Like the shoemaker's children who went barefoot, hers were going to have to pitch in around the house.

Amanda sat down on the side of the bed and waited for Meghan to open her eyes, but vision evidently wasn't a prerequisite to whining.

"I'm not going to waste my day off cleaning and . . . planting!" Meghan uttered the last as if it were some sort of unnatural act.

"Yes, you are." Amanda felt her own anger build. She was turning herself inside out to try to make things OK for her children. It wouldn't kill either of them to help.

Meghan opened her eyes. Still clouded with sleep, they were nonetheless hostile and belligerent. "Why?"

"Because now that I'm working I need your help." Amanda stared down into Meghan's face. She'd told them that she was working on a consulting project with Candace and neither of her children had pressed for details. "And because I thought it would be nice to spend the afternoon together."

Her daughter looked at her like she was a magazine salesman who'd unexpectedly materialized at her front door.

"Well I already have plans." Meghan sat up and huffed her back against her pillows then pulled the covers up to her chin like a shield.

A flash of the conversation she'd overheard between Candace and her mother slipped into Amanda's head, but she shook it off.

"Then you'll have to change them."

Meghan's face darkened. Amanda was extremely sorry she'd come in at all, but it was clear she could not back down now.

"Why do I have to do laundry? Why can't Consuela do it?" Meghan named the maid who hadn't set foot in their home since the day her father left. "Everyone else I know has a maid. Lucy Simmons and Samantha James have a *French* one. Why do I have to spend my Sunday cleaning?"

"Because we can't afford a maid right now. And because

I asked you." Amanda tried to keep her voice calm. "Surely you're old enough to understand what's going on."

"I don't want to understand what's going on!" Meghan jumped out of bed, all too awake now. "I hate what's going on." She squared off in front of Amanda, her dark eyes blazing with pain and fury. "I hate that Daddy doesn't live here and that he's with that stupid Tiffany." Her voice rose with every word. "And I absolutely hate that we don't have money."

She stomped past Amanda and stormed toward her bathroom. "And I hate you most of all for screwing everything up!" She slammed the bathroom door behind her.

Amanda stood alone and shaken while the words Meghan had shouted at her reverberated off the walls and echoed in her head. Then she did some stomping of her own. She stomped to Meghan's bedroom door and yanked it open with all her might.

Wyatt stood in the hallway, already dressed in his practice clothes, a look of horror frozen on his face.

Amanda felt the anger and hurt drain out of her. She closed her eyes and attempted to regroup, searching for words that would somehow make things OK, but it was her son who spoke.

"I'll help you with the flowers when I get home, Mom," Wyatt said so softly it made her want to cry. "And I'll help Meghan, too, if she wants. I bet if we all work together, it won't take any time at all."

Close your eyes and don't look." Candace took hold of Amanda's arm and led her through the back hallway of her home toward the garage.

It was eight thirty on Tuesday morning and Amanda, already dressed as Solange, was afraid she was going to be late for Hunter James's.

They stepped down into the garage and Candace moved her into a final position. She pressed a button and the garage door went up, flooding the three-car garage with daylight. "OK, you can open them," Candace said, real excitement in her voice.

Amanda did as instructed then blinked and looked again, certain her eyes were playing tricks on her.

"What is it?"

"It's Solange's new ride."

Amanda stared at the car. It was a shiny new yellow

Volkswagen Beetle, the paint job so bright she could see their reflections in it.

The words *Maid for You* with a phone number beneath them had been painted on both sides. The *pièce de résistance* was the huge cutout of a vacuum cleaner affixed to the roof.

"It's so . . . yellow."

"Yes, isn't it a hoot?" Candace was positively glowing. "It'll be fabulous advertising and perfect camouflage."

"Camouflage?" Amanda was having a hard time imagining getting behind the wheel of anything that . . . eye-catching. "How can you call something that shouts, 'Look at me, I've got a vacuum on the roof of my car!' camouflage?"

"Well, I figure everybody will be looking at the car. They may feel sorry for the person driving it, but I can guarantee they're not going to be paying much attention to her face."

Amanda took a step closer to the vehicle. "But Solange can't afford a company car. Not even this lovely . . . vacuummobile."

"She doesn't have to. I picked it up for next to nothing from a cleaning business that folded. All I had to do was change the phone number."

Amanda eyed the new vehicle. "It's very . . . cute." It just didn't happen to be the Jaguar she had pictured for Solange.

"I've started booking up, just like you wanted, and I was afraid I wouldn't always be available to drive you where you needed to go." Candace dropped the keys into Amanda's hand and added a remote for the garage door. "Consider this your bat cave; you drive in with the van as Amanda Sheridan and zip out in the vacuummobile as Solange."

"I can't just let you give me a car." It was so hard to believe that a woman she hadn't even known three months ago had become such an integral part of her life.

"Yes, you can." Candace smiled and gave her shoulder a squeeze.

"Why are you doing all this? I know your life would be a lot simpler without my problems planted in the middle of it."

Candace shrugged, flippant as always, but her tone was dead serious. "I've been alone between marriages. But alone with children to take care of and no money to fall back on?" She shook her head. "No woman should have to go through that by herself."

"You're something, Candace Sugarman." Amanda opened the driver's door and contemplated the leather interior and gleaming wood trim. She breathed in the new car smell. "Really something. And as I told you the other day, neither Solange nor I will ever forget it."

The first couple of blocks Amanda felt completely ridiculous. A group of teenagers in a Jeep pointed at the vacuum and hooted with laughter. A toddler in a car seat pointed too. "Look, Mommy," Amanda heard him say through their open car windows. "It's a Wellwoh Bakyoom."

It certainly was.

She did her best to ignore the stares, horn toots, and laughter, and it didn't take her long to notice that Candace was right; while almost everyone she passed stole at least one look at the car, almost nobody seemed to be looking at her.

*   *   *

"Nice car." Hunter James stood in the doorway and smiled. "Though I kind of pictured you in a Jaguar."

He was dressed in business casual, a pair of khakis and a chambray blue button-down shirt, but his cheeks looked freshly shaven and he had that clean male just-out-of-the-shower smell.

"*Merci.*" She patted her dark curls sending Solange's new silver earrings swinging and sashayed into the house. She had on a new uniform too. It was still white polyester and two-piece, but it was a little more formfitting and the pants were bellbottom. A zipper ran down the front of the top.

She fingered the zipper pull as she followed Hunter into the kitchen. Feisty was the only word she could think of to describe Solange's mood today. Maybe the yellow vacuum-mobile was rubbing off on her?

"Would you like some coffee?" Hunter asked as she set down her supplies.

"*Oui, merci.*" She smiled at him, much bigger and broader than Amanda ever would. "I would like eet very much."

"Good," he said. Smiling, he motioned her to the coffeemaker where an empty mug already sat.

While she poured and stirred in creamer and sugar, Hunter cleared his plate and mug from the counter and set them in the sink. "So," he said conversationally, "how long have you been in the United States?"

"It feels like forever," she hedged. "Sometimes I feel as if I were . . . born here." She flashed him another smile, wishing she could ask him the things she really wanted to know. Had he been happily married? Was he as attracted to her as

she was to him? And which one of her did he like better—
Amanda or Solange?

Before she could stop herself, she was offering more information.

"I am zo sankful my cheeldren were born in these country." Oops!

"You have children?" He smiled at her again, that sudden wonderful flash of white teeth in tanned skin. "That's
great. How old are they?"

OK, she definitely didn't need to be inventing a fictional
family or giving out too many details. She really didn't need
to be yammering away at all. Standing here chatting with
Hunter James was a disaster waiting to happen. And she
shouldn't like the way he kept studying her while she talked,
either, as if it was just a matter of time until he figured
her out.

She almost wished Fido would charge in and poke at her
crotch, just to shut her up.

She glanced toward the laundry room, but the door was
open and the room was empty. Fido barked, a faraway sound
that came from the direction of the backyard. She was not
going to be saved by the dog—not that *wanting* a dog to
poke his nose in your crotch was a sign of mental stability.

If her charade was discovered, she'd be humiliated and
jobless. But did Solange care? No, she did not. Solange liked
talking to Hunter James, make that flirting with Hunter
James, despite the very real risk of exposure.

Solange appeared to be both lonely and horny. Solange
was going to have to get over it.

"I have two boys, twins. They are now ten years old," she
caught herself saying. "Very acteeve. They have too much,

what is the word, testosterone." OK, she was starting to sound like Natasha from Rocky and Bullwinkle. The accent was easier to maintain when she kept her sentences short. Nonexistent sentences would be even better. This was not a night at the Improv. This was her life.

"And your husband?" Hunter James asked. "What does he do?"

"No husband." She shook her head adamantly, sending her curls flying. "I don't have one. He's gone. Poof! Gone to Hell." She gestured dramatically. This, at least, was true.

Solange fingered one of the new hoop earrings. She needed to get out of this kitchen and away from Hunter James before Solange said another word. Or did something they'd both regret.

"*Monsieur,*" she said carefully, "if you will excuse me, I weel begin."

"Of course."

She worked quickly and efficiently, eager to be out of there before she said something too revealing. Or allowed Solange to jump Hunter James's bones.

Being in disguise was oddly freeing, but if Amanda was attracted to Hunter James, *she* should act on it and not leave the task to the oversexed Solange. Not that she or Solange were in a place in their lives where a relationship with a man was a good idea.

After all, Amanda had her children to protect, a home to hold on to, and a secret life to hide.

And Solange had those adorable twin boys to raise.

Candace was in her home office the next evening when her doorbell rang. Not expecting anyone, she padded to the door in her stocking feet. Dan stood on the welcome mat with a smile on his face and a bouquet of flowers in his hand, a pretty much irresistible combination.

"I have a floral delivery for one Candace Sugarman," he said as she opened the door.

"Oh?" She feigned surprise. "And who would they be from?"

"A not-so-secret admirer who'd like to take you out to dinner."

"Hmm." She pretended to think about it. "Does this delivery include singing or stripping?"

"It's not in my contract," he replied, stepping into the foyer. "But it could probably be arranged for a small additional fee."

He closed the door behind him and offered the flowers along with a kiss. "My apologies for any grumpiness since you bailed out on me the other day. It's not really my business. I just hate to see you jump every time your mother crooks a finger."

"I know it seems that way because she's such a . . . forceful personality. But she's getting older and needier too. You know?" Candace pressed a kiss to his lips then brought the flowers up to her nose. "Mmmm, nice. Come with me while I put them in water."

He followed her into the kitchen and slid onto a stool at the counter.

"Would you like to open a bottle of this Cabernet?" She set the bottle and opener in front of him and took two wineglasses from the cupboard. Then she pulled out a cut-glass vase and filled it with water, arranging the peace offering while he poured them each a glass of wine.

"Even when I'm angry at the way my mother asks for help, I'm always aware that I'm all she has."

She took the glass Dan offered. "She was never exactly the shy retiring type; she's always liked to pull the strings. But it's gotten worse since my father died. She wants me taken care of, and in her mind the only way that can happen is for me to be married."

"To someone she considers suitable." Dan said it quietly, a simple statement of fact.

"Yes. She refuses to give up despite the fact that all three of the men I married, and she thought were so perfect, weren't. We Bloom women are nothing if not persistent."

He raised his glass to her. "I have to tell you that persistence is more attractive in some of you than others. I mean what sort of woman names her child Candace and then refuses to allow her to be called Candy?"

Candace laughed. "Good question. One day when I get up my nerve, I'll ask her."

Dan smiled and Candace smiled back, the air cleared between them. Giving a final tweak to the flowers, Candace lifted her glass of wine. "To riding out hurricanes and having someone to shelter with in the storm."

"To shelter," Dan echoed.

They touched wineglasses and sipped in silence for a moment. The phone rang. Later Candace promised herself she'd never again answer without checking the caller ID first.

"I'm so glad I caught you." As usual her mother wasted no time on a greeting, but plunged right into the reason for her call. "Ida didn't show up for mah-jongg tonight and we need you to fill in."

"I can't, Mother, I'm—"

"I told the girls you wouldn't let us down. My Candace is not like those other daughters who are too busy to help out their mothers, I told them."

"But I hate mah-jongg." Turning, she caught the wary look on Dan's face. "And I'm busy. I'm just getting ready to go out for a bite with . . . a friend."

"What's going on?" Dan asked, clearly aware that she hadn't mentioned her friend by name.

Candace covered the mouthpiece of the phone. "One of my mother's friends didn't show up for their regular mahj game. They need a fourth or they can't play."

"Say no," he said. "You already have plans."

"But I . . ."

"You can do it, Candace. I know you can."

Resolute, she closed her eyes and spoke carefully into the phone. "I really can't, Mother. Dan's here. We're getting ready to go out for dinner."

This, of course, was the wrong thing to say.

"We've got plenty of food here. And I'm sure *Dan*"—it was, Candace knew, a major concession for her mother even to utter his name—"will understand and applaud you helping your mother. I'm sure he would have done the same for his. If she'd ever been able to get out given all those children." The last was muttered under her breath, just loud enough for Candace to hear.

"Mother, I—"

"You see, Myra, I told you Candace would come through," her mother said off mouthpiece. Then to Candace, "How long will it take you to get here?"

"Mother, that's not fair. I told you I'm—"

"You know Esther barely gets out since Mortie died. She really wants to play tonight."

There was a silence while Candace struggled with what she knew she should do versus what she was conditioned to do. Dan watched her carefully, not pushing, waiting for her to make her choice.

Hannah felt no such restraint. "How long will it take you to get here, Candace? Esther wants to know."

"Twenty minutes," Candace finally blurted out. "I'll see you in twenty minutes. But I'm only doing it for Esther. And this is absolutely the last time I—"

The dial tone stopped her in mid-sentence. Her mother had already hung up. Candace was left to face Dan's disappointed gaze.

"I have to go. They can't play without me. All three of them are just sitting there. Waiting," she said as she hung up.

"For you."

She looked away.

"You were the only possible choice. None of those other women had anyone they could call. Not another friend, a daughter? No one?" His gaze didn't waver from hers.

"Well, they all have children but no one else was . . ."

"It's a power struggle pure and simple. And you, my love, so strong and resourceful in all the other areas of your life, are a complete pushover when it comes to your mother."

Candace winced but remained silent. It was hard to argue with the truth.

"I could understand dropping everything for shortness of breath or a dizzy spell. Hell, we'd be racing there together for a significant chest pain." He looked her in the eye. "But for a game?" He shook his head. Candace all but hung hers.

Dan stood and moved toward her. "So go. We'll eat out another time." He kissed her; an unsatisfactory peck on the cheek. "But you're going to have to do something about this." He walked with her to the door. "I understand that she's your mother. But you're going to have to make her understand that you're entitled to a life too."

Yes, she would definitely do that. Right after she developed a Hannah-resistant backbone.

chapter 18

It was Saturday and the three of them were in the concession stand together when Susie Simmons's name came up.

"What's her gig?" Brooke asked as she finished making change for yet another besotted dad. "I mean she's a divorced single mom too. What makes her act so superior?"

"I don't know. It's weird. I guess it's the money." Amanda rubbed her thumb and middle finger together. "Or as Solange might say, *l'argent*. She walked away from her marriage with everything but Charles's golf clubs, and rumor is she could have had *those* if she'd wanted them."

"Well, you can't fault a woman for hiring a good attorney," Brooke said, looking pointedly at Candace.

"No," Candace conceded. "But I don't like her attitude. Getting a great divorce settlement doesn't entitle you to dis those who didn't. And I don't like the way she keeps trying to set Solange up. Something's not right there. What did she leave out yesterday?"

"A hundred and fifty dollars and some diamond stud earrings," Amanda said. "And I'm glad she's not at the game today. Ditto for Tiffany and Robbie."

"Well, I don't like the way I hear she eyes Hunter James like he belongs to her," Brooke said. "I think Amanda should have him."

Amanda pulled out a long sheet of aluminum foil and began to wrap burgers. Her movements were deft and automatic. One ear was cocked for crowd noise from Wyatt's field; he was the starting pitcher today and his losing streak had left him edgy and nervous.

"He's not a prize to be awarded to the most deserving woman," she said. "I expect he has some say in who he goes out with and what interests him."

"That's right," Candace said. "And we just have to make sure that what interests him is you."

"I don't like that look in her eye," Amanda said to Brooke. "Do you see that look in her eye?" She turned to the other woman. "You're already running a business on my behalf, Candace, you're not responsible for my love life too."

As if she had one.

"I can't be in charge of your love life when I'm handling mine so poorly," Candace replied. "I think my mother's jealous of Dan. And every time they go head to head Dan thinks I choose my mother." She sighed. "And unfortunately he's right."

"So how are you going to get them to play nice?" Amanda asked.

"I wish I knew. Dan's already a lot nicer about it than Hannah, but I kind of feel like a bone being pulled on by two dogs."

A collective gasp from Wyatt's field ended the conversation. Amanda and Candace rushed forward to flank Brooke. Side by side they leaned through the opening and peered out.

Squinting, Amanda could just make out her son drooping on the mound, the bases loaded with runners behind him. A coach was helping a batter up from the ground.

"I think he hit the batter," Brooke said. "Look, the guy on third is walking in."

They watched the runner on third jog home and stomp on the plate.

Amanda groaned. "It just gets worse and worse."

The three of them were still squinting out toward the field when Tyler Mackenzie approached. He ignored Brooke, whose smile of greeting disappeared at the snub, and addressed Amanda. "Wyatt's a mess out there, Mrs. Sheridan. He says his arm hurts. The coach sent me for ice."

Amanda studied Tyler, noting the way he looked at everything except his stepmother. "Brooke," she asked, "can you get the shoulder wrap for Ty? It's the blue contraption in the chest freezer."

"Sure." Brooke moved to the freezer and came back with the bright blue sling. "I pulled a Gatorade for him too." She handed the things to her stepson. "Would you like a drink, Ty? It's my treat."

"Nah." He shot her a look of total contempt. "My mom sent me a water bottle. And I'm not the one who's doing target practice on the other team."

He turned to go, his chiding refusal ringing in the air. Brooke clamped her mouth shut.

"You can't let him talk to you like that," Amanda said after he'd gone. "If you let him treat you that way, he will."

"Yeah, well, I've tried everything I can think of and he's not buying."

"Maybe you need to ask Hap to step in and straighten him out," Candace said.

"He doesn't do it in front of Hap. And I don't want to be some whiny tattletale. It's hard enough getting Hap's attention lately without wasting it complaining about Tyler. That boy's not going to see me as anything beside the Wicked Witch of the East no matter what I do."

"Then get on your broomstick and buzz him with it." Candace's tone was grim. "I don't know much about twelve-year-old boys, but I do know males in general. And you don't want to take their shit, because the more you take, the more they dish out."

"Well put," Amanda said. In the distance Wyatt walked off the mound and toward the dugout, Dan Donovan's arm around his shoulders. The only bright spot was Rob and Tiffany's absence. Rob would undoubtedly have been mad at Dan for pulling Wy no matter what kind of havoc he'd wreaked on the other team; Tiffany would have been chatting with Susie Simmons, probably comparing their cleaning women. Or their manicurists and exercise classes.

"You should talk to Hap and let him know what's going on," Amanda said, "and ask him for a show of support. The thing about boys that age is they can be so rough. Not only on others but on themselves."

Wyatt proved her point on the way home.

"Wow, that was a tough one," Amanda said as they left

the dugout. Wyatt didn't respond. In fact, he didn't speak at all between the dugout and the parking lot. There, he threw his bat bag into the back of the minivan and slunk into the passenger seat, slamming the car door behind him.

He remained silent all the way home from the ballpark. Amanda could feel the waves of frustration bouncing off him, could practically hear the gnashing of his teeth. For a boy who lived and breathed baseball, the Mudhens' losing streak was a personal affront; that his pitching was contributing to that streak made it even more agonizing.

In the garage, she put the van in park and turned off the ignition. She could tell herself it was "only baseball" and "only a game" until she was blue in the face, but to Wyatt it was so much more. How he played was a direct reflection of who he was. He'd been that way since the age of five.

"It's just one season, Wyatt. One season out of so many. Things'll get straightened out."

He put his hand on the door handle. "It's not just the team, Mom. It's me." He was fighting back tears. "I can't believe how bad I suck."

With that he was out of the car and bounding up the garage steps to the kitchen door.

"Wyatt, wait. Don't . . ."

But he was already turning the knob and pushing into the kitchen.

"Wyatt, stop." Amanda scurried out of the car and hurried up the steps behind him. Meghan was sitting at the kitchen table, a bowl of Cheerios and a folded newspaper in front of her. She and Amanda had barely been on speaking terms since Meghan's tantrum the previous Sunday and

Amanda prayed she wasn't going to wade into the middle of Wyatt's meltdown.

She looked up and took in her brother and her mother, then ducked her head and went back to eating. Amanda supposed she should be grateful.

"You do not suck," Amanda said. "But if you're worried about your pitching, why don't you ask your dad to work with you? He's not a professional, but he knows enough. Let him look at your delivery and try to help figure out what's going wrong."

Wyatt slammed down into a chair next to his sister, who was trying to pretend she wasn't listening.

"If you and he put a little extra time in, I'm sure that . . ." Amanda began.

"Dad doesn't have any extra time. At least not for baseball." Wyatt didn't add the "or me," but it reverberated in the room just the same.

"Oh, Wy," she began, "I'm sure . . ."

"He told me that, Mom. He told me he has to put in more hours working now."

His voice was thick with unshed tears. Anger and hurt and love formed a lump in her throat, leaving her speechless.

"He said he'd come to games whenever he could, but that he was going to be working a lot more and not to automatically expect him."

Amanda closed her eyes and drew a steadying breath. She wanted to march over to Rob's and wrap her hands around his neck for getting them all into this mess.

The tears Wyatt had been holding back squeezed out of his eyes and splashed down his cheeks. "I don't even care.

My pitching's so bad I don't *want* him to watch me." Wyatt swiped at his eyes with the back of his hand. "Baseball sucks just like everything else. I don't even know why I'm playing."

Meghan froze, the spoon midway to her mouth. Amanda shot her a look, silently begging her not to make a flip remark, but this time, she needn't have worried. Tears welled in her daughter's eyes, too, just as they did in her own. The magnitude of Wyatt's misery hung over them like a shroud. Any minute there was going to be a Sheridan family cry fest.

"Oh, honey." If only she could take him in her arms as she had when he was small and kiss away his hurts. "This is about so much more than baseball."

Looking into her children's faces, she searched for the words that would make it all better, but there were none. So she settled for the truth. "All three of us have had to face the end of our life as we knew it. Everything's so different and unfamiliar. It would have been a miracle if your pitching hadn't been affected. It affects everything. But we'll get through this. And you *will* get your game back, I know it.

"In the meantime, there will be no quitting. Not right now." She smiled and blinked back her own tears, wishing that she could turn back the clock to before Rob's defection. Reaching across the table, she used the pad of her thumb to wipe a last tear from his cheek and gave Meghan's shoulder a light squeeze. "How many times have I told you there's no crying in baseball?"

Wyatt's hands lay on the table. His fingernails were full of red clay from the ball field. His face and clothes were streaked with it too. It was like the red earth of Tara had been for Scarlett O'Hara, that from which he drew strength.

She'd never let him give it up. If she had to, she'd clean a million toilets to pay for pitching lessons before she'd allow him to quit the game he loved.

Amanda reached over and removed his cap then tapped him lightly on the head with it. "Go take a shower and put on some clean clothes. And don't forget to use the Spray'n Wash on that uniform."

She and Meghan watched him do as he was told; watched him walk slowly up the back stairs, his tall lankiness giving hints of the man he would become.

"Leave those pants in the laundry room, Wy," she called up behind him. "Whoever decided on white for baseball uniforms ought to be taken out and shot."

chapter 19

After four days of cleaning two houses a day, every muscle in Amanda's body ached. And Solange wasn't feeling too great either.

She'd made it home each night just in time to ferry Meghan and Wyatt to and from practices, fix dinner, and fall into bed.

It was now Thursday night, which meant only one more day of kamikaze cleaning before the weekend, at which point she intended to plant herself on the couch and imitate a potato.

With a groan she sank deeper into the bathtub and flicked the hot water lever on with her big toe. With everything aching, it was a major challenge to keep her head above the bathwater. Ditto for the rising tide of her life.

The infusion of warm water added to her drowsiness. As her body began—at last—to relax, she closed her eyes and let her mind and body float.

The shrill ring of the telephone she'd left beside the tub barely roused her. "Um-hmmm?" she answered.

"Amanda?" The sound of her mother's voice yanked her out of her reverie.

"Hi." She scrambled to sit up in the tub and gather her wits about her. "Where are you?"

"We're in New Mexico, darling. I'm just in love with the pueblo architecture. Your father wants to move on to Texas to visit Uncle Don, but I'm lobbying to stay in Santa Fe a few more days."

Amanda had promised herself she'd tell her mother everything the next time they spoke, but given the exhaustion that was now her constant companion, she simply didn't have the strength to explain the state of her marriage or her current career path.

Her command of geography might be a bit sketchy, but surely she could save her bad news until her parents made it to this side of the Mississippi. "Where did you say you were?"

"New Mexico. We're going to El Paso next."

"That's good." Amanda's head lolled back on the inflatable pillow and she yawned.

"Are you all right, Amanda? How are Meg and Wy?"

"We're fine, Mom," Amanda said. She yawned again; she just couldn't seem to stop herself. "The kids are in their rooms doing their homework, and I'm in the tub, but I'll tell them you called."

"Amanda, you don't sound like yourself. We could leave in the morning and drive straight through."

"No!" Amanda straightened so quickly she sent a wave of water sloshing onto the bathroom floor. "I mean, no, there's no need for that." She reached for the towel and dabbed her face with it. "Take your time and enjoy yourself. We'll see you when you get here."

"All right, sweetheart. If you're sure."

"Absolutely." She'd never been surer of anything in her life. "But you *will* give me some warning when you get close, won't you? You know, maybe a day or so?"

"Warning?"

"Um, you know, so I can have the house ready and all. And the kids' schedules cleared." And a complete confession ready to deliver.

"All right. Give Meghan and Wyatt a hug from us. We'll see you soon."

Amanda found a dry spot for the phone and flipped the lever for a last infusion of hot water. Sinking back so that maximum body parts were covered, she cleared her mind and felt her eyes flutter shut. In the quiet of the bathroom, she spiraled down into the warmth and floated for a time.

Until the phone rang again.

"Um-hmmm?" she mumbled into the receiver when her seeking hand finally located the phone.

"Amanda?" She recognized Brooke's voice on the other end, but couldn't summon the energy to pry her eyes open. Thinking was pretty much out of the question. She heard someone snoring lightly and realized with some surprise that it was her.

"Amanda? Did I wake you up?"

Amanda yawned and pried open her eyes. "I guess so."

"Isn't it kind of early to go to sleep?"

"Yes."

The bathwater had cooled, but she no longer had the

strength to lift her toe to turn on the hot water. "And I don't think the bathtub's the best place to do it."

She needed to get up, dry off, and put herself to bed, but that was an awfully long "to do" list for someone as tired as she was.

"The workload's too much for you," Brooke said. "I knew we shouldn't have let you do two houses a day alone."

"No, I'm fine." Amanda worked herself into a sitting position. Reaching forward, she managed to flick open the drain. "I just have two more houses tomorrow and then I'm going to crash for a couple of days."

"Oh, Amanda. I feel so . . ."

"No, it's OK." Amanda yawned again and stretched. "Don't worry about it." She had to get out of this tub and into bed. "I have to go to sleep now."

Placing the phone back on the floor, she watched the water slither down the drain. Then she looked at her shriveled body. It was thinner than she remembered and more muscled. She flexed her arm as she reached for the towel and felt her bicep bulge. Stepping out of the tub, she noticed new definition in her calves.

Eureka! she thought. Maybe she'd come up with an alternative to expensive health clubs and personal trainers. Maybe she should be recruiting other housewives who'd forgotten the physical benefits of manual labor. Maybe she should found a chain of gyms where people could come to perform household tasks.

Or maybe she should just go to bed.

A few minutes later she'd pulled on her pajamas and said good night to the kids. In no time at all she'd drifted off to sleep where visions of vacuuming baseball moms danced in her head.

Brooke dreamt about her mother. In her dream Brooke was a child again, waiting for Cassie to come home with some sort of treat from one of the houses she cleaned; a pair of patent leather shoes two sizes too big, a book already tattered and torn. The smallest extra, transferred from that other world to hers, had been cause for excitement.

Because dreams could not be edited, Brooke also saw the defeat in her mother's eyes, the hunch of her slender shoulders, the utter weariness in her walk as she crossed the weed-strewn front lawn and trudged up the rickety steps of their mobile home.

In the middle of the dream the faces got switched. And the dead eyes and clawlike hands she couldn't look away from became Amanda's.

Before dawn, she stopped pretending she was ever going back to sleep and padded into the kitchen. There she brewed a pot of coffee and carried it out to the back patio to watch the sun come up. The weariness in Amanda's voice last night had been tangible, and Brooke knew that no matter how far behind she'd been trying to leave her past, she simply couldn't spend another day pampering herself while Amanda worked herself into a state of exhaustion.

Determined now, she moved into her closet and riffled through her things until she came up with a simple white tracksuit and her most broken-in pair of sneakers. In the bathroom, she pulled her hair up off her face and pulled out her cosmetics.

Leaving Hap a note that she'd see him at dinner, she

climbed into her car and drove toward Candace's hoping she wasn't too late.

"Well, *mon amie,* are you ready to go?" Amanda considered Solange's reflection in Candace's guest bathroom mirror. "I know you are tired, but today you must be zee whirlwind, zee cleaning cyclone. Tonight you can collapse."

The doorbell rang and Amanda froze. It was eight thirty AM and Candace was already gone. She wasn't sure whether she should answer the door or not.

The bell rang again.

Deciding that she would simply answer as Solange, Amanda walked to the foyer and peered out the sidelight. Brooke stood on the front stoop, an anxious look on her face. Opening the door, Amanda reached for the other woman's arm and pulled her inside. "What are you doing here?"

Brooke was wearing sneakers and a white tracksuit that clung to her long limbs like a second skin. She'd pulled her auburn hair up into a ponytail and applied bright red lipstick. She'd also apparently used black liner around her eyes and added a large black dot near the corner of her mouth—possibly with Magic Marker.

"I, uh, came to help."

"You look like a heavily made-up dental hygienist."

"Well, I'm supposed to be a maid. I thought maybe I could be Solange's cousin or something. I've always liked the name Simone. *Bonjour,*" she said in a passable French accent. "*Comment vas-tu?*"

"OK, then, you look like Brigitte Bardot."

Brooke's face fell.

"But I know what it took for you to come here." Amanda stepped forward and gave Brooke a hug. "And I've never been so happy to see anybody in my life."

"Really?"

"Really." Amanda stepped back and studied her friend. She knew Brooke had slain some serious demons to get here, but she was about as unrecognizable as Michael Jackson in sunglasses. Susie Simmons would take one look at her and the charade would be over. Grabbing Brooke's hand, Amanda led her into the guest bath where she kept her stage makeup and supplies. "We need to deepen your disguise. Let's see what we can come up with."

Ten minutes later, she let Brooke look in the mirror.

"Oh my God." Brooke's fingers touched the slightly beaked latex nose and the layer of pancake makeup that camouflaged its edges. The beauty mark had been enhanced into a mole. "Simone needs to see a dermatologist. This mole needs its own apartment."

Brooke's hands moved up to the shaggy auburn wig with its heavily gelled spikes. "And a hairdresser."

"There's not much I can do about your body," Amanda said.

"For which I am eternally grateful."

"But everybody will probably be so busy trying not to look at that mole that they might not notice," Amanda conceded.

"Yeah." Brooke's voice was dry. "I think the hairs coming out of it are a particularly nice touch."

Amanda smiled. "I'm kind of gifted that way. Just think what I could do for Tiffany."

She ushered Brooke to the garage and into the vacuummobile. "I think you better leave the talking to me," Amanda said, "there's less chance of tripping up that way. But frankly, the way you look now, I don't think your husband would even recognize you."

Brooke batted her eyelashes at Amanda. Her only recognizable facial features were her wide-set gray eyes. "Well, thank the Lord for that."

Susie Simmons let them into the house and was unable to take her gaze off of Brooke's hairy mole.

"*Madame*," Solange said. "Thees is my cousin, Simone. She has come to help me."

Susie ripped her gaze away from Simone's face and escorted them into the kitchen. "Fine," she said. "As long as we agree the total amount stays the same. I didn't contract for two cleaners, just one cleaning."

Brooke made a face at Susie's back.

"*Quoi?*" Amanda feigned confusion.

"Money. *Argent.*" Susie added the word in French. "It doesn't change."

"Oh." Amanda smiled broadly as she mimed the dawning of comprehension. "*Oui.* Of course zee money weel stay zee same. It is only that I have now so many clients and I need zee help."

That was as much explanation as she was prepared to waste on Susie, who offered neither coffee nor interest in either of them once the money issue was settled.

"Come." Amanda motioned to Brooke, who seemed bent on avoiding the sight of her face in any of the kitchen's shiny surfaces. "Bring zee supplies upstairs. I weel show you where we begin."

The phone rang and Susie went to take the call. Amanda and Brooke headed up to the top floor and began to strip the beds.

"You get the sheets and towels from the other bedrooms and bring them to the laundry room." She showed Brooke the upstairs room that housed the washer and dryer. "And be careful you don't accidentally touch or move any of the money or jewelry she leaves out."

"She's still pulling those tricks?"

"Yes. Let me know what's out today. The grand prize seems to go up every week. I'm holding out for the Caribbean cruise."

They separated and with only small bits of direction, Brooke demonstrated her expertise. She moved quickly and efficiently and they were down to the living areas on the ground floor in less than half the time Solange could have made it on her own.

In the kitchen, they worked side by side, wiping down surfaces, straightening what was already obsessively straight. "Wow," Brooke whispered, turning away from the already shiny granite countertops. "If it weren't Susie, I'd feel guilty for taking her money."

"I know what you mean." They whispered so that their unaccented English wouldn't be overheard, although Amanda could hear Susie still on the phone in the study. "What sort of trap did she lay upstairs?"

"Two hundred bucks and a pair of trainer diamond studs that were so small, I'm assuming they must be Lucy's."

Amanda giggled.

"She's going to have to do better than that if she wants to seriously tempt this cleaning crew," Brooke said.

Leaving her to finish the kitchen and family room, Amanda moved into the study. Parking the vacuum cleaner in the open doorway so that Susie would realize Solange wanted to vacuum, she finally had to wave a dust rag at Susie to garner enough attention to gain admittance to the room.

Susie motioned her in with a glance, her attention clearly fixed on the phone. "I think Lucy wants to have a pool party on the last day of school. If Samantha James can come, I'm going to include parents. That Hunter James is absolutely delicious."

There was a pause.

"The Sheridans?" There was a laugh, an unkind bark of derision that straightened Amanda's spine. "No. Whatever for?"

Jaw clenched, Amanda unwrapped the vacuum's power cord and plugged it into an outlet. With a flick of her finger she turned it on and began to vacuum with gusto, her back to Susie, wishing she could aim the attachment at the other woman and suck her right into the garbage where she belonged.

"Solange!" Susie shouted.

Ignoring her, Amanda threw herself into the vacuuming, "accidentally" bashing into the legs of as many pieces of furniture as she dared.

A moment later the other woman was at her side tapping on her shoulder and shrieking in her ear. "Turn that thing off! I'm on the phone!" She waved the cordless phone in Solange's face.

Amanda moved her hand over the vacuum cleaner handle, careful not to smile at the expression on Susie's face.

After a few moments of exaggerated fumbling, Amanda pushed the button and the vacuum cleaner went off, throwing the room into complete silence.

"Ah," Amanda said, smiling triumphantly at Susie, "now I have found eet. Thank God I locate zee switch."

chapter 20

Amanda went to bed on Friday evening and stayed there until Sunday morning.

"Mom?" Meghan's shrill voice intruded into her dreams. A hand clamped her shoulder and shook her hard. "You see?" Meghan said. "I think we should call nine-one-one."

"Maybe we should call Dad again," Wyatt suggested.

There were footsteps nearby. A phone was lifted from a cradle. She could actually hear the dial tone in the quiet.

"No." Amanda roused herself while trying to pry open eyes that felt glued shut. "I'm OK." She got one eye open then the other. Meghan and Wyatt stood next to the bed, panic written on their faces. "I was just really tired."

"Well you scared us to death." Meghan's fear was already morphing into anger. "We thought you were in a coma or something!"

"I'm sorry I scared you." Amanda sat up and rubbed the sleep from her eyes. "I didn't mean to. I just worked harder this week than I'm used to, and I guess my body needed to catch up."

"Well we were stuck here for more than twenty-four hours," Meghan complained.

"We didn't want to leave you," Wyatt said. "Meg put a mirror under your mouth to make sure you were still breathing and then she called Daddy last night and made him come over and check you."

She could picture them calling Rob in a panic; thank God he'd been available to calm them down.

"He said you were just asleep." Wyatt's brow furrowed at the memory. "I was afraid you were dead."

"Dork." Meghan brushed by her brother and turned in the doorway. "Now that it's safe to leave, I'm going to go out and run."

It was Wyatt who fussed over her and settled her out on the deck with a peanut butter sandwich and the Sunday paper. He was in the family room now in front of the television. The sound of the Braves game floated out through an open window.

In the quiet of the afternoon, Amanda took stock of her situation and attempted to reconcile her decidedly split personalities. Where Amanda weighed and considered, Solange acted. While Amanda craved approval and did what was expected, Solange was uncowed by the opinions of others and did what was necessary.

The only thing they had in common was their drive to take care of Meghan and Wyatt and their appreciation of—and attraction to—Hunter James.

She and Solange were in accord about him, but while

Solange, with her more sensual French temperament might be tempted, Amanda knew better.

She was not going to be the divorcée who fell for the first available man, and she was not going to jump into bed at the crook of an attractive finger. Not that Hunter James had actually crooked anything in her direction.

Susie Simmons and Solange could flash their eyes and swing their hips at him all they wanted; Amanda was not about to join that fan club.

She had to remind herself of this vow when the phone rang and his caller ID flashed across the screen. And again while she debated whether to answer or let it go to voice mail.

A truly smart woman wouldn't want to know why he was calling. A really brainy woman would ignore the phone and continue to immerse herself in the Sunday paper and the quiet relaxation of her backyard deck.

Which was why, she reflected as she picked up the phone on that quiet Sunday afternoon, she hadn't actually made it to an Ivy League school.

"Amanda?" Hunter's normally confident voice was tinged with something she couldn't quite identify.

She sat up and pressed the phone closer to her ear while she folded the Living section and tucked it back inside the *Atlanta Journal-Constitution*.

"Is everything all right?" she asked.

"Basically." There was a slight pause.

"Are the girls OK?"

"Yes."

There was a silence in which she studied the shades of green in her backyard and waited for him to speak. She could hear the sounds of a televised baseball game in the background and she realized he was probably watching the same Braves game as Wyatt.

"Hunter?"

No answer.

"What's wrong?"

He groaned. "Samantha wants to have an end-of-school pool party."

She waited for the rest of it, but that appeared to be it.

"And?"

"And she seems to be convinced she needs a woman to plan it."

Chagrin and uncertainty clouded his voice. "I told her it wasn't a problem. I mean we have a pool and she can invite whoever she wants. I told her I'd be glad to order pizzas and drinks." He sighed. "That was when she started crying."

Amanda considered appropriate responses but Hunter didn't seem to be finished. "She said she wanted to plan the party with someone who would understand. Someone, I believe she said, with ovaries."

Amanda stifled a giggle.

"She also wants to invite boys, and she seems to think if I'm the only chaperone I'll be too intimidating."

Amanda suspected that if they were anything like Wyatt, they'd be more likely to line up for autographs. But perhaps Samantha wouldn't like that either.

"Since Meghan was at the top of Sam's guest list, I thought maybe you and she would like to, um, come over and help plan this thing?" There was another pause. "And then possibly help chaperone?"

She caught herself smiling. "When did you want us to bring our ovaries over?"

He laughed. "I didn't mean to put it quite that baldly."

"Well, I have to admit I don't think I've ever heard ovaries mentioned in casual conversation before."

He laughed again. "You can bring the rest of you too. I thought the three of you might like to come over later today and cook out with us. Wyatt and I could do something suitably manly afterward while you all plan the big event."

Words of refusal sprang to her lips. She hadn't showered, her hair was a mess, he made her nervous. But both Wyatt and Meghan would be wild to do this. And she knew deep down that Solange wouldn't bow out. Solange would swing her hips and cart her ovaries on over there and let the chips fall where they may.

She contemplated the unread newspaper and the warming glass of iced tea. As if it was any kind of a contest. The Sunday paper alone on her deck? Or a cookout at the Jameses.

Tomorrow she'd be back to scrubbing floors and making other people's beds. But she could enjoy herself today.

Amanda stood and reached for the iced tea glass. "I'll be glad to help and we'd love to come. Just tell me when you want us and what I can bring."

"I've got the food and drink covered. And I'm guessing Wyatt's not going anywhere until the Braves game is over. Come anytime after that. If there's no answer at the front door, look for us out back. I thought we could have a swim before we eat."

Amanda broke the news to Meghan, who was back from her run and had obviously already consulted with Samantha. Wyatt whooped with pleasure when she explained their plans and wanted to know whether she thought they might get to watch the Cubs' game at seven since Mr. James probably actually KNEW all those players.

Amanda felt a tiny prickle of anticipation herself as she showered and dried her hair. She was even looking forward to it until she opened her bottom drawer and remembered that her most current bathing suit was hopelessly out of style and did absolutely nothing to enhance her thirty-nine-and-a-half-year-old body. The stress of the last months had shaved off some extra pounds and her new occupation had added some muscle, but nothing had perked up her breasts or raised her rear end.

Pulling on the black one-piece, she stood in front of her mirror, wishing it was one of those Miraclesuits she'd seen advertised. She could use a miracle now; a heaven-sent sucking of the cellulite from the backs of her thighs or a flattening of her stomach pooch would confirm her faith in the Almighty.

"It doesn't matter," she muttered as she pulled a pair of capris and a crop top over the suit. Better bodies than hers had undoubtedly thrown themselves at Hunter James during his years in the major leagues. Hell, better bodies were probably thrown at him daily right here in east Cobb County.

She'd just have to think of him as Samantha's father and not as a prospective date. That way there'd be no misunderstandings and no disappointment.

They found the Jameses in the pool. Suffering from none of the shyness Amanda felt, Meghan peeled off her shorts and dove gracefully into the large kidney-shaped pool.

Wyatt kicked off his flip-flops and drew his T-shirt over his head in one fluid movement.

"Go out for a pass!" Hunter shouted from the shallow end. Stepping toward the deeper water, he threw a Nerf football toward her son, who nabbed it in midair and cannonballed into the water with it. Julie whooped and pumped a fist in the air then pulled herself out of the pool and raced to the spot Wyatt had vacated. "Throw one to me, Dad!"

A moment later she'd completed her diving catch and was splashing after Wyatt. Samantha and Meghan were perched on the shallow-end steps, whispering to each other.

Amanda stood at the side of the pool feeling slightly silly, a pot of baked beans clutched to her chest. Hunter placed his hands on the deck and hauled himself out of the water. Straightening, he slicked his hair back and walked toward her, a smile lighting his face. Water clung to the thick lashes around his green eyes and to the mat of hair on his chest.

"You really didn't need to bring anything." He bent to retrieve a towel from a nearby chaise. With one hand he rubbed it over his shoulders and chest then dropped it back on the chair cushion. For a moment, she envied the rectangle of terry cloth.

"It's just baked beans. I can put them on the stove to warm until we're ready to eat."

"Thanks. The kitchen's this way."

He led her through the French doors to the kitchen she knew so well. Fido barked and there was a scramble of claws on wood. Before she could react, the Lab nudged his nose toward her thighs.

"No! Sit!" Hunter grasped the dog by the collar and kept

him from reaching his target. "Sorry. I thought I'd broken him of that but he still does the same thing to Solange."

"No kidding?" Flustered, Amanda turned away and set the pot of beans on the front burner of the cooktop. Without asking, she turned on the burner and moved about the kitchen reaching in a nearby drawer for the pot holders she'd washed last week, moving to the utensil drawer for a big slatted spoon for stirring.

She looked up to find him watching her.

"Glad you're finding everything OK."

Fido's tail whapped the floor and his eyes were on her crotch. The dog had a major thing for her; his owner was looking at her as if he was trying to make some puzzle piece fit. Which was all it took to remind her that while Solange knew this house intimately, Amanda Sheridan had never set foot in it.

"Lucky guesses." She smiled and took a step back, intentionally breaking eye contact. "You wouldn't believe how many of us keep our kitchen things in the same exact place. Why, I bet your measuring spoons are right"—she pretended to look around—"here . . ." She pulled out the drawer she knew they were in with a flourish. "And I'd be willing to bet even bigger bucks that you keep your trash bags in there." This time she intentionally reached for the wrong cabinet and yanked it open to reveal a stash of sponges and cleansers. "Ah well." She pretended disappointment. "So much for that theory."

"It's funny though." He was staring right at her when he said it and she didn't think he was referring to her trash bag search. "If I didn't know better, I'd think you'd been here before."

He kept looking at her, considering her. Fido was whimpering now, straining against the grip Hunter had on his collar.

Amanda felt tongue-tied and uncertain; both drawn to the interest in his eyes and afraid he was going to make the connection between her and Solange.

"I haven't seen Fido since that day at the park." She leaned over to scratch Fido behind the ears and the dog whimpered, this time with pleasure. "How great that he remembers me." And my crotch, she added silently.

Babbling, but moving, she stepped to the cooktop to raise the flame under the baked beans then washed her hands at the sink. After drying them on a paper towel, she moved about the kitchen, trying to put a little more distance between them, realizing, once again, that she looked much too comfortable in a kitchen she wasn't supposed to have entered before.

"Don't move." He held up a finger then began to escort Fido out the door. "I'm going to put him in the dog run. I'll be right back."

She stood, uncertain, waiting for him to return, wishing she weren't so completely aware of him.

When he came back into the kitchen, she looked into the assessing green eyes and knew she was in trouble. He didn't look like a carpool mom or any friend she'd ever had. He looked like rumpled sheets and sweat-soaked bodies. But he was also a father who cared about his children, which made him even more attractive. And twice as dangerous.

"White or red?" he asked as he moved closer.

"Hmm?"

"Wine. We need some. White or red?"

Of course, just when she needed to be thinking quickly, her mind seemed to be slowing down, grinding to a halt. It said, *Alcohol. Hunter. Do not mix.* But her lips were already smiling and saying, "White, thanks."

He pulled a bottle from the small wine refrigerator tucked up under the counter and opened it without fanfare. Then he snagged two wineglasses from an upper cupboard and poured a glass for them both.

"Thanks for coming to my rescue." He held his glass aloft and clinked it softly against hers.

"That's me," she said, "suburban cavalry person and party planner."

He smiled and they both drank. The wine was cool and smooth, with just a hint of fruitiness.

"Well, I'm glad you came. I don't have a ton of experience as a parent. Linda handled everything. It seemed like I was always on the road and then when I finally wasn't, she was sick." He paused, regrouped. "I know they miss her, and I don't know what to do about that either. And sometimes the simplest things—like inviting a couple of kids over to swim—becomes this horrible reminder to them that all they have left is me."

"It must be hard for all of you." She was drawn to both his pain and his honesty. "Girls that age, especially, want their mothers." She looked down into her wine then back up. "But they can be so rough. I find myself tiptoeing around Meghan, trying not to give her an excuse to start something." She wasn't sure why she was opening up to him this way, but couldn't seem to stop herself. "Even though it was Rob who left, she seems to hold me personally responsible."

"I know what you mean. After Linda died, Samantha tortured me at every opportunity." He took a drink then stared out the kitchen window for a long moment. "I guess they have all that emotion pent up and they can only let it out on someone who feels safe."

She looked at him, then, this good-looking guy who by all rights should be shallow and unthinking but seemed to be so much more. "So what do you do now that you're not playing baseball?"

"I have a training facility up in Roswell with a few other ex-players. We give individual and team lessons. And I scout for the Brewers—that takes me out of town on occasion though fortunately not near as much as playing used to. That's one of the reasons we moved here; Linda's parents live in town and they help out when I have to be away."

The shrieks of the kids reached them from the pool, interrupting the moment. "Don't you dare throw that, Wyatt!" Meghan's voice was loud and bossy.

"Eeeeew! Put that down, Jules." Samantha's complaint joined Meghan's. "Or I'm going to tell Dad." It was clear the younger siblings had formed some sort of fighting unit.

A smile lit the corner of his lips. "Well, I'll say one thing about being a parent; it's never boring. I guess we should go out and break things up."

He took a step closer. She could feel the heat from his body and smell the chlorine and sun that had soaked into his skin. "You know," he said, "you remind me of somebody. Every time I see you, I think that."

"Really?" She stepped back, but her spine pressed against the kitchen counter and blocked a full-scale retreat.

He carried himself so lightly that you didn't realize how

big he was until he got close. Her head tilted backward so
that she could meet his gaze when, in fact, she knew she
should be avoiding it. "Maybe I just have one of those common faces. You know, people are always mistaking me for
someone."

"No." He shook his head and stepped closer, not beyond
the bounds of propriety, but close enough so that she could
see the slight stubble on his jaw. "Not common at all."

He dropped his gaze to her lips and she had the disturbing thought that they were both imagining what the other's
lips would feel like. "Pretty." He raised his gaze back to hers.
"Very pretty." He reached toward her and she thought he
was going to touch her, but he just set his wineglass on the
counter beside her. "And very familiar."

Amanda swallowed.

"I'm curious," he said a long moment later. "What do
you think of Solange?"

"Think of her?" Amanda's thoughts flew from the possibility of a kiss to the more immediate fear of exposure.
"Me?"

Her heartbeat kicked up a notch, not that being near
him allowed for a resting rate in the first place. "I think she
does a good job. She's dependable and thorough."

"Doesn't she seem a little . . . flamboyant . . . for a cleaning woman?"

He was watching her closely and she was careful not to
squirm.

"Flamboyant?" Her voice broke on the word. "No, I, um,
think she's just got a lot of *joy de verve*." This time she intentionally mangled the French, hoping to throw him off. "You
know, an indomitable spirit. I think it's very important to

her to earn a good living under her own terms. Maybe she . . ."

Realizing she was offering way too many insights into the possible workings of a maid's mind, Amanda shrugged. "I don't know her all that well, but I've been happy with her work." She raised her glass and drained it in a single gulp.

"Me too," he said. "I'm impressed with her determination to raise her boys single-handedly. It's not easy to be a single parent under any circumstances."

Amanda nodded numbly. This man not only noticed but had empathy for the maid. She was impressed despite herself. Impressed and worried. Because she was not only attracted to him, she actually liked him. And if he was going to be this observant, she and Solange had a problem.

"Da-ad," Julie yelled. "Samantha called me the 'B' word."

Hunter sighed and fell back a step. "Sometimes I think they need a referee more than a parent. It's amazing how ugly they can be to each other."

She heard Wyatt yelp and assumed the older duo was fighting back.

"When are we going to eat?" All four of them chorused from the backyard.

With an apologetic smile, he refilled her glass then took a platter of raw hamburger patties out of the refrigerator. He placed a package of hot dogs in her hands. "Come talk to me while I cook," he said. "We'll get the kids to set the table and organize their drinks. Maybe if we keep them busy, we can avert a full-scale war."

chapter 21

"D on't you think Mr. James is HOT?" Meghan asked on the ride home.

"Hot?" Amanda swallowed. Scorching was more like it. "You mean as in attractive?"

"Yeah. I mean for an old guy, he looks, like, incredible."

Unfortunately, Meghan was right. He *was* incredible to look at. And talk to. And be with. There was that edge of awareness that hummed underneath the simplest communication. But he was easy to be with too. Interested and attentive and completely tuned in to the person he was talking to.

Amanda decided to focus on the age issue rather than the attractiveness factor; it seemed safer. "I don't think forty-three is exactly ancient. It's hardly middle-aged these days." Which made her practically a spring chicken at not quite forty.

Meghan rolled her eyes. "Whatever. The point is he's

totally hot." Her tone changed. "And he seems kind of interested in you."

A small part of her wanted to ask her daughter why she thought that, wanted hard examples of the same thing she sensed, wanted to write his initials on her notebook and squeal with the other girls over him.

Her own excitement made her discount the change in Meghan's tone, because despite her fear of being exposed as Solange, the evening had been fun. Hunter had made a game of flipping the burgers and preparing the meal and had dragged the children into it, even getting them to clean up without complaint so that the two of them could sit and watch the sun go down while they finished the wine.

He'd even made stripping down to her bathing suit and joining everyone in the pool afterward easy. His gaze had skimmed over her as she walked down the steps into the shallow end. His glint of interest had been apparent and gratifying, but he'd made no comment. He'd just asked some question about the girls' upcoming ballet recital that had pulled her mind elsewhere and set her at ease. He was good at that. And undoubtedly good at other things too.

"Oh, honey, I think he's interested in everyone," Amanda said. "In a nice way. But I don't think it's anything more than that."

"Well that's good." Meghan leveled a look at Amanda. "I wouldn't want you embarrassing yourself or anything."

Amanda heard the warning this time and knew her daughter wasn't ready for her mother to be interested in anyone—especially a good friend's father. All the more reason to resist the obvious temptation.

"Yeah, he's cool," Wyatt added from the backseat. "When

we were watching the game, he told me neat stories about everybody. He said his heart used to pound real hard every time they called him up from the bullpen, just like mine does, even after he'd been in the majors for years. He offered to take a look at my pitching, Mom. How cool is that?"

Meghan tossed her hair. "I think the party's going to be awesome. But you and Mr. James have to stay in the background. Samantha says sometimes guys go all weird when he's around. Maybe you can keep him occupied or something."

Amanda coughed. "I'll, uh, do my best," she said, determined NOT to think about all the ways a man like Hunter James might like to be occupied.

She kept the accompanying shiver of anticipation to herself.

Together Amanda and Brooke, make that Solange and her cousin Simone, cleaned houses. Wishing she could offer more, Amanda had made Brooke promise to take 15 percent of each week's earnings and while the work didn't get easier, with Brooke sharing the load two houses a day was manageable. By the end of the first week, they'd fallen into a comfortable routine. If Amanda had ever doubted Brooke's family history, her competence confirmed it. It was like going onstage with one of the Barrymores—you were a little bit intimidated but you knew you were in good hands.

"I've never seen anyone change sheets as quickly as you can," she said to Brooke as she pulled the vacuummobile into the empty bay of Candace's garage. "How did you get so fast?"

Amanda removed the cleaning rags to take home for the

wash but left the rest of the supplies in the trunk. Brooke pulled off her mole and stuck it in her pocket as soon as the garage door went down behind them. "I used to help my mother at the McGinty's on Saturday mornings," she said. "They had about a hundred children and I had to get all of the sheets changed and the new ones washed and dried and folded before I was allowed to leave. That's when I came up with my system."

They walked through the garage door into Candace's guest wing and began their transformations.

"I'll teach you how if you let Simone lose the hairy mole. Maybe she could have surgery," Brooke suggested. "God, I'd love to waltz into Dr. LaPrada's office with this honker on my face just to see his reaction."

"Sorry, no can do. You're already getting closer looks than I'd like. It's that damned body of yours. I should have put you in padding."

"Try it and Simone will be on the next plane back to France."

"Fair enough, but the mole stays. Have I mentioned lately how much I appreciate your help?"

"Yes. A couple of thousand times."

"Well, I mean it."

"I know."

She looked at Brooke who was fast on the way to becoming her glamorous self. "Do you hate doing this?"

Brooke shook her hair out, her smile reflective. "In a strange way it's helping me understand my mother a little better. And while it's not exactly the East End Day Spa, I'm getting a more thorough workout than I was at the club.

And it does keep me from sitting around worrying about whether Hap's losing interest in me."

"In you? No way," Amanda said.

"I don't know. I mean look what happened with Hap and Sarah. He made it thirteen years with her. We've only been married a year and he's already treating me differently."

"Sarah was never you, Brooke. And I'm sure their relationship wasn't similar either."

"But he couldn't get enough of me and now he hardly ever wants to . . ." She sputtered to a stop, clearly embarrassed.

"So this is when you look for other things to share, besides sex," Amanda said. "That animal attraction doesn't last forever. And I think the first thing you need to share with him is the real you. Your outside's pretty impressive, but I think what's inside is even better."

Brooke didn't respond, but her look remained thoughtful.

"Hiding your past from Hap is not a good idea. What kind of partnership can you expect to have if he doesn't know who he's dealing with? I think you're selling yourself and Hap short."

Amanda resisted the urge to continue her lecture. Brooke would have to understand in her own time and her own way. She'd been married for eighteen years and was only just starting to understand herself and the man she'd married.

Pulling out her wallet, she counted out Brooke's percentage of the money they'd earned that week.

Brooke shook her head. "I don't want it. And I won't take it."

"Oh no." Amanda tried to slip it into her purse. "We had a deal."

Brooke handed it right back. "I'm doing this because I want to help you and that's the way it's going to be."

"But . . ."

"I'm not even willing to discuss it, Amanda. Once you're on your feet we'll take a look at this and see what needs to happen next. Maybe I could help you train some other women." She flashed a smile. "Maybe we can branch out and include other nationalities. If we're hiring only French women it's going to be pretty slim pickings."

"But I can't just take from you. I won't be an object of charity."

Brooke snorted. "Charity? Get real. Why don't we call this my tuition? I'm learning a huge amount from you. I could never navigate the suburbs without you and Candace showing me the way. You help me keep my marriage intact and I'll clean my little fingers to the bone for you."

"I think you may have chosen the wrong teacher," Amanda said. "My marriage hasn't exactly stood the test of time."

"Well that's Rob's mistake, not yours." Brooke smiled— one of those full-out affairs that opened up her entire face. "I'm kind of hoping I turn out just like you when I grow up."

At Wyatt's game on Saturday, Amanda automatically sat with her cohorts in grime. Susie Simmons sat up and over to the left and didn't seem at all interested in the three of them. She was gossiping with a group of mothers who barely bothered to greet Amanda. It was as if she'd somehow fallen off the face of their earth and no longer merited their attention. A small sense of loss passed through her, but it was surprisingly easy to shrug off.

Tiffany sat near Susie, but not really a part of the group. Amanda forced her gaze up to the girl's face. It was still startlingly beautiful and was still framed by the lush swirl of blonde hair, but there was an unhappy downward turn to her lips. Perhaps she'd found out about Rob's true financial situation. Or maybe she was tired of sitting in bleachers watching a child she hadn't produced play baseball. Or maybe it was the fact that Rob was standing down at the dugout giving Wyatt last minute advice with his back turned toward her.

Moments later the other team jogged out to their positions on the field. Their pitcher began to warm up.

"Wow, look at that first baseman." Candace leaned over to whisper. "I bet he drove the team bus."

"He must be six feet," Brooke agreed. "Don't they all have to be twelve or under?"

"Yeah, and they're supposed to have the birth certificates to prove it," Amanda said. "But look at that catcher. He's taller than Brett when he's crouching."

Sure enough, the Mudhens' lead off hitter moved into position in the batter's box and even hunkered down in position, the catcher still towered over him.

"I hope Dan is asking to see those birth certificates," Candace said. "That pitcher looks like he needs a shave."

"We are in deep doo-doo," Brooke said.

They watched in silence as Brett struck out and another

Mudhen stepped reluctantly up to the plate. Amanda was staring down at the field watching their next batter take a few practice swings, when Candace whispered, "Speaking of doo-doo . . ."

Amanda followed Candace's gaze. Rob was striding up the bleachers toward Tiffany but surprised them all by slowing to smile at Amanda as he passed.

"What was that about?" Candace asked.

"Beats me." Not knowing what else to say, Amanda focused on the game. Their third batter struck out and the Mudhens took the field. Wyatt jogged out to the mound and from the first pitch it was clear he was struggling.

He walked a batter. A moment later he'd filled the bases.

Stepping off the mound, he removed his cap, put it back on. He took a deep breath and stepped back onto the mound.

"Come on, Wy!" Rob shouted from behind her. "Bear down. You can do it."

"You have to admire the fact that Wyatt hasn't given up," Brooke said.

"I know, but it's so painful to watch. And with the stack of bills I'm trying to work through, I can't even help him with lessons."

Wyatt managed to get the batter to pop up and Drew Donovan flipped off his catcher's mask and snagged it.

"Well, I can." Hunter James's voice took Amanda completely by surprise. Her gaze swung from the field to the man who'd somehow materialized beside her.

A hush settled over the stands as other people began to notice him too. Murmurs and whispers followed as everyone realized who he was.

"In fact, I'm kind of ticked off that you didn't ask me. Especially after I threw myself on your mercy over Sam's pool party." He took a seat next to her, his thigh and shoulder pressing up against hers. "The way I see it, I owe you big time."

"No, you don't. Why—"

"Yes, he does," Candace cut in smoothly. "And you're going to have to let him work it off. Right after you introduce us." She was already leaning over Brooke to extend her hand in greeting. "I'm Candace Sugarman. And I know exactly how hard it is to get her to accept any kind of help from her friends."

"Damn straight," Hunter said affably.

"I'm Brooke." Extending her hand, Brooke smiled at Hunter. To his credit Hunter James didn't point like a bird dog on the scent the way most men did around Brooke.

"I'm Hunter. Nice to meet you."

Amanda was completely aware of his solid warmth beside her. "How'd you know about the game?" she asked.

"Meghan." His gaze moved to the field and Wyatt. "She told Sam how bad things were getting for Wyatt and gave Sam the game schedule. Your son didn't say a word about it to me the other night when we were watching the Cubs." His gaze stayed on Wyatt even as he chided her. "I guess he takes after his mother."

There was a thwack of a ball flying off a bat. A roar went up from the opposing bleachers and Amanda tore her gaze from Hunter's arresting profile in time to see the ball sail over the left field fence. Silence reigned in the Mudhens' camp while the home-run hitter trotted arrogantly around the bases behind the three runners he'd knocked in and stomped on home plate. His teammates rushed out to pound him on the back and swoop him up onto their shoulders.

Wyatt stared down at the pitcher's mound as if he'd never seen one before. Amanda's gaze flew to the scoreboard. Four runs had come in.

Dan Donovan called time and walked out toward Wyatt. His son, Drew, the catcher, trailed behind him. Amanda fought back the urge to run out onto the field and lead her baby off it.

"Aw, come on, Wy!" Rob's voice was too loud and too full of disappointment. "You can do better than that!"

Out at the mound the coach put a hand on Wyatt's shoulder and brought his face close to her son's. They talked for a moment and Wyatt shook his head. Outside the right field fence one of the assistant coaches began warming up another pitcher. There was more conversation on the mound. Wyatt shook his head again, clearly unwilling to come out of the game.

"That's it, son. You hang in there," Rob called out. "Strike 'em out and sit 'em down!"

Rob's voice drew Amanda's attention and her ire. She wanted to take the baseball out of Wyatt's hand and stuff it in his father's mouth, but settled for turning and shooting a warning look up at Rob, who seemed to be splitting his energies between egging Wyatt on and contemplating Hunter James.

"That's rough," Hunter said, his gaze on Wyatt. "But you've got to take the good with the bad in baseball; that's one of the basic principles of the game."

"Well then I'd say we're due for some of the good stuff,"

Amanda said, thinking not only of Wyatt's struggles on the mound. *Way overdue.*

Hunter nodded his agreement. Then he focused his attention on the pitches that followed as Wyatt managed to draw grounders out of the next three batters to get the Mudhens out of the inning.

"Why don't you bring him by my facility up on Roswell Road tomorrow about two?" Hunter said. "I'm not normally there on Sunday, but I can work with him then. I'll drop him at home when we're done."

"That's so kind of you," Amanda began. "But I can't afford—"

"And you don't have to," Hunter interrupted her protest. "Wyatt's a great kid and he's got a good arm. He just needs some help with his mechanics. And maybe a little boost to his confidence." He smiled down at her and she felt a slight flush work its way up her neck to stain her cheeks. "Besides, like I said, I owe you."

"Hi, Amanda." Susie Simmons's voice snapped Amanda's head up. "Too bad about Wyatt's pitching. He's really having a bad day." Having dispensed with the courtesies, Susie turned her attention to Hunter. "Lucy was so sorry Samantha wasn't available to come over to celebrate the last day of school. I think she said she was having a party of her own?"

Susie stared at Hunter James with a look of naked hunger. Whether she was lusting after the man himself or the opportunity for her daughter to form a friendship with a celebrity's child was unclear. What seemed clear was that Lucy's party wasn't happening and Susie wanted her daughter to be invited to the Jameses'.

Amanda was embarrassed on Susie's behalf and irritated
at the same time. She wasn't a big fan of Susie's daughter,
either—she'd been catty to Meghan on more than one
occasion—but she wouldn't like to see the girl excluded.
She knew all too well how that felt. "Meghan and Sam were
working up their lists independently," she said now, nudg-
ing Hunter slightly. "I bet they both thought the other had
asked her."

"Of course," he said, catching on. "I'm sure that's what
must have happened. I'll ask Sam to give, um, Lucy a call."

"Why that is so incredibly sweet of you." Susie's simper-
ing smile and gush of appreciation were directed at Hunter.
Amanda wanted to gag.

"Was there anything else?" Candace asked Susie pointedly. "I'm having a hard time seeing the field."

"Sorry." Susie looked anything but. She didn't move immediately, but turned her gaze between Amanda and
Hunter then back again, obviously trying to figure out
whether something was going on between them.

Hunter smiled easily at Susie. He had a knack for ap-
pearing friendly even while maintaining his distance.
"Which one is yours?" He nodded out toward the field.

"My Chas is over there." Susie pointed to the bench in
the dugout where her son had been sitting for the last several innings. "I think he's in a bit of a hitting slump."

"That's too bad," Hunter said.

"You don't teach batting, do you?" Susie asked brightly.
"I'd love to have Chas take some lessons."

"Sorry." He shook his head, all good-natured friendli-
ness. "But one of the guys I used to play with does." He

handed her a card. "Let me know if you decide to call him, and I'll make the introductions."

"Oh." Susie stepped back clearly disappointed. "Thanks." She returned to her seat where, Amanda assumed, she was already weaving her encounter with Hunter into a story that would show her in a better, more attractive light than was warranted.

Eyes bored into her back, but Amanda resisted turning around. Instead she contented herself with being in the center of her own little support group and told herself she should be happy that for the rest of the game, which they lost, Rob kept the advice he would normally have hurled at Wyatt to himself.

chapter 22

Candace sat in the Buckhead eatery with three women whom she'd known since prep school and hadn't seen in a good six months. Between them, they'd had thirteen husbands and almost as many houses. All three of the others had children in college and empty nests the size of the Taj Mahal. Before Candace's move to the northern suburbs, they had lunched and shopped regularly and taken turns chairing the most prestigious fund-raisers.

"To what do I owe this invitation?" Candace asked after they'd placed their orders.

The three of them exchanged glances and it was Bootsie Birnbaum, who had organized the lunch, who spoke. "We miss you since your move to the hinterlands." Bootsie's recent facelift had left her features in a permanent expression of surprise. "I knew there was something wrong with Nathan when he insisted you actually *live* in the neighborhood he was developing."

"I agree." Sharon Sizeman shivered delicately. Years of dieting had left her with zero body fat; despite the fact that they were sitting out on the terrace on a sunny May afternoon, she had a sweater draped over her shoulders.

Cindy Miller signaled the waiter for more coffee. "You need to come in more often." Like the others, she thought of the suburbs outside of the 285 loop that circled Atlanta as "outside" and the area surrounding Buckhead as "inside." It was much more than a geographical distinction. Candace had once felt that way, too; at the moment she found it irritating.

"How else can we find you a new husband?"

As if there were no available men in east Cobb where she lived. "My mother's already working overtime on that, thank you very much," Candace said. "Don't worry your little heads about it."

"Yeah, but your mother liked Nathan. And he was playing around before he'd finished saying I do." Bootsie's lips moved when she spoke; her face didn't.

Candace rolled her eyes. Her stomach rolled too. "She liked his pedigree and his bank account. I have to admit Nathan looked very good on paper." It was just in everyday life that he didn't stack up. Candace considered the remains of the shrimp salad on her plate. "Does anyone else feel queasy?"

Cindy and Sharon had both had the shrimp salad but shook their heads no.

Candace pushed the plate away and the discomfort from her mind. Everything she ate seemed to disagree with her lately. "To tell you the truth, I'm not sure I want to get married again."

There was a shocked silence.

"But your mother said . . ."

Sharon shot Bootsie a look, which confirmed Candace's suspicions. Then she held a palm to Candace's forehead. "You do feel a little bit warm. Maybe you should see a doctor."

"She's just been in the burbs too long; it's not a target rich environment," Cindy added. "That can seriously lower your expectations."

They all laughed. Or at least the three of them did. Candace bristled. "Actually, I'm kind of starting to like it where I am," she said. "And I'm already dating someone." She waited a beat and then called their bluff. "Did my mother mention that when she asked you to call me?"

The sudden silence was answer enough.

"He's a really great guy who Hannah has decided is not husband material."

"Oh?" Bootsie recovered first. "What does he do?"

"He's an accountant."

"Well that should be a plus in Hannah's book. Which firm is he with?" Sharon asked. "Maybe Steve knows him." Her current husband was a managing partner at Ernst & Young.

"He has his own firm, a small general practice," Candace replied.

The sympathy in their eyes rankled and she felt a fresh flash of irritation. She was not going to apologize to them or anyone else for dating Dan Donovan.

For a moment she toyed with telling them about Dan's Irish heritage and his dedication to the losing Mudhens. They'd laugh themselves silly about her stints in the concession stand and gasp in horror if she told them about Maid for You and her new friends who dressed up like French maids and cleaned other people's houses.

It would be kind of fun to see their expressions of shock and horror. But even as her stomach rolled again, she knew she could never offer up the people she'd come to care about and admire for anyone's entertainment. Or even to make a point.

A part of Candace wanted to march over to her mother's and tell her that her machinations weren't working; that giving birth didn't entitle her to choose Candace's friends or husbands. Instead she turned the conversation. Soon everyone was chatting amiably enough. But it wasn't long before Candace's mind began to wander. The recent designer trunk show at Neimen's and the upcoming spa trip the other three were planning seemed considerably less compelling to Candace than Amanda's struggle for survival and Brooke's attempt to come to grips with the identity she'd created for herself.

Candace's stomach rolled again and she realized with some surprise that she was eager to get back to her house in the suburbs; the place she had somehow come to think of as home.

"Well," Bootsie said as she signaled for the check. "I am just filled with admiration for the way you've adjusted to your new environment."

"Why thank you, Bootsie," Candace replied as she excused herself to go to the ladies' room. "The challenges have at times seemed insurmountable, but somehow I've soldiered on."

* * *

At home that afternoon, Amanda retrieved the mail from the mailbox and trudged up the driveway sorting through it as she went. All she had received were bills, bills, and what looked like still more bills. Which she sincerely wished she could mark "return to sender."

In the kitchen she poured herself a glass of iced tea and carried the phone to the kitchen table so that she could sit and check messages.

The only message was from Rob. "Hi, Amanda." His voice was friendlier than she'd heard it in a long time. "I was thinking about popping by to see the kids." There was a pause. "And, uh, then I thought maybe I could take you out to dinner to, um, catch up a little." A rueful tone moved into his voice. "I think I have one credit card that's still usable." There was a long pause. "Don't worry about calling me back. I'll just stop over at about seven if that's OK."

Thinking about Rob's call, Amanda watched what looked like a family of squirrels race up and down the limbs of the crepe myrtle outside. There were only three of them; a mother, she imagined, looking out for her two children. Maybe the father squirrel had also had a midlife crisis and was currently living in another tree, gathering nuts with a more bushy tailed squirrelette.

Restless, Amanda showered and dressed and popped a frozen pizza in the oven for Meghan and Wyatt. She didn't mention their father's call in case he didn't actually show up, but at seven there was a rap on the kitchen door and Rob walked into the kitchen.

"Dad!" Wyatt jumped up and threw his arms around his father.

Meghan startled and a smile lit her face but was gone just

as quickly. Her anger was an equal opportunity emotion. Although she blamed Amanda for driving her father away, she also blamed him for leaving. "What are you doing here?"

"I came to see you guys and take your mother out for dinner."

"You did?" Wyatt's face lit with excitement.

"You are?" Meghan couldn't pull off her usual tone of feigned indifference.

Amanda leveled a gaze at Rob, which he blithely ignored. She wasn't sure if he had any idea of what his words were now conjuring. At this point even Meghan was picturing him moving back in and their old life slipping back into place.

She gave all three of them a pointed look. "We're just going to eat a meal. Don't go turning it into something it's not."

Rob winked at Meghan and Wyatt. Winked!

Doing a slow burn, Amanda kissed the kids good-bye and grabbed her purse. "Do your homework. No TV. And no talking on the phone until it's all done."

Meghan and Wyatt were too busy imagining things to argue. This was not good.

She managed to hold her tongue until they got to the restaurant, a small neighborhood Italian place they'd often come to as a family.

"*Buona sera,* Mr. and Mrs. Sheridan. How nice to see you again!" Guillermo, one of the owners, led them to a table near the window. "It's been much too long!"

Rob ordered glasses of Chianti and they perused the menu in silence. When they'd given their orders, Amanda looked her husband in the eye. "Why don't you tell me what this is all about?"

He seemed surprised by her question and the anger simmering beneath it. "I just wanted a chance to see how you were doing, how the kids are."

"Is that right?"

"Um-hmm."

"Well, let's see," she said, fingering the stem of her wineglass. "I have a stack of bills in the kitchen I'm afraid to open because I already can't pay the ones I did look at. I'm working on a . . . project . . . with Candace Sugarman to try to create income, but I'm not sure I can ever generate enough.

"Wyatt's so worried he can't pitch anymore and he's become so solicitous that every sweet thing he does breaks my heart or makes me feel guilty. Meghan's hormones and anger are running rampant and I'm never sure whether I'm going to encounter the good Meghan or her evil twin. And I think giving them any thought that we can ever be more than civil to each other is grossly unfair and unkind."

"Wow," Rob said. "You don't pull any punches anymore, do you?" He looked at her more closely. "You've really changed."

"Being abandoned, penniless, and left responsible for two children will do that to a woman."

She tore a piece of bread from the loaf and dipped it into the plate of seasoned olive oil. Her mouth moved in a chewing motion and she swallowed, but for all the pleasure she derived from it, it might as well have been cardboard. "So," she asked, "how are things with you?"

He sipped his wine. When he spoke he didn't quite look

her in the eye. "I don't think I'm going to find another law firm to take me on. Even the smaller practices don't want me. I do have an offer from a commercial real estate company that I'm considering. Whatever I do isn't going to produce serious income for some time."

More good news. "Why are we having dinner tonight, Rob? What's the point?"

"I don't know. I just wanted to see you. I guess when things get hard you turn to the people who know you the best."

She laughed at the irony. "It's funny that you say that, because lately I've been wondering whether I ever really knew you at all."

Their entrees came and although everything smelled heavenly, she had no appetite. She would have thought cleaning two houses a day and running after two children would have guaranteed her a spot in the clean plate club, but sitting across a table from Rob was unsettling.

"Where's Tiffany tonight?" she asked as casually as she could.

"She went out with some of her old friends."

"Oh?"

"I don't think the suburban lifestyle is quite what she was expecting." His smile was pained.

Amanda didn't speak, but she practically held her breath waiting to see what would come next.

"Are you dating Hunter James?" he asked. "I saw him at the ballpark with you and Wyatt says he's helping him with his pitching."

"I think you gave up the right to ask me that when you moved out," Amanda said quietly. She was trying mightily to maintain her calm, but the anger continued to bubble underneath. "And I think you should be glad that a pitcher of his caliber is willing to work with your son."

"Oh, I am." His voice dropped. "I guess I'm just really realizing how much I've given up." The look of regret in his eyes was unmistakable.

"Oh, Rob." She heard a matching regret in her voice and knew a weariness that had nothing to do with the houses she'd cleaned. "I wish to hell you'd taken the time to think before you went chasing off after a new life." She took the napkin off her lap and set it on the table, knowing she couldn't eat another bite.

"Meghan and Wyatt and I are trying to get on with ours. If you want to spend more time with them or help in some way, I'm all for it. But don't go messing with our heads." Lifting her purse from the floor beside her feet, she set it in her lap, eager now to leave. "When you have something specific you want to say to me, I'll listen. But don't waste my time and upset the kids with any more . . . exploratory missions."

chapter 23

Solange was dusting the banister outside Hunter James's home office Tuesday morning when her cell phone vibrated. Pulling the phone from her pocket, she glanced at the caller ID. The name Hunter James scrolled across the front of it.

A glance over her shoulder confirmed he was at his desk, leaning back in his chair with his ankles crossed on the mahogany desktop, a phone pressed to his ear.

Looking up, he caught her staring at him and smiled. Covering the mouthpiece of his phone, he asked, "Do you need to get in here, Solange?"

The phone vibrated in her hand.

"Um, no, *monsieur*. I, uh . . ." She took a step to her side. "I, um, *non*, not now." A few more steps took her out of his line of sight, but it didn't stop her phone from vibrating. Not sure what to do, she speed-walked to the laundry room, pulled the bifold door closed behind her, and squeezed into the corner next to Fido's bed. "Hello?" she said into the phone.

"Hi, Amanda. It's Hunter."

"Oh, hi." She tried to keep her voice down and sound normal at the same time.

"I can barely hear you," he said. "You sound muffled. Almost like you were in a tunnel or a . . . closet . . . or something."

Her gaze flew to the laundry room door, but it was still closed. She didn't think there was anyone in the kitchen, but she couldn't be positive. The washing machine next to her kicked into the spin cycle. Something loud thudded as it was tossed in the dryer.

"I must be in a bad reception area." She felt totally stupid scrunched in a corner of a laundry room talking to someone a room away.

"What's that noise?" The washer whirred beside her. The dryer thumped.

"I, uh . . . I'm in a . . ." If she was going to continue leading a double life, she was going to have to learn to lie faster. "Laundromat," she said. "My, uh, washing machine broke down and I brought the wash here."

"Isn't that funny?" he said. "Solange is doing our laundry right now. Do you want to bring yours over?"

Right. Then she could hand herself her own laundry. Hearing footsteps in the kitchen, Amanda burrowed deeper into the corner. She did not want to be discovered in this ridiculous position, definitely did not want him to learn her secret while she cowered in his laundry room. "No, um, I'm fine, thanks," she said.

The dryer shuddered to a stop and the buzzer that announced the end of the cycle went off. She wondered how long it would take him to notice that the sounds he was hearing through his office wall were the same ones he was hearing through the receiver of his phone. "So, um, did you need something?" she asked.

"I just wanted to see if there's anything else we need for the party. You know, like armed guards to keep the boys and girls at a safe distance from each other. Or 'do not touch' signs for the girls to hang around their necks."

Amanda laughed despite herself. "I believe that's our job." Her laughter reflected her nervousness, but it was hard to sound natural when you were cowering in a laundry room.

"Don't worry," she said. "Everything will be fine. Meghan's so excited about the party she's practically bouncing off the walls. Even better, she's been on her best behavior."

"Yeah, Samantha too," Hunter said. "I haven't seen her smile this much since her mother died."

Amanda felt a warm glow that she was a part of something that meant so much to Samantha. She began to relax in her little hidey-hole, reassured by the sound of Hunter's voice, his sheets and towels all toasty in the dryer beside her.

"That's great," she said as she reached over to squelch the buzzer and pull open the lid of the dryer. "I'm sure all the kids will have a good time."

"What about us, Amanda?" he asked more quietly. "Are the chaperones allowed to have fun?"

Phone cradled against her shoulder, she tried to work out her answer while she unloaded the dryer. Torn between flirtation and self-preservation, she tussled with the need to keep her distance even as she was drawn inexorably closer. She was so focused on this inner struggle and finding an answer that would leave her safely on the fence, she didn't hear the bifold door begin to slide open. Or realize that she was no longer alone.

"Solange?"

She whirled around to find Hunter James standing in the laundry room doorway, his head cocked to one side, the phone still clutched in his hand.

"*Nom de Dieu!*" The one thing she didn't have to feign was her surprise. She'd managed to toss her cell phone in the dryer as she turned, but she wasn't completely sure she'd turned it off first.

In a move she hoped was subtle, she closed the dryer and edged over in front of it.

"Have you been talking on your cell phone?" Hunter asked.

"Me, *monsieur*?" She shook her head unsure whether she still *had* a cell phone given how hot the dryer had been when she tossed the phone inside it. "No, I do not speak on zee telephone." She held her hands up like people on TV did when they were under arrest. Who knew? Maybe she could be hauled in for drying a telephone without a license.

"So, you weren't just talking on the phone while you were in here?" he asked.

"Of course not, *monsieur*." She laughed gaily, sending Solange's latest pair of silver dangles bouncing. "I only do zee laundry. Eet ees too loud to talk in here."

Leaving the phone in the dryer, she picked up the laundry basket and prepared to make her exit. "Do you need somezing?" she asked, unintentionally mirroring the question she'd asked on the phone a few moments earlier.

His eyes narrowed as he considered her and she knew she needed to get out of his sight before he started adding things up.

"Just one thing," he said as she began to move past him. "Would you like to work at Samantha's party Friday night? We could use someone to help with the food and the cleanup."

His gaze stayed on her as she pretended to consider his request. It was one thing to be two different people at two different times; for both of her to be here Friday night would be too sitcomish for words.

"I'm so sorry, *Monsieur* James. That weel be impossible." At last she'd spoken the truth. "I have already plans." Plans she was looking forward to way too much. "But thank you very much for the asking."

Wyatt came home from his second pitching session with his face wreathed in smiles. "Hunter taught me a slider. He said I've got almost perfect balance, which is crucial for a pitcher, and that all I need is a few more weapons."

He stuck his head in the refrigerator and came out with the milk jug and a slice of apple pie.

"Honey, it's almost dinnertime, don't . . ."

He poured the milk and grabbed a fork then clambered onto a kitchen chair and prepared to dig in. He looked so happy she didn't have the heart to argue about the snack. And given his current appetite, it wasn't as if anything less than a full side of beef was likely to spoil his dinner.

"He said he'd teach me a curveball when I'm thirteen

and he gave me a bunch of exercises to do to build up my arm strength." He slid a huge hunk of pie into his mouth and chewed happily. He appeared to be tethered to earth by the slimmest of threads.

"That's so great, sweetheart. When you're done with your snack, I want you to take care of your homework. I'm going to start dinner."

"OK, Mom." He rinsed his plate and at the first raising of her eyebrow, actually put it, and his empty glass, into the dishwasher. Slinging his backpack over one shoulder, he pounded upstairs to his room, whistling as he went.

Without thought, Amanda picked up the phone and punched in the James's phone number. Hunter picked up on the second ring.

"Thank you," she said as soon as she heard his voice. "Thank you for what you're doing for Wyatt. I haven't seen him this happy since . . ." She paused for a moment. "Since his father left."

There was a silence in which she knew they were both thinking how closely her comments mirrored his about Samantha. How strange that so many people she hadn't even met until a few months ago were having such a positive impact on her life.

"I'm glad," Hunter said, his reflective tone matching hers. "He's a great kid. I'm getting a real kick out of working with him."

Amanda felt a warmth that she was beginning to associate with Hunter James. It started in her chest and then, if she were honest, dipped considerably lower.

"Well, I appreciate it," she said. "It's wonderful to see

Wyatt so happy. Meghan and I are both looking forward to the party tomorrow night."

This, of course, was a complete understatement. Meghan was vibrating so intensely Amanda was afraid she might levitate right out of her skin.

"Yeah, us too," he said as she prepared to say good-bye. "Oh, I almost forgot." A lighter note stole into his voice. "You don't happen to have a cell phone number for Solange, do you?"

She swallowed and her heart plummeted downward.

"I've been trying to figure out if she owns one."

On Friday afternoon Candace set her dining room table for a traditional Shabbat dinner. She used her grandmother's cut lace tablecloth and filigreed silver candlesticks. To this she added a bent-lipped silver kiddush cup from Israel that a relative had sent as a wedding gift, though she couldn't remember which marriage it had been intended to commemorate.

In the kitchen a pot of matzo ball soup simmered on the stove. A brisket of beef cooked with potatoes and carrots in the oven. A mound of chopped liver surrounded by crackers sat on the kitchen counter. A bottle of Manischewitz waited nearby.

The mouthwatering smells pulled her back to the Friday night dinners of her youth. When her grandparents had been alive the meal had been a weekly ritual. In her mother's household it had occurred more sporadically. In Candace's, with no children to indoctrinate, the practice had been almost nonexistent.

Tonight she was using the ritual meal as a mediatory

measure. She'd invited only two guests, neither of whom was expecting the other.

Dan was the first to arrive. He'd come from the office and wore a pair of gray slacks with a button-down shirt, sleeves rolled up over his forearms, no tie.

"Mmmm," he said as he kissed her and followed her back to the kitchen. He'd brought wine and chocolates, which he placed on the counter. "Something smells fabulous."

She poured him a glass of Merlot without asking and handed it to him. He was going to need it.

"That's the brisket you're smelling," she said. "It's a traditional Friday night favorite. The women in my family do it with a tomato-based sauce, but brisket recipes vary from family to family. Nathan's mother used an onion soup base; I never could get used to it. I should have paid more attention to that brisket before I agreed to marry him."

Dan took his usual seat at the counter. He looked right at home there. She hoped he didn't bolt before the evening was over.

"Here try this." She slathered some chopped liver on a cracker and handed the hors d'oeuvre to Dan, watching intently as he popped it into his mouth.

"Chopped liver," she said in response to his questioning glance. "As in the complaint, 'what am I . . . ?' "

He smiled and popped a second appetizer into his mouth. "Who else did you invite for dinner?"

She was congratulating herself on how easily he'd handled the chopped liver hurdle and trying to decide whether to warn him or not when the doorbell rang.

"Be right back." Drawing a deep breath, Candace walked

to the foyer and opened the door. Hannah stood on the step, a bakery box in her hands.

"I only saw one other car in the driveway," she said as she kissed Candace on the cheek and followed her into the house. She stopped before they reached the kitchen and sniffed. "You made brisket?" Her surprise was evident. "What's the occasion?" Spouting questions without waiting for answers, she preceded Candace into the kitchen. "I don't understand what all the mystery's"—she spotted Dan and stopped in her tracks—"about."

Dan and Hannah eyed each other from across the room. Neither of them spoke.

"You're probably wondering why I called this meeting," Candace joked.

Neither of her guests smiled.

The kitchen smelled warm and wonderful, but there was none of the chatter or laughter that was supposed to accompany those smells. What there was was silence, thick and uncomfortable. Which Candace felt compelled to fill.

"You're here," she said as she poured her mother a glass of wine and replenished Dan's, "because you're the people I care most about." She cleared her throat, trying to dispel her nervousness. "And I, uh, think it's time you got to know each other. I think you have all kinds of things in common and could have lots to talk about if you'd just give it a try."

They stared at each other. Then they turned to stare at her.

"OK," Candace said. "So maybe we'll just skip over the shmoozing and get to the main event." Ushering them into the dining room, she directed them to their seats. "Mother, I'd like you to translate the blessings for Dan as I do them."

For a moment she thought Hannah, who was eyeing the doorway like a prisoner searching out a hole in a chain-link fence, was going to refuse. Not giving her the chance, she took a book of matches from the table, lit one, and held the flame to the first of the Sabbath candles. "Mother?"

"*Baruch atah adonai . . .*" She and the reluctant Hannah recited the blessings while Dan, standing politely behind his chair, looked on.

Another awkward silence followed.

"Now we eat," Candace said. When her mother moved to help, Candace waved her back. "You two sit and get better acquainted. I'll bring the food."

From the kitchen she heard Dan's voice several times, but heard nothing from Hannah in response. They were eyeing each other in silence when Candace got back with the bowls of soup.

"That looks as good as it smells." Dan directed his comment to Candace. "I've always wanted to try a matzo ball."

Hannah snorted. "You should have started him on gefilte fish," she said, also to Candace.

"He passed chopped liver with flying colors. I don't think we need to make him jump through fire his first time out." Candace retrieved her own bowl from the kitchen then sat at the head of the table between them. She felt like a UN negotiator attempting to bring two hostile nations into line.

"All right then," she said. "Maybe we could each share a little bit about ourselves; something that might help you know each other better."

They both looked down at their food.

"Or maybe we should eat first." Candace dipped her

spoon into her soup and her guests, clearly relieved, followed suit.

"This is great," Dan said. "Really delicious."

"It *is* very good, Candace," her mother said, "though I think it could use a little more seasoning."

OK, at least they were talking. Not to each other, of course, but the fact that words were leaving their mouths must be an indication of . . . something. Surely if she tried hard enough, she could help them find some common ground.

"Mother," Candace said, "I think I mentioned once before that Dan is very involved in charitable causes. Walter Green and Todd Williams"—she made a point of mentioning two names she knew Hannah would recognize—"made donations to the inner-city baseball program that Dan initiated."

"That's nice." Hannah's tone was grudging, but at least she'd responded.

"Dan," Candace said into the silence that followed. "Why don't you tell us a little about the program and your philosophy about mentoring and youth sports?"

Dan did. And he did it with gusto. Candace could tell he wanted to help, but she could also feel him coiled and ready to defend her if he deemed it necessary. Prepared for combat was not quite the same as open to possibility.

Candace had imagined that if she just got them in the same room together somehow things would work out, but their mutual distrust had turned the evening into a mini-version of the Cold War.

Watching them closely for any sign of thawing, Candace led them through a carefully orchestrated three-course meal. By the time they'd finished coffee and dessert, they had each divulged their personal biographies, their pet peeves, and their political philosophies.

But each exchange was hard won. No one was firing nuclear warheads yet, but no one was about to call for shots of vodka either. Next time she was going to add Henry Kissinger to the guest list.

Candace felt as if she'd run a marathon. And finished last.

When her mother finally pushed back her chair and said she had to leave, Candace was relieved.

Dan insisted on helping her clean up. Numb, she worked beside him in the kitchen trying to figure out what she could have done differently. "What a waste," she said as she shoved a last coffee cup into the dishwasher. "For all this meal achieved, we could have driven through McDonald's."

"It was a valiant attempt." Dan dried his hands and walked with her to the door. They faced each other in the foyer. "And I'd like to say I'll try harder. But she doesn't make it easy."

"No kidding." Candace's entire body felt heavy with failure. "She just can't seem to see you as anything but a threat."

"I'm afraid I'm not the biggest issue here, Candace; I'm just a symptom. You need to find a way to make your mother respect your choices."

"Oh, I don't think it's really a lack of respect. She's just lonely and . . ."

"From what I can see, Hannah is living her life exactly as she pleases." Dan kissed her good-bye and reached for the doorknob. "Don't you think she should let you do the same?"

chapter 24

That same Friday night, Amanda and Meghan arrived at the James's thirty minutes before the party was supposed to start. Fido greeted Amanda with his usual enthusiasm. Hunter and Samantha were also glad to see them, but showed a little more restraint.

"I don't know what it is, but that dog has a real thing for you and Solange." Hunter gave her a light hug and took the containers of appetizers from her, setting them on the counter. "Don't you think it's odd?"

"That he's so attracted to my crotch? Absolutely. And I'm thinking about having a talk about it with him."

He laughed. "I meant isn't it odd that he does the exact same thing to both of you and no one else?"

Amanda walked past him to the counter where she began to arrange the appetizers on the trays she and Meghan had brought. "I guess so," she said carefully. "Maybe we wear a similar perfume or something."

The girls left with their heads bent together, the whispers and giggles already started. Looking at them, Amanda was reminded of Rose White and Rose Red, Meghan's long dark hair and Samantha's blonde curls tilted so prettily toward each other as they practically skipped out to the pool.

"Red or white?"

She looked at him, surprised, thinking he'd somehow read her mind—which would not necessarily be a good thing—and saw the wine bottles he held aloft.

"I've got a Chardonnay and a Merlot."

"Oh. I don't know. I didn't think we'd drink. We really need to stay on top of things."

He laughed. "I'm not planning to overindulge, believe me. I just don't think I can handle all the raging hormones we're about to encounter without softening the edges a little bit."

"Good point." She finished filling the first tray of hors d'oeuvres and started on another. "So we're going for slightly desensitized but not completely anesthetized."

"Exactly." He held up the bottles again, and she pointed to the white. "Relaxed, but upright," he agreed as he removed the cork from the chosen bottle.

Finished with the trays, she took the proffered glass and clinked it against his.

"OK," he said, setting the bottle in a wine cooler on the counter. "You're in charge here. I'm going to go outside and get the girls to pick music for the sound system. Then we can get some rock and roll cranking out back." He rubbed his hands together in anticipation. "It's a good thing the Smiths are out of town and the Wadells are in their eighties and hard of hearing. I warned the Carlyles across the street, and I promised we'd keep the kids on our property."

Amanda took another sip of wine and let his enthusiasm wash over her. Other fathers, Rob included, might have helped their daughter give an end-of-year party, but few would have been as ready to throw themselves into it as Hunter appeared to be. They would have been there out of a sense of love and duty, would have smiled and taken pictures and done whatever they were directed to do, just as they had at the earlier birthday parties at Chuck E. Cheese's and Celebration Station. But it was unlikely that it would have occurred to them that they might actually enjoy it.

She puttered around the kitchen, setting things up, dumping the cans of soft drinks she found into an already iced cooler. Fido eyed her occasionally, but kept his nose to himself. She felt good, she realized, as she gave the counters a final swipe, happy almost.

True, the growing stack of bills was never completely out of mind, but deep down where it mattered most, she was beginning to believe that she had what it took to protect herself and her children; that she was a fighter and survivor; that she had real value that had nothing to do with being somebody's wife, or somebody else's mother.

The music snapped on outside followed by whoops of laughter. The front doorbell rang and Roses Red and White, out of breath and flushed with excitement, speed-walked through the kitchen and made a beeline for the door.

"Oh God, it's starting," Meghan said to Samantha. "Can you believe it?"

And then Samantha's equally breathless, "I hope it's Joey

and Brent. I *so* want them to see us before our hair gets all wet."

And then there was more excited babble, and a steady stream of teenagers traipsing through the kitchen with waves and nods, on their way out to the pool.

Squaring her shoulders and affixing a smile to her lips, Amanda kicked into parent/hostess/chaperone mode. Outside, at his station in front of the grill, Hunter James did the same.

Sometime after ten P.M. Amanda's energy began to flag. Wandering out to the pool, she found a vacant chaise and lowered her weary body into it. It was a perfect night; the dark sky was littered with stars and a sliver of moon dangled in the midst of them. Music still played, but the selections were quieter now, more reflective; the booming rhythms of Green Day and Bowling for Soup had been replaced by the haunting melodies of Norah Jones and Michelle Branch.

A handful of kids stood in the shallow end of the pool talking. Others lingered in the shadows of the deep end in that eternal teenage quest for privacy. The majority had changed out of their swimsuits and headed down to the basement where Hunter had been staked out for the last hour.

Amanda tilted her head back and stared up into the stars, the words of the song twining itself through her thoughts. *Don't know why I didn't come* . . .

"How are you holding up?" As if summoned by her thoughts, Hunter dropped down onto the lower end of the chaise near her feet. The moonlight glinted off his hair and threw his face into shadows.

"I'm still kicking," she said. "I'm just not kicking quite as high as I was a few hours ago. I don't think the Energizer Bunny has anything to fear from me."

"I know what you mean." He sighed. "I don't normally feel particularly old, but I haven't been around this many teenagers at one time before. I'm feeling like Father Time."

Amanda laughed. "Yeah, there's nothing like twenty-five fifteen-year-old girls in bikinis to make a middle-aged woman's life pass before her eyes. I can barely remember being that young."

"Well, I can. And that's what's keeping me on my toes," Hunter said. "I caught two boys eyeing the liquor cabinet, one couple trying to sneak into the downstairs guest room, and I had one girl give me her mother's phone number."

"You're kidding."

"No. Lucy Simmons seems to think her mother would be perfect for me. She wanted to write the number on my hand in permanent marker."

Amanda laughed again. "Poor man. You must be so tired of women throwing themselves at you." She smiled and shook her head. "But I guess it's understandable. There aren't a lot of single men in the suburbs and most of them don't look like you. And, of course, as it turns out, you *are* famous."

His lips turned up in a smile. "Yeah, but dating in the suburbs is kind of like high school. All the ones you're not interested in are hot on your trail. And the one you want?" He speared her with a look that left no doubt who he was talking about. "She doesn't give you the time of day."

Amanda studied Hunter James. In the moonlight, just like in the light of day, he was wholly masculine and completely attractive. He was also kind, considerate, and easygoing, but with that sharp bite of humor that kept things interesting. And, of course, he was busy dealing with his responsibilities, not trying to escape them.

The way he was looking at her made her want to give him way more than the time of day. If they weren't surrounded by teenagers they were supposed to be chaperoning, she'd hand him her entire watch, fob and all. Why she might even allow him to reset her second hand or ask him to check her battery.

"So what time is it?" she asked quietly.

"I wish it was time to take you upstairs and show you my etchings," he said.

Amanda felt a brutally swift kick of desire, which she attempted to fight off.

"But I'm afraid it's actually time to make another swing through the basement. I can hardly wait to hear their groans of annoyance when they catch sight of me."

Amanda smiled and told herself she should be glad she wasn't about to view Hunter's etchings or anything else. "If you help me up," she said, "I'll go torture some kids too." She put her hand in his and he pulled her out of the chair and set her directly in front of him.

Their bodies were close, too close. She could feel waves of heat pulsing between them. Before she could stop herself, she was imagining his arms wrapped around her with all those hard planes and angles pressed tight against her.

"All righty then." She removed her hand from his and drew a deep breath as she waited for him to step back. But he continued to look down at her, their faces so close they wouldn't even have to move for their lips to meet. "I guess it's time to go check on the kids."

Neither of them moved. But something completely visceral passed between them.

"This party can't last forever," he whispered. "Midnight is only"—he glanced down at his watch and back up into her eyes—"an hour and a half away." He rested his hands on her shoulders.

Amanda knew she should step away and pretend not to notice the current surging between them. The trouble was she didn't *want* to move and neither did Solange, who seemed to be trying to stage some sort of takeover. *Think of all you've been through,* that inner voice said. *After all the hurt and rejection, don't you think you deserve* one *night?*

"That's ninety minutes until midnight," she finally said. "Why is that starting to feel like an eternity?"

They spent the next sixty seconds of it staring into each other's eyes.

"I say we synchronize our watches and do our best to get everybody out the door by twelve-oh-one," he said.

His eyes were dark and bottomless. Above his head the stars still glittered and the moon still hung, suspended in the night.

She felt suddenly sexy and sure under his regard and uncharacteristically bold. And she no longer cared which one of her was in control.

"I'm with you." Her gaze still locked with his, she went up on tiptoe and pressed a kiss to his lips, just a small opening salvo in a campaign she couldn't wait to wage.

"It's ten thirty-three," she murmured against his lips. "Only eighty-seven minutes to go."

* * *

For Amanda, the rest of the party passed in a rush of antic- ipation. Where the first two hours had, in fact, stretched out into infinity; the last hour and a half telescoped and flew. And through every moment of it, she was completely aware of Hunter James.

He handled the boys with a casual acceptance that puffed their chests up with pride, and flirted with the girls in a nonthreatening way that made even the least attractive of them preen. He stayed so calm and attentive, so com- pletely in the moment for Samantha, that Amanda would have thought he wasn't counting the minutes like she was. Until she'd look up and catch his gaze on her, an incredibly sexy smile hovering on his lips, his eyes sparkling with promise.

He made her feel like the most attractive woman in the world; made her aware of her body in a way she hadn't been in too long to remember. She wanted to do a happy dance and a striptease at the same time. Her mind practically shouted, *You're going to have sex! This Greek god, who could have any woman he wants, wants you!* And Solange added, *Admit it, Amanda, you know you want him too!*

She wanted him all right, so much that it scared her. Her fear dredged up the evil and insidious what-ifs: What if she didn't remember how? What if when he saw her naked he changed his mind? What if they had mind-boggling sex and she never heard from him again? What if Meghan noticed what was happening between them and freaked out?

The Greek god who wanted her sent her a saucy wink across the room and the what-ifs scrambled for cover.

* * *

At midnight parents began arriving to pick up their kids. The only one who attempted to linger was Susie Simmons, but by twelve thirty everyone but Meghan, Samantha, Hunter, and herself, was gone.

The girls yawned in unison. Amanda followed suit. Hunter was right behind her.

"Wow, I'm beat," he said too quickly.

Amanda yawned again. "Me too," she said.

They looked at each other over the girls' heads.

"You two get to sleep." Hunter stood and moved toward her. "I'll see Amanda home."

"You don't have to do that." Amanda protested because she knew that's what she would have said to anyone else. "I'm not even a mile away."

She stole a glance at Meghan, but her daughter appeared too euphoric over the party's success to tune in to the undercurrents swirling around her or to make anything of the fact that with both she and Wyatt spending the night out, Amanda and Hunter would be in their house alone.

Ignoring her halfhearted objections, Hunter patted his pockets for his keys, scooped Amanda's purse from behind the kitchen counter, and grabbed her hand. "You girls get ready for bed," he said. "I don't want to hear a peep out of you when I get back."

Before Amanda could protest further, they were out the door, and he was helping her into her car. When she was settled behind the wheel, he leaned in and kissed her, a searing kiss that promised all kinds of things she sincerely hoped he was going to deliver.

Her hands actually shook on the steering wheel as she

drove, her gaze trained on him in her rearview mirror, her mind fantasizing forward to what might happen next.

Her clock was so tightly wound she was afraid her works might pop out.

At home she pulled into the garage and barely waited for him to pull to a stop next to her before she sent the garage door flying down.

"OK," she said as she climbed out of the van.

"OK," he repeated as he clambered out of the Escalade and strode around it toward her.

They stood in front of each other for all of two seconds before they were in each other's arms. His mouth covered hers, warm and insistent. Their tongues met and parried.

He slid his hands down her sides then slipped them beneath her buttocks to lift her up for an even tighter fit.

"Hmmmm . . ." She pressed against the bulge of his erection, rubbed her breasts against his chest. Details seemed unimportant; it was the touching that mattered.

"Wrap your legs around me," he said, "and hold on. We need to go inside."

She did as instructed and he carried her toward the kitchen door, his erection pressing more insistently against her with every step.

"Do you have the keys?" He groaned when they reached the door. "God, you feel good."

She thought that must be an understatement, because at the moment she was way better than good and on her way to great. She did not, however, know where her keys were. "They must be in the car."

With another groan he carried her back down the garage steps to the car. With one hand he pulled the van door open and fumbled around for the ignition, his mouth still glued to hers and their bodies still wedged together. His free hand supported her bottom.

When he'd managed to get hold of the keys, he retraced his steps, still holding her against him, his mouth still moving on hers. At the top of the steps he broke the kiss long enough to put the keys in her hand. "Inside. Now," he croaked.

It was her turn to fumble, but she finally got the right key in the lock. They pushed through the doorway into the house. As the door slammed behind them, he turned and braced her against it, deepening the kiss.

Panting with need, she tore her lips from his. "Bedroom," she said. "Upstairs."

Following her breathless directions, he carried her up the flight of stairs and into her bedroom. Not bothering to pull back the comforter, he laid her on the bed and looked down at her, visibly struggling for control. "Are you OK with this?"

She didn't want to think about OK versus not, didn't want to analyze, debate, or—God forbid—talk herself out of this wondrous thing that was about to happen. She nodded her head and held her arms up to him.

He smiled. Good Lord, the man's smile was almost as big a turn on as the rest of him. Her body quivered with anticipation.

In one smooth movement, he removed his shirt and dropped it on the floor. Kneeling over her, he began to unbutton her blouse. Before she could catch her breath, they were both naked from the waist up.

His eyes on her made her nipples harden. He smiled and

traced them with his fingertips then leaned over and circled them with his tongue.

When he straightened, she reached for the snap of his jeans. Staring into his eyes, she pulled the zipper down and reached for him.

The glow in his eyes was its own form of foreplay. As he eased off her to step out of his jeans and underwear, she felt an answering wetness between her legs. When he slid her panties down her legs, she held herself very still, afraid she'd come before he'd done anything more than look at her.

"I, uh, haven't done this for a while," she said.

"No?" A smile played around his lips as he knelt in front of her again and spread her legs. "Then we'll have to make it very, very good."

He lowered his mouth and opened her with his tongue. Mini-waves of pleasure rippled through her. "Oh, thank, God," she managed, as her body tightened. "I was so afraid you weren't going to give it your all."

She thought she felt a burble of laughter against her clitoris, but he brought his thumbs up to brush her breasts at the same time and she was too distracted by how good everything felt to be sure.

Every touch, every flick of his tongue drove her closer to the precipice.

She tried to hold on, tried to resist the inexorable freefall that beckoned, but Hunter's hands and mouth moved in tandem. His hair brushed across her bare skin.

Her eyelids fluttered shut and she teetered on the verge, exquisitely taut, until she was forced to let go.

He held her while she orgasmed in a rockslide of pure sensation.

Long, gasping moments passed before she remembered to breathe. When she was able to open her eyes, she stared up into his and saw the haze of lust that filled them.

"Come here," she said, pulling him closer. "I want to give you what you gave me."

He raised his body forward so that his penis rubbed against her. "You're the boss," he said. "All we need is a condom."

She expected him to locate his jeans and whip one from the pocket. She was ready to help him put it on; could probably break land and air speed records doing it. Anything to prolong the sensations pulsing through her. And make sure he experienced them too.

"Do you have one?" he asked.

Given all the blood that had rushed to her sexual organs, she thought maybe she had misunderstood. "Me?" she asked. "A condom?"

"That night at the grocery store you had hundreds of them," he said more urgently. "Tell me where they are, and I'll get one."

Amanda closed her eyes and drew in a shaky breath. Her body wanted Hunter James buried inside her and it wanted him now.

But there was a small problem. "I, um . . ." She forced herself to meet his gaze. "I don't have any. I, um, I tied them all to a tree."

He blinked. It was the only part of him that moved. "I hate to be critical at a time like this," he finally said, "but I think you've got things a little bit confused."

She couldn't decide whether to laugh or cry.

He rolled off her. "We're not on *Candid Camera* are we?" he asked.

"No," she said. "I frittered them away in a twisted attempt at revenge and now, when I would sell my soul for one, I am condomless."

He sat up and swung his legs over the side of the bed. "I can tell this is a completely fascinating story, and I hope you'll tell it to me later." He stood, naked and glorious, and pulled on his jeans. Then he was moving purposefully toward the door. "But right now I'm going to check the glove compartment, my wallet, and anywhere else I can think of for some form of protection."

She would have liked to toss her head back and laugh at the ridiculousness of the situation, but she simply couldn't believe this was happening. A moment ago she'd been in the throes of a ten-point orgasm and now she was alone in bed, watching the man who'd given it to her scrambling for the door.

He stopped in the doorway and turned to face her. Seeing her expression, he strode back to the bed. "Don't move." He smiled at her, his eyes frantic, yet warm. "If I have to, I'll hit the Kroger on Upper Roswell. It's open twenty-four hours."

He leaned over and kissed her, a long deep kiss that made her body tingle with renewed anticipation. "When I get back, we'll do whatever it takes to put you back in the mood. That, you can count on."

Then he turned and pretty much sprinted for the door.

chapter 25

He did come back, right?" It was Sunday afternoon and Candace was completely ignoring the line of people awaiting her attention at the concession stand. "After my own Friday night fiasco, I need to know that somebody's evening worked out."

Amanda nodded and blushed, which, Brooke realized, she'd been doing a lot of since they'd arrived to open the stand.

"Oh God, your cheeks are all red." Candace turned to Brooke. "I may not know how to negotiate a settlement between Dan and my mother, but I knew Hunter James would be good in bed."

Amanda nodded again. If possible, her cheeks grew redder.

"Here, I'll take the window." Amused, Brooke pushed Candace away from the front of the concession stand. "I can see you're determined to wring every tiny detail out of the poor woman." She smiled at the little girl clutching her dollar bill and moved to get the Icee she requested. "But speak up. I don't want to miss the good parts."

"I am not sharing details," Amanda insisted. "It's wrong to kiss and tell." Brooke turned to get a hot dog from the warmer and saw Amanda grin evilly. "Besides it would take way too long. They were *all* good parts." She fanned her flaming cheeks. "I wonder if this is what a hot flash feels like?"

"I don't think so," Candace said. "None of the menopausal women I know look anywhere near as happy as you do when they're having one." Then Candace's face flushed and she, too, began to fan her cheeks. "I'm kind of starting to wonder whether I'm going through the change early. My whole system seems to be out of whack."

There was a whoop from the stands nearby and the three of them rushed to the window.

"Can you see what's happening?" Amanda asked. "I thought I heard Wyatt's name."

"No, but here comes Tyler." Brooke hated the sense of dread that accompanied the approach of her stepson. No matter what she said or did, he seemed to take it as an insult.

"Hi, Ty." She greeted him as jovially as she could when he reached the concession window, but he looked right past her toward Amanda. "Hi, Mrs. Sheridan," he said, all smiles now.

Brooke bit back a gasp at the insult.

Amanda greeted him in return then stepped close to Brooke, turning her body away from the window. "Lesson number one in suburban motherdom: don't let him treat you that way," she whispered near Brooke's ear. With a subtle squeeze of Brooke's shoulder Amanda moved toward the back counter, leaving Brooke to face Tyler.

"I agree," Candace said quietly. "It's time to take a stand. If he's going to treat you like the evil stepmother anyway, you might as well have your say."

She went to join Amanda at the back counter, which was far enough away from the front window not to get involved, but close enough to hear.

Brooke cleared her throat and straightened her shoulders. Amanda and Candace were right. Keeping her mouth shut had accomplished nothing. It was time to speak; if nothing else he'd know her true feelings. If he rejected them, well, at least she would have said her piece.

Screwing up her courage, Brooke looked Tyler directly in the eye; something, she realized with surprise, she couldn't remember having done before. "I guess if you actually want something, you're going to have to deal with me," she said.

There was a silence. Studying him, she noticed that his brown eyes were identical to his father's and so were the set of his jaw and the shape of his brow. This wasn't just some hostile teenager to whom she had no connection, this was Hap's child, his own flesh and blood; there had to be enough of Hap inside to give her something she could tap into.

"Really, Ty, this can't continue. You don't have to love me."

A look of abject horror washed over his face.

"I guess you don't even have to like me, although I hope one day you will."

Still Tyler didn't speak. But because she didn't look away,

she saw the barrage of other emotions that flashed across his face. First there was anger followed by hurt, fear, and uncertainty. In the end he went with his old standby, hostility.

"I know this isn't easy for you," she said. "Hell, if I were you, I'd probably hate me too."

Tyler's look of hostility was replaced by one of surprise.

Brooke wanted desperately to make him understand. Not knowing how else to get through, she simply put all that she was feeling into her words and prayed he'd hear the truth. "The thing is," she said, "I really love your father." She swallowed. "And I know you do too." She tilted her chin a notch. "I know it would mean a lot to him if we could at least be cordial. That's all I'm looking for right now, Ty. Basic courtesy on both sides." She looked him straight in the eye again. "Maybe somewhere down the road—and I'm on this road for the long haul so there's no point thinking I'm just a temporary irritant—somewhere down the road, maybe we can have more than that. I hope we will, but that'll be up to you."

In a movie, Brooke thought, the music would swell and Ty would throw himself into her arms in a big gushy embrace and vow to meet her more than halfway.

Brooke watched his face closely. Behind her Amanda and Candace stopped wrapping burgers. She could feel them holding their breath, just as she was.

But this was the real world and Tyler Mackenzie was not going for an Oscar. He simply shrugged, just a casual lifting of the shoulders as if none of this really mattered at all and he didn't know what she was making such a fuss about.

"OK," he said. "Whatever. We don't have to make a big deal here. I just want a Gatorade and a pack of gum."

Brooke shot him a look and instead of growling at her, he smiled. "Please," he said.

Brooke smiled back and her heart lightened. With a nod, she went to get the things he'd asked for.

Amanda stepped forward and gave Ty a smile too. "So what was the shouting about out there?" she asked.

"Wyatt struck out the whole side, Mrs. Sheridan," Tyler said. "Three up, three down. It was beautiful."

"You're kidding." Amanda was already untying the apron she wore. "Did he really?"

"Yep." Tyler nodded sagely. "It was totally awesome. Mr. Sheridan went absolutely crazy."

Amanda set the apron on the counter and ran a hand through her hair to straighten it. "Is he pitching the next inning?"

"We're in the bottom of the fifth," Tyler replied. "Coach thinks we might actually win this one."

"I've got to get out there," Amanda said already heading for the concession stand door. "This is one victory I intend to witness myself."

Watching Amanda and Tyler hurry down to the field, Brooke crossed her fingers and offered up a little prayer on Wyatt's behalf. She'd had her own small victory today. She wanted the Sheridans to have one too.

That night after the kids went to bed, Amanda sat at the kitchen table and faced reality. It was not a pretty sight.

First, she forced herself to open all the bills she'd been avoiding. Staggered by their total, she divided them by category and sorted them into piles in an effort to lessen the overall impact.

Then she looked at her income. Based on two homes a day, five days a week—assuming she continued to accept Brooke's help and generosity—she could make the most critical ongoing bills on a monthly basis.

What she couldn't do was pay off the dauntingly large lump sum that was owed on the credit cards—even making the current minimum payments wasn't going to happen.

If she could just add a few more houses, do three a day a few days a week for a month or so, she could make a dent in them. None of this, of course, allowed for emergencies or anything unexpected, but it would at least put her on track to whittle away the debt. And then?

Feeling panic threaten, Amanda reached deep down in search of her inner Solange.

Several deep breaths later, that inner voice began to chastise her. *Don't borrow trouble,* it said. *Just focus on creating extra income.*

The split personality thing was becoming a tad worrisome, but Solange, of course, was right. There was no point in worrying about the "then" until she took care of the "now."

Picking up the phone, she dialed Candace's number. "Ees that you, *Candee ass?*" she asked when her friend answered.

Candace groaned at the nickname, but didn't bother to correct her. "It's *moi,*" she said dryly. "What's going on?"

"I need you to add a third client on Fridays and Mondays. I know it's too late for tomorrow, but do you think we could start this Friday?"

"Booking the jobs isn't going to be a problem." Candace hesitated but then, being Candace, forged ahead. "But how are you going to handle that kind of workload? And what will you do about the kids now that they're out of school? Isn't tomorrow the first day of summer vacation?"

"Very good questions, *mon amie*." Amanda pulled the calendar from another pile of papers; the one she had filled in for her children with the wiliness of Machiavelli. She'd arranged for Meghan to get a ride to afternoon dance practices all week and signed Wyatt up for a hitting clinic that Drew Donovan was attending. The rest of the summer was similarly accounted for.

"I've got the kids pretty much covered and Rob has promised to pitch in when he can. I need those extra houses, but I don't want Brooke coming along. She's doing more than enough already. I'll handle the extra cleaning on my own."

"Amanda, I'm not sure that—" Candace began.

"Well, I am," Amanda interrupted with Solange's determination. Then more quietly she said, "Just book me, Candace. And don't say anything to Brooke. Solange and I will take care of it."

For the rest of the evening, Amanda kept one ear cocked for the phone. If she hadn't slept with Hunter James—and didn't still remember just how many condoms they'd gone through—she would have been the one calling him to share the news of Wyatt's pitching breakthrough. But the truth was she was too embarrassed to call. And with every hour that the phone didn't ring, she became more convinced that sleeping with him had been a massive error in judgment.

*   *   *

On Tuesday morning Amanda stood on the James's front step dressed for work. Hunter still hadn't called and despite the protection of her disguise, her heart pounded when Brooke rang the doorbell. Her palms went slick with sweat as they waited for him to appear at the door.

But there was no approaching shadow through the sidelights, no hint of Hunter's voice from inside. Torn between relief and disappointment, Amanda reached under the welcome mat and pulled out the key. "I guess he's not home," she said needlessly.

Brooke followed her into the house. There was no coffee, no Fido hurtling toward her, nothing but the hush of an unoccupied home. An envelope of cash with Solange's name scribbled on the front sat on the counter. Under her name he'd written: *Work emergency. Girls at grandparents. Out of town. Please leave key with Amanda Sheridan.*

Well, at least that was convenient.

"See," Brooke said. "He wants you to have his key."

"No, he wants the maid to drop it off with the closest person she knows. It's not exactly a telling action."

Brooke raised an eyebrow, which made the mole shift slightly. "A little testy, aren't we?" she asked.

Yes, she was. Because she wanted him around to flirt with—and possibly to sleep with again—not traipsing off somewhere conducting business.

She was looking for validation that what they'd shared was more than random lust. She wanted specific lust, aimed directly at her. Oft-repeated lust would be even better.

"I'm not . . . testy," Amanda insisted. "I'm just a little disappointed that he's not here, that's all."

And extremely disappointed that she didn't know when

he'd be back. Even a determined optimist needed something to look forward to.

That night Brooke and Hap had dinner at The Thai House, a tiny restaurant tucked into a strip mall around the corner from their house. The décor was starkly modern—black lacquer tables and chairs—with a few plaster Buddhas strategically placed for atmosphere.

Brooke's gaze zeroed in on the closest Buddha's belly as Hap placed their order. It was smooth and white like the white polyester uniform Simone would wear to Susie Simmons's in the morning. As happened more and more, thoughts of Simone led Brooke to thoughts of her mother—an alarming tendency given how completely she'd believed she'd cut Cassie Blount from her current life.

"Honey?" Hap's voice broke through her reverie.

"Yes?" She turned to her husband. "I'm sorry. Did you say something?"

He looked at her strangely, as if she'd somehow managed to surprise him. "I was wondering what you did to Tyler?"

"What I *did* to him?" She couldn't tell from his tone whether he considered whatever she'd done good or bad.

The waiter brought their drinks then placed a bowl of fried noodles between them.

Hap picked up his beer bottle and tilted it toward her in salute. "If I'm not mistaken, his hostility quotient seems to have dropped a bit."

Brooke sat back in her chair and studied her husband. "And all this time I thought you hadn't noticed."

"I love that boy," he said. "But I'm not blind. It was about time you read him the riot act."

"Well, I'm not sure I'd put it in those terms." She remembered how Candace and Amanda had encouraged her to speak up and Tyler's surprise at her candidness. "I just told him how I felt about you and that I wasn't planning on going anywhere so he might as well get used to me."

"Good for you." He flashed a smile of approval. "I was hoping you'd find a way to pull him in line. It's better coming from you than me. He needs to respect you for yourself."

Pleased at Hap's praise, she considered him from across the table. What would happen if she just opened her mouth and told him the secrets she'd been guarding so carefully? Would his smile grow wider or disappear altogether? Could he possibly know all there was to know about her and love her anyway?

He took a sip of the Thai beer. "Tell me how you're filling your days. I haven't heard you mention going back to work for a while now. What have you been doing with your time?"

As openings went, it didn't get much better than that. Mouth dry, she reached for her tea and took a drink as she considered her response.

He'd asked. Maybe she should just tell him. She could start with her part in Amanda's cleaning business and segue right into the fact that she came from a long line of cleaning women. Then she could explain that she wasn't actually estranged from her mother; just too ashamed of where she'd come from to let her current and past worlds intersect.

But how could she say something that didn't even sound plausible in her head?

Brooke set her cup down, the moment gone. "I'm actually working on a, um, project with Candace and Amanda," she finally said, trying not to lie outright this time.

"That's great," Hap replied, his tone signaling that his attention had already begun to stray.

For once that was OK. Because her thoughts had moved on too. Or rather back. To all the things she might have told him. And now probably never would.

While Brooke searched her soul, Candace searched her closet for something a French maid might conceivably wear to work.

As she perused the possibilities, she fought back the nausea and lethargy that continued to plague her. If she was coming down with something, she wished she'd get it already so that she could spend a few days in bed or take an antibiotic and get over it.

Studying the designer pants suits and coordinates, she attempted to push the memory of her failed Friday night dinner from her mind. She'd gone over and over what she might have done differently and had come to the conclusion that the whole dinner concept had been much too subtle. The next time she had the opportunity, she planned to knock their heads together and tell them to grow up. Just thinking about Dan and her mother made her want to cry. Of course, so did Hallmark commercials. She'd become an absolute emotional basket case.

"OK," she muttered to herself. "Take a deep breath and focus. Right now, all you have to do is find something you can wear to clean houses tomorrow."

This, of course, was not an eventuality she'd ever shopped for, and at first it appeared that none of the designers she favored had ever considered creating a line of "Housekeepingwear" either. But at last she found a white Donna Karan from a couple of seasons ago that she thought might pass as a uniform. She'd leave it to Amanda to disguise her from the neck up.

Giving in to the exhaustion she couldn't seem to shake, she laid out the pants suit and crawled into bed knowing she'd need all the energy she could muster in the morning. And, of course, she really needed to come up with a name for her new persona. Solange was about to acquire a new relative. If Amanda thought Candace was going to let her handle all that extra work alone, she had another thing coming.

chapter 26

B*onjour, mes amies.*"

Amanda and Brooke turned from the guest room mirror where they were adjusting their disguises at the sound of Candace's voice. It was hard to tell whose jaw dropped farther.

"What?" Candace asked, sounding amazingly like Maurice Chevalier. "You are not happy to see Chanel, your long lost cousin?"

"Chanel?" Amanda asked. "As in the designer?"

"But, of course." Candace gave a deep-throated laugh. "My mother the runway model, she named me after her."

"And what you're wearing is?"

"A leetle beet of thees and a leetle beet of that."

What it looked like was a designer pants suit that, even though it had been smudged strategically with dirt, still looked like it cost as much as the vacuummobile. Candace's wig, which moved freely as she shook her head, was a long frosted blonde number. It, too, had probably cost a fortune.

"I figured you could just add a few features to disguise my face and we could be off."

"Off?" Brooke asked. She stepped closer to Candace. "You don't seriously intend to try to clean houses in that getup, do you?"

"Do you even know how to clean a house?" Amanda asked.

"Well, not exactly," Candace said, "but I'm sure I can . . ."

Brooke looked from Candace to Amanda. "What's going on? Aren't I covering enough ground?"

"You're fabulous." Amanda hastened to assure her. "I just told Candace to book a third house for me on Fridays and Mondays so that I can try to pay off some of my debt and she must have decided to try to help."

"Weren't you going to tell me?" Brooke actually sounded hurt.

"No," Amanda said. "You're already doing way too much. I can't bear for you to do any more. I told *Candee ass* I could do it myself." She rounded on Candace. "I hate to sound unappreciative, but I don't think you can waltz into a house in designer clothing and six-inch nails and expect to accomplish very much."

"Have you ever scrubbed a toilet?" Brooke asked.

"No." Candace's wig swung about her shoulders as she shook her head.

"Mopped a floor?" Amanda added.

"Er . . . no."

"Used bleach?" Brooke threw out.

"You mean besides on my hair?" Candace quipped.

Amanda and Brooke rolled their eyes.

"What, so now there's a bar exam for maids?" Candace huffed. "I realize I'm not an expert, but neither were you when you started, Amanda. You'll just have to teach me. Come on, go ahead and do my face so we can go."

"Candace, I'm really moved that you want to help. But I'm cleaning houses because I *have* to. You don't. Brooke has been kind enough to help temporarily, but she knows what she's doing. We're already late and I have three houses to do today. There aren't any jobs you can do without running the risk of breaking a nail, messing up your clothes, and possibly even working up a sweat. I just don't see how..."

"Wait a minute." Brooke folded her arms across her chest and leaned back to study Candace. "There are things she could do to help."

"Like what?"

"Well, let's say I'm doing the laundry—she could strip the beds and gather up the sheets and towels and drop them in the machine. I'll handle the detergent and bleach ratio, even the separating. When we do the floors, she could throw out the dirty water and clean out the bucket afterward. I'm sure she could push a vacuum. There are certainly enough unskilled"—she shot a look at Candace— "tasks that we could direct her through to at least help us pick up our pace and work in that additional house."

"Well . . ." Amanda was having a hard time picturing the elegant Candace in any of these scenarios, but it was getting late and there wasn't time to argue.

"And about that third house?" Brooke said. "Don't even think you're going there without me."

"That's right." Candace nodded emphatically. "It'll all go faster if we do this together."

Amanda looked at Brooke and Candace. She smiled through a blur of tears. "OK already. I'm convinced. And I'll never forget what you're doing for me."

She took hold of Candace's shoulders, turned her toward the mirror, then settled her on the makeup stool. "Let's see," she said as she riffled through her tackle box. "Chanel deserves a special disguise. Because with her in the mix we weel be like zee three musketeers. All for one and one for all."

Gingerly, Candace felt the slightly bulbous nose and the latex padding that extended her chin. She opened the visor of the vacuummobile and confronted her new reflection in the mirror. "Did you really have to make me look like Gerard Depardieu?"

Candace was riding shotgun in the vacuummobile, which was, in fact, almost as humiliating as having been made up to look like the oversized French actor. Cars whizzed by and in almost every one of them the passengers were laughing. The less well-bred folk laughed *and* pointed.

A lifetime of dignity swept aside by a single act of compassion.

Candace's gorge rose and she fought it back down. The only thing more embarrassing than riding around in this disguise in the bright yellow "look at me" mobile would be opening the window and losing her breakfast out the side of it.

Or being recognized.

"Has anyone else noticed that Amanda is the only one of

the de Papillon girls who's attractive? How come she got better looking and we got worse?" Brooke asked.

"Hey," Amanda protested. "I went to great pains to give each of you a signature look. It took real talent to create that hairy mole and bulging nose."

"Not to mention chutzpah," Candace pointed out.

Brooke laughed. "OK, so you struck a blow for first wives everywhere." She peered at her reflection in the rearview mirror. "Actually, after all the years of relying on and worrying about my looks, it's liberating to be this ugly. Do you know what I mean?"

"Actually, I do," Amanda replied. "That's kind of how I feel about Solange. She's a lot freer and surer of herself than I am."

They turned onto the Simmons's street. "But both Solange and I hope Susie's not home today," Amanda said as they neared the house. "I absolutely hate the way she follows us around and treats us like we're either potential jewel thieves or ignorant thugs.

"I mean for all she knows Solange and Simone could have come from a fine French family fallen upon hard times. Or we could be former rocket scientists reduced to scrubbing floors in order to bring the rest of our family over."

Brooke shot her a look. "OK, now you're starting to scare me. Besides I thought we were part of a small family. Just me and you and those poor fatherless twins."

Amanda pulled the vacuummobile into the driveway. The garage door was up and Susie's SUV was in it. "Ugh. She's here. And Lucy and Chas are probably still sleeping.

Even with a third person, it'll take twice as long to work around everybody."

"My, you are whiny today," Brooke observed. "Still no word from Hunter?"

"What makes you think I'm whining about him? I have plenty of things available to whine about," Amanda said. Like Rob's sudden reappearance and the mountain of bills she was trying to climb. "Everything I do and think is not about Hunter James."

Just every other thing. Which was really starting to irritate her. Amanda tried to shrug off her bad humor. Arriving at Susie Simmons's house in this kind of mood was like taking coals to Newcastle; she normally didn't feel this bad until she was leaving.

Susie greeted them at the door, the phone to her ear. "It's the French contingent," she said into the receiver. "And it looks like they've added a third musketeer."

Amanda kept Solange's cheery smile plastered on her face, but she could tell by the rigidity of her friends' shoulders that Brooke and Candace were also reacting to Susie's snide tone.

"*Madame*," Amanda said. "Thees is also my cousin. Her name is Chanel."

"Like the designer?" Susie seemed to find this hilarious.

Solange, Simone, and Chanel turned up their faux French noses and sniffed in unison.

"But of course," Candace said, still sounding unfortunately like Maurice Chevalier. Or a foghorn. "Most French women they are simply born with zee sense of style." She shrugged a completely Gallic shrug. "American women must try so much harder." She looked Susie up and down and sniffed again. "And so often they do not succeed."

They left Susie with the phone frozen next to her ear, her laughter stifled, but saved their high-fives for the laundry room.

"I can't stand that woman in any language," Amanda said, "but we are not going to let her ruin our day or slow us down." She took a deep breath and let it out. "All we have to do is draw the good thoughts in." She inhaled again. "And let the bad thoughts out." She exhaled.

Brooke and Candace followed suit. They breathed together for a while in the closed laundry room, probably sucking all the oxygen right out of it, and then looked at each other.

"I'm dizzy. I need to sit down," Candace said, lowering herself into the laundry room's caned-back chair.

"I think we should accidentally wash her best outfit in hot water and make sure it ends up in the dryer," Brooke suggested.

There was a knock on the laundry room door. Amanda opened it and poked her head out. Susie Simmons stood on the threshold. "Chas is up." She mimed someone opening their eyes and stretching.

Amanda kept her own eyes wide. *"Oui, madame?"*

"I want you to come strip his bed now." Susie mimed a motion that might have been hoeing a garden or rowing a boat.

Amanda furrowed her brow enjoying the show.

"Oh, for goodness sake!" Susie grabbed Amanda's wrist and led her to Chas's room then walked her to the side of the empty bed. "Change the sheets now," she demanded.

"At thees moment?" Amanda asked.

"Yes." In one rapid movement, Susie reached down and pulled the sheets off the bed and stuffed them into Amanda's arms. Then she shook the pillows out of their pillowcases and added them to the pile.

"*Merci, madame,*" Amanda said when Susie had finished stripping the bed. "I appreciate zee help."

Muttering under her breath, Susie marched in the opposite direction and tromped down the stairs.

Feeling a little cheerier, Amanda tossed Chas's sheets in the washing machine then directed Candace to strip all the other beds and bring the sheets to the washer.

They met up about ten minutes later in the master bedroom.

"Look at this." Brooke motioned them over to the dresser where the weekly "pot of gold" had been planted.

This time it consisted of three hundred-dollar bills, the diamond studs they'd snubbed the week before, a strand of 5 mm freshwater pearls, a square cut diamond surrounded by baguettes in what appeared to be a platinum setting, and a lapis lazuli necklace.

"She's starting to get serious," Brooke said. "What do you think we're looking at? Fifteen hundred bucks? Two thousand?"

Amanda wasn't sure of the accumulated value, but she knew the increased stakes spelled trouble.

"I don't have my loupe with me." Candace picked up the ring and held it up to the light. "The diamond looks a little cloudy. It's only average color with a number of imperfections. But the setting's nice, and the baguettes aren't bad." She set the ring down.

"Where do you think you are? The sales counter at Tiffany's?" Amanda ushered Candace and Brooke away from the cache. "This is a trap and we don't want to be anywhere near it. For all we know, Susie has a camera pointed this way."

"So do you think we should act tempted?" Brooke asked.

"Act tempted?" Candace said.

"Well, if we were really who we're pretending to be, this might be very attractive. Maybe we should act out Chanel wanting it and Simone or Solange stopping her. You know, kind of like Good Maid, Bad Maid."

"Hey, how come I'm the bad maid?" Candace put on a hurt expression. "I want to be the good maid whose real reason for coming to this country is to make her bad cousins give up their life of crime."

Amanda laughed. "We are not going to stand here and worry about whether we're offending Susie Simmons by not wanting to steal her jewelry. And I'll handle the dramatic scenarios, thank you.

"Now let's get this job done and get out of here." Amanda checked her watch. "It's getting late and we still have to do the Glantzes' and the Sullivans'."

"Here." Pulling a bottle of ammonia from the bucket of supplies, Brooke handed it to Candace. "Go put about a half a cupful in each of the upstairs toilets. Let each sit for about five minutes and then use this to scrub the bowls." She handed her the toilet brush.

"*Oui! Oui!*" Candace saluted smartly and went into the master bathroom. But when she unscrewed the cap and leaned over to pour the ammonia into the toilet, the sharp odor made her gag. Before she could stop herself, she was vomiting into the toilet she was supposed to be cleaning.

Amanda found her in there on her knees. She called Brooke in to help her and they half carried Candace to the master bedroom chaise. "Consider yourself off toilet duty," Amanda said. "Are you all right?"

"Sorry. I must be coming down with something." Candace looked around. "I'm OK, though. Give me something else to do; something without chemicals."

"Here." Brooke pushed the vacuum toward her. "Why don't you catch your breath and then start vacuuming?"

Candace opened her mouth preparing to protest, but Brooke waved her off. "Look, we don't have time to debate this. If you can vacuum all three floors, it'll be a big help. When you get done with that, take the feather duster and hit the most obvious spots. We'll rendezvous in the foyer at eleven thirty prepared to move on."

Amanda had just picked up the envelope of cash from the counter and was joining Brooke and Candace in the foyer when a shout reached them from upstairs. "Stop! Thief!"

Lucy's voice joined her mother's in perfect schoolgirl French. *"Au voleur! Arrêtez!"*

The three musketeers froze.

Feet pounded down the back stairs.

"They've stolen my jewelry!" Susie shouted.

Amanda, Brooke, and Candace looked at each other. For about two seconds, Amanda considered turning and standing her ground.

"Forget it!" Candace said, seeing her hesitate. "I am not going to be exposed on my virgin outing."

As one they picked up their cleaning supplies and sprinted for the front door.

"Chas, call the police!" Susie Simmons shouted, her voice growing louder as she got closer. "Lucy, go through the garage and try to head them off!"

"Oui, Maman!" Lucy shouted in beautifully accented French.

Racing outside, the de Papillon girls ran toward the car. "Forget the trunk," Amanda shrieked. "Just throw everything in the backseat with Brooke."

She tossed in the vacuum and threw the bucket of rags on top of it. Slapping a hand inside the purse that flapped around her shoulder, she found the keys and slid into the driver's seat. Brooke was in the back and Candace just pulling the passenger door shut when Amanda turned the key in the ignition and stomped on the gas. But when Amanda reached for the door handle to pull her door shut, there was a body in her way.

"Oh, no you don't!" Susie Simmons wedged herself more firmly between Amanda and the door. Lucy did the same on the passenger side.

"You give me back my jewelry!" Susie shouted.

In the distance, a police siren sounded. Amanda's heart thudded in her chest; her foot hovered over the gas pedal. If she put the car in gear and stomped down on it, they might get away in time, might even be able to ditch the vacuum-mobile at the bottom of the nearby Chattahoochee River and make it home undetected.

Of course, taking off would mean dragging Susie and Lucy along and possibly even running them over, which while appealing, seemed a lot more serious than an unfounded accusation of theft.

Except that as Solange, Simone, and Chanel they wouldn't be able to defend themselves. Or show any ID.

Amanda's life flashed before her eyes. She pictured it ending in a high speed chase, the video on all the nightly news programs. OJ had had his Bronco. The de Papillons could find their fifteen minutes of fame in their bright yellow vacuummobile.

She was still pondering these horrible case scenarios when Susie reached her hand inside the car to grab hold of, well, Amanda never knew what she was reaching for, but what she got was Solange's wig.

"Oh my God!" Susie shouted as she pulled Solange's dark curls aloft.

"Oh my God!" Amanda, Brooke, and Candace shouted as the police car screeched to a halt and two armed policemen raced toward them with their guns drawn.

"*Mere de Dieu!*" Lucy shouted.

The cops just shouted, "Freeze!"

chapter 27

Well, at least they didn't strip-search us," Candace said when they were finally allowed to leave the Cobb County Adult Detention Center five long hours after they'd arrived in the back of a police van.

"That might have been the only thing that would have shut Susie up," Amanda said. "She's still insisting we stole her money and jewelry. If she hadn't created such a scene, we wouldn't have been hauled in in the first place."

And fingerprinted, and photographed.

"It's a good thing they put her in a separate holding cell; I was ready to tear her from limb to limb," Candace said.

This was what prison did to a woman.

They were limp with exhaustion and drenched in disbelief as Hap and Dan escorted them through the lobby of the building toward freedom. Candace had insisted on paying her bail, so Amanda had used her phone call to reach Rob and ask him to meet the kids at the house. So far she'd kept the details sketchy. But she simply couldn't believe this had happened. Arrested! Put in a holding cell. Let out on bond!

"Why do you think they took my shoelaces? Did they really think I could hang myself with them?" Candace asked numbly.

"I don't know," Amanda replied. "Did they give them back? A quick hanging by shoelace is sounding awfully appealing." She looked down at her bedraggled disguise. "I'll never be able to go out in public again."

"You?" Brooke gasped. "They photographed me on the way in with that horrible mole on my face!"

Hap had his arm around Brooke's shoulder, but even though her face had been scrubbed of her disguise and the wig removed, he kept looking at her as if he didn't recognize her.

Dan appeared somewhat amused, but so far both men had kept surprisingly quiet.

Candace groaned. "I'm finished," she said. "My mother will probably have me committed to an insane asylum— right after she disavows any knowledge of my existence."

Dan smiled.

"Please God"—Candace raised her eyes heavenward— "don't let this story leak out of east Cobb. I'll never be able to travel south of 285 again."

Brooke cast a fearful look at Hap, and Amanda knew what she was thinking. She leaned over to whisper words of reassurance in Brooke's ear.

At the entrance they paused to gather themselves. Amanda felt incredibly weary. She had no idea how Rob would react, but she was more worried about Meghan and Wyatt. They were going to hate this and, possibly, her. And all that she'd tried to build to protect them would undoubtedly come crashing down.

She was pathetic and about to become a laughingstock; a grown woman running around in disguise cleaning other people's houses. And how many of her current clients were going to want Amanda Sheridan cleaning their homes instead of Solange de Papillon?

A crowd waited out front. There was a news van with the satellite dish raised high.

Candace slung an arm around Amanda's shoulder. "Hang in there," she said. "We'll get through this. We may have to change our names and move to another country. But we'll survive."

"I can't afford to move to another country. And after this I won't be able to afford to live here either. What in the world were we thinking?" Amanda asked.

With Hap and Dan trying to run interference, they stepped out of the building and into bedlam.

"Hey!" someone shouted. "There they are! It's the Desperate Housewives!"

The mob surged toward them and more flashbulbs went off. "Why the disguises?" someone shouted. "Are you a ring of thieves or a den of housekeepers?"

There was laughter.

A television reporter with his cameraman tight beside him called out, "Look this way! Can you tell the *Live at Five* audience why you did this?"

Their heads turned and Amanda could just imagine how they probably looked—bedraggled and guilty; three suburban housewives who'd gotten their jollies masquerading as French maids.

Hap and Dan shoved their arms forward to hold the reporters off and escorted them through the crowd to the parking lot.

Hap and Brooke left. Amanda slipped into the backseat of Dan's car behind Candace. She felt limp as a wet dishrag, with barely enough energy to speak.

"What both of you need is a nice hot shower and a meal," Dan said jovially. "I'd also recommend a couple of shots of whiskey."

Candace turned to him. "How can you joke at a time like this?"

"How can I not?" He leaned over and placed a kiss on the top of Candace's head that made Amanda feel even more alone. "I'm sure you're going to explain this in your own good time. I don't see that any real harm's been done, other than to your pride."

Candace just groaned. "How did I end up dating such a happy-go-lucky optimist? You have no idea what lies ahead."

"What do you think's going to happen now?" asked Amanda. "I mean with the business."

Candace shook her head. "I don't know for sure," she said. "But I don't see how Maid for You can survive as long as Susie keeps shouting 'theft.' I think we need to be prepared for the worst."

It was pretty hard to imagine anything worse than what she'd just been through, but as it turned out, she was wrong.

Because when they pulled up in front of Amanda's house, every light was on inside and parked right beside

Rob's car in the driveway, was her parents' shiny new motor home.

"Do you want us to come in with you?" Candace asked.

Yes, actually, she did. But the exhaustion was clearly etched on Candace's face and there was nothing Dan or Candace could do that was going to make this any smoother. "Thanks for the offer. But I'm afraid I'm going to have to tough this one out alone."

Drawing a deep breath, Amanda let herself into the house. Her entire family was gathered in the foyer waiting for her.

They stared at each other for a long moment, all of them sharing a similar look of amazed horror. Dumbly she kept thinking that her parents were supposed to have called before they came. As if she might have picked another day to get arrested.

"So," Amanda finally said. "I gather you've all heard about my business venture."

Meghan's eyes were red and swollen. Her gaze swept over Amanda, taking in the uniform, the crumpled wig clutched in her hands, the streaked remains of Solange's heavy makeup. Amanda kept her chin up, but she could feel herself trembling.

"And a few other things you failed to mention," her mother admonished, nodding at Rob. "I wish you'd taken us into your confidence, Amanda. We could have helped."

Her mother stepped forward and hugged her fiercely. Her father did the same.

Tears she'd been holding off all day clouded her vision. "I just couldn't tell you," she said. "I was so ashamed."

"Tell me about it," Meghan scoffed. "I thought Lucy was

making it up when she called, but you've actually been cleaning her toilets. And mopping Samantha James's floors." Her daughter's voice rang with horror. "We saw it on *Live at Five*! I can't believe you did this to me." She shook her head in distress. "I won't be able to show my face in public!"

Amanda's cheeks stung as if she'd been slapped. The unfairness of it was a sharp, clean stab to the heart. Before she could form a response, Meghan was already up the stairs and slamming her bedroom door behind her.

Wyatt considered her, his expression somber. "It *is* gross, Mom, picking up after all those people. Wasn't there something else you could do?" Head hanging, he, too, went to his bedroom, leaving her with Rob and her parents.

Trying to gather herself, Amanda looked past them at the home she'd gone to such lengths to save. Had all her hard work been wasted? All her subterfuge for nothing?

Thoughts of all she'd done to spare her children, to protect them, washed over her. She'd been prepared to face disapproval and even ridicule, but not from her children. That they could condemn her so easily and with such little regard for her feelings, was the worst cut of all.

Rob all but shuffled his feet; his discomfort was palpable. But whether he was uncomfortable because her parents were there or embarrassed at what she'd been doing, she didn't know and didn't have the energy to ask.

"I'll pick up the kids in the morning and keep them for a few days until things blow over," he said. "I, uh, I'm sorry I put you in a position that forced you to do something like this. I, uh . . ." He paused then seemed to think better of what he was going to say. "I'm sorry."

They watched him leave.

Numb, Amanda turned to her parents. "I'm going upstairs," she said. "I'm sorry you walked in on all of this, but I just can't talk about it anymore right now."

Weary, she climbed the stairs, hauling herself and the twin weights of hurt and humiliation with her. In the sanctuary of her bedroom, she stripped off Solange's uniform, laid her wig and hooped earrings on the dresser, and wiped off the rest of her disguise.

She stood in the shower under the hot spray of water wielding the loofah with all her might, trying to rid her body of jail and humiliation and everything else that had happened to her that day.

Her limbs were heavy, her head throbbed. As she pulled on her pajamas, the phone rang continuously but she didn't pick it up. Whether her parents were fielding the calls or letting them go to voice mail she didn't know or care.

There was a knock on her bedroom door. At her invitation, her mother entered. Without asking she pulled back the comforter and top sheet and fluffed Amanda's pillow.

Amanda wanted to weep; this time with gratitude.

"Oh, Mom," she said as her mother actually tucked her into bed. "Everything is so messed up. I feel like I've failed at everything."

"Hush." Her mother smoothed her hair back as she had when she was a little girl then lowered herself to sit beside Amanda on the bed. "The only thing that I can see you should have done differently is let us help you. When I think of how desperate you must have felt." She shuddered. "We would have been here in a heartbeat."

"I wanted to tell you. I was going to tell you before you

got here. It's just that you and Daddy have such a successful marriage; I couldn't admit mine was such a shambles."

Her mother looked down at her, her expression regretful. "Oh, honey. Our marriage hasn't been so perfect. I love your father dearly, but no marriage is always smooth."

"But I never heard you fight." Amanda sniffed. "And I'm fairly certain Daddy didn't take up with anyone named Tiffany."

Her mother smiled, but it was tinged with irony. "That's because I was always so careful not to let you overhear anything. Maybe I was wrong not to let you see the reality, but my parents took such delight in shouting at each other that I always thought they were on the verge of splitting up. It was awful." Her smile turned sad at the memory. "I swore I'd never do that around any child of mine—no matter what the provocation.

"There were no Tiffanys, but we had our share of problems. I almost left your father a thousand times. A couple of times I actually did."

"I don't remember you going anywhere." Amanda searched her store of childhood memories, but there was nothing.

"Well." She smiled ruefully. "I usually came back before you got home from school." She smoothed Amanda's hair one more time. "But my point is no marriage is without its share of trouble. What you have to decide is whether yours is salvageable or not. And if it's not, we're behind you."

"I wish the same could be said for my children."

Her mother sighed. "They're teenagers and being embarrassed in front of their friends feels like a fate worse than death. They'll get over it. But you have to be straight with them. No more hiding or disguises. What you did, you did for them, and if I were you, I'd make sure they understand that. Even if you have to kick a little butt in the telling."

Amanda smiled at the image. Right now though the only thing she could even contemplate was sleep.

"Good night, sweetheart." Her mother cupped her chin and kissed Amanda's cheek. "Sleep tight. Tomorrow is soon enough to start figuring things out."

She reached over to unplug the phone then left the bedroom, closing the door behind her.

Amanda pulled the covers up over her head and burrowed into the muffled darkness. It wasn't exactly the Bat Cave, but it would do.

Candace's mother was also waiting for her at her house when she and Dan arrived. The sight of her car in the drive sent Candace's stomach lurching.

"Oh, God. I can't take this right now," she whispered.

"Come on." Dan walked around the car, opened her door, and helped her out. "I'm not afraid of Hurricane Hannah. And you shouldn't be either."

Dan put his arm around her and escorted her to the front door. She felt weak and shaken, every one of her emotions practically straining against her skin. She hadn't even gotten the key out of her purse when the door swung open.

Her mother looked her up and down, took in the soiled pants suit, the heavy makeup, the wig sticking out of her purse. "It's true then. When Myra called me and told me she'd just seen you on *Live at Five,* I thought she was joking."

She stepped back so they could enter, but she barely

spared a glance for Dan. All of her considerable energies were focused on her daughter.

Candace, who hadn't shed a tear in front of her mother since her turbulent teenage years, wanted desperately to cry.

"To think that my daughter would parade around pretending to be a maid—and a French maid at that! Picking up people's dirty clothing!" She shuddered. "Scrubbing their toilets!"

Candace felt an urge to throw up—she always felt nauseous these days—but she was too busy trying not to cry to give in to it.

"If it'll make you feel any better," she said, "I never actually scrubbed Susie Simmons's toilet. I mostly knelt in front of it."

Hannah Bloom's look of horror grew. Turning, she focused on Dan for the first time. "Of course it would be you."

Her words vibrated with disapproval. Candace could practically see her mother replaying the whole Irish routine in her head. Scrubbing toilets AND an Irish boyfriend. If she were Hannah Bloom, which would she find more troubling?

"And what do you make of my daughter's behavior, Daniel?" her mother asked in a deceptively friendly tone, by which Candace was not deceived.

Candace wanted to sit down before her knees buckled. Or go screaming from the room—either action would have suited her at the moment. Instead she cowered under Dan's arm, a ready-to-weep, emotional basket case. What in the world was wrong with her?

"I think she's fabulous," Dan said without hesitation. Or,

fortunately, an Irish lilt. "She stepped up to help a friend when a friend was in need. I'd think as a mother you'd be proud that you'd raised a child who would do that."

"She's made us both a complete laughingstock, is what she's done," Hannah countered. "I don't know what's come over her."

Neither did Candace. But Dan didn't seem bothered by this. In fact, for someone so mellow, his voice was infused with a surprising amount of certainty. "Of course, Candace isn't exactly a child anymore is she, Mrs. Bloom?" He pulled Candace closer to his side while Hannah glared at both of them. "She's forty-two. I'd say that's old enough to make her own decisions."

This of course was the point at which Candace should have straightened beside him and shouted out her own emancipation proclamation. "Free at last! Free at last! Great God almighty, I'm free at last!" But she was so used to judging herself through the filter of her mother's approval that she didn't know how to stop. And she couldn't tear her gaze from her mother's face.

To her abject horror the tears she'd been holding back burst free in a scalding torrent. They flowed down her cheeks like lava from a volcano, taking the last particles of Chanel's heavy makeup with them.

"Look what you've done to her," her mother scolded Dan. "Look what she's been reduced to."

Putting his hands on her shoulders, he turned Candace to face him. The tears washed down her face and splashed onto the marble floor. A small puddle seemed to be forming at her feet.

"All I've done is love her."

They all stood there absorbing that.

"Candace," he said quietly, ignoring her mother as she fervently wished she could. "Look at me." He placed a finger under her chin and tilted her face up so that her eyes met his. "Tell me what you want to happen right now. Should we ask your mother to leave?"

This sounded like an incredibly wonderful idea. Because then she could collapse into Dan's arms and ask him whether he'd actually meant to say the "L" word to her. Or whether it was just a ploy to drive her mother out of the house.

But she couldn't seem to find the strength to answer. Nor could she avoid turning to see the expressions now flitting across her mother's face. There was hurt and horror and ultimately a look that said, "I gave you life and everything else. You cannot turn your back on me."

It was the "I gave you life" look that did her in.

Sadly, Candace shook her head. "I can't do that."

Dan looked deeply into her eyes. After a long moment he dropped his hands from her shoulders and took a step away.

"Your mother has her own life and friends. Don't you think you're entitled to the same?" he asked her, still quietly, though she knew her mother was straining to hear. "It's time to grow up, Candace." His smile was almost as soft as his voice. "And I meant it when I said that I love you."

Then he moved toward the door and put his hand on the knob. "When you're ready to live your own life, give me a call."

And then she was staring at his back as the door closed behind her.

Aghast at what she'd just done, or rather failed to do, she turned back to face her mother and caught the look of triumph that spread across her face.

Her final thought, just before she raced to the bathroom to throw up, was how lucky Brooke Mackenzie was that her mother wasn't around to muck up her life.

chapter 28

It was an indication of how rattled Brooke was that she actually wished her mother was there on the long silent ride home.

She at least would have understood why her daughter had made up such a carefully crafted new identity and just how appalled she was that it had been jeopardized.

Amanda's advice played in her head. But she didn't see how she could possibly tell Hap the truth now when he was looking at her the way he was. What were the chances that someone from her distant past would see her in the paper and feel a need to point out the irony? No, her old secret was safe if she could just ride this out. So people would turn up their noses at her for this little escapade. As long as Hap didn't, she'd find a way to tough it out.

Whenever they hit a red light or a stop sign, he turned to consider her. But he never actually said anything. He'd just look at her and then slowly shake his head as if to say, "Doesn't she beat all?"

By the time they pulled into the driveway, she couldn't take the silence anymore. She needed him to speak, even if she didn't like what he said.

When they entered the house, Tyler was lounging on the couch watching TV. "Hey," he called out, "I saw you on *Live at Five*. Which one were you, Chanel or Simone?"

She didn't bother to answer. Instead she took Hap's hand and drew him along with her. In the bedroom, she closed the door and turned to face him. "Aren't you going to speak to me?" she demanded. "I swear if you shake your head at me one more time, I'm going to jump out of my skin."

Hap blinked in surprise, as well he might. Never once since the day they'd met had she ever raised her voice in his presence. As Amanda had pointed out, he didn't know her at all.

"I've been trying to figure out what to say, but nothing seems to come to mind," he admitted. "I actually think it was nice of you to try to help Amanda. But you look so not like you in that getup. And you're not acting like yourself either. I mean dressing up like a cleaning woman and mopping other people's floors? I've never even seen you with a dust rag in your hand. I can't imagine how you could ever bluff your way through something like that. Didn't any of your clients complain?"

He laughed and it was then that she knew she had to tell him. Because she loved him and wanted him to love her. But the real her, not the cleaned and sanitized version.

It hit her then like the proverbial ton of bricks, though it had, in fact, taken her nearly thirty years to figure it out.

Her mother had not been a failure; she'd been a strong woman like Amanda, who had done what was necessary to take care of her child. There was no shame in that. Brooke would not be ashamed any longer. Not of her mother or herself.

She looked Hap in the eye and it was as if someone turned on a water tap: the truth simply began to pour out. "I wasn't bluffing, Hap. I'm an expert with a mop and a broom. I come from a long line of cleaning women."

She told him everything then. About how far and how hard she'd run. How difficult it had been to offer to help Amanda. Because she had been so afraid of this very thing.

"But I can't be silent anymore," she said when she'd run out of words. "I love you. More than anything. And I hope to Hell you'll still love me now that you know where I came from."

She stared into his eyes, willing him to understand.

"Wow." Hap shook his head as if to clear it. "I just can't seem to take it all in." He sank down on the side of the bed and considered her carefully. But the smile of love and acceptance she was waiting for didn't come.

"How am I supposed to know which parts of you are real and which aren't?" he asked finally.

"I'll tell you anything you want to know, Hap. Really, I will. But you already know my deepest darkest secret. My mother is a maid. And so was my grandmother." She was trying for a light tone but couldn't quite pull it off as her panic rose. "It's not exactly a criminal offense, is it? I mean I've always treated it as if it was, but it isn't, right?"

Why was he sitting so still, his face so devoid of expression when she was dying for him to smile and take her in his arms and tell her it didn't matter?

"And are you and your mother actually . . . estranged?" Hap asked. His tone, like his voice, was frighteningly neutral. "Or is that just part of the fairy tale too?"

"Not formally. I just don't see her too often." She dropped her gaze. "And I didn't think you'd want to be obligated to have a relationship with her."

"Even though she's your mother."

It sounded so wrong the way he said it. As if she'd been trying to do anything but save him from embarrassment. "Well, she's uneducated. And quite young—she was only sixteen when she had me. And she, um, drinks too much." Her heart was thudding painfully in her chest. She wanted to scoop up all the words she'd poured out and stuff them back inside her. Anything to have Hap back, instead of this unemotional stranger.

"But she's your mother and you didn't trust me to know her." This, too, was delivered in a calm, measured tone, but she could hear the undercurrent of accusation all too clearly.

Her head snapped up. "It wasn't like that. It was . . ." Her voice trailed off.

"It sounds exactly like that to me, Brooke. You say you love me, but you don't have enough faith in my love for you to believe I could accept your less-than-idyllic background?"

"No, I . . ."

He stood and moved toward the closet. "I already had one marriage to a woman who didn't trust me. I believe I mentioned that to you when we met." When had Hap

Mackenzie become such a king of understatement? Each simple pronouncement carried the weight of a shout. Or maybe that was just her guilty conscience?

"There is no element in marriage more important than trust. At least not to me."

"Oh, Hap, I . . ."

"I've got to run Tyler to his mother's now. And I think I might stay over at the club for a bit, to sort of think things out." He pulled out his overnighter and stuffed some clothing into it while she watched, speechless. Then he opened the door and prepared to walk through it. "I do love you, Brooke. At least, I've always believed I do. But I'm not too sure how we get past this. Maybe we both need to give it a little time and thought."

Then he was gone, taking Tyler with him. And Brooke was left in the perfect house with the picket fence all alone.

On Sunday morning a shot of the three musketeers—taken as they entered the detention center, before they'd had a chance to remove their disguises—ran on page one of the *Atlanta Journal-Constitution.*

Brooke stared at the hairy mole on her face, which was impossible to miss given its position just above the front page fold.

The caption carried their full names along with their cleaning aliases. The headline screamed,

DESPERATE HOUSEWIVES DON DISGUISES
AND CLEAN UNSUSPECTING FRIENDS'
HOMES!

The cancellations came fast and furious. Candace thought afterward that the clients called not out of courtesy but because they were afraid if they didn't, the three of them might actually show up. Susie was still claiming to anyone who would listen that they had stolen from her, even though they'd been arrested for disturbing the peace—as had Susie—and not for theft.

There were only two clients who hadn't canceled so far; Candace's neighbor, Sylvia Hardaway, who had informed Candace that "I don't care whether she's French or Albanian. She does a damn fine job and she thinks I have style." And Hunter James, who Amanda figured was still out of town and hadn't yet heard the sordid news. And who, she said pointedly, had apparently gone somewhere on earth where they didn't have phones.

So all three of them laid low that week, dealing as best they could with the specters that had risen to haunt them. The vacuummobile sat in Candace's garage, its shiny yellow paint dimming under a light layer of dust.

To add insult to injury, Candace had absolutely no appetite but still seemed to be putting on weight. And Dan didn't call, though she'd fallen into the habit of sitting by the phone wishing that he would. Nor were there invitations to lunch or to functions. Her phone remained accusingly silent.

Toward the end of the week, her mother reappeared. Hannah's brown eyes were determined and her mouth was set in a grim line. Two trips to the hinterlands in one week had to be some sort of record, but this time Candace was too uncomfortable and too miserable to comment.

"What's wrong with you?" her mother asked. "You look awful."

"Thank you." It didn't help that she knew her mother was right.

"You can't just lie around like your world is coming to an end. You need to get out there, start dating, hold up your head."

Only she couldn't and didn't want to. And it seemed like her life was, in fact, over. For once nothing her mother said made any difference. Candace felt thick and mule-like; the more her mother talked, the more obstinate she felt.

Hannah walked over to stand next to the couch Candace was lying on and peered down at her. "I'm going to call Dr. Epstein and make you an appointment."

"I'm not sick. I'm just tired." And unhappy. And lonely.

"Well, I won't have it." Hannah all but stamped her size six foot. "No daughter of mine is going to moon over some silly Irishman like he was the catch of the century."

Her mother wouldn't have it? Candace thought she must have misunderstood. After all she'd given up, her mother expected to control her mood as well?

Then Candace woke up. She still felt queasy and uncomfortable, but the flash of anger buoyed her. She sat up on the couch and looked at her mother.

"You won't have it?" she asked.

They both froze in shock at Candace's incredulous tone. This time Candace recovered first. "You think you can decide what I feel and for how long?" She stood and stepped up to her mother. Even in her bare feet, she towered over her. "You told me it was you or him and I did what I've always done, I chose you. But that's not enough for you, is it?

You have to control every little thing, every thought, every action." Her rage began to grow. In the span of a few minutes, it dwarfed them both. She was tired of doing what her mother told her. Tired to death of living the life her mother thought she should live.

Dan Donovan was right. She was way too old for this shit. "You know," Candace finally said, "I'm not sure how we got this way." She lowered her voice and took a step away. "But I don't think it's good for either of us. You've got too much power. And I've got too little. It's time for things to be more balanced."

"I haven't the faintest idea what you're talking about." Hannah tried to maintain her imperious tone, but Candace could tell that she was shaken. Never once in forty-two years had she spoken to her mother this way.

"Well, you don't really have to understand all the details," Candace pointed out more calmly. "What matters is I'm ready to live my own life and make my own choices. And if that happens to include an Irishman with a fair to middlin' amount of ambition, so be it."

"Candace, darling, you can't be serious. Why . . ."

But Candace was already taking her mother's arm and escorting her toward the front door. "But I am, Mother. I'm as serious as a heart attack."

They were in the foyer. Candace opened the door and motioned her mother through it. "Thank you so much for stopping by. I'm really feeling much better now." Happily this was the truth. "But in the future if you want to visit, I'd really appreciate it if you'd call ahead and make sure that it's convenient."

There was a gasp of indignation and a "Well, I never!"

And then Hannah Bloom swept out the front door and down the flagstone walk.

Wishing that Dan had been there to see her kick tush, Candace watched her mother leave.

Brooke sat in her perfect house trying to enjoy the perfect silence. But all it felt was empty without Hap in it. She walked through the rooms, all neatly arranged and oppressively tidy. She never thought she'd say it, but she even missed Tyler.

She talked with Amanda and Candace every day, but other than her daily workout, she was completely alone. She had no idea what she could do to convince Hap of her love and trust in him. If he expected her to bring her mother to meet him or, worse yet, take him to the double-wide she'd once called home, he'd be waiting for a lifetime.

But there must be some way to introduce him to the real her without frightening him too much.

In the bedroom she found herself on her knees next to the bed, feeling around underneath it. When her fingers felt metal, she grasped on to the handle and pulled out her steamer trunk; the one she'd taken with her to college. It was old and banged up, but it had been her first personal possession and at the time that her mother had bought it for her, it had been shiny and new, symbolic of all that lay ahead of her and all that she couldn't wait to leave behind.

She opened it now, and looked through the things inside smiling over some of the sillier mementos, shaking her head over others and wondering what had made them seem important enough to keep. The ticket for her first university football game, her cafeteria pass, all four of her University of Georgia yearbooks.

Underneath all that was a cigar box that she'd gotten when she was five. It had always been the repository of her most prized possessions; there hadn't been many and they'd easily fit.

As she removed the rumpled reminders and the bent-cornered pictures, she had an idea. Her heart beating with hope for the first time since Hap had left, she spread them out on the coverlet and began arranging the photos in order, from the shot of her as a wailing baby in her teenage mother's arms to the auburn-haired college girl clad in cap and gown. There weren't a lot of photos—hers had not been a picture-snapping, vacation-taking life—but still they told a story. Going to their wedding album, she pulled out her favorite shots from both the simple ceremony and their honeymoon in St. Barts.

Later that day she went out and purchased a grainy leather photo album in which she arranged the story of her life.

Then she picked up the phone and punched in her husband's cell phone number.

Rob came over the night before Amanda's parents left. His excuse was to drop something off for the kids, but not even Meghan and Wyatt were fooled. He stayed to have dinner with them, a meal that almost captured the sense of family they'd once had, and then asked to speak to Amanda alone when her mother and the children began to clear the dishes.

They went out on the back deck, completely aware that the eyes of the family were glued on them. Amanda walked to the railing and turned her back on the house. Rob came to stand beside her. Together they stared out over the trees of the wooded backyard.

"I imagine you have some idea of what I'd like to talk about." Rob wiped his hands on the sides of his pants and cleared his throat, and she realized just how nervous he was.

Her own palms turned sweaty and her pulse kicked up a notch, but she just cocked her head in his direction and waited for him to speak.

"I, uh, have some good news," he said. "It looks like the position with the real estate developer is a done deal. I'm going to have a base salary, plus a lot of growth potential. It'll take a while, but I'll have a chance to get back on my feet."

"That's great, Rob." She felt a burst of relief as she realized that some of the financial pressure would lessen. Between what Rob would be able to pay and what her parents insisted on loaning her, she'd still need to work but she would no longer be facing imminent eviction.

"Yeah. I can't tell you how relieved I am that I won't be driving a garbage truck like Anne Justiss suggested." He smiled, but it was forced.

She studied her husband, knowing what was coming next, wondering why she didn't feel more excitement at the prospect. "So, um, I was wondering if you'd have me back. Maybe let me move in and see if we can start over again."

She waited for her heart to swell with happiness, or her feet to break into a little happy dance, but the request didn't even generate a sigh of relief.

Her mind said she should be happy that her husband

wanted to come back to her. Her bruised and bloodied heart wanted to know why.

"What's happened to Tiffany?" she asked.

Rob shifted uncomfortably beside her. His gaze was locked on a scraggly fir tree. "She's gone," he said.

Now there was an interesting bit of news.

"Gone out of town?" she asked. "Gone on a trip? Gone from your life?"

"Yes." He turned and tried to look her in the eye, but he sort of caught a part of her shoulder and the edge of her earlobe. "All of those things."

She did not, she realized, really want to know this. But she felt compelled to ask. "And if she hadn't left you, would you still want to come home?"

She held her breath while she waited for his response. She didn't have to wait long.

"Yes. I screwed up and I dragged you all through my mess, but I'm sorry and I want to come back."

He spoke without hesitation, finally meeting her eye, his voice ringing with conviction. But Tiffany's defection rankled. How would she ever know whether what he was saying was true? And if she did take him back, how would she know that there wouldn't be another Tiffany?

She felt like she was getting a really great price on a used car—a car she wasn't even sure was right for her anymore.

She looked more closely at the man who was still technically her husband. What she saw was a man who had left her for another woman; a man who'd been able to walk away from his children because his panicked libido was stronger than his paternal commitment. She saw the officer of the court who had cheated his clients out of money and never really been forced to pay.

"What's the matter?" he asked, puzzled. "I thought you'd be excited about getting back together."

"Yeah," she said, feeling almost as puzzled as he sounded. "So did I."

Meghan would be thrilled if Rob came home and so would Wyatt. If for no other reason, she should be saying yes right now. She opened her mouth to speak, but she couldn't make the words come out.

He'd trampled on their love and treated them as if they didn't matter. And now that Tiffany had left him, she was supposed to quiver with joy and welcome him back into the fold.

She took a step back as the realization struck her.

She might be able to interface with Rob Sheridan on a surface level, but she could never really trust him again. Her well of love for him had been sucked dry.

"I know it would make Meghan and Wyatt happy," she said as she struggled to come to grips with her decision.

His face lit up and he took a step closer.

She surprised them both when she put a hand out to stop him. "But that's not reason enough for us to be together."

They studied each other in the falling twilight. This day had reached its end. Tomorrow would be brand new. "You'll still be their father, Rob, whatever house you live in. And I hope you'll be a good one." She looked him deep in the eye. "But . . ."

"Amanda," he said, interrupting, "you can't seriously mean to say no." It was clear he couldn't fathom that she would choose to be alone rather than with him. She was kind of blown away by that fact too.

"I expect I should be grateful for the offer," she said at last as the day faded all the way to black. "But I think I'm going to have to pass."

chapter 29

The idea of driving to a distant ballpark on Sunday and sitting in the stands while everyone talked about her was about as appealing to Amanda as double root canals. Rob had the kids and was taking them to the game, but she'd be bringing them home with her. Still, she was more than reluctant to expose herself to public scrutiny. She couldn't figure out why Brooke and Candace appeared so eager to get there.

"Remind me why we're going to this game today?" she asked.

"Because your son is pitching and nobody, especially Susie Simmons, sends the three musketeers into hiding."

"Right." The idea of seeing all those people and them seeing her made Amanda's stomach churn.

"You have absolutely nothing to be ashamed of," Candace reminded her.

"I know. I keep telling myself that. But somebody needs

to convince my children," Amanda groaned. She and Meghan had been in a state of armed truce since her parents had driven off in their motor home.

"I would, but they need to hear it from you," Candace said.

Brooke checked her watch for about the twentieth time. She was lugging a carryall with something bulky inside.

"You two look like you've got something up your sleeves," Amanda observed.

Brooke smiled. "Let's just say if everything goes well, Candace and I won't need a ride home."

When they arrived at the field, the game was already underway. Trailing behind Candace and Brooke, Amanda felt like a condemned prisoner being led to the gas chamber.

Everyone stared and their gazes on her were like a physical thing, heavy and pervasive. Refusing to look away or down at her feet, Amanda raised her chin and looked each one of them in the eye. A few of them turned away or dropped their gazes. Susie Simmons glared at her then leaned over to whisper something to Karen Anderson. There was laughter.

She wanted to get in Susie's face and remind her that she, too, had been arrested. She imagined standing up and expounding on all the embarrassing and petty things she'd learned about the people who thought they were superior to her. She glared back at Susie Simmons and realized with a sudden flash of clarity that that was probably what they feared most.

Meghan sat beside her father, her gaze on her fingernails. Amanda willed her to look up and meet her gaze, but she kept her head down and hid behind a curtain of long dark hair. Rob waved hello, a small friendly gesture that made her breathe a tiny sigh of relief.

Candace and Brooke slowed slightly as they passed the Mudhens' dugout, and if Amanda wasn't mistaken, the two were clearly, and pointedly, strutting their stuff. Dan and Hap watched them go by.

Amanda raised a hand in greeting to Wyatt. He didn't turn away, but he didn't come over to the fence to speak to her either. He watched her move toward the stands, his eyes overlarge in his face, then turned his attention back to the field.

Amanda told herself it didn't matter. Somehow she'd find the right words to make her children understand. They were hurt and angry. But, she realized, so was she. In her effort to protect them, she'd forgotten to protect herself.

When they reached the stands Amanda turned her attention to the game, which seemed to be going slightly better than her life. The score was tied, but when his teammates took the field, Wyatt warmed the bench. He sat much like she did, with his shoulders straight and his chin tilted at a stubborn angle. But she doubted he was as focused on the game as he pretended. Or that he and Meghan were any more immune to the stares and whispers than she was.

"Hey, Broom Lady!" The shout came from the back of the stands. "I dropped my burger. Do you want to come clean it up? Or maybe your daughter would like to do it!"

Amanda's head snapped up and she swiveled in her seat. Behind her, Meghan, at whom the taunt had also been aimed, sat frozen in her seat while Rob glared at a teenage boy Amanda didn't recognize. She wanted to go up there and smack the boy silly. Or grab him by the ear and drag him from the bleachers and out of the ballpark.

"Jerk." Candace put a hand on her shoulder.

"Yeah, but look at that," Brooke said.

As they watched, Rob got up and walked over to the boy. He leaned down and said something. A moment later, the boy got up and skulked off. Rob went back to his seat and put an arm around Meghan. After a few moments, talk resumed.

Two innings later, Amanda was still trying to calm down. Her thoughts flitted from problem to problem, as her brain worried at them seeking solutions; how to straighten things out with the kids, how she might get Maid for You back on track now that Susie's accusations had derailed it, her surprising decision not to take Rob back. Where in the world Hunter James had disappeared to.

A collective groan drew Amanda's attention back to the action on the field. The Mudhens were now up by two runs but the other team had the bases loaded.

"Riley walked the last two," Candace said, pointing toward the Mudhens' pitcher. "And that's their number five hitter coming up."

"We've got two outs on them. We need to get out of this inning. Now." Brooke, too, had become a real fount of baseball knowledge.

"Definitely time for a pitching change," Brooke observed, swiveling in her seat. "Do you think he'll warm up Wyatt?"

Amanda searched the dugout for Wy.

"He's over there," Candace said, pointing to the sidelines where Wyatt was, in fact, already throwing to Drew.

Dan called time then walked out to the mound. He slung his arm around Riley Calhoun and clapped him on the back. The boy handed Dan the ball and headed off the field.

Wyatt began a slow, agonizing jog to the pitcher's mound. Drew Donovan came in to catch for him.

There were whispers. Someone laughed. She felt movement on the bleacher beside her, and Rob, with Meghan in tow, sat down in the vacant space beside her. Meghan still didn't speak, but Rob's presence signaled his support. And gave her hope that even divorced, they could still be a family unit.

Amanda's gaze returned to their son. When he turned to face the plate, the fear in his eyes was evident, and she knew what he was thinking. Maybe his improved pitching was a fluke. Maybe he couldn't do it again. Maybe this guy was going to hit a grand slam and bring in four more runs.

Drew Donovan squatted behind the plate. The batter stepped out of the box so that Wyatt could take his warm-up pitches from the mound. One skidded past Drew in the dirt. Another flew over his head.

Amanda closed her eyes and offered up a small prayer. When she opened them, she saw Rob doing the same.

"He's going to be fine, Amanda," Rob said. "All he needs to do is put his head in the right place."

She hoped with all her heart that Rob was right. She willed Wyatt to tune out the chanting for "one more out" that rose from the stands.

The pressure was palpable. As she often did, she wished she could go out and pull him from the mound and rescue him from the possibility of failure.

But there was no place in baseball for self-doubt. As in

life, it was Kilimanjaro and Everest combined. It could fell the most ardent climber.

It was so much easier to avoid potential failure and embarrassment, much easier to take a flatter, more circuitous path. But sometimes, Amanda realized as she watched her son, you had no choice. Sometimes the mountain sat right in front of you and you had to scale it. Even if you did little more than cling to the rock face and inch your way up, you had to commit to the climb.

Just as she had when she created Solange and began cleaning houses. And as she had the other night when she'd turned down Rob's offer.

Wyatt finished his practice pitches and waited for the hitter to step into the batter's box. Drawing a deep breath, he angled his body and brought his arms down into the set position.

She held her breath as he stepped back and began his motion. She was still holding it when he threw his first pitch.

The batter swung and missed.

"Yes!" Brooke and Candace shouted in unison.

"That a boy!" Rob called out beside her.

Amanda exhaled. Four words repeated themselves over and over in her mind. *You can do it! You can do it!* Every fiber of her being was focused on sending this mental message to her child.

His next ball was his reworked changeup; the one Hunter had helped him develop. The batter missed that too.

"Oh, yeah," Amanda whispered. "That was sweet."

Amanda folded her hands in her lap and tried to still her racing heart.

The stands were quiet now as everyone watched Wyatt. He shook off the first two signals that Drew sent him then slowly nodded at the third. He was completely focused on the batter; totally committed to scaling the mountain at hand.

"He's going to use his slider," Rob said. "And he's going to sit him down with it. Our boy's a fighter."

"Yes he is," she breathed.

"Just like his mother," Rob said.

She took her gaze off Wyatt for just a moment to consider the man whose desertion had forced her to learn how to stand on her own two feet. If they were lucky, they could forge some kind of friendship that would make things easier on the kids.

Some good things had come out of the turmoil she thought now as she watched Wyatt stare down the batter. Candace and Brooke topped her list; having them covering her back had gotten her through the toughest times. Hunter James, if in fact he ever resurfaced, could be a positive. It was too bad he wasn't here today to see what his coaching had done for Wyatt.

So everyone knew that she'd been forced to clean houses. So what? So her children had been embarrassed and ridiculed. That hurt the most, but it was something they'd have to live with. So Susie had accused her of stealing and was trying to ruin her reputation. Was she just going to sit back and let that happen?

No, she was not. She wasn't finished, not by a long shot. And neither was her son.

For his third pitch, Wyatt did, as Rob had predicted, go with another off-speed pitch. His delivery was smooth and flawless. Everyone—including the batter—watched in amazement as the ball whizzed toward the inside corner, seemed to dance in midair, and then somehow swooped across the far edge of the plate.

"He's out of there!" the ump yelled.

With whoops of joy, the Mudhens surrounded Wyatt. They pounded him on the back then dragged him off the field and into the dugout. The crowd jumped to its feet.

"Oh my God," Amanda breathed, "did you see that?"

"He sure as Hell pulled it out of there," Rob said, already heading toward the dugout to congratulate Wyatt.

Brooke and Candace nodded happily. The three of them wrapped their arms around each other and just kind of swayed together.

"Somebody stop me," Candace said. "I'm feeling an irresistible urge to start the wave."

"And I," Amanda said with a smile, "am feeling an irresistible urge to clear Solange's name."

"Count us in," Candace said. "But after the game Brooke and I have our own preemptive missions to take care of. Let's rendezvous at my house tomorrow morning at oh eight hundred hours."

Amanda left the ballpark with Meghan and Wyatt. Candace squared her shoulders and headed down toward the dugout where Dan was gathering up the team gear.

Brooke kept her gaze on Hap and Tyler. Afraid they might pass her by, she moved to intersect them as they left the dugout and planted herself in a spot where they couldn't miss her.

An uncomfortable look passed over Hap's face as they drew near. Taking a tight rein on her nerves, she turned a bright smile on her stepson who at the moment seemed the most approachable.

"Great game, Tyler," she said as they drew to a stop in front of her. "That was a fantastic catch in the third inning."

"Thanks." The word was mumbled, but he did say it and looked her in the eye at the same time. For Tyler Mackenzie, what came next was the equivalent of the Gettysburg Address. "I saw the picture of you in the paper," he said, nodding his head. "That mole was *ugly*. I didn't think somebody as pretty as you could look that bad."

Brooke blinked. "Um, thanks," she said. "I think."

Hap stood behind his son watching her. It was a fine irony that after a year of unrelenting hostility it was Tyler who was waxing eloquent. Her hairy mole seemed to have made a major impression.

"I mean I've never seen anything as gross as that," Ty continued enthusiastically. "It was humongous. It needed its own zip code. It—"

"Thank you, Tyler," she said. "I think you've made your point."

Still Hap watched her.

Brooke turned to face her husband. *Please God*, she thought, *don't let him reject me. Not here. Not now.* Oh, who was she kidding? There would be no time or place that would make such a thing OK. She pushed the negative thoughts from her mind and drew herself up to her full height. It was do or die time.

"My ride seems to have left," she said to Hap. "And I, uh, have some other pictures I thought you two might like to see." She pulled the photo album out of her carryall and handed it to Hap like the present it was meant to be.

She smiled, trembling lips and all. "If you thought Simone was ugly, just wait until you get a load of the place I grew up in."

"Cool." Tyler turned to his father. "I'm starving. Can we stop at Steak n Shake and get something to eat? Maybe Brooke could show us her pictures there."

Hap looked down at the album he held in his hand and then back up at Brooke. "Sure," he said, reaching in his pocket and tossing Tyler the car keys. "Go stow your gear. I want to talk to Brooke for a minute. We'll be right behind you."

They watched him leave. Afraid of what Hap might be planning to say, Brooke rushed to speak first. Her words practically fell over themselves in her need to get them out.

"Hap," she said. "I never meant to trick you. Or lie to you."

She looked over his shoulder to the playing fields that stretched out behind him. Clean and beautifully mani-cured, they were a far cry from the hardscrabble play-grounds she'd known as a child. "But the truth is you were right. I didn't trust you." Nibbling on her lip, she forced her-self to go on. "I didn't think anyone would be able to see be-yond where I'd come from if they knew. And I was so afraid of losing you."

"Aw, Brooke." Shaking his head, he opened his arms and pulled her into them. He was big and solid and she could feel the album against her back as he held her. She thought about the pages of pictures that lay between them; what she'd always thought of as her ancient history—a separate time and place that could be sealed away and forgotten.

"I just wanted you to know who I became—without anything clouding it, you know?" she said, raising her gaze to meet his. "I want you to love the me I am now. I've spent my whole life becoming her."

Hap's smile lit his face and she loved seeing herself reflected in his eyes. "I understand," he said. "But we all carry pieces of where we came from with us, Brooke. And while I don't intend to hold your past against you, I'm glad you've decided to share it."

Relief coursed through her as he pulled her closer. They walked arm in arm toward the car where Tyler waited. Brooke drew in a deep breath of happiness and smiled up at her husband. "You know what's really strange?" she said.

"What's that?"

"That after all these years of running from my past, I seem to be following in my mother's footsteps."

"As a parent I expect she might like to hear about that." Hap gestured toward Tyler who had turned on the radio and was bopping in the backseat to a Nelly tune. The car lurched up and down to the beat.

"Speaking of your child," Brooke said, a teasing tone in her voice, "I can hardly believe what a great equalizer that hairy mole of Simone's turned out to be."

He smiled down at her as they neared the car and she could tell he was going to kiss her.

"Yeah," he said as his lips swooped down on hers. "You

can never underestimate the gross-out factor where a thirteen-year-old boy is concerned."

Candace lowered herself onto the dugout bench and watched Dan shove equipment into a bag. Drew had apparently ridden home with someone else, which should have made things easier, except that the normally affable Dan didn't look like he was planning to help her through this.

"That was a great game today," she said as a conversation opener. "The team looks like it's starting to come around."

"Yep." He continued stowing the gear, making a big deal out of fitting the lid down on the bucket of practice baseballs, picking up the stray trash.

"Wyatt's pitching was first-rate," she said, looking for some sign that he was glad to see her. "It was a nail-biter but he really came through."

"Yes he did."

She folded her arms across her chest and stared up at his cleanly chiseled face, irritated. "So what is it you want me to do now, Dan?" she asked. "Grovel? Throw myself on your mercy? Would you like to give me a little baseball quiz to see if I'm worthy?" She was starting to heat up now, the anger grabbing hold of her with a speed and intensity she wasn't prepared for. Her feelings were so close to the surface all the time now, she could hardly keep up with herself.

"You told me to come when I was ready. And here I am." She stopped talking when she heard the strident tone of her own voice. In a minute she'd be shouting. Shaking her head in disgust, she tried to calm down.

"I'm sorry," Candace said. "I seem to be so out of control lately. One minute I'm shrieking, the next I'm crying." She snorted in disbelief. "And I can't seem to hold on to a train of thought. It's like someone sucked out some of my brain cells when I wasn't looking."

Dan moved closer, a strange look on his face. "How's Hurricane Hannah?" he asked tentatively.

"I'm not sure," Candace replied. "I haven't heard from her since I threw her out of my house."

"You threw your mother out of your house?"

"Well, I didn't pick her up and toss her out bodily, though I'll admit I was tempted." The anger gone, Candace smiled at the memory. She'd felt like a prizefighter winning a first KO when she'd escorted her mother to the door. "But I did inform her that I was going to be making my own decisions from now on."

He was still contemplating her as if she were a series of numbers that didn't add up.

"And one of those decisions is you." Suddenly shy, Candace looked away, afraid that he might have somehow changed his mind while she was figuring out hers.

He came and sat next to her on the bench. They stared out through the chain-link face of the dugout as the grounds crew came out and started dragging the field.

Just when she was beginning to fear that she was, in fact, too late, he reached for her hand. "I'm impressed." He smiled full out, the same flash of white he'd used on her mother that night at the fund-raiser. "And it's glad I am that me girl has found her senses at last."

He lifted their joined hands and kissed her knuckle. She'd barely turned her lips up in a smile before tears were skidding down her cheeks.

"Are you crying?" he asked, concerned.

She rolled her tearstained eyes and sniffed, embarrassed at the raw emotion that gripped her. "I'm sorry. I don't know what's got into me." She sniffed again. "One minute I'm furious at the tollbooth operator for telling me to have a nice day and the next I'm sobbing over the lyrics to a song."

Dan shifted in his seat and his gaze became more intent. He squeezed the hand he'd just kissed. "So you're telling me that your emotions are . . . out of whack."

"Completely." She sniffed and nodded. The tears continued to roll down her face. "And I'm always nauseous or exhausted, or both. Sometimes it's so bad I can barely get off the couch."

"Does anything else seem . . . different?" Something in his voice made her look up. Suddenly she saw in his eyes the very thing she'd been afraid to even think.

"You mean like the fact that I can barely eat and I'm putting on weight?" she asked. "And that everything about me is getting . . . rounder?"

They stared at each other for a long moment there in the dugout. And then Dan Donovan's blue eyes started to twinkle.

"No," she said, shaking her head. "It's not possible. I'm too old. I've never been able to . . ."

He put a finger to her lips to shush her, and his smile was heartbreakingly gentle. "I'm not exactly an expert, Candace," he said. "I've only had one child."

"Oh, you don't think . . ."

"But I am the oldest of seven." The teasing Irish lilt was

back and his smile was blinding. She could feel the warmth of it all the way inside.

"We might want to stop by the drugstore and buy a kit for confirmation. But if I'm not mistaken, you may just have my bun warming in your oven."

chapter 30

Amanda's euphoria over Wyatt's performance and Rob's acceptance began to fade as the silence from the backseat became louder.

A glance in her rearview mirror confirmed that Wyatt still glowed from his triumph. He was undoubtedly reliving each and every pitch of the game in Technicolor in his mind.

Meghan also appeared lost in thought, but her face was closed and hard.

"Wasn't Wyatt's pitching incredible, Meg?" Amanda asked.

Meghan's face didn't change. "Yeah, it was great." Her tone was polite and . . . frigid.

Amanda felt separated from her children by more than the car seat. The outing of Solange was a three-hundred-pound elephant wedged between them. And it was nothing compared to the looming divorce from their father.

"Did you enjoy having Grandma and Grandpop here?"

"Yeah, it was great." Meghan's tone was devoid of emotion; she was clearly unwilling to give Amanda the satisfaction of real interest in anything.

Amanda sighed. She was too tired and too emotionally drained to have it out with Meghan now. But somehow she was going to have to make her children understand why she'd done what she'd done. Then she was going to have to make it clear that as much as she loved them, she would not let them sit in judgment of her.

At home, they retreated to their rooms. Amanda spent what was left of the evening girding her loins for the next day. If they were going to build a cleaning business—and she still felt Maid for You was viable even without the French connection—Susie Simmons was going to have to retract her accusations. Amanda hoped the other woman would do the right thing. Her whole attitude toward Solange seemed unwarranted and her coldness to Amanda unjustified. They'd never been best friends, but they'd always been cordial. Somewhere along the way, Susie had begun to change; Amanda didn't know why or exactly when.

Just after eleven that night, Amanda left her room to lock up downstairs. Wyatt's room was already dark. She slipped in quietly and walked over to the bed. He slept with one arm flung out in abandon. The other clamped across his stomach. Today's game ball sat on the nightstand within easy reach. He murmured softly in his sleep as she bent over to pull the covers up over him and kissed his cheek.

Meghan's door was open a crack, allowing light to spill out into the hallway. Amanda paused in a sliver of brightness. Through the opening she saw Meghan standing in front of the closet mirror, the prom dress clutched to her chest, her nightgown hidden by the silver sheath.

Meghan's face in the mirror reflected none of the joy that had shone on it when she'd come down the stairs the night of the prom. Her brown eyes were tinged with sadness and she worried her lip between her teeth.

Drawn by her daughter's unhappiness, Amanda opened the door and stepped into Meghan's room.

Their gazes met in the mirror. "How many toilets did you have to clean to pay for this dress?" Meghan asked.

Amanda moved closer. Meghan continued to hold the dress up like a shield.

"I'm sorry you were embarrassed," Amanda said quietly. "But I'm not sorry that I did what I had to do."

Meghan looked away. "I wanted this dress so badly, and I"—she glanced down at the silver sheath—"I appreciate you buying it for me."

She picked up the hanger from the bed and carefully hung the dress back on it then placed it back in the closet. She turned to face Amanda. "But wasn't there anything else you could do?"

Amanda's heart actually hurt, but she would not make excuses. "I'm afraid not," Amanda said as she moved to the door. Turning, she stood in the doorway, considering her daughter. "And if cleaning houses will allow us to keep our home and buy the occasional prom dress, I'm going to continue to do it. So I guess you're going to have to get used to it."

"But why can't Dad come home? He said he's sorry and I know he's not seeing Tiffany anymore."

"Oh, honey." Amanda closed the distance between them.

In three long strides she was there, pulling her daughter into her arms.

Meghan's body was stiff and unyielding. "I want Daddy to come home and make things like they used to be."

"I know Meg." Amanda held on tightly. "I know."

Finally Meghan shuddered in her arms and began to cry, great heaving sobs that racked them both. Amanda hung on while Meghan sobbed, letting out all the agony she'd kept so tightly inside.

Closing her eyes, Amanda simply held on and let Meghan cry. "It hurts, doesn't it? It hurts like Hell."

Time passed, Amanda didn't know how long. Nor did she care. When Meghan's sobs began to grow quieter, Amanda still hung on, rocking gently as she had when her firstborn had been small enough to hold in her arms.

They clung together in the center of the room. "I wish I could put things back the way they were for you." She smoothed back her daughter's hair and bracketed Meghan's tear-streaked face in her hands. "But things went too far. I can't live with your father again. I have to go on and build something new."

"But . . ."

"But your father is still your father and he loves you. And he's going to be there for you, Meghan. You and Wyatt can spend as much time with him as you want."

They studied each other in silence. Meghan took a step back and then she turned away.

At a loss, Amanda went to the door and stopped. "If you're finished downstairs I'm going to go down and lock up," she said over her shoulder. Then she left the room, pulling the door closed behind her.

* * *

It felt incredibly odd the next morning not to become Solange; odder still not to be headed to the Menkowskis' for her usual Monday morning sex education class.

She showered and dressed and made her bed. Applying her own understated makeup rather than Solange's more flamboyant palette, Amanda contemplated the dark curly wig and swinging silver earrings that still sat on the bathroom counter and reminded herself that she didn't need the disguise to tap into Solange's practical boldness. Everything she needed to get through this day lay inside her.

She was halfway down the stairs when the unexpected smell of brewing coffee hit her. She stopped mid-step as frantic whispers reached her from the kitchen below.

"Pull the waffles out of the toaster, moron, they're going to burn."

"Don't tell me what to do, Meghan. Warming syrup in the microwave doesn't exactly make you the Iron Chef."

Amanda double-checked her watch, surprised that her children were not only awake but making conversation— even of a hostile nature.

"Hurry up," Meghan whispered. "I think she's coming."

Amanda waited for the scurrying in the kitchen to stop. Then she walked into the room and came to a stop in the entranceway.

The table had been draped with one of her best cloths. On it sat a place setting of her good china, a cloth napkin folded beneath her best silver. A vase of freshly picked flowers sat in front of it. The morning newspaper had been unfolded and set at the perfect angle for reading.

"Is it somebody's birthday?" Amanda asked.

Meghan pushed Wyatt forward. They were both in their pajamas, but Wy had a dish towel draped over his forearm and a Magic Marker mustache drawn over his lip. "No, *madame*," he said in a really poor French accent, "this is a small token of our love and . . . esteem." He turned to Meghan looking for assurance that he'd gotten the word right.

At her nod, he pulled out a chair and motioned Amanda into it with a grand wave.

Meghan carried the coffeepot to the table. "Would *Madame* care for some *café*?"

Amanda smiled at their earnestness. "*Oui*," she said in Solange's voice. "*Madame* would."

They made a show of vying with each other to grant her every wish. Her greatest fear, that her children wouldn't be able to understand the choices she'd made, began to dissipate and a sense of calm settled over her. She drew her first completely easy breath since the debacle at the Simmons's.

Their French accents disappeared midway through the fruit course and the formality decamped soon after. Wyatt cleared away the empty bowl and Meghan placed a dinner-sized plate in front of her with a flourish.

They took their usual seats across from her. Amanda looked down at her plate and her heart wrenched.

Two Eggo waffles sat not on top of each other, but side by side in an apparent effort to afford enough room for the syrup-scrawled message.

We're sorry, Mom oozed across the top. *We love you AND Solange* was crammed underneath it.

She looked up at her children through a haze of tears.

"I'm sorry, Mom," Meghan said. "I just couldn't believe it when Lucy called. And then people kept calling me a broom baby. I was so embarrassed that I didn't really stop and think."

"Oh, sweetie." Amanda reached out to both of them, grasping their hands across the table.

"Me too," Wyatt said. "How come you didn't tell us what you were doing?"

Amanda blinked back the tears as she tried to explain. "I was so scared that I wouldn't be able to hold on to the house for you. After everything that had happened, I didn't want you to be scared too."

Amanda looked down for a moment. The message was beginning to slip down the sides of the waffles, but she would never forget her first sight of it or the gesture they had just made.

"Daddy said that it was his fault and that you were doing the only thing you could to take care of us." Anguish shone in her eyes. "I feel so horrible. I wanted the prom dress so much and then I made you feel bad about what you had to do to buy it for me. And I just couldn't understand why Dad couldn't come home. I'm not really ready to give up on that yet."

Wyatt swallowed and his voice broke. "I don't care if we have to get another house. I don't care how little it is either. But I want to stay right around here so I can keep playing with the Mudhens. And see Dad."

"I don't care where we live either," Meghan said. "And I'll even help you clean if you need me to." She looked Amanda in the eye, her jaw set. "If Lucy Simmons or anyone else

•

doesn't like it, they can just . . . well . . . I don't care what they think."

Amanda held on to her children's hands, her heart so swollen with love for them that it hurt.

"You'll be nice to Dad, won't you?" Wyatt asked.

"And at least give him a chance to show you that he's changed?" Meghan asked.

Amanda sighed. She understood their reluctance to abandon hope of a reconciliation between her and Rob. All children wanted their parents together. But now was not the time to debate that issue.

"It's all going to be OK," she promised, and this time she knew it was the truth. "I love you guys completely and so does your dad.

"Things are going to turn around for us. I started cleaning out of desperation. But I'm really good at it and with Candace and Brooke's help I think I can turn it into something big enough to support us."

She gave their hands a final squeeze. "But first I have to repair my reputation and get my customers back. That means Susie Simmons is going to have to confess that nothing was stolen."

"How are you going to get her to say that, Mom?" Meghan asked.

Amanda ate her breakfast as they talked. It felt so fabulous to be able to share her ideas and goals rather than trying to hide them.

They were a team, just as she and Brooke and Candace were. She didn't have to go it alone.

"I'm not exactly sure," Amanda admitted. "But the three

musketeers are going to pay her a little visit. And we won't
be leaving until the issue is resolved."

The three of them met at Candace's house and decided to
take the vacuummobile for old times' sake.

"Do we have a plan?" Brooke asked as they piled into the
bright yellow Bug.

"Not really," Amanda said, slipping into the driver's seat.
"I thought we'd just ring her bell, step inside, and explain
what we need from her. We'll only use brute force if we
have to."

"That's too bad." Candace looked truly disappointed.
"I've been dying to smack Susie Simmons up against a wall
since I met her."

"She wasn't always like this," Amanda said as she headed
north on Johnson Ferry Road. "When we first met, she
was—well, not completely warm and fuzzy—but kinder
and gentler. Ever since her divorce she's become so bitter
and judgmental. I don't know why."

"Well, I don't care why," Brooke said. "You've been
treated worse than she ever was and you haven't gone all
hostile."

"I've been too busy to get hostile," Amanda pointed out.
"But I'm working up a good, clean mad right now. Susie's
lies could destroy everything. The only clients who haven't
canceled so far are Sylvia Hardaway and Hunter—and I'm
afraid that may be because he hasn't heard about our arrest yet."

"God, that man is hot," Candace said.

"Yes, he is." Amanda smiled, but his continued silence
had made her question his sincerity. "I'm trying not to be

hurt by the fact that he's so totally disappeared, but I'm really not sure what to make of him."

She put on her blinker and changed lanes.

"You don't have to make anything of him," Candace said. "He looks pretty well formed to me. Just enjoy yourself. You deserve it."

Amanda eased into the middle lane as they neared Upper Roswell. It felt strange to be in the bright yellow Bug without Solange's uniform and makeup. When she pulled out to pass a silver Mercedes, the driver pointed to the three of them, nudged her passenger, and laughed.

Amanda waited for the burn of embarrassment, but nothing happened. "Hey," Amanda said. "Those ladies think we're funny." She pointed to the twosome in the silver car.

"They don't know the half of it." Candace turned in the passenger seat and stuck her tongue out at the Mercedes' occupants as they flew by. She actually put her hands up to either side of her head and waggled her fingers at them. The only thing missing was the "nya nya nya na nah."

The driver's mouth puckered into an O of shock and disapproval. The Mercedes sped off.

"Damn straight," Candace said. "They're lucky I didn't moon them."

Amanda looked at the elegant Candace. She was still perfectly turned out and had dressed with obvious care for their confrontation with Susie. But something about her was different.

"What in the world has happened to you?" Amanda asked. "You actually seem to be not only understanding, but interested in baseball. Yesterday you had an urge to lead the wave. Today you're talking about mooning two total strangers."

Amanda met Brooke's gaze in the rearview mirror. "What do you think, Brooke? Have aliens inhabited Candace's body?"

Amanda waited for the expected retort, but none came. She turned to Candace, concerned. "What is it? What's happened?"

"Well, something has sort of invaded my body."

Brooke leaned farther into the front seat. "Are you OK?"

Candace blushed. *Candace!*

"It's a baby," she said.

"What?"

"I'm, uh, pregnant." Candace's smile was both mocking and filled with wonder. "Forty-two-year-old, allegedly infertile me is going to have a baby."

"Oh, my God." Amanda turned into Susie's neighborhood then found a place to pull over. "You're joking, right?"

Candace shook her head.

"Is it . . ." Brooke began.

Candace nodded, her face still split by her smile. "It appears that mild-mannered Dan Donovan's sperm are a hell of a lot more potent than the macho men I was married to."

They sat in silence for a moment, absorbing the news.

"Are you OK with this?" Amanda finally asked.

"I'm better than OK," Candace said. "I'm just a little off-kilter. And these mood swings sneak up on me when I least expect them. But the nausea seems to be over, thank God."

Still absorbing the news, Amanda pulled back on the road and headed toward Susie Simmons's.

"Frankly," Candace said, "I wouldn't want to be Susie

Simmons right now. Because if she doesn't behave herself, I'm going to turn my hormones loose on her. And believe me, it won't be pretty."

"What do you want?" Susie stood in her doorway and glared at each of them individually. Her hair and makeup were flawlessly done. Her lipstick-covered mouth turned downward. "I'd think you'd be too embarrassed to show your faces here."

Amanda didn't wait to be invited in. She stepped forward, practically into Susie's face. The other woman dropped back.

Candace and Brooke pressed into the foyer behind her. The door closed and the three of them formed a solid wall in front of Susie. "Obviously you thought wrong." Amanda took another step forward, intentionally crowding the other woman. Candace and Brooke stepped up beside her. "About a lot of things."

A look of panic washed over Susie's face. There was a noise up on the landing.

"Are you all right, Mom?" Lucy Simmons's voice quavered with uncertainty. "Should I call the police?"

"Why don't we have her do that, Susie?" Amanda asked quietly. "And when they get here, we can ask them to search for the jewelry and money you claimed was missing."

She stared Susie in the eye adding a silent challenge to the one she'd just issued.

"That's, um, not necessary, Luce," Susie finally said. "I'll handle this."

"Good move," Candace muttered.

"I'll say." Brooke gave her a menacing look.

"Why don't we continue this in your office?" Amanda took another step forward. "Unless you want Lucy to hear how you tried to set up your poor unsuspecting maids for something they never did."

Susie fell back another step and then another. With a sigh of what Amanda thought might be resignation, she turned and walked into her office. Amanda, Candace, and Brooke followed.

Susie took a seat behind her desk. The three of them sank down on the sofa across from it.

Once again, silence reigned.

"So, what's going on, Susie?" Amanda asked as calmly as she could. "What did Solange—or I—ever do to you?"

Susie stared back in silence. Every item on her desk was aligned at a perfect angle to something else. The books on the shelves formed perfectly straight rows, the bindings lined up according to height.

"All I've done is try to keep a roof over my children's heads," Amanda continued. "I didn't do you any harm. Or attack you in any way. I cleaned your house, and I was happy to have the work."

Susie flushed, but whether it was with embarrassment or disdain, Amanda didn't know. "Your accusations are threatening my ability to take care of my children. As a mother, I'm sure you understand I can't have that."

Still Susie remained silent. Beside her, Candace took a breath as if to speak, but Amanda laid a hand on her arm to stop her.

"I'm not here to beg for your friendship, Susie. I have to make a living and Maid for You is the way I intend to do that. If you don't want someone you know cleaning your house, that's fine. But you have to clear my name.

"We all know that your things weren't stolen. I expect you to take back the accusations and I want you to tell me, right now, why you made them."

Still no response.

"Jesus, Susie." Candace couldn't take it anymore. "You walked away from your marriage with a sweet deal. Why behave so viciously to someone who didn't?"

"Let's go, Amanda." Brooke stood. "It's clear she isn't going to . . ."

"My deal wasn't so sweet," Susie said. "In fact, there was no deal."

The three of them froze where they were.

Susie studied the paperweight on her desk as if it held some sort of answer. Then she moved it several inches to the left. When she looked back up at them, her mask was gone. "I got screwed too." Her mouth twisted in bitterness. "Worse than screwed." She looked at Amanda. "Charles spent years hiding his assets before he finally divorced me. Fucking years, making sure I didn't get anything."

"But everyone said . . ."

Susie looked weary, as weary as Amanda felt. "Everyone repeated what I told them. I couldn't stand for anyone to know what he'd done, how stupid I'd been." She smiled, but it was tight and bitter. "So I pretended." She aimed the smile at Amanda. "You dressed up in a disguise and cleaned houses. I pretended I had money I didn't."

"But, how did you live?" Brooke asked.

"My grandmother had left me money when she died. We lived off that for a while, but I couldn't figure out how to scale back and maintain the fiction. The money's almost gone now." She dropped her gaze to the paperweight. "I was going to sell some of her jewelry, but you never really get what it's worth. And it was all I had left of her." Susie sighed and closed her eyes. "I needed the insurance money."

They sat in stunned silence for a while.

"So, what do you want me to do," Susie asked. "To prove that Solange and her cohorts are innocent?"

Amanda studied Susie Simmons. Without her mask of frightened arrogance, she looked much more like the woman Amanda had once known. Susie had lashed out at the very thing she'd been most afraid of, as if calling attention to Amanda's misfortune would somehow keep people from guessing her own.

The truth was Susie Simmons had been every bit as much a victim as Amanda. And she had covered and protected her children in the only way she'd known how.

It wasn't their place to try to punish her for it.

"Why don't you just 'find' the missing things and let everyone know you were mistaken?" Amanda said. "That would work for me."

"But . . ." Candace and Brooke began.

"I don't know if you've given any thought to what you might do next." Amanda gestured around the scarily immaculate office and then looked pointedly at Brooke and Candace. "But Maid for You is getting ready to expand."

She waited several seconds for her partners' reluctant nods. "I think the company could benefit from the services of an . . . anal-retentive of your magnitude."

"Me? Cleaning houses?" Susie laughed, but this time

with amusement rather than derision. "Would I have to dress up and develop an accent?"

"Nope," Amanda replied. "There'll be no more dressing up or pretending. And you don't necessarily have to clean houses unless you want to. I, myself, have found it very therapeutic, but you could help with training if you prefer."

Amanda considered Brooke and Candace who flanked her on either side and thought of all they'd been through together and how much still lay ahead. She might be single in suburbia, but she was not alone. Her life, and the opportunities that filled it, stretched in front of her, a veritable smorgasbord of possibility.

"I can promise you one thing," Amanda said as she stood and prepared to leave, her friends at her side. "Whatever we do from here on out, we're going to do it as ourselves."

And that included her next stop.

After dropping her partners back at Candace's, she drove the vacuummobile to Hunter James's house. It was, Amanda reflected as she drove the peppy little Bug through the streets of east Cobb, a vehicle she could relate to; a much better fit than the sagging-seated Volvo she'd once left idling in the car lot of her life.

Confirming that his SUV was in the garage, Amanda walked up the front steps and rang the bell.

There was no bark from Fido, but she heard footsteps and then Hunter's shadow appeared in the sidelight. The door opened. *"Bonjour, Solange,"* he said in beautifully accented French. *"Comment vas-tu?"*

She blushed, which seemed to be a regular occurrence whenever he was around. "So, you heard?"

He smiled and there was no censure or judgment in it. "Amanda," he said quietly. "It wasn't exactly a revelation."

He motioned her inside. A suitcase and laptop sat just inside the door.

"I recognized you the first time Solange sashayed into my house. Anyone who didn't recognize you in her just wasn't looking. I liked Solange right away. She's feisty, a real fighter. Fido's not the only one who knows a good thing when he sees it."

Amanda blushed again remembering that Hunter James had had his face in her crotch too.

"I'm a little worried about her twins though." He smiled. "Will somebody be looking after them?"

Amanda was still trying to absorb the fact that he'd known, not to mention how well he spoke French. The invitations she'd issued when she'd thought he couldn't understand her rushed back to smite her. "But . . ."

"Amanda, I spent six years playing ball for Montreal." His smile broadened. "You didn't say anything in French that I wasn't thrilled to hear."

"Fine," she replied. "So you knew. Then where have you been? Hasn't anyone told you it's not nice to sleep with a woman, even if you know she's your maid, and then not call her again?"

"I left you a note and the key to my house."

She rolled her eyes.

"And I did get that one call through to your house despite the most unreliable cell phone service I've ever encountered. I spoke to Wyatt." He noted her look of surprise. "Whom I take it failed to mention that I called?"

She nodded, wishing she'd known.

"I was sent to look at a prospect in the Dominican Republic. The Phillies were after him, too, and we were afraid he was going to sign. I barely had time to stash Fido and the girls at their grandparents'. I just got back from the airport; I haven't even gone to pick them up yet."

He smiled and the glint of amusement was back in his eyes. "I can promise you if I'd known you were going to go and get yourself arrested while I was gone, I would have left you an emergency contact number."

They were both smiling now and whatever language they were thinking it in, she could tell they were thinking the same thing. "*Viens ici*," he said. Come here. He reached out and pulled her close. "*Je veux te faire l'amour.*" I want to make love to you.

He lifted her in his arms and carried her to his bedroom. And then he told her in flawless French exactly what he intended to do to her.

Hunter flipped burgers and hot dogs on the grill on Amanda's deck while Dan Donovan and Hap Mackenzie tipped back their beers and gave him pointers. It was late September and the leaves were just beginning their turn to yellow and gold.

Wyatt, Tyler, Drew, and Julie threw baseballs to each other in the backyard, debating the Mudhens' recent try-outs and the four new players they'd taken on. Every five seconds they demanded to know when the food would be done.

"Do you think your dad will be our pitching coach next year?" Wyatt asked Julie, who he'd already admitted threw really well "for a girl."

Meghan and Samantha lounged in chaises, a bowl of potato chips between them, their noses buried in the latest issue of *Teen People*; Rose Red and Rose White dishing over the relative merits of the latest teen heartthrobs.

In the kitchen, Amanda, Brooke, and Candace did their own dishing while they prepared the side salads and set the table for dinner.

"God, I wish I could have some of that." Candace eyed their glasses of Merlot. "I wasn't that much of a drinker, but now that I can't have any, I'm craving it big-time." Her hand rested on the swell of her belly. Despite her complaints, her face glowed.

"Yeah, you look completely miserable," Amanda said. "Dan's in here fussing over you every other minute, you're CEO of one of the fastest-growing residential cleaning companies in Georgia, and"—Amanda held up Candace's hand with the gleaming diamond solitaire—"you're about to be married to the world's nicest, and evidently most virile, guy."

"Too true." Candace beamed. "Today when I tried to tell him my thoughts about our honeymoon, he told me not to worry about it; he'd already booked an island getaway."

"Which makes him romantic and persuasive." Amanda smiled. "He's definitely my hero."

"I know." Candace rubbed her stomach again and stared out the kitchen window at the man who'd so surprised her. "He's even got Hurricane Hannah coming around." She turned away from the window to eye the bottle of wine. "You know our grandmothers' generation drank all the way through their pregnancies."

"Forget about it." Amanda took the bottle and moved it out of Candace's line of sight then helped Brooke put large serving spoons in the bowls of potato salad and coleslaw. Together they pulled condiments out of the fridge.

"Hap and I are going to visit my mother next week. He's

offered to move her up here." She, too, smiled with happiness. Her beauty remained, but it glowed more softly now—not an asset to be cultivated and clung to, just part of who she was. "I can't wait to tell her I'm in the cleaning business. Maybe we can make her a consultant or something."

Amanda concurred. "All I know is putting Susie Simmons in charge of the new recruits was a stroke of genius. She's put a whole manual together—and she makes all of them memorize it."

"I had ten new inquiries this week," Candace said. "The fact that our force is so thoroughly trained really appeals. All the side services we've added put us in a whole other league. We're going to have to add some more cleaning squads."

The three of them were still happily talking business when Hunter backed through the kitchen door with the tray of burgers and hot dogs in his hands. Fido followed at his heels.

Hunter set the tray in the center of the table and leaned over to drop a kiss on the top of Amanda's head. "The hungry hordes are about to descend. Do you think we have enough meat?"

She waggled her eyebrows at him and smiled as saucily as she knew how.

Of all the good things that had happened, he was way up there. Their physical attraction remained so strong that it surprised her at times, but it was his easygoing acceptance of her and what she was that made him such a keeper.

The fact that Wyatt worshipped him and Meghan

considered Samantha her long lost sister made things that much sweeter.

They chowed down around her kitchen table then sat talking late into the night. The mountains just two hours north of Atlanta were about to burst into full color and plans were afoot for a long weekend at Dan Donovan's cabin. It would be a glorious time, Amanda knew, but so was this one. She wished this moment, and this evening, could go on forever.

It was after eleven when everyone left. Dan and Candace took all the boys to Dan's for a sleepover. Brooke and Hap offered to drop the girls at Hunter's on their way home so that Hunter could stay and help her clean up.

They'd just finished the last of the dishes and wiped down the counter when Hunter came up behind her. He slipped his arms around her waist and pressed against her. His lips were warm on the side of her neck.

"You know," he said as he nibbled on her ear, "I'm kind of missing Solange tonight. Those swingy silver earrings and the way she used to bend over and show me her ass were a real turn-on."

Amanda turned in his arms, pressing up against all that fabulous male hardness. "She did no such thing. Why all that poor girl could think about was making enough money to take care of those precious twin sons of hers."

He kissed her again and then trailed his lips back down the side of her neck. "She was definitely coming on to me. She was hot for my form."

He reached down to unbutton her blouse and dropped another kiss on the hollow at her throat. "I used to fantasize about making it with her in my laundry room. Or when she was down on her hands and knees scrubbing the floor."

A wave of lust rippled through her. "She used to fantasize about you too." A smile tugged at Amanda's lips. "But there were those who thought her a bit flamboyant."

Their lips met and their tongues followed suit. She was startled, as she always was, by just how much she wanted him.

"Do you want to go upstairs?" she asked, her voice turning husky. "I've still got the wig and earrings and that extra sexy polyester uniform."

He smiled and the movement of his lips tickled her skin.

"Just speak French to me, *mon amour,*" he said as he bent her back over his arm like Gomez Addams used to do to Morticia. "You know it drives me wild."

"Whatever you say, *monsieur,*" she whispered as he lifted her in his arms and began to carry her toward the bedroom. *"Voulez-vous couchez avec moi ce soir? Voulez-vous couchez avec moi?"* Do you want to sleep with me this evening? Do you want to sleep with me? She delivered the lyrics of Patti LaBelle's immortal song "Lady Marmalade" with a straight face and a seductively raised eyebrow as if she were composing them on the spot.

He did stumble halfway up the stairs, clearly biting back his laughter, when she got to "coochi, coochi, yaya, dada. Coochi, coochi, yaya, here."

When he laid her on her bed, she very sensibly shut her mouth so that he could kiss her.

But her *coeur*—her heart—beat very, very fast.

About the Author

Wendy lives with her husband and two sons in a testosterone-laden home in the suburbs of Atlanta. When not at one ballpark or another, she spends her time either writing or attempting to invent an automatic toilet seat-dropping device.

Readers can contact her through her website at www.authorwendywax.com.